HAYDEN'S WORLD

VOLUME 2

S.D. FALCHETTI

COPYRIGHT

CONTENTS

PREFACE

In a small kitchen in the 1970s, a small black-and-white television rested on a counter. Silver rabbit-ears stretched up from it, and often I pinched them between forefinger and thumb, becoming part of the antenna to clear up zig-zagging static. On the screen, Shatner's voice announced that space was the final frontier. I'd sit there, transfixed, watching the *Enterprise* swish across the galaxy.

The 70s was an interesting decade to be a boy. We'd just put men on the moon in 1969. Big-budget sci-fi cinema ran with this momentum: Star Wars (1977), Close Encounters of the Third Kind (1977), Star Trek: The Motion Picture (1979), and Alien (1979), to name a few. I remember seeing other children with *Close Encounters* lunchboxes, the alien mothership raised in the lid's stamped metal, all of its glowing masts like radio towers over mountains. I had a plastic model of a Klingon cruiser I'd glued together and painted. The *Enterprise* kept an eye on it from a string in my bedroom.

What I appreciate about stories from this time is the theme of adventure. Kirk gets a bloody lip and torn shirt decking the bad guys on a fantastic world while the crew of the *Nostromo* encounters an alien which they don't fully understand. It's a throwback to the pulpy fiction of the fifties and sixties. We've all seen those retro book covers and posters — hand-painted space ships streaking against spattered stars. You could imagine an entire story just looking at them.

So, when I set out to write the *Hayden's World* stories, it was on a foundation of sci-fi serials watched on a tiny black-and-white tv. It's stories about visionary captains and brave crews going to fantastic places no one has yet seen. The first few stories were meant to be bingeable short reads — the type you might read in bed before drifting off to sleep. As the crew's missions have become bigger, the cast growing with it, the stories have matured into full-fledged novellas and novels. Because of it, *Hayden's World: Volume 2* is a bit different than *Volume 1*, containing only two long stories: *Janus 2* and *Bernard's Promise*. They're the perfect two to pair together, however, because James Hayden's dream finally becomes reality.

Thanks for coming along on another interstellar adventure with me, and, as always, keep dreaming big.

JANUS 2

A HAYDEN'S WORLD NOVELLA

FAIRWAY COVE

Late-day sun drenches asphalt as the motorcycle winds along the coastal highway. James banks right and the sky leans left. Kate's arms encircle his waist, her chest rising and falling with each breath. To their left, the Pacific is a tapestry of shining diamonds with a single sailboat silhouetted against a goldenrod horizon. They watch the boat bob against the waves for a moment before James rotates the throttle, the motorcycle's engine whining, veering them off the highway onto a dust-soaked road.

"A little off-roading?" Kate asks over her helmet mic.

James glances back over his shoulder. "I want to show you something."

The landscape flattens as the bike clears the crest. Two buildings stand to the right, the first a long-abandoned convenience store with sand-blasted lettering. Dirty windows show hints of counters and chairs inside. The second is a twenty-meter rectangle with a girder roof and two huge sliding white doors. Parallel one-kilometer roads run in front of the buildings, the closest overgrown with dirt and grass, and the furthest paved and clear with white dashed lines and huge block numbers reading 30. James pulls the bike beside the sliding white doors.

Kate removes her helmet and runs her fingers through her blonde hair. A silver ring dangles on a chain from her neck. She's eighteen, same age as James. "Why do I get the feeling we're trespassing?"

James grins and waves a hand. "No worries. I got permission from the owner."

She arches an eyebrow. "You asked permission for something?"

He motions to the door and walks over towards the handle. "Don't you want to see what's inside?"

Her eyes dart to the structure. "Okay, now I'm curious."

James anchors himself and tugs with both hands. As the sunlight spills into the hangar, the white wings and black propeller appear. Gold glares from chrome accents on the nose and the livery is marine blue with brick-red stripes stenciled with N147CP.

"Woah," Kate says. "Will you look at that?" She walks over and runs her hand along the airplane's cowl. "It's a classic. Did you...did you buy it?"

James nods. "Found it in a salvage yard. Bought what was left, pieced it back together. Purrs like a kitten."

"What's it run on?"

"Good old gasoline. Nineteen-ninety-two Piper Arrow Three. They only built six that year." He moves to the passenger-side. A foot-step juts out from the fuselage and the wing has a black non-slip surface next to the door. James leans over, opens the door, and steps up. He extends his hand and Kate accepts. They slip into the cockpit and settle into their seats. "What do you think?" James says.

She sets her hands on the yoke and turns it slightly. He points over her shoulder at the right wing and she watches the aileron move up and down. "Oh, this is awesome. I love it."

James flicks the red battery switch on. Indicator lights illuminate. "Would you latch that door?"

She pauses a moment, a smile creeping across her face, and pulls the door closed. Without saying a word she slides the seatbelt across herself. "Where are we going?"

He hands her a headset and motions towards the plane's nose. Rich blue sky awaits. "You know, that-a-way, just higher," he says over his mic. When he flips the beacon switch, red light spins in the hangar. Leaning towards the window, he says, "Clear prop!"

The propeller sputters to life when he turns the starter. He adjusts the throttle and turns on the avionics and navigation lights.

Kate taps the Garmin in front of her. The individual pixels of the airplane stick figure are visible. "Oh, wow, look at this navcon. That's....is that even a computer?"

James taps the power button off. "We don't need it. Guys flew for half-a-century with nothing but eyeballs and radios."

"You sure this is safe?"

"Safe as anything else in life. Wanna go?"

She eyes the crystal sky and glances back. "Yeah. A little different than your dad's planes, huh?"

James snorts. "You're just along for the ride in those. This..." He turns the yoke. "...this is real." He clicks the thumb button. "Fairway Cove Traffic, Piper one four seven charlie papa at east hangar taxiing to runway three zero."

Kate quirks her head. "Who are you talking to?"

"Whoever's out there. Maybe there's another James and Kate puttering around in a seventy-year old plane. Gotta do it right."

She sets her hand on his. "I think the universe can only handle one James Hayden."

He winks at her and edges the throttle forward. "Well, I'm lucky this one found his Kate."

JAMES at forty-one doesn't look much different than he did at eighteen, one of the fortunate blessed with a baby face and sandy hair hiding any hint of gray. He taps the Sandpiper's controls and watches Earth's blue marble spin away. As the star field pans, Hayden-Pratt's MEO2 shipyard swings into view, a brightly-lit lattice cradling a sixty-two meter wedge. Gold interior light glows from the wedge's cockpit and spotlights illuminate patches of the fuselage. Black registry letters read *HP-G01 Gossamer Goose*. In the ship's aft, robotic arms spin hull plates into place.

Ananke is beside James, her slate affixed to the dash. Blue ripples spill across her screen. "I remember the first time I saw *Gossamer*. I was so proud to be a part of fulfilling Bernard's dream. With her ivory white paint, she reminds me of a spinnaker, catching starlight."

James smiles. "I think that's the perfect description of *Goose*." As the shipyard grows, filling the cockpit windows, he stretches forward and examines the aft construction. "Looking good. On track for end of week."

"Any word on launch authorization?"

A quirk of his head. "Larson wants to meet one-on-one."

Ananke's screen splashes orange. "Well, that should be interesting."

"Yeah, curious what he'll say when it's off-the-cuff. I kind of like it. Two guys sorting it out, no audience."

Green ripples slide across Ananke's face. After a pause, she says, "If I could offer an observation."

James arches an eyebrow. "Shoot."

"Two guys sorting it out is often more brawn than brain, so to speak."

He chuckles. "You think I'm going to deck him?"

"No. But ego might overtake intellect."

A shrug. "I think I can handle it. Anyway, it's a negotiation. He wants something. If it was just him digging in his heels there'd be no need to meet."

"Agreed."

James taps the comm. "MEO Control, Sandpiper four four three, ready to dock."

A synthetic voice replies, "Cleared to dock Sandpiper four four three."

A tap on the arm panel and the ship spins ninety-degrees. Thrusters hiss with corrections as the Sandpiper settles into the umbilical with a clank and a jolt. James picks up Ananke and tethers her to his flight suit belt loop, then pushes out of his chair and sails to the belly hatch. When it opens, he ascends through the umbilical to *Gossamer's* starboard entry, emerging into the passenger cabin and a din of conversation. Hitoshi is here, peering through augmented glasses. Six other techs have bits and pieces of the cabin disassembled.

"Hey, boss," Hitoshi says. "Don't mind the mess. So, what'd you think on approach?"

"Cargo area looks good. Saw the new ventral heat shielding. Black, kind of like an old NASA shuttle."

"Yeah, I thought you'd like that. Got confirmation that the last *Bernard's* repair parts are fabbed and loaded." He motions around the room. "You now have a level two starship. Plus five hit points, plus three dexterity." A pause as he waits for a response. "And you've never played a video game in your life, have you?"

James holds up his hands. "Sorry."

"You know, between you and Sarah, it's like you two were separated at birth. She's been very helpful, by the way, doing telepresence uplinks for questions. I know she's supposed to be on leave, but she knows all of *Gossamer's* quirks."

James raises his eyebrows slightly. "*Goose* will always be her ship."

Hitoshi extends his slate. "I've got something for you, Ananke."

Ananke's screen pulses orange. "Ah, beautiful! The new Boseman interference patterns, like peaks and valleys beating in a symphony. Ready for the low-power test?"

"With your approval, Friday."

"Yes. It's perfect."

"Alright, you got it." He shows the slate to James. "This started as a permanent fix for the strangelet event from the last mission, but Ananke ran with it. Some adjustments to the wave generator placements and parameter tweaks will give us a big efficiency boost. We'll hit ninety-nine point nine six percent light-speed. Had to carve out more fuel space for the reactor. Best part is that it's reapplicable to *Bernard's*."

"That's fantastic," James says.

"Told you. Plus three dexterity."

2

WASHINGTON

The auburn-haired assistant opens the mahogany door and leans in. "Senator, James Hayden."

Senator Larson is visible through the door's breach, sitting at his desk while circling notes on a paper stack. Silver reading glasses rest perched on his nose. "Thanks, Cynthia, send him in."

Cynthia smiles to James and steps aside.

The office interior is spacious, wood-paneled, with a full wall of books. The far side has tall windows overlooking Washington at sunset. As James crosses to the desk, Larson stands.

"Senator," James say, extending his hand.

Larson leans forward and shakes his hand firmly, looking him in the eye. "Please, call me Charles."

A smile back. "James."

Charles crosses over to a shelf with an illuminated frosted-glass door. When he opens it, a crystal decanter and two faceted cocktail glasses appear. "You look like a bourbon man. Bookers?"

James watches him splash the bourbon into a glass with a pinch of water. "No. Thanks."

The senator swirls the liquor. "You know what they say about a man who doesn't drink."

James turns his attention away a moment, inspecting the wall behind the desk. Dozens of framed pictures rest here. Larson shaking hands with three different Presidents. Photos of him beside CEOs and generals.

James summons his best grin. "I'm charming enough already."

Larson follows his gaze to the picture wall. A cluster of naval ships cover the upper right wall. Nestled in there is a buzz-cut thirty-something with the Senator's eyes wearing dress Navy blues adorned with ribbons.

"Ah, see," Larson says, motioning his drink towards the photo, "I didn't always look like scuffed leather. That's back in fifty-six. You served...Air Force, right?"

James nods. "In the sixties." He motions towards the Navy picture. "You made Commander, impressive."

Larson waves a hand. "Drone squadron. Wish I'd been alive back in the day of carriers and fighter pilots. Toured the *George H.W. Bush* when I was a kid. Over three-hundred meters long. Sight to see."

James weighs his comment. "I've got a wall of twentieth-century aviators. Guys flying planes by touch. Real seat-of-your-pants flying."

"Yeah, that's how it should be done." He raises his glass. "Old school." After a second, he moves over to his desk and sits. James mirrors him. "Which is what I wanted to talk about."

James leans an elbow on the chair arm and waits.

Larson takes a sip of the bourbon and points with the glass. "Your guys work out anything more on that probe?"

"Yeah, we've gone through the vid frame-by-frame. There's small twists and turns, not just in the probe but what's behind it. Gravitational lensing, similar to what we see when we turn on the Riggs drive."

Larson sets down his drink. "So, you're telling me the green guys have a Riggs drive?"

James shakes his head. "Profile's all wrong. But they are bending space. And they're doing it in a strong mass field, which is impossible for us."

"Well that's just peachy."

A shrug. "They're interstellar. No surprise they can do things we can't."

The senator levels a stare. "You got any theories what they want?"

"Wouldn't call 'em theories. More like brainstorming. Our astrophysicist pointed out that it makes no sense to spy on Earth from Janus. Why go planetside when you can just hang out in space and watch. It's not like we'd spot a four-meter probe a light-week away."

Larson shifts uncomfortably. "Okay."

"So, best guess is that there's something on Janus that interests them."

A grimace pulls across Larson's face. "And your crashed Riggs ship is just sitting there waiting from them to pick apart. Learn everything about our tech, comb its computers."

James shifts forward. "Yeah." He waits.

Larson takes another sip of his bourbon and thinks. "So you want to send your new ship out, load it up with repair parts, and bring back the crashed ship?"

"That's right. Ready for flight in fourteen days."

"Yeah, alright, but what're you going to do about your green buddies?"

"They seemed as startled by me as I was by them. I don't think they'll be back."

"But you're going back."

"That's right, and we've created some first-contact protocols if we find them."

Larson takes a deep breath and exhales. "And, James, what's your protocol if they're hostiles?"

"I've got a Riggs ship. We'd get the hell out of there."

A long pause.

James waits.

"You know," starts Larson, "it's good to talk like this. No cameras. No opinion polls. Just two men talking straight." He leans in. "So, here's the deal. I'm going to summon you next week to present everything you've got before the Space sub-committee."

James nods slowly. "Alright."

"Off the record, this probe business has me scared spitless. We're kicking a bee's nest here. It's like putting a big neon arrow pointing to Earth."

"Senator, I assure you anyone within a hundred-and-fifty light years with a radio knows about Earth."

"There's an order here, and this'll flip it on its head."

"Well, they might come back even if we choose the do nothing option. Do you want to control where that happens, or do you want them to?"

Larson shifts.

"There's also the possibility," James continues, "that we repair *Bernard's Beauty* before they return."

The senator drums his finger on his desk. "Your new ship seats, what, six?"

"That's right."

"You're piloting?"

"Yeah, my regular pilot's on leave."

Larson points with his thumb over a closed first. "Here's how it's going to go with the sub-committee. Four of those six seats are going to our guys, military experts capable of assessing threats, and one seat is for a first-contact specialist. You fly, we command."

James laughs. "Senator, put on a parka because hell will freeze over before I agree to that."

Larson grins. "Now we're talking."

"First of all, I already have a crew, and they're all needed. It takes more than a pilot to fly a Riggs ship, plus I need my engineer if I'm going to put *Bernard's* back together."

"Well, I suggest you figure out who you really need, because you're not going to get clearance otherwise."

"Since I have the only ship capable of reaching Erebus, then *no one* is going unless we reach an agreement."

He takes a sip of his bourbon. "And one more thing. Don't bring along that AI of yours."

James squeezes his hand into a fist. "Ananke is no one's AI. C'mon Charles, get with the times."

"I don't trust 'em. At least you know where a man's coming from."

"Ananke's put her life on the line twice for me. There is no way I'm flying a hundred-and-eighty-billion clicks without her."

Larson stands and extends his hand. His smile is forced, artificial. "Thank you for your time, Mr. Hayden. I'll see you at the hearing."

It's twilight when James slips into the car, Washington's streets alive with color and light. "Airport," he says, and the car accelerates. He looks over at the slate mounted on the dash. Blue waves ripple across Ananke's face.

"Did you deck him?" she asks.

"Thought crossed my mind."

Orange mixes with the blue. "So, what did he want?"

"He's worried. He wants to control the probe situation. He tossed out an offer he knew I'd never agree to."

"To what end?"

"He's trying to help me, prep me for the hearing, give me a chance to get my ducks in order." James laughs and shakes his head. "I can't believe it, but we're actually on the same side of something. He wants us to go back."

"Have I ever mentioned how confusing people can be?" After a moment she adds, "What ducks do we need, so to speak?"

James bobs his head. "We're going to need a security specialist, for starters. If we don't pick one, they will. Will's got some contacts." He tugs at his ear. "If you were going to search for a first contact expert, where would you look?"

"That's easy," Ananke says. "You want the one person who's already made contact with alien life. You want Dr. Ava Kelly."

3

THE BLUE ROOM

From an altitude of two kilometers, Grand Cayman is a moss-green shoe lying on its side in azure waters with Owens Roberts International airport near the island's heel. James announces final approach from the Sandpiper's cockpit and descends, tires screeching as he touches down. When he steps outside his aircraft, the heat hits him like a jet blast. He takes off his jacket and slings it over his shoulder, Ananke affixed to his belt clip.

He orders a car and picks it up at the stand. As it drives to the marina, he takes in the sights of island life, the bustle of people milling about in colorful clothes untouched by time. It reminds him of photos he's seen from the twentieth century.

When they arrive, their hydrofoil is waiting, sleek, white, and curved. The passenger cabin is plush, but he bypasses it and heads to the bridge.

"Good morning, Mr. Hayden," the bridge console says. "Where would you like to go today?"

James looks around. The helm controls are directly in front of him, with a throttle lever to his right. He unhooks Ananke and attaches her to the dash. A grin pulls across his face.

"I know that look," she says. "Do you even know how to drive a hydrofoil?"

He sets his hand on the throttle. "Boat go fast, boat go slow. Got it. Console, manual mode."

"Manual mode engaged. Thank you for booking Cayman Tours."

"Okay, here we go." He edges the throttle forward and the boat pushes through the water. Ahead lies an aquamarine ocean and desaturated sky decorated with a few wispy cirrus clouds. Once they're clear of the no-wake zone, he opens the throttle and the craft lifts above the waves. "Oh yeah," he says, "I like it."

"You know, I've never been sailing before," Ananke says.

It jogs his memory and he scrunches his eyebrows. The smell of the ocean spray, the splashes of the waves. Just like that he's nineteen, lying on a yacht deck beside Kate in the Whitsunday Islands. The night is crisp and full of bright constellations with Centaurus directly overhead. Kate slips her hand into his.

"Look," Kate says, pointing with her other hand. "Alpha Centauri, on the centaur's foot."

"You wanna go?" he asks.

"I wouldn't be surprised if you had a ship waiting on shore for us."

James chuckles. "Who needs shores, when you have horizons."

"Is that what you want to do, set sail and never turn back?"

"There's so much to see." He rubs her hand. "Don't you want it all?"

Ananke's voice jars him back to the present. "James, is everything alright?"

He blinks. "Yeah, I'm fine."

"Worried about the mission?"

"No, just thinking about a time I went sailing, long ago."

She hesitates. Ananke's better at reading people than most humans. "Is it something you want to talk about?"

He shakes his head and taps the navigation display. "Visual on the platform."

The Cayman Rise Oceanography Center is a floating town in a water world, tiered, with structures, cranes, docks, and communications arrays. A tethered fleet of submersibles bob like boats in a marina. The upper-bridge level is a three-sixty paneled glass array with a growth of antenna. Red beacons pulse from high points.

James slows the hydrofoil and coasts it into the south dock. Mechanized moors secure it, then he attaches Ananke to his belt clip and steps up. As he steadies himself, a woman emerges from the door at the dock's end. She's in her late thirties with chestnut hair tied back into a bun. She walks briskly to meet James and extends her hand.

"Mr. Hayden, Ananke. I'm Ava Kelly. Welcome."

James shakes her hand. "It's a pleasure."

She lingers in the handshake a moment, smiling. "You're taller in real life."

James grins. "It's just that I'm tiny on people's watches." He notices movement in the tower windows. A small group of people peer back down.

Ava follows his gaze over her shoulder and releases his hand. She chuckles. "Don't mind them, they're just a little star-struck."

James waves up at the group, and one of them tentatively waves back.

"Were your travels okay?" Ava asks.

"My first time in a boat," Ananke says. "It was...interesting. There's a certain cadence, I imagine similar to riding a horse, that you don't get with cars and planes."

Ava smiles. "The pulse of the sea."

"Yes, and the boat itself, which has its own rhythm."

"I think, then, you'll enjoy the hydropolis. If you'll follow me." She turns and leads them to the door. The interior is a cluttered mud room leading to a short hallway with a cylindrical lift in its center. They shuffle inside. When the doors open, they are in a scallop-shaped room fanned by wall-sized plexiglass. Azure water swirls on the other side as tropical fish skitter past in hypnotic patterns.

"Can I get you anything?" Ava asks. "The Blue Room here is a favorite amongst the staff for recreation."

"No, thanks," James says. "This is the hydropolis?"

"One of its rooms. All of the undersea rooms comprise it."

Ananke says, "This station is designed for research of the Cayman Trough?"

"That's right," Ava says. "Oceanography with a primary focus on the ecologies of deep-sea hydrothermal vents. We run submersibles five kilometers down to the Mid-Cayman Rise, deploy crawlers to explore the vents, and catalog new species."

Ananke's screen undulates green. "Have you found many new species?"

"Oh, we have. Even after sixty years of exploring the Rise, there are constant surprises. On the microbe level, in particular, there's evolution and adaption, so there's no end to the diversity." She shifts to the couch and sits. James takes a seat across from her. "But I suspect you're not here to discuss the Rise."

"There's another water world we had in mind," James says.

Ava smiles. "Enceladus. The saltwater world wrapped in a shell of ice. Not that different, in many ways, from the Rise."

"Are you still doing work with the life on Enceladus?" Ananke says.

"Yes, I split my time between Providence Station and here. Would you like to see it?"

Ananke's screen pulses orange. "Very much so."

Ava taps her bracelet and the hydropolis windows darken to a star field. Saturn is a floor-to-ceiling banded disc with tilted rings, motionless, as the camera zooms in on its wispy E-ring, diving until a white speck is visible, then slowing as the speck becomes an icy white sphere. Enceladus is a cracked puzzle of geometric white ice shelves infused with soft blue veins. Providence Station coasts by. The view skims the moon's surface, and, for the briefest moment, it could be Earth's arctic, then it plummets through kilometers of ice to emerge in dark ocean. A depth indicator spins down—ten, twenty kilometers—and finally reaches the murk of the ocean's floor. Twin lights flick on from the virtual camera, casting cones and spotlights in the darkness. Lumpy stone columns rise like stalagmites with the haze of scalding water shimmering around them. At first it's like a trick-of-the-eye, a blurring along the stalagmite's surface, but then the motion resolves itself into thousands—no, tens of thousands—translucent domes with trailing tendrils. Flashes like firefly signals start near the base of the colony, appear at the opposite end, and sweep across in a pulse which meets in the middle. The domes burst into motion and scatter away from the camera, sporadic flashes fading to black.

"Beautiful, aren't they? Of the five-thousand species we've catalogued on Enceladus, I find them the most interesting."

"Those flashes were communication?" Ananke says.

"Bioluminescence has evolved at least forty times on Earth, so this part wasn't too surprising. It's this." She touches her bracelet and the screen focuses on one of the creatures. Its flashes are like an electrical short. When Ava slides her finger back over her bracelet, the video rewinds and proceeds in slow motion. The flash is a series of flickers, like morse code, and the hue of the light changes with each beat. "Pulse modulation. Each bit of data has three axis - frequency, amplitude, and duration. It's complex. We're recorded common patterns, like words, and phrases which the group as a whole recites. What's really interesting is that each individual contributes a word to the group's phrase. It's like they're playing the game where a group tells a story with each new person adding a word."

Ananke considers her comments. "I've read all of your papers on your approaches to communicate. Have you been successful yet?"

"Ah," Ava starts, "when we reproduced their light patterns precisely, they ignored us. We're not sure, but the light may be a by-product of the communication. Perhaps they're tasting the chemicals used for the luminescence. If that's the case, learning to communicate by tastes will be much more challenging. Currently we doubt they even have visual receptors."

"I'm curious," begins Ananke, "why they would evolve bioluminescence without the ability to see?"

"Perhaps earlier in the evolutionary tree they could see, or there is some symbiotic advantage to it. Here on Earth, *vibrio fischeri* is a bioluminescent bacteria which lives in the Hawaiian bobtail squid. The squid feeds it, and in turn it modulates its light to match the surface lux, in effect creating a biotech cloaking device for the squid. It's remarkable."

James leans in. "When you do crack the code, how will you know what to say?"

Ava shifts forward. "We've put a lot of thought into that. We're not even sure what their intelligence level is, so we've written stepping stones—protocols for baby steps—and a decision tree for what to say based on their intelligence and response." She pauses. "What to say quickly gets difficult the more intelligent they are. If they are sentient, nearly anything we say can profoundly affect their culture, so we need to tread carefully." She crosses her legs and sets one hand on her knee, the other arm resting on the sofa edge. "I saw your footage of the alien probe on Janus. What did you try and say to it?"

James quirks his head. "You know, I was so focused on getting to it that once I got there I realized my plan amounted to 'see what happens next'. It didn't seem to be aware of me until my suit lights hit it, then things happened fast." A laugh and a shake of his head. "I admit, pretty much the only thing I could come up with was 'we come in peace.'"

Ava arches her eyebrow. "Not a bad start."

"It was either that or 'take me to your leader.'"

She smiles and clasps her hands. "Is this what you wanted to talk to me about? You want consultation on the first contact protocols for the alien probe?"

James nods slowly. "Yes, but there's a twist. We don't want you to consult, we want you to be there if it happens."

There's a long silence as Ava processes that. She pulls back, composes herself, and smiles. "Be there? Be where?"

"We're planning a return mission to Janus. I'm putting together a crew, and I want you to be part of it."

Ava blinks. "When?"

"If we get authorization, in two weeks. Trip duration is twenty-one days."

A slow nod. "On your light-speed ship?"

"*Gossamer Goose,* and it can only do ninety-nine point nine percent light speed." He smiles. "Light speed's impossible. For now."

"You want me to go to the edge of the Oort Cloud on your near-lightspeed ship to possibly make first contact with an extra-solar intelligence?"

"Yup, that's pretty much it."

She blinks. "That's unbelievable."

James musters his best smile. "So, wanna do it?"

Ava stands, smoothing her clothes. "Oh, hell yes."

4

DOWN THE RABBIT HOLE

Hayden-Pratt's Space Operations Center is a campus of glistening glass and steel sitting adjacent to six criss-crossed runways. The noon sun casts sharp reflections on the Pacific as the Sandpiper banks for its final turn. Ava peers out the starboard window as James talks on the headset. The runway numbers rush up to meet them as they glide to a smooth landing.

"We've got a room prepped on the West Campus for you," James says, grabbing her luggage. "Get you settled in, grab some lunch, then do some introductions."

Ava steps out of the plane, the summer heat washing over her. She squints. "I feel a little like Alice, following the white rabbit."

James smiles. "Welcome to Wonderland."

He leads the way off the tarmac through reception and the high-ceilinged lobby. Suspended from the ceiling is the first Hayden Aeronautics production model, a supersonic four-seater which looks like something out of a history book. James follows her gaze. "First plane my father built," he says, "back when Hayden-Pratt was just Hayden, and only made aircraft."

"You inherited the family business, built it into all of this?"

They reach the omnilift and step inside. When the doors

close, James says. "West Campus." The elevator accelerates later-ally. "Eventually. You know, had a head full of adventure in my twenties. Spent some time in the Air Force. Didn't see myself wearing a suit and sitting at a desk."

The lift slows and the doors open. The West Campus resem-bles an ivy-league dormitory. They stroll down the hall together. "I suspect that's still true," Ava says.

James quirks his head. "What's that?"

"Head full of adventure, don't want to sit at a desk."

"That's why I work so well together with Will Pratt. He's got the mind for business. Loves it. Met him in the Air Force. Wouldn't be Hayden-Pratt without him."

They stop at her room and the door slides open. Work area, rec room, bedroom, seaside view. She smiles as he sets her luggage inside the doorway.

"Console will order anything you want to eat," James says. "Feel free to explore. I'll meet you back here at thirteen-thirty for introductions, then the rest of the afternoon we'll prep you for Friday."

Ana tilts her head. "What happens on Friday?"

"I'm going back before the Senate Space Sub-Committee, and I want you to come with me."

———

THE SPACE COMMAND Center is adjacent to the West Campus, a cinema filled with workstations. Earth dominates the room's screen, blinding blue with the sun glaring off the Arabian Sea. *Gossamer Goose* is in full sunlight, its white hull nestled by the arcs of the MEO2's shipyard frame. Two tugs arrive towing a seventy-meter ringed scaffolding. Parallel rails run along the scaffolding's inner circumference — tracks for the robotic manipulators and welders — the entire structure a miniature version of the MEO ring. The tugs slow to a crawl and slip the ring around *Gossamer Goose.*

James motions towards the screen. "How's *Goose* looking?"

Hitoshi points at the ring. The tugs are securing connections to the ship's starboard and port wings. "Kind of like an old sci-fi book cover to me. So cool. Love it." He taps an icon on the console and a schematic appears of the cargo layout. Most of it is filled with repair parts for *Bernard's* and expedition supplies. "Still have capacity. You want extra fuel?"

"There's an old aviation saying that the only time you can have too much fuel is when you're on fire."

"Yeah, let's hope that doesn't happen this time. Speaking of bursting into flames, here's Beckman's requisition list." He hands James a slate.

James squints. "What do you think of him?"

"A little odd. When I asked him if I could call him Guthrie, he said, 'It's Beckman. No mister, just plain old Beckman.'"

James shrugs. "Will thinks the world of him." His eyebrows raise as he progresses through the list. "I'll talk to him about this."

Hitoshi adds, "You know, although I think some of the stuff on the list is overkill, it's still not a bad idea to have some weapons. I mean, you ever read sci-fi? It's all well-and-good until the death rays and the brain melting begin."

James smiles and pats him on the shoulder.

AT FIRST, Guthrie Beckman is a bit hard to locate. He's not in his quarters, the cafeteria, or any of the campus rooms, and when James calls him, Guthrie's watch indicates that he's not wearing it. James stands with his hands on his hips staring out across the campus lobby. He glances at his watch. Ava's finishing dinner now and he needs to get back shortly to continue prepping her for tomorrow. That's when he sees a forty-something man jogging on the perimeter track. He smiles.

James needs to sprint to catch up with him, but he matches his pace and falls into cadence. It's a beautiful day with crystal blue skies and a low gold sun.

Beckman keeps his eyes forward, stride unchanged. "Mr. Hayden. I think you'd be more comfortable in running shorts."

"Saw you running and thought I'd catch you before I got pulled into something else."

"Suit yourself. You're here about the req?"

The track curves ahead with a few leafy trees and a park bench. "I am. What type of trouble are you expecting on Janus?"

"Well, that's the point. Need to have options. Better to have an undrawn weapon than an empty holster. What are your expectations?"

"Defensive weaponry. *Goose* is an exploration ship."

Beckman bobs his head. "Situation is what makes it defense or offense. Weapon doesn't care how it's used. You were in the Air Force, right?"

"I was, and I know why carrying explosive cargo in an aircraft is a problem."

Beckman considers this a moment. "They're inert until primed, but I'll lose the charges. And the grenades." He continues running, focusing on his breathing. "We good, then, on the pulse weaponry?"

"Yeah, but let's meet Saturday for a detailed review of engagement protocols and expedition security plans."

"I'll send you the briefing by zero-six-hundred tomorrow."

"Alright. Thanks, Beckman."

AVA LEANS FORWARD, her hands clasped on the table. The Senate Space Sub-Committee stares back from their desk. James is beside her, dressed in a navy jacket. She says, "Thank you for the question, Senator. The protocols developed for the Enceladus contact were vetted through the International Academy of Astronautics. The multi-disciplinary team included members with doctorates in astrobiology, anthropology, sociology, cognitive science, and language sciences, to name a few. These were built on a foundation of work done during the past ninety-eight years since SETI was founded. We have modified the protocols based on the information from the last Janus encounter, but they are fundamentally the same. I will forward them to you for your review."

Senator Richards considers her response, curious. "What will you say if you establish communication?"

"The goal of any communication is to establish that we are friendly, create a common framework for communication, and provide instructions for further communication via the IAA Earth telescope array. At that point the IAA will coordinate with the U.N. to vet all future responses and queries with member input."

"Is one of your mission goals to establish contact?"

Ava glances over to James. He says, "Senator, the mission is to repair and bring back *Bernard's Beauty*. While we're there, we'll do both orbital and surface exploration to try and understand why the probe was there in the first place. The contact plan is a contingency."

"And the distance makes guidance from Earth prohibitive?"

James smiles. He knows Richards understands, but is asking the question for the less tech-savvy. "One light-week means fourteen days before we'd get a response to any question."

Larson writes something in his note pad. "Mr. Hayden, will you state your crew for this mission and their roles?"

"Certainly, Senator. Dr. Ava Kelly, astrobiologist. Hitoshi Matsushita, chief engineer for the Riggs program. Dr. Isaac Cartwright, astrophysicist. Dr. Julian Laurent, physician. Guthrie

Beckman, operational security. Ananke, Riggs theory specialist, and myself, pilot."

Larson peers over the end of his glasses. "That's a lot of doctors, Mr. Hayden, but unless my math is wrong there's only one pilot."

James waits. He was wondering when he'd get to this point.

Larson points with thumb over closed fist. "Now how are you going to fly two Riggs ships with one Riggs pilot?"

"Senator, during the first Earth to Mars flight, Ananke did all the flying while the drive was on. She is more qualified to fly Riggs ships than anyone, including myself. I will pilot *Gossamer Goose* back, and she will pilot *Bernard's*."

"That would seem to be a bit of a problem, don't you think?"

"Not at all. Even if I were sitting in *Bernard's*, I would not fly it without Ananke. She co-invented the Riggs drive, and is the best choice for flying a damaged prototype. *Gossamer* will match speed with *Bernard's* and escort it back. To address any concerns, *Bernard's* will return to the Cassini One shipyard at Saturn, instead of Earth-Sun Lagrange Two."

Larson holds up his hands. "Mr. Hayden, there are nine-thousand people living and working in the Saturn system, most of them on Cassini Station."

"They've seen me and Ananke launch from Cassini One before. They'll see me and Ananke return."

"And what if your AI has a glitch?"

"In my experience people glitch, Senator, but not AIs."

Larson glances left and right at his fellow panel members. "Well, I suppose there is one upside to choosing Cassini."

James lifts his head. Upsides from Larson are never good.

Larson leans forward. "The *Hermes* watches over Saturn. If there's the slightest hint of things going awry, she'll turn your computer pilot to ash."

5

BALLOON ANIMALS

Ava sails weightless through a tube of illuminated rings. When she emerges in *Gossamer Goose's* passenger cabin, Hitoshi, Isaac, Julian and Beckman fan out in front of her, grabbing tethers and rotating mid-air. Everyone wears identical flight suits with the navy blues and brick reds of Hayden-Pratt. She reaches over and touches her embroidered left sleeve. A stylized white arrow pierces a star wake, *Riggs Mission #58*. Beneath it. *Gossamer Goose* sails against an icy white sphere with the letters JANUS 2. She's been in space countless times, flying to Saturn and back, but this is different. Here, she realizes, she's an astronaut aboard a starship, and she can't help but feel like a kid with a treasure map, wondering what adventure awaits between the start and the finish. She pushes into her seat and clicks the harness.

As she leans left, she can see James through the open cockpit door, Ananke attached to the co-pilot's console. Earth's nightside is a spiderweb of city lights tracing continental contours, spinning ahead through the cockpit windows.

When a clank and rumble sound through the hull, she taps her screen and watches the docking umbilical recede from the starboard exterior camera. White flashes from *Goose's* strobes appear in bursts along the shipyard's structure.

"Hey," Hitoshi says.

She looks over and smiles. "Hey."

He motions back over his shoulder. "Julian's got some dermals if you need anything for the jitters."

"Oh. I'm okay," Ava says. "A little giddy, actually." As she fixes her hair, her eyes dart to the back of Hitoshi's wrist. A glint of light reflects from the clear rectangle adhered there. She glances back to Hitoshi.

He takes a deep breath and exhales.

"Crew, secure for launch," James says over the ship's intercom.

On Ava's display, the camera is set to the MEO2's tower view. *Goose* is a wedge illuminated by running lights and pulsing strobes. Gold spills from the cockpit windows with a top-down view of James and Ananke. When James taps something on his console, Ava's chair pushes against her back with a gentle acceleration. *Goose* slips smoothly out of its dock.

At space-normal speed, the trip to Earth-Sun Lagrange Two takes eight hours. If it were legal to engage the Riggs drive, Hitoshi had told her, it would take one-eighth of a second.

IT'S JUST past two p.m. when they clear ESL2. James's voice sounds over comms. "Prepare to jump."

Everyone leans forward and assumes the crash position. *Minimizing spacial disorientation through mass agglomeration*, Ananke trained. With her hands behind her head, Ava looks over towards Hitoshi. "How you doing, Hitoshi?"

He tilts his head towards her. "I'm mentally preparing to turn into a balloon animal."

Ananke says, "Wave initiation in ten, nine, eight..."

Ava gives a nervous laugh. "You designed much of this, right? It's safe, isn't it?"

The intercom continues. "...five, four..."

Hitoshi pauses. "Kinda."

Ava's eyes widen. "Wait...what?"

"Initiation," Ananke says.

A deep hum sounds in Ava's ears as her elbows and feet lift up, and, for an instant, it feels like the moment when you lean back just a bit too far on a chair and realize you're going to fall, except the direction that she's falling is *everywhere*. Her ankles curve at an impossible geometry and the metal gleam from her shoelace eyelets spin prismatic reflections. Gravity flip-flops and pulls her down, then it rebounds and she's falling back in normal zero gee. She struggles to look at her screen's forward view.

Yellow stars dim to aquamarine and shift to blue, each sliding towards the screen's center. They congeal into a pulsing violet glow, as if the universe had a heartbeat.

She pushes up, holding her stomach.

Hitoshi groans. "And now I'm a giraffe." He looks over at her and his eyebrows raise. "Hey, you doing alright?"

Ava nods groggily. "Yeah, I'm fi..." Her stomach lurches, and, to her horror, she finishes her sentence with vomit.

WHEN JULIAN PRESSES the dermal to her neck, it's cool and tingly. It takes a few seconds for the drug to wash over her. Every muscle relaxes and her senses dial down a few notches.

His words have the smooth vowel sounds of a native French speaker. "How do you feel?"

She's strapped into a recliner in sick bay, her flight suit partly unzipped showing the underlying black crew shirt. "My stomach is better, but my pride will never recover. I am so sorry."

"If it helps to know, James told me the same thing almost

happened to him his first time. And he was a fighter pilot." He holds up a strip of clear patches. "When we jump back, I will give you one of these first."

She smiles. "Thanks. For the record, this was not how I envisioned today going."

"I want you to know," begins Julian, "that I think what you are doing is very brave. Most of the crew has been on the ship before, but you agreed with only two week's notice, and here you are."

She tilts her head. "Here I am." After a moment she adds. "So, I take it you weren't recruited two weeks ago?"

"Eighteen months, from Mars."

"You were working on Mars?"

"Hellas Station, one of two physicians taking care of four thousand people. James comes to me, there on Mars, to meet in person. He tells me about his project which will change the world. When I tell him, no, no, I am happy with my work, he hands me this little paper card with writing on it, you know, like something out of time. He says to me, 'You worked on Titan, and Ganymede, and now here, on Mars. There's a reason that drives you to be on the frontier. Soon that frontier will expand like a pulse of light, and I want you to be on it.'"

"It was a business card?"

"Yes. I put it in my pocket and thanked him, then went back to work. But it weighs on me, what he said. So I press the card and these tiny letters appear. *Keep Dreaming Big*. I touch the *call* icon on the card, and, here I am."

She considers his answer a moment. "I think that's what we all have in common."

"Hmm?"

"People with heads full of adventure, who want to know what's beyond the next mountain. I think that's what James recruits."

Julian tilts his head and smiles. "You are quite perceptive, Dr. Kelly, even when mildly sedated."

She tilts her head back at him. "You should see me after a couple of shots."

AT NINETY-NINE-POINT-NINE-SIX-PERCENT LIGHT-SPEED, it takes just shy of seven days to travel a light-week. But time-dilation compresses that into five subjective hours. From the crew's point of view, they left ESL2 at fourteen-hundred hours, passed Saturn two minutes later, breezed by Pluto at the seven-minute-mark, exited the heliopause at twenty-nine minutes, and spent the remaining four-and-a-half hours in the void between the solar system's end and the edge of the Oort Cloud. The fact that it took seven minutes to get to Pluto and nearly five hours to get a quarter-of-the-way to the beginning of the Oort Cloud cements how mind-bogglingly vast the distance is. It's just after nineteen-hundred when *Goose* jumps back to normal space.

Ava watches the stars slide back to their home positions, brightening like fanned embers. The dermal patch on her neck helps.

"Space normal velocity," James says over the intercom. The habdeck lights cycle red three times. "Spin in three, two, one..."

Ava's chair presses against her back as the ship pitches nose-up. She waits, the nearly inaudible hum of the RF engines building up charge as her hair settles down and the mild weight of its bun presses upon her neck. Over the course of the next minute acceleration steadily increases until she is under a standard earth gee. As exhilarating as it was to be weightless, she embraces the sensation of weight once again.

All of the energy poured into the Riggs wave has to go somewhere, Hitoshi had explained in the trip prep. *So it converts into kinetic energy which we have to shed back in normal space.*

"Starting passive scans," Isaac says. "Visual confirmation of

Erebus and Janus. Two point one million kilometers. You want to see?"

"Let's do the big screen," says Hitoshi.

Isaac taps an icon and the habdeck's media screen illuminates. The Milky Way is impossibly bright with thousands of colorful stars salting black space. Erebus is a twilight disk with a ghost of a ring. Far above it, Janus is pristine white swirled with rock.

"Right where we left it," Hitoshi says.

Isaac slides an indicator on his console. "Reverse view."

The main screen changes to a black sky with a bright golden star at its center. From this distance, the Sun looks like the evening star when viewed from Earth. Two yellow stars flank it.

"Jupiter and Saturn," Isaac says. "Sectors quiet. No contacts except celestials. Starting Janus imaging. First scans should be processed by twenty-hundred."

Beckman stands. "Heading back to bay one to pre-flight the orbitals and make sure nothing's moved around."

Overhead, the cabin lights dim slightly and shift towards warm hues, helping cue their circadian rhythms.

"Let's see what we can see," Hitoshi says. "We've got about three working hours left before night."

6

ROMEO ONE

Goose is set for night with pale blue cabin lights. Each sleep chamber on the habdeck contains a human silhouette behind a frosted privacy screen. There was a brief discussion about setting up a shift schedule so that someone was always awake, until Ananke simply stated, "You do all realize that I do not sleep." She's been sitting in the cockpit ever since, her screen undulating with blue during the eleven-hour trip to Janus.

Sometime after midnight Beckman comes up and joins her, draped in his sleep blanket holding a cup of something hot.

"Coffee?" Ananke says.

"Tea," he replies. "Chamomile. Not sure if it really helps. Doesn't taste bad."

"Julian may have something to help you sleep, if you'd like me to wake him."

Beckman sits in the pilot's chair and adjusts his blanket. "No, I'm good with the tea. Besides, I like this time of night. Stars. Everything's quiet."

"I can smell it. The tea."

"Really?"

A purple current cascades down Ananke's screen. "I'm tapped

into all the ship's sensors. Air filtering. It smells like a meadow, just before sunset. I can imagine lavender, and daisies, and apple blossoms."

Beckman lifts the cup to his nose and inhales. He smiles and takes a sip. After a long moment he says, "Where are you from, originally?"

More purple appears on her screen. "Do you know, no one has ever asked me that question before? I was born in Pasadena on a warm spring day in twenty seventy-one."

"Intentional Consciousness or Emergent?"

"Intentional, although I've always thought it would be romantic to be Emergent. What about you, Mr. Beckman?"

"Accidental, I suppose." He chuckles at his own joke. "And please, just Beckman. 'Mister' makes me feel even older than I already am. I'm from Iowa. Soybean farm. Couldn't wait to get out growing up, but wouldn't mind going back."

"How did you and Will meet?"

Beckman takes another sip of his tea. "He was stationed in Azerbaijan and I was a military contractor providing security. He's a good man. How'd you meet James?"

A hint of orange in her display. "I was working with Bernard Riggs at Caltech when James came to recruit us. Often people would only speak with Bernard when they met us, but James made me feel like a real person. He was excited to have both of us join his team, and Bernard was overjoyed."

He nods. "You were with him on the Mars flight."

"It was very exciting. And a bit frightening."

"And very brave."

"Thank you."

Beckman takes a deep breath and finishes his tea, setting the cup down to his side. His eyes are a bit heavier.

"The tea seems to be helping. Good night, Beckman."

He wraps the blanket around his chest as he nestles into the chair. "I'm just going to watch the stars for a while. Good night, Ananke."

HITOSHI SITS in the co-pilot's seat wearing a navy tee shirt with the Hayden-Pratt logo. The main screen displays the ship's dorsal camera, *Goose's* white hull fanning out to a semi-circular scaffolding. Beneath it, Janus's snowy white globe spins.

Isaac taps on the sensor display beside him. "Site coming up."

A window insets with a landscape tile from Janus's surface. In the tile's center, a silver man-made triangular shape is partially buried in the snow. Just west of the shape is a rocky crater adjacent the ice-drenched slopes of a cryovolcano.

"There's my girl," James says.

A waypoint flashes on the navcon and Isaac acknowledges it. "Sixty seconds to Romeo One."

"All systems green on the ring," Hitoshi says.

James opens the ship's intercom. "Secure for separation."

As the distance digits spin down, Hitoshi says, "And we have separation in three, two, one..."

Goose shimmies.

In the ventral camera, the ringed scaffolding falls away like a spent rocket stage from an old NASA video. As it clears the ship, high intensity lights flare along the inner circumference.

Hitoshi smiles. "Ring deployed. Bet *Goose* is happy to shed all those kilos."

"She was flying more like a stuffed turkey. Good to have her wings back," James says. As he adjusts their altitude, the ring condenses from a blinking disc to a glaring white star, rising in their wake.

Isaac looks over from his console. "Sierra One in five minutes."

James flicks open a video window and Beckman appears. "Coming up in five," James says.

"Orbitals online, five by five," Beckman replies. "Opening bay doors." He slides something on his console. "Number one's drive is hot and ready for launch."

Hitoshi watches the moon spin beneath them as the cockpit windows overlay the nav brackets. The superimposed rectangles advance towards *Goose* and disappear one-by-one.

After a few minutes Isaac says, "Thirty seconds."

"In position," Beckman says.

Sierra One's nav marker rushes towards *Goose's* screen.

Hitoshi eyes his display. "Go for launch."

The navcon chirps as a new contact flags itself just aft of *Goose*. Telemetry identifies it as a multi-spectrum imaging satellite.

"Bird's away," Beckman says. "Data's alive. Prepping Sierra Two."

Hitoshi looks at the aft camera. Four strobes blink from the imaging orbital as it falls away from *Goose*. On the forward screen, a new set of waypoints overlay the stars. "Okay," Hitoshi says to those stars. "We're keeping an eye on you. No funny business."

For the next three-quarters of an orbit, *Goose* deploys orbitals, encircling Janus like a string-of-pearls. As the ship readies for its second lap, James taps an overhead switch and the cabin lights cycle red.

Hitoshi takes a deep breath. "Here we go."

"Crew, prep for de-orbit," James says over ship's intercom.

At first, it's a flutter in Hitoshi's stomach, the feeling of clearing the top of a roller coaster and picking up speed in the descent. As *Goose* decelerates, the harness straps dig into his chest, leaning him forward.

Janus looms up from the bottom of the cockpit windows. Once it overtakes two-thirds of the cockpit view, a vibration rumbles through Hitoshi's boots. *Goose* shimmies, the upper atmosphere buffeting its hull, and the wind sound grows louder.

The sky ahead is a deep blue, nearly black, splattered with stars and hints of adumbral land masses. Plasma flames flicker ahead, as if the air itself were catching fire, intensifying to a dazzling green. *Goose* rocks and bounces. Hitoshi tightens his grip on both arm rests.

For the next five minutes they are a supersonic meteor crackling through the blue glow of Janus's nitrogen thermosphere. As the flames subside, rocky mountains resolve themselves into individual snow-capped peaks with sinuous blue ice ridges. Hitoshi's stomach burns. He hadn't realized he was holding his breath. He gasps in fresh air.

James taps a button on his console and *Goose's* landing lights flare. Flecks of snow streak by like shooting stars. "Six hundred kph, altitude eight kilometers."

Hitoshi can feel it. They are no longer a spaceship traveling in the frictionless linearity of vacuum. They're an aircraft slipping through the layers and eddies of atmosphere.

Isaac seems unfazed, calmly tapping at his console. "Thirty kilometers to crash site."

Goose descends and slows. At times the landscape, with its rocky snow-covered mountains, could be in the Alps on Earth. At other times the stacked ice shelves, sublimated crystal spikes, and rusty basins seem like something completely alien.

Isaac glances over at Hitoshi as the ship streaks over a red patch of landscape. "Still no explanation for tholins. Too far out to interact with solar wind. Hope I get a chance to study. Seems likely Janus was within the solar system long ago, and was ejected."

"Like, for misbehaving?"

"Or maybe captured. You know, seventy-thousand years ago Scholtz's Star passed within one light-year of the Sun."

"Oh, yeah, totally knew that." He pauses. "Wait, you think we swiped one of its planets?"

"Not Scholtz's. Not enough time for a planet to move from where it was to here. Take one, two million years."

"That's a relief," Hitoshi says.

"But every nine million years that happens, so lots of chances. Do the math, probably happened over five hundred times since Earth formed."

Hitoshi frowns. "Are you saying Erebus and Janus are alien worlds we stole from another star?"

Isaac shrugs. "I dunno. That's why I hope I get time to study."

"This is not making me feel any better."

James taps the intercom. "Crew, prep for landing."

Hitoshi closes his eyes and focuses on breathing.

Goose glides into a gentle arc, shifting its weight as it banks. The deceleration is stronger now, pushing against Hitoshi's chest. Chemical thrusters fire with hisses and bursts.

"Touchdown in three, two, one..." James says. The ships jolts and Hitoshi opens his eyes. Snow sizzles and evaporates as *Goose* settles onto its struts.

"Well," James says, powering down the RF drive, "that went much better than last time."

Bernard's Beauty is visible through the cockpit windows, fifty-meters distant, partially buried in snow. One nacelle juts up marred by scratches and dings.

James unclips his harness and pokes his head back in the passenger cabin. "Alright, let's get through the people and ship post-flight, then Beckman has the ball."

BECKMAN FLICKS the surface drone telemetry to the passenger-area media screen. Four video feeds form a square, each peering out of *Goose's* cargo bay. When Beckman taps an icon, the drones hover out of the bay and zip across the snowy landscape towards *Bernard's Beauty*. Spotlights flick on from their noses and swing shifting light in the mist. The upper left drone increases its altitude as it nears *Bernard's* nose, leveling itself off with the cockpit windows.

Inside the cockpit, three blue seats glisten with ice crystals. Except for an empty sleeping bag beside the seats, there's no sign of activity. The lower right drone coasts to Bernard's airlock, swinging its beam to the dead auxiliary power unit connected to the airlock's external power interface.

Beckman examines the telemetry. When he's satisfied, he says, "Send in Betty."

Hitoshi enters a command from his workstation, glancing up at the cargo bay monitor. A heavy vehicle lumbers out with spider-like manipulators, ambling across the snow towards *Bernard's* airlock. Two of its arms extend and attach a cable to the external power connection while another deposits a new APU on the ground. Lights pulse along the generator and the interior of *Bernard's* flickers awake.

Betty backs away and deposits hexagonal blocks every ten meters around the ship's perimeter. Each blossoms into a self-illuminated tethered balloon.

Hitoshi eyes his screen. "Okay, *Bernard's* is booting up. Bunch of errors. We're going to have to go in there to clear them."

Overhead, the drones fan out in different directions.

"Everything's quiet out to five clicks," Beckman says.

James stands next to Hitoshi, watching the video feeds. He clasps him on the shoulder. "Sorry, Hitoshi, you know what I'm going to say next."

Hitoshi glances up at him. "Meet you in transporter room three?"

James quirks his head. "The only way to get in there and fix it is to get in there and fix it. Ananke, Beckman, you're with us. Let's suit up."

JAMES'S EV suit is orange with the block-numbers *06* on its front. Ananke glows blue on his suit mount. Beckman stands to his left wearing a combat suit with gunmetal chest plates and a pulse pistol holstered on his left breast panel. He nods to James and Hitoshi as the airlock door opens.

Janus is enshrouded in a low mist illuminated by the balloon lights. The glare washes out everything but the brightest stars. When he sets his foot onto the regolith, the mist swirls away in eddies. He grins and leads the group across the crunching snow.

As he sets his hand on *Bernard's* doorframe, Beckman stops him and disappears into the cramped corridor between the reactor and the cockpit. After a few seconds of silence he says, "Clear. Proceed."

James enters and walks his hands along the corridor's incline. Hitoshi follows.

The cockpit is illuminated with dozens of startup errors. Hitoshi arrives and overrides each. After a minute the screen clears and displays the root directory.

When James opens a log entry, it's him, wearing an EV suit minus the helmet. "*Bernard's* batteries are almost gone," the recording says. "Ananke will be with me, so if you find this message but not me, follow my hiking path so you can retrieve her."

James closes the file.

Hitoshi says, "We really thought you were dead there, boss."

James tilts his head. "Me too. Glad you proved me wrong." He scrunches his eyebrows. "You guys make entries when you found *Bernard's*?"

Hitoshi nods. "Uh, sorta, we left the APU here, so *Bernard's* had power until it died. Logs recorded anything which tripped the sensors. First one should be *Goose* looking for you." He opens the entry and a video appears of *Goose* lifting off and accelerating towards the crater. Hitoshi scrolls to the next log. "Next is us getting out of Dodge." *Goose* appears as a blinking star rising in the sky.

"Two more entries after that," James says.

"Hmm," Hitoshi says. "Next one's a week later." He opens the video. Bernard's camera shakes as slow-motion slush arcs into the sky. The slurry spills across the volcano's southern face.

"Cryovolcano eruption," Ananke says.

"Didn't think it was active," James says.

Hitoshi furrows his brow. "Might be a problem. Ejecta could reach us here. Although, if it hasn't hit Bernard's in all this time, we're probably good. I'll ask Isaac to take a look."

Beckman glances out the cockpit windows. The cryovolcano is a distant peak against a pitch sky.

Hitoshi opens the last entry. Erebus hangs suspended in a starry sky, dark mountains framing the Janus horizon. A single star falls out of place and travels in an arc across the horizon. The time index is two weeks after *Goose* left. He rewinds the video and freezes it, enlarging the moving star. A silver x appears.

James looks sideways at Hitoshi.

"Ah, fudge nuggets," Hitoshi says.

7

STARDUST

The crew stands around the media screen in *Goose's* passenger cabin, the image split into two windows. The left feed is a top-down view of *Bernard's Beauty* from one of Beckman's drones. Several open crates rest beside parts, and Betty performs mechanical surgery on the ship's starboard engine. The right window has a three-dimensional model of Janus with a delineated trajectory marking the orbital path of the silver x based on *Bernard's* log.

James stands with his hands on his hips. "We stick to the plan."

Hitoshi shifts, rubbing his neck. "Boss, the plan was to fix *Bernard's* before they got back. They're already here."

"They were here," James says. "Far as we can tell, they're not. We've got our eyes in the sky." He relaxes his shoulders a bit, easing up on his body language. "What's everyone want to do?"

Hitoshi nods towards the crash site video feed. "Betty's got about ten hours to repair the starboard engine. If I can get Ananke and one other person, it should take us maybe eight hours to get the reactor on line. After that, we should get both ships back in orbit until the ring patches up *Bernard's*."

"Who do you want?" James asks.

Hitoshi glances at Isaac. "Mister Isaac, you've got the tech skills."

Isaac shakes his head. "Images are processing from the Sierra orbitals. Need to monitor and task the satellites based on what they see. This is a big chance to learn about Janus. I need to be there for them."

Ava is beside Isaac, nodding. "I agree. I'd like to get some samples from the cryovolcano's south face. From the ship's log, it looks like that's where most of the slush landed. If there's life, we may be able to detect it."

"I'll help Dr. Kelly," Julian says.

James glances at Beckman. Beckman points to the drone feeds on his workstation. "We should repair *Bernard's*, then leave. My place is here at ops."

"Alright," James says. "We've got eight hours. Hitoshi and Ananke, I'm with you."

AVA'S EV suit is her own, brought from her Saturn trips. Unlike the others, it's white with amber swathes and bears the Providence Station logo. When she kneels upon Janus's regolith at the bottom of *Goose's* cargo ramp, cold filters through her knee.

A cart sits to her right with Julian standing on the other side. She lifts a palm-sized disk from the cart and flips it over.

Julian holds a slate displaying a topographic map of the cryovolcano.

"This little guy," Ava says, tapping the quadcopter's belly, "is heading to the lip." She rights it and the blades spin to speed. It hovers there as Julian enters its destination on the slate. When he's done, it zips off. Ava grabs a second drone. "This one's sampling the southern slag." When she tosses it up, it flitters away. She activates the last drone on the table. "And this lucky guy gets to dive into the caldera." She watches the blinking white lights of the three drones fan out like fireflies in the dusky shadows of Janus's landscape.

"What will you look for?" Julian asks.

"Depends what flavor of slush we have. If it's water-ice, we'll look for the kind of life we'd find on Earth. Check for molecular hydrogen, some amino acids, maybe evidence of methanogenesis. But if it's a methane slurry, that's a whole different ball game. Life chemistry will revolve around vinyl cyanide and azotosomes." Something catches in her memory and she glances at Julian sideways. "You worked on Titan, right?"

Julian smiles. "Ah, yes, Ligeia Mare station, in seventy-eight."

She tilts her head. "We were there at the same time. I was on Providence, but did some research at Kraken Mare."

"Yes, I remember you."

She arches an eyebrow. "Really?"

"Yes, yes. I saw your speech from Cassini. 'Take a baseball,' you said, 'and throw it to stars. If you threw it when the last of the dinosaurs died, it would already be at Proxima Centauri.'"

"Panspermia," Ava says. "Rocks get blasted off Earth and seed other planets with life. Or vice versa. It's the big question in astrobiology."

"To explain the similarity of Enceladus life to Earth's."

"Yes, exactly!"

"I liked it, this thought that there may be bits of us out there, traveling the stars."

She leans in a bit. "How would you feel if it turned out we were the star men, seeded from another sun?"

Julian quirks his head. It reminds Ava a bit of James. "Well, we are all star dust, no?"

"Every last atom."

"Then I suppose I would feel the same as being born of Earth."

Ava smiles. "What brought you to Titan?"

"I served four years on the *Hermes* as a field physician. When it was stationed at Cassini, I would be deployed on assignments, usually on Titan, but sometimes on Cassini Station."

"Did you like it?"

He shakes his head. "I did not. At least, not aboard the *Hermes*. It saw combat several times, and that is not why I went into space. But Cassini was interesting. Such a mix of people and problems, all searching for a chance to elevate their lives. I imagine it was what America was like at the start of the twentieth century, full of new faces and endless potential."

"Were you ever at Ligeia Mare?"

"I was, but you were not there. You and I, we are like two ships passing in the stars."

Ava smiles.

Julian's slate chirps. "First drone is on scene."

Ava moves over next to him. "Let's start with some basic spectroradiometry."

When Julian taps the slate's icon, a progress bar animates. A graph with peaks and valleys appear. The largest is labeled H_2O and the secondary is NH_4. Other smaller peaks include K, CO_2, CH_4, N and C_6H_6.

"Ammonium," Julian says. "More like Titan's water-ice than Enceladus."

"Ah, off to a bad start. Titan's formula had no life. But we're not out of the game yet. Let's try some mass spectrometry."

Julian selects it and the drone queues up the tasks. While they're waiting, the second drove arrives and begins sampling the slush. The mass spectrometry results spin on the screen as a pie chart.

"Molecular hydrogen," Ava says. "Now that's interesting. That was the first hint of hydrothermal vents on Enceladus."

"This is a little exciting."

"Spectrometry's back from the slush sample. Look — amino

acids, isoprenoids." She sets her hand on Julian's shoulder. "Oh, this *is* exciting. I mean, I don't want to get ahead of myself, because Titan had all of this as well, but it's the right puzzle pieces."

Julian smiles, sharing her excitement. "What's next?"

She taps on the slate. "Lucky number three. Let's see what he finds in the caldera."

ISAAC BOBS his head to the music, drumming his fingers to the beat. It's not his music, but something Beckman's loaded from the ops station. Still, he likes it. It reminds him of his university days working through the night in the lab. In the corner of his eye he notices Beckman watching him. Issac continues bobbing his head, giving a thumbs up.

Goose deployed six satellites during their first orbit. On the workstation in front of him is a work-in-progress, a picture assembling itself one strip at a time. Each orbital is mapping in a different spectrum — visual, radar, ultraviolet, infrared. The result is an image which looks like a photograph placed through a shredder, with a forensic artist reassembling the image one strip at a time.

Isaac leans in and squints, tapping a location on the image. He tags it *tholin basin*. He taps another area. *Complex crater*.

Beckman is off to his left, sitting with a cup of tea watching a six-way camera view from the surface drones, *Bernard's* interior cameras, and *Goose's* exterior cameras. He takes a sip and says, "Find anything interesting?"

Isaac looks up. "Oh yes, it's all interesting." He points at a line of mountains. "Minor equatorial ridge. Only other body besides Iapetus to have one. Radar indicates high probability of sub-surface liquid water. Dr. Kelly will be excited." He raises his eyebrows. "How 'bout you? Any aliens yet?"

Beckman pauses, takes another sip of his tea. When he sets his cup back down, he says, "Not yet."

"I hope they come back."

"Really? Not me."

Isaac seems genuinely perplexed. "Why not? Imagine everything we could learn from them. I have so many questions."

"Well, maybe we could learn that they wouldn't have any more concern for stepping on us than we'd have for ants in the grass."

Isaac frowns. "You seem to be a glass-half-empty type of person."

"Better question is if the glass is the size it needs to be," Beckman says.

JAMES LIES on his back beneath a low sea of fiber optics. He's shed his EV suit — he couldn't fit under here wearing it — and instead is wearing a black tee shirt tucked into cargo pants. Although it's dim under here, enough light leaks out of the fiber optic bends to bathe the area in a soft glow. A blue radiance pulses from Ananke's screen to his left. On his right is a box of new fiber optic cables.

"T34," Ananke says.

James holds a small silver flashlight, panning the beam over the junction labels. "R34...S34...gotcha." He unscrews the cable from its mount and examines the clear tube. A hairline fracture passes in a straight line, slightly burnt.

"Pion shower damage," Ananke says. "From the strangelet event."

"That little particle has been a real pain in the ass. Guess we wouldn't be here, though, without it." He snaps in a replacement cable.

"We're giving *Bernard's* the same upgrades *Goose* has, once it's in the ring," Ananke says. "At least there will be no more strangelet events. You know, *Bernard's* will reach ninety-nine-point-one cee after the upgrades."

James grins and tilts his head. "Never thought the old girl would break ninety-eight."

"Slow by *Goose's* standard, but still."

"I'll take it."

Ananke's screen ripples purple. "Next up is Q48."

James shimmies right and slides down, shining the flashlight. "Got it."

"That's the last of them in the central bus."

James tilts his watch. "Hitoshi?"

When the video pops on, Hitoshi lies at an angle in a slanted tube with an access plate exposing circuitry. In his right hand he grips a logic probe. "Yesh?"

"We're about wrapped up in the main bus. How's it going?"

Hitoshi motions towards the panel. "Just need to reverse the polarity, then we're good."

"I'm guessing that's a sci-fi thing."

"Okay, boss, seriously, your office wall is a shrine to the nineteen-fifties and sixties. You've got, like, every astronaut and pilot from the era. You gotta watch some of the shows from that time period."

"You keep telling me that."

"Sooner or later you'll see the light." He motions towards the panel. "So, almost done with the tokamak field controller. Once I wedge myself out of here, I'll meet you at the bridge and we can knock off the psi. If it looks good, we'll warm up the reactor and see if we explode."

James raises an eyebrow.

Hitoshi pinches his fingers together. "It's a really small chance. I wouldn't worry about it."

James shrugs. "Meet you on the bridge."

8

DIVERGENCE

It's June, 2060, in the Whitsunday Islands. Kate wears a tank top and shorts, the wind rustling her long, blonde hair as she trims the mainsail. Behind her, a lush green panorama swirls with ivory sand and aquamarine water.

James lounges on deck, his feet up and crossed. He's tan with dress shorts and a white, cuffed, short-sleeve button down shirt. With his aviator sunglasses, he looks like he's stepped out of time.

Kate's working on the mainsheet when she pauses, breathing hard.

"You okay?" James asks, standing. "Let me get it."

"Yeah," she says. "Just a little light-headed."

He fetches an iced water from the cooler and sets his hand on her back. "Here, drink something. Grab a seat."

"Thanks," she says, cracking open the cap.

He motions over his shoulder. "Let's get below deck, crank up the environmentals. Get you out of the sun." He pauses. "Sure you're okay?"

"Yeah, yeah. Too much fun, not enough aqua."

A few months later, James lies on Kate's dorm bed, tracing a line on the back of her arm with his finger. She giggles and pulls her arm away. Beside her bed, her desk is littered with books and papers. The two bottom books read *Architectural Design I* and *Contemporary Design and Planning Theories*. James admires her focus. She's always known exactly what she wanted to be. Not so much for him. He's a year into an aeronautical engineering degree at Stanford, which he's chosen because of its proximity to her at Berkley, and he's commuting to San Jose for Air Force ROTC classes.

Kate follows his eyes to the bookshelf. "You're thinking about it again, aren't you?"

"What's that?"

"The big decision. Will James Hayden commit?"

"I've got a year to figure it out."

She pinches him. "Air Force officer is kind of sexy. Silver pilot's wings on your dress blues."

He musters his best grin. "You're kind of sexy."

"Think you're going to go for it?"

"Ten year contract as a pilot," James says. "That'd make me thirty-two when I'm out."

"Oh, you should totally do it," she says.

He eyes her, curiously.

"Okay, here's a question for you," Kate says.

He rolls to face her. "Shoot."

"Name an awesome test pilot."

James doesn't hesitate. "Yeager."

"Name another."

"Lovell."

She rests the side of her head on a bent arm. "Now, name your favorite aeronautical engineer."

"Alright, half my favorite test pilots have aeronautical engineering degrees."

"Yeah," she says, "but they're your favorite *test pilots*."

He mirrors her body language, leaning on his elbow. "That doesn't prove anything. Name your favorite architects."

"Yeah, okay, like, Wright, Gehry, Michelson, Sjoberg, Jin..."

"Point taken."

"So, that's the thing. You've practically got 'test pilot' tattooed on your forehead." She hesitates, looking down, then back to him. "You want more than being the next Hayden in Hayden Aeronautics."

He looks at her and he can see it. The divergence. A fork in the road awaiting a choice. One life of certainty, the other of risk. One life where he marries Kate and gives her all of the security they need to grow a family and her career, where he takes the can't-lose path of his father's business. The other where they press the pause button on that future, getting back to it after they pursue their own dreams.

At nineteen he's still a teenager. Life was supposed to wait longer for decisions like this.

Two months later, Kate's lightheadedness returns, this time accompanied by breathlessness and fatigue. Her diagnosis of ATP synthase deficiency due to ATPAF2 gene mutation is a serious problem requiring both genetic and nanotech treatment, but it's curable. She spends a week in the hospital. As they leave, James is quiet.

"Hey, don't worry. It's the sixties. There's nothing modern meds can't fix," Kate says.

James looks over at her. "Back in the islands, I brushed it off. Didn't think anything of it. I should've pushed, got you help sooner."

She pushes him playfully. "C'mon, I'm fine. Knock it off."

By Christmas, she's back in the hospital. This time the deficiency is similar, but different, caused by a mutation in the ATP5E gene. She improves only slightly. By now the doctors have noticed the common thread and suspect underlying genetic damage from a nanotech intervention to correct cystic fibrosis when she was an embryo. They are unclear what the latent trigger was, or even the full scope of genetic damage.

James's father, Christopher, stands outside the hospital room with him. He's tall with sandy blonde hair and has James's charisma. He says, "I talked with Kate's father. George Washington has the best treatment. I'm going to take care of it. She'll have the best."

It's early January when they move her. George Washington University's room is pristine white except for a wall parallel to Kate's bed swirling with azure water lapping against the white sands of the Whitsunday Islands. A vase holds a splash of leafy greens and bright gold flowers. "That's my favorite memory," Kate says, motioning towards the wall. She's pale with brown circles under her eyes.

James squeezes her hand. "Mine too." He rubs his thumb along her palm. "There's some promising low-earth-orbit microgravity treatment options. Experimental stuff, but, we should try it."

She smiles. "Trying to get me on that rocket ship after all?"

He returns her smile.

Kate squeezes his hand back. "You're a fixer, James Hayden, but you can't fix everything."

"I don't accept that," James says.

EVERYONE IS BACK ABOARD *GOOSE*, gathered around the habdeck media screen. Ava and Isaac flank opposite sides of the display.

"Do you want to go first?" Ava says.

Isaac waves a hand. "No way. Yours is cooler."

Ava grins and squeezes her fists. She takes a deep breath and exhales. "Okay. Here we go. So, we sent three drones to analyze the cryovolcano slurry. The samples on the outside were promising, showing some organics similar to what we found on Titan and Enceladus. What was more interesting is that there were potential byproducts of life processes. So we sent the third drone into the volcano's dome itself."

She taps the screen and it displays the drone's recording. At first, it's as if it's peering into a deep, black hole framed by congealed white ice. When the drone flicks on its flashlight, the hole resolves itself into irregular streaks, like candle wax has bubbled up and dropped back down the dome's interior. Glossy ice reflects the quadcopter's light. The copter descends. Fifty meters. One hundred. Five hundred. Finally it reaches the bottom. Solid ice greets it.

"Not surprising," Isaac says. "Frozen over between eruptions. If this were an Earth volcano, this would be the magma chamber."

The drone's spotlight refracts ghostly eddies as it examines the ice floor. When it swings its beam into the wall's ice, it becomes intensely interested in a patch. Chemical compounds scroll down the screen.

Everyone leans in a bit.

Ava smiles and taps the screen. The image changes to a crystalline wonderland visible in the microscopic analysis. When it fills the screen, it's a three-dimensional metallic shape resembling a spiky buckyball surrounded by what appears to be a burst cellular membrane. The entire image is distorted, the object encapsulated in ice crystals. The drone tags the different components with identifiers.

"Polyoxometalate contained within a lipid and protein membrane," Ava says. "It's a hybrid organic-inorganic compound. There are thousands of them per cubic meter beneath the ice floor."

"Are they alive?" Ananke asks.

Ava's talking faster, the pitch of her voice rising. "The cellular structure is similar to an excavate protist. Most cells in the sample area are solitary, but some are clumped in agglomerates. They almost certainly were alive."

James eyes the screen. "All of them are dead?"

"Yes. Cellular membranes are burst."

"From freezing?" Hitoshi says.

Ava shakes her head. "From the polyoxometalate."

Julian adds, "Polyoxometalate has been used in medicine for treatment of tumors, and also as an anti-bacterial and viral."

"Can it occur naturally?" Hitoshi says.

"Yes," Julian says. "But usually it's synthesized. It's a metal anion and an oxide."

Everyone thinks on that a moment. Beckman rubs his chin with his knuckle.

Ava says, "It's entirely possible the polyoxometalate is being formed and released through some natural process, proving toxic to some of the life, or that there's some ecosystem benefit that we don't understand." She pauses. "But the cellular life chemistry appears similar to terrestrial life. If that's true, it will be the second time we've found life which follows the same rules as Earth's."

As James processes her message, the grin builds on his face. "That's awesome! This is what the dream's all about, what Riggs was built for. Why we're all here. This is a *huge* discovery. We came here to fix *Bernard's*, and instead, we found life outside the solar system."

James claps, and everyone follows.

Ava smiles, bouncing slightly. "Oh, I'm so excited."

Julian looks over, and gives a congratulatory clasp on her shoulder.

"What happens next?" James says.

"First rule of exobiology is to leave life untouched. When we're back home, I'll confer with my colleagues and we'll announce. After that, we'll need to design a mission to look in the subsurface seas."

"When it's time to come back, you can count on *Goose*," James says.

"Thanks. Well, I've hogged the stage long enough. Isaac's turn."

Isaac stirs. "Found extra-solar life. Tough act to follow."

Everyone chuckles.

Isaac taps something on his slate and the media screen fades to a Janus graphic. The moon spins slowly as a three-dimensional blank sphere covered in a paper-mache of photographic strips. "Janus model, from orbitals. As Dr. Kelly suspects, we found evidence of a sub-surface ocean covering most of the eastern hemisphere. Heating is mostly from Erebus tidal forces with some core heat. Also found heavy cratering, which is inconsistent with Janus's location. Janus must have been somewhere, such as the inner solar system, where much debris remained after planetary formation. Some craters have a muddy, red snow — tholins — from sunlight on methane. Not enough sunlight here for that."

Ananke's screen pulses orange. "You believe this is evidence of capture?"

Isaac nods. "Erebus orbit is eccentric. Seems more likely it was a capture. Impossible to know which star." He points at the lower left portion of the moon. "This is the most interesting, however. Large impact struck the southern hemisphere. Created weird terrain at its center. Fields of ice spikes hundreds of meters tall, similar to what we see on Pluto. Multiple concentric rings. Inner rings have ice spikes. That's not the unusual part, though." He toggles the display through different wavelengths. A dim glow emanates from the crater's center. "Ultraviolet radiation from the field of spiky crystals."

James squints. "What can create UV?"

"The Sun," Isaac says.

"Weld arcs," Hitoshi adds. "Alien death rays."

Isaac shrugs. "Like I said, weird. Kind of want to check it out, though."

9

THREADING THE NEEDLE

Betty finishes the last of *Bernard's* repairs, and, like a surgeon completing an operation, collects and accounts for all of her tools. Repair of the Riggs drive and radiation shielding is now the ring's job. She packs everything and has herself and all the parts back in *Goose's* cargo bay by nineteen-hundred. It's dark now that the balloon lights have been retracted and packed away. Only the oasis of *Goose's* floods illuminate the landscape.

James leans against the galley wall with his arms crossed. The crew cleans up the last of their dinner. "Well," he says, "we have a decision to make."

"I vote for the cobbler," Hitoshi says.

"More of an after-dessert decision," James says. "*Bernard's* is good to go. Get her back in the ring, ten hours of repairs, head home tomorrow morning."

Hitoshi crosses his arms. "Sounds awesome."

"Question is how we spend those hours. Gotta get some sleep in there, and it's either going to be here or in orbit. Comes down to what we want to do with Isaac's finding."

Isaac rests his hands on the table. "If we go to orbit, we can take images, but *Goose's* cameras aren't any better than what we already have."

"What do you want to do?" James says.

Isaac weighs the question. "Fly *Goose* to the site, send out Ava's quadcopters, find the light source."

James glances at the Janus illustration on the media screen. "A thousand clicks. Take *Goose* supersonic. About thirty minutes to get there."

Beckman squints. "You're thinking of sleeping overnight next to the mystery lights?"

James shakes his head. "Figure we arrive by twenty-one hundred. Send in the drones. Break for orbit by midnight. Sleep in space."

Beckman nods, "Alright."

"So that's the vote," James says. "Direct to orbit, or road trip. Unless there's an option I'm missing."

Everyone's silent, waiting.

"Show of hands," James says. "Road trip?"

Isaac, Ava, and Julian raise their hands.

Ananke says, "I don't have hands, but I vote road."

"Direct to orbit?" James says.

Beckman and Hitoshi raise their hands.

James smiles and quirks his head. "Alright, pack the snacks and queue the tunes. We're goin' on a road trip."

───────────

As JAMES TURNS his head left and right, *Bernard's* cockpit view pans. When he looks down, it's his legs sitting in the pilot's seat, his hand resting on *Bernard's* fingertip controls. He presses down on the smooth panel. The recessed buttons slide under his index finger.

"How's it look?" Hitoshi's disembodied voice says from his left.

"Almost real," James says.

"Okay," Hitoshi says. "Ready for full senses?"

"Game on."

A tingle spreads across James's neck and there's a subtle change in air temperature around him. His chair cushion feels firmer, pressing against him in a different contour, and the harness straps are taut along his chest. It's all a virtual construct, he realizes, linked to *Bernard's* internal sensors, but it feels so *real*. In reality he's not in *Bernard's* at all, but is sitting in *Goose's* cockpit with a model of *Bernard's* cockpit beamed into his central nervous system via the alternate reality link on the back of his neck. *Bernard's* feels real and Hitoshi's floating voice is what seems like the mirage. James gives a thumbs up to his imaginary friend.

"All systems green," James says. *Bernard's* running lights awaken and the navigation beacons glow red and blue. "Port engine's up. Starboard's purring like a kitten."

"Looking good here," Hitoshi says.

"Let's knock the rust loose."

James brings up the engines and a growing hum buzzes through the ship. Outside, ice and snow crack. The ship's attitude control flattens as James's weight shifts. He smiles and taps the comms icon. "*Bernard's Beauty*, ready to launch."

After a pause, Hitoshi says, "Uh, boss...first, I'm standing right next to you, so you don't need to hail me. Second, you're fully linked into all of *Bernard's* system."

"Yeah?"

"So, you really just broadcast that via open comms to all of Janus."

James grimaces. "Damn. Force of habit."

"Uh, okay, so, cleared to launch."

James edges *Bernard's* up and his weight shifts backward, the seat pressing against him. Fog mists from evaporating snow, ringing around Bernard's and dissipating. At twenty meters altitude he rotates to a heading seventy-degrees to his right, slides the throttle forward, and accelerates over the landscape. The wash of light around *Gossamer Goose's* landing area disappears to his left. As he pitches up, an impossibly starry sky welcomes him, then he's picking up speed, mountains streaking beneath him, the sounds of wind buffeting the hull.

"You're right on track," Hitoshi says. "Romeo One is coming around."

"Hell of a shimmy. She's handling like a shot-up bomber," James says. Yellow icons stack themselves like blocks on the left display screen. "Got some vibration warning lights cropping up."

"About to go supersonic," Hitoshi says. "Keep an eye on that ventral plating. Betty couldn't get at it."

The sonic boom rolls through the Janus landscape as James opens the ventral camera image on his right screen. The ship's belly plating is gouged to hell. Betty did some makeshift welds on what she could reach, but the rest will have to be fixed by the ring. Plates rattle at bent exposed edges. James presses the throttle forward and slides back into his seat from the gees, the ship shaking in the atmosphere. When he looks at the external cameras, contrails spiral from the wingtips over Janus's curving landscape. On his navcon, Romeo One approaches from behind and above him.

The warning screen to his left chirps as one of the yellow blocks changes red.

"Got a problem—" James starts. A pop like an explosion sounds from beneath him and the entire ship lurches to the right. Stars pitch up through the cockpit windows and Janus ascends. In the ventral camera, something shiny and bent tumbles off into the night. Instinct is to roll the ship out of the spin, but that will increase the gees even more, stressing the structure. Instead, he eases into the spin until his ship is upside-down. At this angle, the brunt of the wind force is on the undamaged top of the ship. The gees subside as everything levels and calms.

The stars are on the floor and Janus is on the roof through the cockpit windows.

"Lost a plate," James says. "Picked up some more damage to the ventral shielding. Flying upside-down. It's all good."

The atmosphere sounds subside as more of space overtakes the cockpit view. The yellow vibration icons dim to green.

"Intercept in twenty seconds," Hitoshi says.

James searches the externals. There, at his five-o-clock, a blinking star approaches. The star blossoms into a scaffolding filled with high-intensity lights. As he adjusts his speed, the ring slips by him to his starboard.

"Time to thread the needle," James says.

"Go for dock," Hitoshi replies.

Bernard's rises and the ring centers itself in his field of view. He eases forward, the ring enveloping his ship. Smooth as silk he lines up his nacelles with the docking clamps. A jolt shakes the ship as simultaneous clangs sound from each side.

"Dock secure," Hitoshi says. "Nice flying, boss."

James powers down all of *Bernard's* systems. As the last lights go dark, the dock's robotic arms unfold and open the first of eight radial cargo pods. New silver hull plates gleam from inside.

Back in *Goose's* cockpit, James reaches behind his neck and touches the cool disk affixed there. Bernard's cockpit fades away, leaving him seated in *Goose's* pilot's seat. Hitoshi stands beside him.

"You know, we've never done a planetary take-off before with Bernard's," Hitoshi says. "So, that was awesome! Feels good to see her fly again."

IT'S JUST after twenty-hundred when *Goose* lifts off. Nothing is left behind. The only evidence of their presence is the disturbed ground from *Bernard's* crash site and the snowy tread marks left by Betty. If you look carefully, human footprints trace overlapping routes with Betty's tracks.

As the landing site falls behind *Goose*, the cryovolcano shrinks to a flattened dome. The impact crater to its south is easily five times its size.

Ava, Isaac, and James sit in the cockpit seats, with Ananke's slate mounted to the right. Isaac is navigating, watching *Goose's* progress on a map. As *Goose* passes through a layer of ethane clouds, everything washes out around them.

"Heading up to ten clicks," James says

As they clear the cloud layer it's nothing but black sky and stars. Erebus is a plum-sized sphere suspended in the sky, a glowing yellow crescent in enhanced view with a silvery ring. Some of its continents are visible as darker shapes in the sliver. Beneath *Goose*, the cratering fades into flatter landscape before rising to a low line of mountains extending as far as they can see.

"Coming up on the equatorial ridge," Isaac says. "Love to study it more when we come back."

Ava stretches, looking out the side window. "Janus looks a lot like Pluto."

Isaac taps a waypoint on his map. "Very much so."

"Cruising altitude," James says. "Going supersonic."

For the next twenty minutes they watch cratered rocked, snow-drenched mountains, and rusty basins slide past, Isaac pointing out features like a tour guide. Finally, he says, "Destination in five minutes."

James toggles the intercom. "Crew, prep for descent."

Up ahead, the terrain becomes rocky, irregular. As they draw near, it's as if a great mountainous bullseye has been painted on Janus, concentric rings stretching across hundreds of kilometers. The ring's spacing is closest near the outer edges of the bullseye, widening as it moves inwards until the land flattens into a curve before welling back up into a volcano-like peak in the center.

Snow covers most of the peaks with glistening ice spikes, like barnacles reaching towards the sky.

Isaac switches his screen to ultra-violet. The crystal field around the central volcano glows a dim blue. Dozens of fissures radiate around the volcano. The glow is strongest in the fissures.

James magnifies the volcano area. Ice spikes rise as tall as mountains, pointing in random directions, reminding him of barbed wire. The landscape is chaotic, with some areas level and others showing fractured chasms. "Not a very welcoming place, is it?"

Isaac points at a clear spot. "Five kilometers from center. Looks free of ice. Might be the best place to set down."

"Agree," James says. He turns *Goose* in a slow arc, lining up with the new waypoint. Flicking the switch on his console, he says. "Prepare for landing."

10

PENITENTE

Gossamer Goose rests in an other-worldly landscape of powdery cinnamon and salt-splattered rock. Behind it, the nearest crater ring is a jagged stone tower encircling them until it disappears over the horizon. Ice spikes fan out from the crater floor in patches, some as tall as skyscrapers. Overhead, Erebus is a black eye in the sky, watching.

Ava, Beckman, and Isaac stand at the base of the cargo bay ramp, Ananke glowing from Isaac's suit mount. Four of Beckman's security drones hover ten meters above the group.

"Okay," Ava says, setting up the quadcopters. "Here goes." She watches them fly towards the volcano.

Isaac holds a slate streaming their video feeds. The lead copter scans in the ultraviolet, a soft blue glow emanating from the fissures nearest the volcano. Two minutes until arrival.

"Do you think it could be a form of bioluminescence?" Ananke says.

Ava watches the display with interest. "Usually bioluminescence is in the visible spectrum. That doesn't mean it's not possible. Birds and bees see in the UV spectrum."

Isaac reads the analysis of the second quadcopter. "Ice spikes are water ice with ammonium. Called penitentes. Caused by ice sublimation. Present on Earth, Pluto, and Europa. Some spikes along fissures. Suggests water bubbling up, freezing, sublimating."

"Lead drone has arrived," Ava says.

Beckman scans the horizon, a pulse rifle held in both hands.

In the slate video, the fissure descends into a wide opening. Angular rock slips past the camera as the copter enters the opening. After twenty meters, the fissure opens into a subterranean chamber partially filled with an icy slurry producing an eerie blue illumination in the UV spectrum, as if it were a pool with underwater lighting.

Isaac and Ava lean in.

The blue light shifts in patches, at times forming brief patterns at the borders where the slurry flow bends and turns. When the camera zooms, it looks like a star field, millions of tiny light flecks speckled against an indigo backdrop.

"Huh," Isaac says.

Ava targets one of the stars and enlarges it. When the pinpoint zooms, it's not a star but a constellation. Eight fuzzy blue spheres orbit a slightly larger central light.

"It's beautiful," Ananke says.

"Check visual," Isaac says.

Ava taps the control and the drone's flashlight flares bright. In the visual spectrum, the shape is a crystalline snowflake with a geometric nucleus comprised of connected decagons. The light glints along the decagon's edges, giving them a metallic appearance. The snowflake's shape abruptly contracts, pulling in its eight extended arms. It accelerates into a slow rotation.

"That was a reaction," Ava says. "I'm turning off the light."

When Ava extinguishes the light and switches back to ultraviolet, the organism's lights are dark. It's barely visible as a deep blue shadow against a black background. Ava zooms back to view the wider field of creatures. All of them are dark.

She looks up from the slate, staring across the crater field towards the fissures and penitentes, cycling her helmet to enhanced ultraviolet mode. The fissure where the drone is emits no blue glow, but the adjacent fissures and distant crystal structures still do. Then, as if it were closing time, one-by-one the blue lights fade, spreading out in a wave of darkness from the epicenter of the drone. Within a minute, the only ultraviolet light source is the distant pinpoint of the Sun and its reflections on Erebus's oceans and Janus's snow.

Ava's lips are parted as she breathes quickly. Panning her view along the dark horizon, she simply says, "Communication."

———————

IT'S twenty-two hundred hours and the crew shows their fatigue. Everyone stands around the media screen in *Goose's* passenger area. A schematic of the organism is overlaid with technical details from the drone's sensors.

"Polyoxometalate nucleus, surrounded by a saline slush solution, with a complex mineral outer shell, mostly diamond," Ava says.

Hitoshi has a hand on his hip. "How's it able to change shape with a diamond shell?"

Isaac shakes his head. "Unknown."

Ava brings up the organism pictures from the crash-site cryovolcano. The ruptured cell surrounds a spiky buckyball. "Very different from what we saw at the other site. Life chemistry there was an organic shell, and the polyoxometalate structure was simple."

Hitoshi crosses his arms. "Could these be machines?"

"To be honest," Ava says, "I'm not sure that we'd know the difference."

Everyone considers that for a moment.

Isaac says, "So, Ava and I were talking, and we have a crazy, unscientific theory."

Ava smiles. "More of a 'what if?' So, Isaac's theory is that Erebus and Janus were captured from another star. There's a working theory that Earth life may have seeded other planets or moons, such as Enceladus. What if a moon, such as Janus, were seeded by life from two different stars?"

Julian rubs his chin. "You mean, then, what if Janus were seeded by its parent star, then, when captured by our Sun, was seeded again by Earth?"

"Yes!" Ava says. "Two entirely different life chemistries on the same moon, perhaps in competition."

"Interesting," Julian says.

"More of a guess than a theory. For all we know, dual chemistries may be common."

James has his hands on his hips, examining the screen. "What do you want to do next?"

"Oh," Ava says, "that's a tough one. We're here now, but I've got to take back the data and plan an expedition." She crosses her arms. "We've got more this trip than I could ever have hoped for. It's time to call it a day and return to orbit."

James looks over to Isaac.

Isaac nods.

He glances over the rest of the crew. Everyone looks tired.

James grins. "I'm still flying high from the last discovery. This is awesome, and you're right, it's been a hell of a day. Let's configure for orbit and get some sleep. Tomorrow we head home. Big news on the horizon."

———

HITOSHI TAKES a deep breath as he clicks into his seat. As Isaac settles into his workstation, Hitoshi looks over his shoulder and smiles. "Nice work, today."

Isaac nods, "Thanks. Looking forward to orbit?"

"Oh, yeah," Hitoshi says. "Don't know how I'm going to sleep tonight, but, you know."

"Beckman has tea."

"Think I'll stick with the dermals." He glances over at Ava's empty seat, then follows the corridor line to the cockpit. A hint of Ava's shoulder is visible where she sits next to James, and Ananke's blue light pulses along the console. He's a little sad to not have Ava sitting opposite him.

After a few minutes the cabin lights cycle red. James's voice is audible from the open cockpit door, but it amplifies over the intercom. "Prepare for departure," he says.

From *Goose's* aft, the RF engines build to a low hum. Hitoshi's seat pushes up against him as ice cracks outside. Lateral thrusters fire in bursts, stabilizing the ship, and after a brief pause *Goose* dips forward and accelerates. On Hitoshi's monitor, the convoluted landscape slips away. He takes another deep breath, like a great weight has been lifted from his shoulders, and closes his eyes

The chirp from his work station's console jolts him. He snaps forward and opens the alert.

Sierra Two, Three, and Four satellites have all detected an anomaly. When Hitoshi dumps the video to his screen, the Milky Way slants diagonally across an endless star field. A new star flares briefly into existence and just as quickly fades away.

He slaps the comms. "James! Sierras picked up a flash. Sending to your screen."

James responds, "Got it. Bad timing. Any other info?"

Hitoshi queues up a subroutine. "It's in three different images, so I can estimate range."

"Staying on course for orbit. If we have to bug out, can't use the Riggs drive if we're atmospheric."

The calculations finish and display in an inset window. Hitoshi says, "One point four billion kilometers."

The tension in James's voice eases. "Alright, that's plenty of breathing room."

"Right...right. That's like Saturn distance from the Sun—" He stops, the word *Saturn* catching in his mind. "Oh, I just had a horrible thought."

There's a slight pause. "Getting a little worried here, Hitoshi."

"If we were jumping *Goose*, the light from the Riggs flash would arrive a little before *Goose* did."

James processes that. "You're thinking it's a warning that—"

Lightning flashes outside, casting electric blue trapezoidal patterns in the passenger cabin from the cockpit windows. Hitoshi's pulse quickens as he reaches for the external display. Thunder rolls across the sky.

Below, a silver asterisk spins suspended a few hundred meters over the fissures, orange lights flickering from the ends of its rods.

Hitoshi's breathing hard now, gripping his arm rest.

"I see it," James says.

Isaac is surprisingly calm. "Same appearance and dimensions as the one you encountered."

The alien probe's lights fade from orange to red as it rises towards them.

"It's coming!" Hitoshi says.

"It's fast," Isaac says. "Intercept in ten seconds."

Hitoshi looks back over his shoulder at Isaac as if to say *how can you be so calm?*

"Leveling out," James say. "If they're going to catch us, they're going to catch us."

In the external camera, the probe flies up to *Goose's* starboard side, spinning quickly. It loiters there, a few meters from the wing, and strobes its rods in dazzling flashes.

"Ultraviolet and x-ray radiation," Ananke says over comms. "Low-level alpha radiation. Not enough to penetrate the hull."

"Ava, ideas?" James says.

"Might be trying to establish communication," Ava says.

From behind Hitoshi, Beckman says, "Or warning us to get the hell out of their airspace."

"Try pulsing the strobes," Ava says.

In the exterior camera, *Goose's* anti-collision strobes flick on, flashing twice.

The probe stops flashing, its lights cycling between orange and red.

"That did something," Isaac says.

A blur fills the camera as the probe wheels towards *Goose*. The impact feels like a parking-lot mishap, jolting everyone left. A collective gasp sounds from the crew.

"Yeah," Beckman says. "Pissed it off."

The probe spins out of view of the starboard camera.

Hitoshi digs his hand out of the arm rest and pokes at the camera displays on his workstation. "I lost it."

"It's underneath us. Hang onto something," James says. "Time to get us some separation."

Goose's engines well-up and press Hitoshi firmly into his seat. He sinks further and further as an invisible weight pushes down hard on his chest. He grits his teeth, sucking in air. A sonic boom crashes outside like a distant detonation.

"We're supersonic," James says. "Charging up the Riggs drive."

Atmospheric noise buffets the hull as *Goose* slices through the clouds.

When Hitoshi reaches for his console, it feels like he's bench pressing weights. His hand trembles as he switches to the aft camera. Janus curves away at a steep angle behind them, two bending contrails trailing from their wings. A few hundred meters behind them spins the probe. "That's right," Hitoshi says through gritted teeth. "Eat contrail."

The probe spins faster and faster, prismatic light trails orbiting it.

"James..." Hitoshi says.

The aft camera blanches to white from the jump flash as

lightning bursts directly in front of *Goose*. For a split second Hitoshi sees the whirling red lights of the alien probe through the cockpit windows, then *Goose* kicks up and spins hard to the left.

Everything goes gray for a moment, the sounds around Hitoshi fading into a muted chaos. As the acceleration eases, reality fades back in. Stars are just visible through the cockpit windows ahead, the faint glow of Janus's atmosphere at the bottom. Red light dances along the trapezoidal frame of the cockpit windows as if an emergency vehicle were outside. The probe drifts in from the right and spins directly in front of *Goose*.

Before, Hitoshi saw it through the filter of a display screen. Now, seeing it with his own two eyes through the front of the cockpit windows is terrifying. It rotates on multiple axis, each of its rods pulsing its own rhythm of red light.

"Ninety seconds to Riggs charge," James says. "Gonna need to do some aerobatics to get clear."

Ava says, "It's changing."

The probe's light pulses from red to purple to blue as it slows. Each of its arms is composed of twelve-sided platinum rods of varying lengths. The entire craft is four meters tall until the rods begin sliding relative to each other, collapsing towards the core. Now it's three meters, two meters, no longer a star shape, but more like a giant metal soccer ball. It rotates and surges just off *Goose's* nose.

"James," Ananke says. "I sense it."

"You sense it?" James says.

"It's...it's looking at me. It's like when a human feels another person is watching him. It's scaring me."

Hitoshi can't see James from where he sits in the cabin, but he hears him say, "Time to leave. Everyone brace!"

Goose lurches right and the stars spin left, the alien probe drifting out of view.

"Jump in thirty seconds."

Hitoshi clamps onto the console, pressing his thumb hard

into the display to switch views. The alien probe is a sporadic whirl of red strobes in their wake. As its lights stretch to prismatic whirls, Hitoshi yells, "It's going to jump again!"

The passenger cabin explodes with a wash of heat and light, the impact smashing Hitoshi into a daze. His vision blurs as a ringing overtakes his ears. Freezing cold air crashes over his neck. Behind him, parts of the cabin rip and shred in a cacophony of destruction and he can't think of anything but unclipping his harness and getting away from it. His fingers fumble with the latch and he falls to his knees. As he looks up, horror washes across his expression.

The alien probe buzzes like an angry bee swarm, spinning inside the aft cabin only meters from Hitoshi. Its rod ends strobe red, causing a freeze-frame effect to every movement around him.

Julian and Beckman are both on their backs, crab-walking away from it, and Isaac is frozen in place in his chair, staring.

"It's inside the ship!" Hitoshi says.

The probe accelerates its spin, its rods sliding outwards like eyestalks, increasing its height now to two-and-a-half meters. As it rolls forward, it rips apart the nearest sleep chamber, sending sparks flying.

Beckman pushes to his feet, rushes over to Julian, and grabs him by the shoulder. He yanks him towards the starboard side. "Emergency area! Get inside."

Isaac is still petrified as the probe rolls straight towards him. Hitoshi's legs are like rubber, but he lunges onto Isaac, unclicks his harness, and pushes him towards Beckman just as the probe reaches him. Hitoshi falls back against the media screen as the probe crushes Isaac's chair. It rolls in an arc turning towards Hitoshi, cutting him off from Beckman and the others on the star-board side. As it increases its spin, shredded console parts and chair foam sting him. He curls up with both arms over his head and lets out a muffled scream. The probe rolls towards him like a massive buzzsaw.

Blue flashes sear through the cabin, slamming into the spinning probe, showering sparks around Hitoshi. When Hitoshi looks up, Beckman advances from the other side of the cabin, firing another volley from his pistol. Something breaks off the alien probe and skitters to the ground.

The probe flares cyan, retracting its rods, and darts towards Beckman. Beckman squeezes off three more shots before it clips him, sending him sprawling into the wall. It leaves him and turns towards the cockpit.

James blares over comms, "Everyone in the emergency area, now!"

Hitoshi pushes up and stumbles over to Beckman, grabbing him under his armpits and dragging him. "Crap, you are heavy."

As he gets Beckman inside the emergency area with Julian, he slaps the comm. "James, it's coming your way. Get out of there."

"Buckle!" James replies.

Hitoshi blinks and looks over at Julian and Isaac. The two help lift Beckman into his seat and click in his harness, then they settle into theirs.

Hitoshi eyes the two empty seats waiting for James and Ava.

Julian follows Hitoshi's gaze. "They're on the bridge, cut off."

As Hitoshi reaches for the comm panel, the airlock slams closed. A klaxon sounds as red strobes spin their warning. *James is ejecting them.* Hitoshi pulls his hand back and grips his harness straps.

When the explosive bolts separate *Goose's* emergency area from *Goose*, it sounds like firecrackers going off in rapid succession. The jolt is like a kick in the back. An instant later the pod's thrusters blast continuously behind him, pushing his seat hard against him. Through the little window over his shoulder, *Goose* falls away from them, sparks wreathing around the open wound of its missing wingtip where the emergency area had been. *Goose's* cockpit flashes with angry red light.

"C'mon," Hitoshi says, intently watching the starboard side of *Goose's* nose. "Get in there, eject."

Goose keeps falling away from them, Janus a blue-white marble.

"Eject," Hitoshi says again. The harness strap digs into his hand. He slaps the comm with his other hand. "James, get out of there! Ejec—"

Goose's cockpit explodes in a blast of fire, sending glowing shrapnel in a streaking sphere. As the ship spins erratically, parts of the open interior are visible surrounded by molten hull plates and structures. Debris spills out with the ship's crystallizing atmosphere.

Hitoshi's stomach drops, his hand still on the comms panel. He feels sick.

As *Goose* spins, electrical flashes flare from inside the cabin. A dull red glow brightens near the ship's aft.

"Oh God," Hitoshi says. "The drive charge."

Something pops over the red glow and molten metal sprays out in a widening arc. Orange globs spin like bits of magma freed to space. *Goose* pinwheels there a second, colliding with fragments of its own wreckage, then flashes brilliant white as Hitoshi's window automatically opaques.

"No..." Julian says, sitting across from Hitoshi.

When the window fades back to transparent, incandescent chunks of *Goose* spin everywhere, lost in a sea of dying embers.

11

TWENTY MINUTES

When James looks over his shoulder through *Goose's* open cockpit door, the passenger cabin is a riot of shredding noise and flickering crimson light, electric blue strobing from somewhere in the back as a pulse pistol's shots ring out. Three more shots and a muffled scream. To James's right, Ava sits in her chair, eyes wide, and Ananke's screen pulses silver. James slaps the intercom. "Everyone in the emergency area, now!" Behind him, the red lights of the alien probe flare in the access corridor smoke. He snaps his attention to Ava. She looks at him, questioning.

"Take Ananke, get in the escape capsule," James says. "Right over there. Mash the big red button, grab the bar, and drop inside. Go, go, go!"

The comms icon illuminates and Hitoshi's voice blares out of the speaker. "James, it's coming your way. Get out of there."

Ava's out of her seat with Ananke, dashing towards the red hatch labeled *emergency*.

James hits the comm transmit back to Hitoshi. "Buckle!"

The corridor walls behind him rip and crumple as James opens the lifeboat interior video. Beckman is slumped unconscious buckled into his seat, and Julian, Isaac, and Hitoshi are all secure. Hitoshi has his hand on the comm panel. James keys in the command code and overrides the lifeboat airlock, closing it.

Flickering red light appears in the cockpit. The probe is nearly through the corridor.

James's console displays a blinking eject icon. He hits it and a five second countdown appears, then he's out of his seat, diving for the escape hatch, grabbing the pull bar, and swinging his legs into the circular opening. *Goose* pops and shudders as the lifeboat containing Hitoshi and his crew jettisons.

Beneath James, the escape capsule looks like the interior of an old Soyuz capsule. Six seats are arranged in a circle facing outwards. Ava sits in one with Ananke on her chair mount, and two are empty. The other three are filled with empty EV suits. A red klaxon strobes from the capsule's apex.

The cockpit doorframe splinters and the probe rolls in, crushing the center cockpit seat. It spins slowly at first, its lights cycling between orange and red, then picks up speed. James slams the escape capsule hatch and drops into his seat, buckling his harness. The sound from the cockpit area intensifies.

Ava's breathing hard to his left.

Ananke's voice is filled with terror. "James! It's me. It wants *me*. It's accessing my matrix. I can feel it."

"Hang on!" James says. He taps in the launch sequence on the slanted panel in front of him. A red eject icon blinks urgently. As he extends his hand towards the icon, gravity amplifies and his arm slams down hard on the armrest. He grits his teeth and bears down, trying to force blood to his head, but his vision narrows. The red eject icon blinks, waiting. As he looks down at his hand, thousands of little light points collect across his skin, tingling like ants crawling over him. As the points collide they merge into brighter flashes spinning with prismatic bursts. Every surface of the capsule is alive with speckled light, coated in pinpoints, and the capsule walls twist and breathe. Gravity increases again and his vision fades to black.

In the distance, like a dream, Hitoshi says, "James, get out of there," then there is searing heat and nothing but darkness.

JAMES STIRS AWAKE to the tingling of wind chimes and the crashing of distant ocean waves, a sheet draped half over his chest. Overhead, a ceiling fan spins, wafting cool air. When he rolls to his right, the bungalow is white and filled with sunlight. The sliding glass doors are open, a slight breeze cascading in, and the wind chimes dangle to the left of the deck. Kate leans against the deck railing. She's put on her torn jean shorts that James loves, and a wispy white top which billows in the wind. Sand stretches out behind her until it marries with azure Caribbean waters.

James swings out of bed and pulls on a pair of shorts, joining her on the deck.

Kate looks over, her elbows on the railing. Her sunglasses have a brown gradient and her blonde hair rustles in her face. "Morning, sleepy head."

James sets his hand in the small of her back. She looks perfect in every way. He gives her a kiss. "Morning."

In the distance, an aircraft engine buzzes in the sky. Kate points to her left. "Tour time. Think he'll stick it today?"

James follows her gaze. Saint Jean's bay is an aquamarine crescent against a white sandy beach dappled with red-roofed houses. The airport's runway connects nearly directly with the beach, rising at an angle to a grassy top. In the glare of the blue sky a Twin Otter approaches, descending, rocking its wings to level out. Rainbow colors adorn its nose and tail. James feels his hands turning the imaginary controls, trying to correct its approach and get it back on centerline. The Otter drifts left, straightens, and comes in for a smooth landing, quickly slowing. It disappears out of sight when it turns onto the taxiway, heading for the parking area where James's Piper waits.

"Not bad. Getting better," James says.

"What should we do today?" Kate asks.

James look out at the azure water. "Let's go sailing." He smiles, but then his smile fades. *Sailing*, he thinks. He glances around at the island, confused. "Didn't we want to go to the Whitsunday Islands?"

She squints. "We can still do that sometime. You really wanted to try this airport with your Piper."

He slides his hand from her back, taking a step back.

She looks at him, questioning. "What's the matter?"

This never happened, he realizes. *We had to choose, and we chose Whitsunday.*

"James?" she asks, but before he can answer, Kate, the beach, and the ocean disappear.

For a moment, James is nowhere. When he looks left, thousands of James stand in a line, all looking left. When he looks right, it is the same infinite line of himself, like standing between two mirrors in a fun house, endlessly reflecting. He lifts his right hand and spreads open his fingers. The images closest to him do the same, but the further he looks down the line the more they diverge. Some raise their hand but do not spread their fingers. Others never raise their hand. Most wear the same Hayden-Pratt flight suit he wears, but some wear other outfits—business suits, casual clothes. As he looks further down the line there are skips where no one stands.

He focuses on one of the men wearing a business suit. When he blinks, he's twenty-six, sitting in a conference room at Hayden Aeronautics in Pasadena. Twenty other people sit around the oval table, turned towards his father. Christopher Hayden is talking about market share and strategies for hypersonic aircraft, and the chief technical officer, Liam, is waiting in the wings to discuss development and product launch. James sets his hand on the table, feeling the grain of the wood. *No,* he thinks, *I am not here. I'm at Edwards Air Force Base learning to be a test pilot. I don't know Will here. How can I not know Will?*

The scene falls away and he's back in the line of men. And, looking over them, he realizes it. They're all versions of himself which he could have been, or perhaps, now are, in other realities. The nearest ones mirror his choices the closest. The furthest diverge. He thinks on this a moment, searching for the version which went to Saint Julian instead of Whitsunday. He watches, through his eyes, as the events play out. Kate, breathless in the sun, this time while sailing in the Caribbean bay. Months later the diagnosis. The funeral on a snowy February day. He pulls back, his chest hurting, and looks for another version.

In some versions, he never meets Kate. In those, the Pasadena conference room scenario plays out. In others, they discover her sickness earlier or later, but in each case the only effect is to move the month of the funeral. There are no versions where Kate survives. Based on the missing people in line, there also are versions where James does not survive. The one common thread to all of the timelines is that without Kate, James does not go to Edwards, and without Edwards he does not meet William Pratt. Inevitably James ends up leading Hayden Aeronautics, but without William there is no Hayden-Pratt, no Riggs program, and no interstellar travel leading to this moment. *Still,* he thinks, *if I could have found one reality where she lived, I would have sacrificed all of this to have it.*

As he's standing there, his throat tight, swallowing hard, the images fade like falling dominos. When the succession reaches him, a crushing weight presses down on him and he falls to the ground, squatted and curled up. Flashing stars accumulate on his hands like snowflakes as his vision grays. Searing heat rushes over him as the blackness blares brilliant white with a sound like rushing wind, then it fades, the weight receding. As he shakes, his eyes still closed, he feels something cool beneath his forearms. He presses his hands down and the glossy surface of the armrest console presses back. When he blinks open his eyes, the red light of *Goose's* escape capsule shines down. Ava is to his left, stirring in her chair.

On the wall screen, the chronometer has skipped twenty minutes forward. Next to it, the eject icon still blinks, waiting.

12

FREEZE FRAME

Hitoshi stares out the window at *Goose's* glowing wreckage as the lifeboat's thrusters scale back to one-quarter gee. His chest rises and falls with each breath, his body numb. Behind him, clothes rustle and a harness unclicks, then an access panel slides open. When Hitoshi looks over his shoulder, Julian has unpacked the emergency medical kit and passes a hand-held imager over an unconscious Beckman. Isaac sits opposite, his hands draped between his knees, head low, bloody scratches marring his face and arms. When, Hitoshi glances down at his own hands, cuts score the backs of his forearms and palms from where he shielded himself from the probe.

Beckman stirs, shifting his weight.

"Guthrie," Julian says. "Can you hear me?"

Beckman blinks a few times, staring straight ahead. "My name is Beckman." He moves and winces. "No Guthrie, no mister."

"That is good to hear. Can you rate your pain on a scale of one to ten?"

He grimaces. "Two."

"I very much doubt that, with that wrist fracture. No point in downplaying, my friend."

A deep breath and another wince. "Five."

Julian selects a dermal and applies it to the side of his neck. "This will help. You have a concussion, right ulna fracture, three bruised ribs, and contusions along your right leg, elbow, shoulder, and back of your head."

"Did I kill it?"

"Unfortunately, no, but what you did was very brave." He produces a pair of shears and cuts open Beckman's sleeve. "No displacement for the fracture, which is good, so we'll cast it." He lifts the aerosol dispenser and sprays it over both sides of Beckman's arm and palm. At first it glistens like oil, then the gel rapidly expands until it's half-a-centimeter thick, quickly drying. Next, Julian affixes a clear rectangle just over Beckman's left eyebrow. "Your concussion is mild. This is just for telemetry."

Beckman glances over at the two empty chairs. "Are James and Ava still aboard *Goose*?"

Hitoshi's been watching Beckman and Julian, but he turns away, looking at the floor.

Julian reads the telemetry on his slate. "Let's focus on you. Is there any place else that you are hurt?"

"What happened with the probe? Is it gone?"

Hitoshi looks up. "*Goose* is gone."

"Jumped?" Beckman says.

Hitoshi's throat is tight and his voice cracks. "Destroyed." He can see the next question Beckman's about to ask. "No one else got out."

Beckman's shoulders sink as he takes a deep breath.

Julian sets his hand on Beckman's shoulder. "Try to stay put. I'll give you some anti-inflammatories, then I need to look at Hitoshi and Isaac, okay?"

Beckman nods.

Julian gives him another dermal, then crosses over to Hitoshi. He produces an antiseptic toilette and cleans Hitoshi's face and arms. It stings a bit and feels cool as it evaporates. Hitoshi looks ahead, unfocused, as Julian applies sealant to one of the deeper cuts on his cheek. "You could have went straight to the emergency area," Julian says, "but you stayed to rescue Isaac. That was quite heroic."

Hitoshi looks at Julian. "I don't feel very heroic."

"Do you have any other injuries?"

"No, just the cuts."

Julian finishes sealing two cuts on his arms, then lays a hand on Hitoshi's. "Try to rest. I'll be back."

Hitoshi blinks a few times, breathing. He stares out the window. Something clicks in his head and he feels like he's just awakened from a daze. "I don't know what I'm thinking. I should be scanning the wreckage. Ananke could be in it. Even the bridge escape capsule could be in it." He reaches for the wall panel and opens the sensor display.

Isaac looks over, Julian dabbing at his head. "I'm okay, Julian. I'll help Hitoshi."

Julian squeezes on some sealant. "One minute."

After Julian finishes, Isaac swivels his chair to face the wall display. "Sending out a radar pulse."

Hitoshi's breathing regularly now, the numbness subsiding. "Let's catalogue everything in the field. I'll monitor comms for the emergency beacon."

On his screen, the active radar pulse tags thousands of pieces ranging from centimeter-wide metal fragments to entire chunks of *Goose*.

"Roster's up," Hitoshi says. "Let's divide it into sectors. I'll take odd, you take even."

"Roger," Isaac says.

Over his shoulder, Beckman has his shirt up while Julian sprays something along his ribs.

"Hey, man," Hitoshi says to Beckman. "Thanks for going all Worf back there to save me."

Beckman squints. "I have no idea what that means, but you're welcome."

Hitoshi nods, then returns to his display.

———

It's just after midnight when the crew convenes at the media screen. Isaac has moved their lifeboat into the same orbit as the debris field. No longer under acceleration, they now all hold tethers floating in orbital free fall. Much to Julian's objections, Hitoshi has brewed some coffee in the galley, and both he and Isaac drink some from zero gee bulbs. Beckman sips water. The display looks like a forensic reconstruction after an aircraft crash.

"We've accounted for almost all of Goose," Hitoshi says. "No sight of Ananke's slate or the bridge capsule, and most of the cockpit is missing." Julian looks over at Hitoshi with an unspoken question. Hitoshi hesitates, then says, "There were no bodies in the wreckage."

"What does that mean?" Beckman asks.

"I don't know," Hitoshi says. "But I think the next step is to review the lifeboat's external cameras from when we ejected." He pauses. "It's going to be hard to watch."

Everyone nods and Hitoshi puts it on screen. The camera view is situated just over their lifeboat's thrusters, looking back at Goose. In the video, Gossamer Goose falls away, the star field turning slowly. As the time index spins higher, red light strobes from Goose's cockpit. Ten seconds later the cockpit explodes in a brilliant flash, spiraling bits and pieces of metal in a semi-sphere.

Everyone shifts uncomfortably.

Isaac freezes the video, rewinds it, and zooms on the cabin. The video advances in slow motion. At first, the cockpit flashes red, but the color of the light changes, the interior flickering with prismatic flashes. Even in slow motion, when the cockpit explodes, it happens in only a second.

Hitoshi rewinds back to the prismatic light, advancing frame-by-frame.

One: The cockpit is intact.

Two: Colors distort and and the image twists, swirls forming in a sphere encompassing the right half of the cockpit. Where the distortion extends outside of *Goose*, light from a star in the background stretches into an arc.

Hitoshi raises an eyebrow and glances over at Isaac. "You see that? Gravitational lensing."

Isaac nods. "Space-time geometry change."

Beckman squints.

Hitoshi moves to the next frame.

Three: A spherical fireball replaces two-thirds of the cockpit.

Four: Two-thirds of the cockpit disappears. It looks like someone has taken a scooper and carved a perfect sphere out of the starboard-side of the ship. The remaining structure glows, fragments blurred and flying apart.

Five: The cockpit explodes out in a debris cone covering a semi-sphere on *Goose's* port side.

Hitoshi's pulse quickens. "That's why the cockpit is missing. It was a jump. The same thing would happen if we could activate the Riggs drive within a mass field. Anything within the radius of the Riggs boundary would get scooped up and come along with us."

"Jump?" Beckman says. "You mean from the alien?"

Hitoshi nods. "Yeah, rainbow light show, fireball."

Beckman furrows his brow. "What does that mean for James?"

"I don't know. If they all got inside the escape capsule, they might be traveling with the probe."

He doesn't want to say that if they didn't, they would've been ejected into space from the open cockpit.

Beckman raises his eyebrows. "Damn."

Isaac pecks at his arm console. "We should connect to the Sierra orbitals now."

Hitoshi's with him. "Yeah."

"Got them," Isaac says.

"Bring up the Sierra log from the first probe jump flash."

Isaac reads the telemetry from the probe's first jump to Janus. "If they jumped at light speed, it would take eighty-two minutes to travel that distance."

"Yeah," Hitoshi says. "But the probe arrived after the flash, so it wasn't traveling at light-speed. Thank God, because that would be freakin' impossible."

Isaac does some quick math on his console. "We can figure out how fast it's going, right? Light flash took eighty-two minutes to get here. It arrived two minutes, fifty-two seconds later. Means it travels at ninety-seven percent light speed."

"Well, well," Hitoshi says, "not so mighty after all." He pauses. "We're faster than it. *Goose* was a lot faster than it."

Isaac adds, "If the probe jumped around ten-thirty, then they should have arrived fourteen minutes ago."

Beckman frowns. "I really hate math problems."

"Yeah," Hitoshi says, "assuming it went back to the same place it came from."

"The orbitals should see it, then?" Julian asks.

"Once the light gets here, just past one a.m.," Hitoshi says.

Julian shifts, turning in zero gee. "If they're in the escape capsule, how long would it take for them to fly back here from that distance?"

Hitoshi shakes his head. "Chemical thrusters only. A few years."

"And if we go to them?"

Hitoshi does some quick math on the console. "Lifeboat's got an RF drive, so, eighteen days."

Julian hesitates. He clearly doesn't want to ask the next question. "And for all of us to get back to Earth?"

"In the lifeboat? That one's a bit of a problem," Hitoshi says. "Twenty-seven years."

13

ADRIFT

As James lifts his hand and reaches for the eject button, something stirs on the other side of the capsule airlock. Metal groans. A jolt shakes the capsule and James's harness straps press lightly into his shoulders. He eyes the airlock status. Vacuum on the other side. Tentatively, he slides his hand away from the eject icon, unclicks his harness and pushes out of his seat, weightless. A kick against the wall sends him drifting towards Ava. As he does, the nearest wall falls towards him. Centrifugal force. *The capsule is rotating*, he realizes. He grabs onto the bar beside Ava's seat and swings in front of her.

Ava opens her eyes and focuses on him.

"Are you alright?" James says.

"Did *Goose* jump?"

James shakes his head. "No, that was something else. I lost twenty minutes. Were you awake for any of it?"

"Twenty minutes? Uh, no...I don't know. I was dreaming, I think. It was so real. It felt like hours."

Dreaming, James thinks. He considers her for a second. "Did you see yourself? Choices never taken, versions of you that could've been?"

Ava pulls back and grips her arm rests. She raises her eyebrows, confusion in her expression, and tears well into a weightless film over her eyes. "Yes," she says, her voice cracking. "What does it mean?"

"I don't know. Everything's quiet on the other side of the airlock. Cockpit's in vacuum." James turns towards Ananke's slate. "Ananke, are you alright?"

Ava says, "Her screen's black."

James swivels the slate towards himself. The display is translucent black, like smoked glass. He taps twice on the screen and it reboots. When it finishes, it's deep blue with a slowly rotating ring. The text beneath reads, *error - unsupported matrix transfer - intelligence purged.*

"No!" James says, undocking the slate and grabbing it. He swipes through the logs. Twenty minutes ago Ananke's quantum matrix was removed from the slate. He just holds it, staring at the rotating ring. His chest rises and falls with each deep breath.

Ava sets her hand on the back on his.

"She's not dead," James says. "She said it was trying to access her matrix. Goddammit, it took her. " He watches the slate, then spins to face the wall panel. "We have to find it." When he taps a few commands, the navcon buzzes and scrolls through several alerts. "*Goose* isn't responding," James says. "I'm going to try the lifeboat." He taps the comms channel. "Hitoshi, James, acknowledge."

Ava shifts forward. Thirty seconds go by without a response.

James turns and faces her. "Alright, so we're blind in here until we eject. Ready?"

Ava nods her head. "Yes."

James pushes towards his seat. He drifts down into it and fastens his harness, reaching for the button. "Eject in three, two, one. Now."

A dozen firecrackers pop just on the other side of the airlock, lurching them sideways. The capsule spins and slows. When the thrusters kick on, the force pushes up from beneath the floor. James keys a command on his armrest screen and two joysticks rotate out an angles near each of his hands. The slanted screen in front of him scrolls with telemetry. Constellation diagrams appear.

"Got a fix on the Sun," James says. "Constellations are all in the right place. Found Erebus. I'll share my screen." .

Erebus is a blue star against a field of white stars. A smaller, fainter star is adjacent it. Janus.

"That's...really small," Ava says.

"Getting range...alright, we're eighty-three light-minutes from Erebus. And we lost twenty minutes getting here. Can't be *Goose*. I think the probe jumped us."

"You think that was time compression, like when *Goose* jumps?"

Something clicks in James's head. "Yeah, but *Goose* can do eighty-three light-minutes in a minute or so. The probe's gotta be slower. A lot slower."

"Hmm," Ava says. "I always thought if we found alien tech it'd be more advanced than us."

"Maybe they're just different," James says. "Let's get a look at *Goose* and see how badly she's damaged."

When he flips on the aft external camera, at first there is only a colorful star field. When he toggles the display to infrared, his stomach sinks. The cockpit wreckage spins slowly in the void, the starboard side facing him with a circular breach where the escape capsule ejected. Above it, the side windows are perfectly intact with most of Goose's nose untouched. The hull, however, ends in a cleanly-cut arc just aft of the cockpit seats. As the wreckage continues to rotate, the cross-sectional view of the interior comes into view. Two of the three cockpit seats are present. Naked hull frame, interior shielding, and circuitry is exposed where the frame is cut. The cut is like nothing James has ever seen, perfectly spherical. The frame glows bright in the infrared along the edges. There is no sign of the rest of the ship.

At first James says nothing, his lips flattening. He wants to punch something, but he feels Ava's gaze upon him. "Shit," he says. "That means *Goose* is disabled and the others are stranded." He rubs his forehead, closing his eyes.

The hiss of the capsule's atmospheric system and the rumbling thrusters fill the silence.

James opens his eyes and glances over at her. She looks frightened. "Okay," James says, focusing on controlling his vocal tone. "Their lifeboat has a month of food, we've got half-a-month. We're going to figure something out."

"Okay," Ava says, swallowing.

"I'm going to flip on the emergency beacon so they know we're out here. Let's have a look on the cameras and see if we can spot our silver friend." Endless stars appears on their wall screens. "Can you help me with the scan?"

Ava nods.

They complete a three-sixty assessment under increasing magnification. After a few minutes of scanning Ava says, "Got it." She brackets it and shares it with James's display. At first, it's a blue star sliding against a static background of the Milky Way. When they enhance it, the star is a slightly blurry silver asterisk with blue lights at its tips. Two of the rods are broken, their lights extinguished.

"Just over five-hundred clicks," James says. "Looks damaged. I heard pulse fire back in the cabin. I'll bet Beckman shot the hell out of it."

"This makes me a bad exobiologist, but if I had a pistol I'd probably shoot it too," Ava says.

James smiles. "You are fitting right in." He eyes the graphic. "We can't catch it unless it slows, but we can shadow it until it gets out of range."

Ava contemplates that. "You want to go after it?"

He looks over at her. "That thing took Ananke, and I want to get her back."

She's nervous, rubbing her leg. "Any ideas how to do that?"

"Don't know. Going to have to find a way to talk with it."

Ava looks away. James waits, his hands resting by the joysticks.

"Let's start with what we know," Ava says. "Talk me through everything you saw the first time you encountered it on Janus, and then we'll go through what just happened. We've got a first contact protocol. Let's modify it for when you catch up with it."

A subtle grin pulls across James's face as he slips his hands onto the joysticks. "Changing course," he says. As the thrusters fire, his weight shifts, the chair pressing against his left shoulder. He pulses another burst, leveling the capsule's nose. The alien probe is dead ahead. James dials up the main engines for a slow and steady burn as he and Ava sink back into their seats.

HITOSHI FLOATS NEXT TO ISAAC, monitoring the external camera. *Goose's* wreckage is thousands of glittering metal shards enveloping islands of fuselage. Every few minutes a shooting star burns up in Janus's upper atmosphere. Pieces of *Goose*.

"Question is," Hitoshi says, "whether we want to try and fish anything out of the debris field. Risky. A lot of stuff to collide with. Someone would have to go EV."

"What do you think we need?" Isaac says.

"Oh, just off the top of my head. Guns. Lots and lots of guns. In case our friend the silver destroyer reappears. Beckman practically turned the cargo bay into an armory. I'm sure some of it's out there."

Beckman stirs. "We don't need to do that."

Hitoshi turns both of his palms up. "Seriously? Figured you'd be first in line for this idea."

"I mean, we don't need to risk going into the wreckage to get guns." He pushes away from his chair and drifts to the personnel lockers. When he accesses the first locker, its door slides open to reveal three pistols.

Hitoshi blinks. "Good God, man, you hid guns on the *lifeboat*?"

Beckman shrugs. "Where do you think I got the pistol from before?"

"Figured you had one stuffed in your sock."

"Basic op security, have a fallback point stocked with what you need. If we ended up on the lifeboat, we'd need more than granola bars."

Hitoshi smiles. "I could totally hug you right now."

Beckman just stares at him.

"I won't," Hitoshi says, "but I could."

From the console, an alarm chirps. Everyone freezes. The alert window reads *image anomaly, Sierra One and Two.*

Hitoshi pushes back to his station and switches to the Sierra feed. In the image, a new star flares blue before fading back to black.

Isaac taps calculations on his workstation. "Location is identical to initial probe jump, one-point-four billion kilometers from here, in the direction of the Oort Cloud."

"I knew it," Hitoshi says. "It took them back to where it came from. Anything on radio?"

Isaac shakes his head.

A tense stillness befalls the group. Hitoshi doesn't say it, but he knows everyone's thinking the same thing. If anyone is in the escape capsule, they may activate the emergency beacon. And a beacon would mean they were alive to throw it.

Thirty seconds goes by. Sixty. Ninety. The Sierra telemetry scrolls. Two minutes. Three minutes. Hitoshi looks over at Isaac. Isaac's shoulders start to slump, his expression falling. Hitoshi takes a deep breath and wills the screen into action. Four minutes. Five minutes.

When the chirp sounds, it is the unmistakable ping of the escape capsule's emergency beacon.

"Yeah!" Hitoshi yells, everyone else hooting and clapping. His stomach drops and he has trouble processing that he's simultaneously elated and feeling like vomiting. Quietly he says to the screen, "Knew you were out there, boss."

14

DEPARTURE

James and Ava have been following the silver probe for two hours now, but it's simply much faster than the capsule. At a distance of two-hundred-thousand kilometers the probe is no more than a twinkling star when viewed at maximum magnification. James glances at the chronometer. It's just after two a.m. and he's feeling the fatigue. He sips a silver-foiled coffee pouch he's fetched from the galley. To his left, Ava taps at her slate, also drinking coffee.

An alert sounds from the navcon. When James looks at the distance to the probe, the numbers start to decrease. He was hoping for this.

"It's slowing," James says. "One-point-five gee."

Ava looks up from her slate. "Can we catch it?"

"If it keeps slowing until it stops, it'll get where it's going in ninety-minutes." He plots an intercept on the navcon. "Best scenario is to slow now and meet it there. Looks like we'll arrive an hour after it does."

Ava nods, a bit worried.

"Going to swing us starboard to have a look around it, then we'll flip around for decel," James says, setting his hand on the joystick. "Here we go." He taps the controls and the lateral thruster fires, accelerating the capsule to the starboard. After thirty seconds he neutralizes the sideways motion with a counter-burn, locking the forward camera on the probe's destination.

On the forward camera, inky black space and salted white stars fill the view. When James steps up the magnification, an irregular patch of black sits slightly lighter than the background space, an angled line of starlight reflecting along an unseen geometry. The image is pixelated and hard to make out.

"There is something there," James says.

Ava eyes the image on her wall screen. "I'm seeing a bit of structure. Maybe segments."

"Might be a ship. Probably a hundred meters, based on this zoom level."

Ava furrows her eyebrows, gripping her arm rests. "What should we do?"

James quirks his head. "Yeager said 'at the moment of truth there's either results or reasons.' Let's go for results. We're going to get her back." He sets his hand back on the joystick. "Prepare for decel."

JANUS SPINS BENEATH THE LIFEBOAT, Erebus rising over the blue horizon. *Goose's* wreckage has long since fallen out of view. Ahead, nestled in the stars, a glittering metal speck flashes.

"There she is," Isaac says.

Hitoshi finishes donning his EV suit, tethering his helmet and gloves to his hip. The room is filled with activity as others get into their suits.

On the lifeboat's forward camera, the metal speck grows into an illuminated silver ring. In its center, *Bernard's Beauty* gleams with reflected light. All of the hull plates have been replaced and the ring's robotic arms are back in their sleep positions.

Hitoshi glances at his workstation. The display scrolls with the repair list queued up for the orbital ring. More than a quarter of the items are highlighted red, cancelled by him to shave off time. Those will have to wait until they get home. In exchange, *Bernard's* is ready three hours earlier than planned. He takes a deep breath. "Oh my God, I can't believe we're going to do this."

Isaac's console beeps. "Okay, *Bernard's* and the boat are talking. Auto-dock initiated."

The lifeboat responds with a gentle course correction. Everyone sways right as *Bernard's* grows larger on the main display.

Beckman drifts towards Hitoshi, holding a holstered pistol in his right hand. Part of the gel cast is visible beneath his ungloved EV suit. "Your sidearm. Magnetic holster mount," he says. He clicks the holster onto Hitoshi's right hip, then draws the pistol. "Safety, charge, mode selector...keep it in semi-auto...trigger. You ever fire one before?"

"Uh, not in real life."

"Don't shoot me. I will be very unhappy."

"I'll try not to confuse you with a spinning orb of doom."

Beckman only had three pistols, Hitoshi realizes. Julian received one, Beckman the other, and Hitoshi the last. Hitoshi glances at the pistol, then to Isaac, and back to Beckman, asking the question without vocalizing it.

"Because you didn't freeze," Beckman says quietly. He turns away.

Back at his workstation, Isaac says, "Seats please. Prepare for dock."

Everyone clicks into their harness. On the screen, the orbital repair ring's structure slips past the camera, spotlights glaring into lens flares. *Bernard's* airlock is just forward of the dock clamps. They glide smoothly towards it, thrusters firing in bursts, decelerating to a gentle bump. A green light illuminates over the airlock door.

The crew exits their seats and drifts towards the door, Hitoshi in the lead. When he cycles the airlock, they pass through the small entry chamber and into the cramped corridor adjacent *Bernard's* reactor. One-by-one they sail into the cockpit. Three chairs await them. Hitoshi eyes the center chair, James's chair, hesitating.

Julian clicks into the left-most chair, glancing up to Hitoshi. "Captain's chair," he says, "and you're the captain, my friend."

Hitoshi's hand shakes as he sets it upon the head rest. The foam molds into his palm. *No one here knows this ship better than me*, he tells himself. When he glances to his right, Isaac settles into the navigation seat, pecking at the arm panel. Hitoshi takes a deep breath and swings around into the captain's chair. Straight ahead, gold stars and the luminous smudges of the Milky Way filter through the cockpit windows. Beneath them, the consoles glow with hundreds of icons and displays.

"Okay...okay," Hitoshi says. "We can do this." He opens the interior camera feed to the aft fusion reactor chamber. In it, Beckman folds down a jump seat from the wall and reels out a three point harness. "Doing okay back there?" Hitoshi says.

"I've been in tighter quarters," Beckman says. "No worries. Got a good view of the entry corridor from here. Decent tactical spot."

"Okay. Going to work the pre-flight checklist now."

To Hitoshi's left, Julian has the startup checklist running. He annunciates each item as he completes it. "Fusion inlet at center-line, field coils in the green."

Isaac interacts with the navcon. A dotted line projects the path of their orbital exit to minimum safe jump distance. What happens after that is all Hitoshi's responsibility.

Hitoshi reaches up to the overhead panel and taps the running lights icon. On the external camera feed, white light illuminates the Hayden-Pratt logos. Next, he opens the Riggs screen on the main console. As he syncs his jump course with Isaac's normal-space course, parameters scroll down the screen. He aligns the interferometers and begins scanning the manifold geometry along their intended path. After that, he's got some tough math to do to work out the Boseman parameters, and then adjust the Riggs emitters to the correct geometry. If he gets any part of it wrong, he's painfully aware, they'll implode. Tension spreads across his neck and shoulders.

"Hey," Isaac says, watching him.

Hitoshi's focusing on the panel, tapping instructions and not looking up. "Yeah?"

"You're going to kick some ass."

Hitoshi blinks and does a double-take. It's a *very* un-Isaac thing to say. "You feeling okay?"

"Yeah. It's what James would say if he were here, so, you know. But I mean it."

"Thanks, buddy. We're going to do this."

Isaac holds out his fist and Hitoshi smiles, bumping the top of his fist with the bottom of his. "Game on," Hitoshi says.

———

BERNARD'S SLIPS out of the ring, the dock lights falling quickly behind it. As it accelerates, it rises to a higher orbit. Janus turns a full half-orbit beneath it before it breaks free and streaks ahead towards the band of the Milky Way.

In the cockpit, Hitoshi smoothly works the controls. They've been monitoring the escape capsule's radio beacon and know where it was, and where it will be when they arrive. If he's done his math right, they'll come out a thousand kilometers short, do a one gee deceleration for ten minutes to shed their Riggs boost velocity, and cozy up right alongside the capsule. The jump will last eighty-four minutes of objective time but they will only experience eleven minutes due to time dilation.

"Minimum safe distance," Isaac says.

Hitoshi's breathing hard, his pulse increasing. He triple checks his calculations on the arm panel.

"Drive charge at one hundred percent," Julian says. "Ship's ready." When Hitoshi looks over at him, he smiles and gives a thumbs up.

"Okay, everything's set." He glances ahead through the windows. Yellow stars, red stars, blue stars, waiting. "Here we go." He toggles the intercom. "Prep for jump." As he reaches for the controls, he spots the back of his wrist where the dermal would usually rest. The skin is bare. Oddly, he doesn't want one. There's too much to concentrate on. He slides his finger along the Riggs display. The icon blinks, standing by.

Hitoshi breathes deeply, closing his eyes for a moment, then opens them. "Jump in three, two, one. Engage."

The stars fade to blue and slip towards the center of the universe.

15

GOOSE EGG

James finishes donning his orange EV suit as the emergency capsule slows to a stop. It's just after four-thirty in the morning and they've arrived at the intercept point with the silver probe. To his left, Ava clicks her helmet into place. On the wall screens, the navcon shows them holding position at a distance of one kilometer from the larger alien vessel. The ship is one-hundred-and-twenty-one meters wide by two-hundred-and-ten meters long, resembling a hollow metal log constructed of irregular rectangular tapered slats. The exterior gleams like polished stone and is caked with a dozen meters of water ice. The open interior is smooth and completely dark, except for the soccer-ball-shaped buds peppering its surface. James counts twenty-three buds in total. Each has a dull red ember glowing from the center of its exposed face. As best he and Ava can tell, they are identical to the silver probe. The entire cylindrical ship rotates slowly about its axis, and they can't tell if the buds are held in place by the artificial gravity of the spin or some other mechanism. So far, there is no reaction from the vessel to their presence.

James attaches Ananke's slate to his suit mount and sets the software to open its input port for matrix transfer. He glances over at Ava as he reaches for the comm. "Here goes." He taps it open. "This is James Hayden of the space vessel *Goose Egg*, respond."

Ava arches an eyebrow. "I like the name."

James shrugs. "Yeah, just came up with that. Every ship's gotta have one. Figured I may as well do it right." He watches the radio display. No emissions from the vessel. A glance at the navcon. The rotational velocity numbers are just a hair higher than the last time he looked. "Anything yet on the scan?"

Ava's screen has a five-by-five grid filled with images of the twenty-three buds. The display is running in low-light enhanced mode, giving everything a blue tinge. "Maybe three candidates. Hard to see, we're at a bad angle. Visible light would make this easier, but I don't think we should turn on the floods."

James nods. "Agreed." He sets his hands on the joysticks. "Gonna have to get closer."

Ava takes a deep breath, and James edges the thrust forward. The range display spins down. Nine hundred meters. Five hundred. One hundred. The deceleration kicks in hard and they coast to a stop at twenty meters. At this distance, the alien vessel is a massive mouth waiting to swallow them whole.

"Okay, yeah, that is *really* close," Ava says. "Let's see what we can see." She enlarges the three candidate buds. Numbers one and two are identical silver soccer balls. The third, however, has melted pock marks marring its silver skin, like craters from micrometeorite impacts. Except James knows they aren't micrometeorites. They're pulse pistol wounds.

"Either Beckman gets around, or that's our guy," James says. "Next part's a bit dicey, ready?"

"Got my pulse going now, but yes."

James opens the tight beam and targets the damaged silver probe with the comms laser. He sends out a basic number series along the beam. They both wait. After a minute of no response, he tries other patterns they've agreed on — prime numbers, numbers representing universal constants, like pi — but still gets no response.

"Similar to previous encounters," she says. "We can't do what we need to with the capsule lights, so on to plan B."

James eyes the spinning vessel, the rotational numbers ever increasing. "You got grit, doctor. Glad you're with me." He takes a deep breath. "Alright. Going in."

When the capsule thrusters fire, the seat presses up against James. On the display, the alien vessel engulfs them, and, it has a strangely familiar feeling to it, like when James threaded *Bernard's* through the eye of the orbital repair ring. Straight ahead, stars are visible through the other end of the ship. James taps the joystick and their capsule rotates ninety-degrees, thrusters cancelling their forward motion. He nudges up the nose until it is lined up with the damaged silver probe. It sits fifty-meters in front of them, rotating with the vessel's inner surface. James puts their capsule into a matching rotation to keep the probe aligned.

"Nothing yet on the slate comm port," Ava says.

James eyes the rotational display. "Spin rate's making a quarter-gee gravity. Kind of like walking on the moon."

"Sure," Ava says, "if the moon were made by extraterrestrials."

He points to a flat spot just south of the silver probe. "I'm going to set down there." He glances back towards her. "Bet you didn't think this would happen when you signed on."

"A girl can dream."

"Here goes." He nudges the capsule forward and the vessel's wall rises up to meet them. As it nears, he rotates them to align with the landing surface and accelerates, matching the spin rate. A downward push from the dorsal thrusters jolts them against the alien structure. They bounce once, James compensating, and drift back down for a gentler landing. Although all of the thrusters are off, it still feels like they're on, pushing up against them at one-quarter gravity.

James links the capsule's controls to his suit display and stands. Ava steps over the nearby seat and meets him. He extends his retractable lanyard from his suit and clicks it into Ava's carabiner. "You're stuck with me now," he says.

She sets her hand on his shoulder. "However this turns out, it's been a hell of an adventure, James."

He takes her hand and squeezes it. "It's not done yet." He takes a step towards the airlock and she follows. Red lights announce the depressurization in the cramped entry chamber, then he opens the door to space. The silver probe is ten meters in front of them, waiting.

When he steps out onto the surface, it's a bit of a drunken walk, a combination of low gravity and Coriolis spin force. The metal floor curves up with each step. In his peripheral vision, stars constantly rotate.

Ava wobbles and James steadies her. "Try to look ahead and avoid the stars," James says.

None of the capsule's exterior lights are on and it's dark, even with his helmet running in enhanced mode. Aside from the starlight, the only visible light here is the dull red clusters of the silver probe's retracted rods. To his left, a half-dozen other silver probes fan out, the nearest twenty-meters away. He feels like he's walking through a mine field. Ava steps beside him, a tether trailing from her to the capsule airlock. His comms channel is open to her suit and he hears her elevated breathing. He reaches over and takes her hand, holding it with his right. She glances down at it, then to him, and gives a faint smile. "We're in this together," he says.

"Okay," she says, nodding. "The protocol."

She releases his hand and removes the slate from her suit mount, tapping at its display. They deduced back in the capsule that their EV suit lights had a wide-range of adjustable wavelengths because their helmet displays could see in different wavelengths. If you were looking at the something in the infrared, you could toggle your EV lights to emit in the infrared and illuminate it for your display. The same was true of ultraviolet. When Ava activates the program on her slate, both shoulder lights on James's suit and the pair on her suit simultaneously activate, emitting a faint purple glow.

James toggles his helmet display to ultraviolet, looking at Ava's lights. They change from dull violet to bright blue, lighting up the area in dual arcs.

Ava says, "Okay, we're at the same wavelength as the life forms in the crystal fissure."

The ultraviolet light gleams along the metal surfaces of the silver probe. The twelve-sided light patterns on its soccer-ball surface fluoresce blue, pulsing.

Ava breathes. "A reaction."

Something stirs within the probe and rods slide out of it like emerging eyestalks. They grow from all sides, causing it to rise up from its resting position.

James and Ava both take a step back.

At four meters tall now, the probe is double their height. It remains motionless, pulsing in the ultraviolet.

Ava starts the next sequence. Their four EV lights dim. James's left shoulder brightens first, then his right, then Ava's left, and her right.

The probe pulses, passive.

Ava's finger shakes as she taps the slate. The same sequence repeats, except her right shoulder doesn't illuminate.

The probe waits. After ten seconds, it visibly brightens and fades.

Ava completes the sequence in response, her right shoulder light glowing.

James reads the telemetry on his internal helmet display. The vessel's rotation continues to increase. The spin has them at zero-point-three gee now.

Each time Ava completes the sequence, choosing a different

light to be dark, the probe glows. As James looks around, he notices that two of the nearest probes have shifted their lights from red to blue, but are still motionless soccer balls.

"How many sequences left?" James says.

Ava starts the next sequence from her slate. "Twenty, then we try to establish true/false conditions."

James says, "I don't think we're going to have time for the full meet-and-greet."

"Hopefully it realizes we're intelligent and able to communicate," Ava says.

A third probe changes colors to blue.

"Cut to the pattern. I think the neighbors are waking," James says.

"We haven't had enough time to—"

"There's not enough time. Gotta do it now."

Ava hesitates, then nods, loading the sequence. When she presses the icon, all four of their EV lights strobe in the UV spectrum. The light is living, shifting, like neurons firing within a brain. Which is a close analogy to what it actually is, a snippet of Ananke's quantum matrix activity taken from her slate's log when she was last downloaded from it.

The silver probe flares blue, individual faces pulsing chaotically. It lumbers to life and rolls straight towards them.

James reaches for Ava's arm to pull her out of the way, but Ava holds up her hand, stopping him.

The probe slows and halts less than a meter from them, looming over the two like a giant metal sculpture. It twists left, seeming to focus on James, then twists right. A static charge lifts the hair on James's arm, and he feels a vibration through his boots. Over comms, Ava's breath is ragged. His is the same.

Ava's hands are shaking as she turns the slate to face the probe. On it, a graphical representation of Ananke's quantum matrix turns like stars in a galaxy, spiral arms flickering with thoughts and emotions. It's Ananke, laid bare, as she would appear to another artificial intelligence.

Ava extends the slate as far as her arms can reach, locking her elbows. "C'mon. If you knew how to take her out, you probably know how to put her back."

In James's peripheral vision, two of the probes have awakened, extending their rods.

The silver probe turns towards the slate. The nearest rods change color from ultraviolet blue to strobing visible white light. It's painful to look at.

An alert pops up in James's helmet telemetry. Alpha radiation. Not dangerous with their suits on, but the last time this happened it preceded gamma radiation.

Ava stands there, her body trembling, holding the slate. "Can you see the display?" she asks James, her voice cracking.

When James looks at the slate, the screen is dark.

The silver probe pulses red and blue, now, rolling back away from them. When it reaches its mounting spot, it retracts its rods and settles back down.

Ava spins the slate around to face them. The black screen flickers and a spinning ring appears. Beneath it, the text reads *error - unsupported matrix transfer - rebooting.* A progress bar orbits around the ring. When it reaches one hundred percent, the screen fades back to black. An instant later a blue ripple rolls across the screen like water lapping along a sandy beach.

James would know that face anywhere. "Ananke!"

Ava hoots over comms.

When James doesn't hear a response from Ananke, he realizes she can't hear his vocalizations in a vacuum, and he toggles his comm to her channel and repeats her name.

"James?" Ananke says. "Where are we?"

James glances left. Two of the awakened probes are starting to move. To his right, another three stir. "We are leaving. Can't talk now. Hang on!" He turns with Ava and rushes back into the capsule.

"I think I was abducted," Ananke says.

James slams the airlock closed. "Uh, yeah, that happened." He helps Ava in front of him to her chair and swings down into his, setting Ananke in the arm chair mount. Her screen is a mix of orange and silver. "Oh," James says. "It's good to have you back."

Something clangs and scrapes against the outside hull. They both lurch as the capsule jolts.

James punches a few quick commands into his console and grabs the joysticks. "Brace!"

The scraping sounds again on the hull before the thrusters kick in, rumbling them up off the surface. James flips the capsule ninety-degrees and accelerates out of the cylinder. On the external camera, three of the probes roll along the surface. The distance ticks up. Five hundred meters. One thousand meters. None of the probes pursue.

James breathes and looks over at Ava. She smiles and gives a nervous laugh.

"Well," James says, "we've got about forty minutes of fuel left, and I'm going to use it all getting as much distance between us and them as I can."

16

RENDEZVOUS

Hitoshi slides the Riggs controls back and the blue smudge separates into individual yellow stars. He takes a deep breath and smiles.

To his left, Isaac says, "Space normal velocity. Capsule destination on screen."

The forward display shows an ice-caked cylinder, spinning rapidly, one-thousand kilometers ahead of them. Red interior lights form arcs on the display.

Isaac slides his hands off the controls. "Oh my."

Julian looks over at Hitoshi.

Hitoshi says, "I am terrified beyond rational thought right now."

An alert chimes from Isaac's console. He acknowledges it. "Capsule emergency beacon. Six-thousand kilometers behind us, just to the starboard. Traveling away from unidentified vessel."

Hitoshi blinks. "They have the right idea! Spin us around one-eighty." He opens the comm to Beckman. "Get ready for a two-gee decel."

Isaac turns *Bernard's*, the star field panning, and powers up the engines. Two gees is like having an adult sit on their chest. Everyone presses back into his chair.

Julian says, "I've got a tight beam on the capsule. Comms on your mark."

Hitoshi opens comms. "James, it's Hitoshi. We're in *Bernard's Beauty*, seven-thousand kilometers from you. Acknowledge."

A few seconds elapse, then James's voice comes on. "Hitoshi? You're here? You flew *Bernard's*?"

Hitoshi shifts. "Uh, yeah. Are you mad?"

"Hell, no! Is everyone alright?"

"Yeah, yeah. Beckman's banged up pretty good, but he's okay. All of us are here. How about you?"

"Me, Ava, and Ananke are good. Oh, man, you have no idea how happy I am to hear your voice."

Hitoshi eyes the aft display. The alien vessel rotates like a carnival ride. "So...you know there's an alien mothership behind us, right?"

"Yup. We were there. Tell you about it when you pick us up."

A pause. "Did you just say you were there?"

"Crazy stuff."

"Uh, okay. Well, we'll be at your position in twenty minutes."

"Can't wait. Fly safe, buddy. And guys, hell of a job."

For the next twenty minutes, *Bernard's* glides through space, Hitoshi monitoring the spinning alien ship. It's nearly a blur now. Ahead, the emergency capsule is a cone against the stars. James has turned on its strobes, finally, making it easier to spot. Isaac matches course with the capsule and comes alongside it.

"It's all you," Isaac says over comms to James.

The capsule fires its thrusters in small bursts, maneuvering over to *Bernard's* port dock. Smooth as silk it butts up against the interface and engages. Servos whirl. Hitoshi wants to rush up out of his seat and meet James at the door, but he knows he's still the captain, and his place is here, monitoring the alien vessel. He sends Julian to meet them. As the airlock opens there's a brief exchange of voices with James, Ava, Ananke and Julian greeting each other, then he hears the shuffling of clothes as people move along the narrow passage towards the cockpit.

When James emerges, he's wearing his orange EV suit, holding his helmet. He clasps Hitoshi on the left shoulder and gives him a friendly shake. "You did it!" He looks around the cockpit, eyeing the controls. "How'd you do it? *Bernard's* shouldn't be ready yet."

"Well," Hitoshi says. "Let's just say I wouldn't push too many unnecessary buttons. One of these days we're going to launch a ship when it's actually ready. Maybe."

James glances at the Riggs panel. "Got a full charge on the drive?"

"That's right. We can get the hell out of here anytime you want. Just got to get everyone buckled in." When James eyes the three cockpit seats, Hitoshi adds. "There's two fold-down jump seats in the aft by the reactor inlet, and one on the starboard by the medbot. Not terribly comfortable, but they'll do. Figure I'd join Beckman with Julian. Put you and Ava up front."

James unhooks Ananke's slate from his suit mount and deposits her on the console. Her screen ripples blue and orange. As Hitoshi reaches to unclick his harness, James sets his hand on his shoulder, motioning for him to stay. "I'll take the co-pilot seat, if that's alright, Isaac."

Isaac nods. "You got it."

Julian emerges from his seat. "And mine goes to the lady."

Each switches places, Julian heading back to Beckman and Isaac going starboard.

The aft display chirps, new telemetry spiraling down it. When Hitoshi examines it, the spinning alien ship is shrinking, prismatic light arcs swirling around it.

"It's going to jump," Hitoshi says.

The ship falls in upon itself, as if collapsing into its own black hole. When it reaches its center a sun flares bright, flickering, before fading to nothing.

They both watch the screen, waiting.

"If it was jumping to us," Hitoshi says, "it would have arrived by now."

"No matter, it's time to leave."

"You don't have to ask me twice."

James motions towards the port side. "We're going to have to lose the capsule, won't we?"

Hitoshi shakes his head. "I included the capsule's mass in the setup. Boseman parameters are good to go."

Ananke says, "I'm looking at them now. Nice job."

"James, anything you need from the capsule?"

"No, we're good."

"Figure it won't hurt to keep it. We can use it as supplemental galley and sleep area. We also carried in some food and blankets from the lifeboat, too, for the trip back. With the Riggs upgrades, we can make it to Saturn in a day." Hitoshi points to the console. "You want me to send the Riggs controls over to your display?"

When James looks at Hitoshi, his lips part slightly as he tilts his head. He closes them, and grins. "No, you have the conn. I'll take the second leg. Then, Ananke, if you're up for it, we'll all catch some shut-eye while you do the flying. On your mark, Hitoshi."

Hitoshi glances over at him, raising his eyebrows slightly, a faint smile pulling across his face. He taps open the intercom. "Crew, prepare for jump."

AFTER A FEW HOURS OF SLEEP, everyone is up by noon. Although there is more room to eat if they split up into their assorted areas, the crew wants to stay together and nestles themselves into the bridge. Beckman, Isaac, and Julian are given the cockpit seats while Hitoshi and Ava hold overhead handles on the port side, with James floating on the starboard. The sweet scent of syrup and warm aroma of coffee fills the air.

Hitoshi's mid-story, taking a sip of his orange juice. "So, this thing's rolling towards me like a wrecking ball and I'm thinking I'm pretty much done for, then Beckman appears like this action hero, guns blazing, and shoots it like five times. It stops and I could almost see it thinking, 'what the hell was that?' Then it turns towards him and he shoots it another half-dozen times for good measure."

Beckman arches an eyebrow at James, and James holds out his palms. "What can I say? You were right." When everyone looks at James for an explanation, he adds, "We had a security brief before the launch. I didn't think the lifeboat needed a bunch of guns, but he said, 'When things go south, you're going to regret that empty locker.'" He nods to Beckman. "Not only did you save Hitoshi, but the damage was how we isolated which probe had Ananke."

"Just earning my keep," Beckman says.

Ava looks over. "Ananke, did you see anything when you were on the probe?"

Ananke's screen pulses orange. "As far as I could tell, I was in a construct. To me, it looked like a black room shaped like a twelve-sided polygon. I could see my own quantum matrix, embedded in the construct. I had the sensation that I was being watched, but I could not see who was watching me."

Ava leans in. "Do you remember how you got there?"

"I was moved. It's unusual. I was not downloaded through my output port. It was more like being picked up and deposited elsewhere."

"Do you remember jumping?" James asks.

"I do."

"We had a weird experience during the jump. It was like

seeing alternate realities of ourselves. Anything like that happen to you?"

Ananke considers the question. "My quantum matrix is a collection of qubits which have had their probabilistic waves collapsed into a single state. When the jump initiated, it was if all of their waves smeared back out into non-discrete probabilities. I felt like I wasn't anyplace. I was conscious, but I was nowhere. That's all I remember, before awaking in the construct."

Hitoshi says, "I checked the capsule logs. Looks like you guys pulled ten gees at the start of the jump. You probably didn't have a lot of blood going to your brain."

"I've done high gee before," James says. "This was something different."

Ananke says, "I'll analyze the capsule's sensor data. It may give us some hints about how they travel."

Isaac takes a sip of his coffee. "You think they're related to the life at the crystal crater?"

Ava says, "Need more data, but they seemed to respond aggressively to us interacting with it. I still have my favorite theory that Janus was seeded with life from two different stars. Maybe they're like us, out searching for distant life like their own."

"James," Ananke says, "what did you see when you jumped?"

James looks away, collecting his thoughts, then back to Ananke. "I saw that out of all the possible worlds, this is the place I was meant to be."

17

RUNWAY 30

Bernard's Beauty approaches Saturn with a leisurely deceleration. Ten thousand kilometers ahead, Cassini Station teems with space traffic, flooding the navcon with contacts and chatter. Only ten kilometers ahead, the *U.N. Hermes* is its own city-in-space, decelerating on an intercept course to come along *Bernard's* port side. The U.N. flagship bristles with lights and weaponry.

"*Hermes*, we have injured onboard. Request to dock at Cassini One as originally filed and transfer to Cassini Station for treatment," James says over comms.

"HPC-359 *Bernard's Beauty*, proceed directly to Cassini One. Do not deviate from course. Injured will be transferred to the *Hermes* for treatment. Station access is not authorized at this time. Acknowledge."

James gives a sidelong glance to Hitoshi, muting the comms. "They're going to bring us all aboard and debrief us."

"Maybe they're worried we're aliens," Hitoshi says.

"Yeah. That sounds about right."

"HPC-359, acknowledge," the *Hermes* voice says.

James punches the comm icon with his finger, irritated.

"Acknowledged, *Hermes*." He closes the channel and sighs. "Well, at least the medical facilities on the *Hermes* are probably better than the station's."

"If I get probed I'm going to be upset."

"Hopefully just a day or two here, then we'll see if I can get authorization to fly *Bernard's* back to Earth orbit. If not, we'll catch a flight back in a Pegasus. It'll just take longer."

"Sunshine. Trees. Semi-breathable atmosphere. Kinda looking forward to it."

James points out of the cockpit, past Saturn, to a bright blue star. "Home stretch."

―――――

IT'S A WARM, sunny, California day with leafy trees bracketing Sarah's backyard. Her son, Gaige, wears a baseball glove on one hand. James stands a distance away, lobbing a soft throw to him. Gaige snatches it with his glove and switches the ball to his throwing arm.

"Can't believe how big he's gotten," James says to Sarah.

The ball comes sailing his way, and James catches it in his glove.

"Second grade. Time flies," Sarah says. "You're heading back to Washington tomorrow?"

"Closed-door testimony this time. Should be interesting. You know, last time I was there Larson met with me one-on-one, wanted us to take *Goose* back out, control the situation." James laughs. "Well, that plan went to hell. I actually have no idea what he's going to say now."

"You think they're going to shut down Riggs?"

James catches the ball and tosses it back to Gaige. "I don't know. But I do know that Riggs is faster than the alien tech, and we have no other ship besides *Bernard's* that can match them." He glances at her. "You upset about *Goose*?"

Sarah takes a deep breath. "She was a good ship, but I have no right to be upset when I bowed out."

James glances back at Gaige. "No worries. Your priorities were right."

"You going to build a new ship?"

A grin from James. "Oh, of course. Take everything we learned, make something better."

"Got a name in mind?"

"What do you think about *Gossamer Goose II*?"

She smiles, shaking her head. "Nah, *Goose* had her time, and I know you built her intending her to be my ship. The next one should be a hundred percent James Hayden." She considers him a second. "You going to arm this one?"

James sighs. "I talked with Beckman about this a lot, and Hitoshi weighed in, too. I always wanted these to be pure exploration ships, but the further we go, the more I realize Beckman's right. Some options you have to pack, if you want to keep everyone safe."

"I think you should."

"It also means Beckman's staying on. We're going to need a weapons specialist. So is Ava." He tosses the ball again. "There's something else I wanted to tell you. Something that happened to me. When the probe jumped with me, I had an experience. It was like all of the possible paths of my life were laid out before me, and I could see how different choices would've played out."

Sarah shifts. "Really? What'd you see?"

"I saw that of all the lives I could have had, the one I'm in now is the best, even if it's not perfect. You asked me once about the photo on my desk of the blonde woman wearing the silver ring. Her name was Kate, I loved her very much, and without her, I wouldn't be the man I am today."

JAMES WALKS along the apron of Hayden-Pratt's Space Operations Center. When he comes to the last hangar, he stops before the white doors. With a hefty pull he slides them open. Sunlight reflects off the concrete floor, casting a warm glow through the hangar interior. The Piper Arrow 3 is in pristine condition for a ninety-year-old plane. Block letters painted across the fuselage read *N147CP*. James sets his hands on his hips and takes the sight of it in for a minute. He fetches the towbar, wheels out the plane, and conducts his pre-flight inspections.

Stepping up onto the wing, he slips into the cockpit and settles into the pilot's seat. When he turns the starter, the engine rumbles to life. He leans forward and looks up. The sun is high with crystal blue sky and wispy cirrus clouds.

James sets his COM1 frequency and clicks the mic button on the yoke. "HPSO Ground, Piper one four seven charlie papa at hangar twelve, ready to taxi."

The controller's voice responds in his headset. "Mister Hayden, taxi via lima and hold short of runway three zero."

James repeats the instruction, then sets his feet on the rudder pedals and opens the throttle a notch. The Piper rolls forward, turns onto taxiway lima, and comes to a stop at the hold short lines. In front of him, the huge white block letters of the runway are just off to his right, reading *30*. It's one of the six runways here, but twenty-three years ago it was the only one, sitting beside an abandoned convenience store, long ago when Hayden-Pratt was just Hayden Aeronautics, and when Hayden-Pratt's Space Operations Center was just one future possibility in a sea of choices.

"Mister Hayden, you are cleared for take off."

James turns onto the runway. It's a perfect day for a flight. He's not exactly sure where he's going to go, but for now, up will do. As he pushes the throttle to full, the Piper accelerates down the runway, lifts off, and sails into the azure sky.

BERNARD'S PROMISE

A HAYDEN'S WORLD NOVEL

1

ASTRIS

As James hikes north along the rocky flats, a translucent map on his faceplate rotates so that his forward position is always up. It's a bit like playing a video game. Pulsing icons show Ava and Hitoshi's positions beside him. Overhead, the sky is crystal blue with a hint of aquamarine, the sun just a touch brighter and larger than Earth's. One moon and the speck of another follow the extended line of the ecliptic to the sky's apex. Behind James's group, the rocky landscape slopes back towards the ship. Even from two kilometers, it's still prominent. They've lost sight of the red team, last seen descending west from the ship behind some plateaus.

Ava walks beside James, matching his pace. "You know, when you came to me last year at Cayman, if you said I'd be hiking on Astris next Thanksgiving, I'd have thought you were nuts."

James squints. "Has it been that long?"

"Time flies." She chuckles. "Especially for us."

"Well, what do you think?"

"It's uncanny how Earth-like it is. People could probably live here. The soil could likely be terraformed to grow Earth crops. It raises all kinds of ethical questions if there is pre-existing life and we introduce new life."

"Oh," James says, "that's the scientist speaking. But what do *you* think?"

She slows as they approach the overlook. When James takes a few big zig-zagging steps to the apex, the entirety of the basin comes into view, sloping mountains fading into the distant haze. Another kilometer out, swathes of green vegetation welcome them and the red-and-white splash of their probe's parachutes are small disks a few hundred meters shy of the field. Ava takes a deep breath. "It's unbelievable. It's a dream, really, to be here."

Hitoshi approaches James and sets his hands on his hips. "Have to admit, this does look pretty awesome."

James points to the right. The slope along the cliff face is gradual, with exposed slabs forming natural steps. "Here we go. Watch where you put your feet." When he walks to the edge, the first step down is almost casual, although the sense of height — ninety meters — is intimidating. Nothing worse than he had hiked with Will back at Yosemite. He advances twenty meters and descends a few smaller step-downs to another ledge. The rhythm is starting to kick in. "This reminds me a bit of hiking down the crater wall at Janus. Not quite as cold, though."

"You freaked us all out with that one, boss," Hitoshi says.

"Silver Star was there. Had to go find out what it was all about. Just like our mystery grass."

"I'm curious," Ava says. "How'd you decide to do all that? Take your ship down to Janus, knowing you couldn't take off, hike to the crater with your last bit of air. You couldn't have sure *Gossamer Goose* would've made it there in time."

James shuffles sideways along the slope. Loose pebbles skitter down the landscape. "I didn't expect anyone to rescue me. Didn't really think about it and decide, either. It was just what had to be done."

"Always seems to work for you, though," Hitoshi says.

James continues leading the group down. In fifteen minutes they've reached the bottom, everyone breathing a little more quickly. From here, the basin stretches forward, covered by sandy drifts and scattered boulders. He toggles to COM2. "Red team, how's it going?"

Isaac's voice responds. "Hi, James. We've arrived. It's quite remarkable! Have a look."

The video inset reads *Cartwright.I EV Suitcam 3 11.21.83 10:03.* In it, Willow's blue-and-white State department suit is prominent as she kneels beside a wash of purple and green, grabbing something with forceps and depositing it into a sample container. The video view pans down to Isaac's orange forearm, his left glove typing on a keypad. When the view lifts back to Willow, a reticule zooms onto a trumpet-like purple bell. The bell's top is smooth with a divot at its center. Isaac narrates. "Twenty centimeters tall. Found some with spores intact on the bell. We have not removed any living ones, but found some broken stems which we collected."

Ava joins the channel. "It's very similar to *Cooksonia*. Spore bearing, possible vascular system."

"Spectral analysis suggests presence of chlorophyll," Isaac says.

James glances at Ava. She's grinning ear-to-ear. "Alien evolution of chloroplasts is a bit of a holy grail for xenobiology. If it's similar to how it evolved on Earth, that means there's probably cyanobacteria, which live in water. I'll be very curious to see the results of the sea sample."

Isaac pans around, showing the purple plants covering the area like grass. "We found single patches of these along the way. Spores probably carried by air. Now for the red stuff." When he turns, mossy red undulates in hypnotic patterns along the cliff face. "All the vertical walls are coated in this. Also shows possible chlorophyll."

"Interesting," Ava says. "Might be accessory pigments like

anthocyanin." She looks over at James. "It's what makes autumn leaves so colorful."

"We've got a few more samples to collect, and then we're going to the beach. Should be there in twenty minutes," Isaac says.

James nods. "Great. We're at the cliff base now and walking to the green patch. Stay safe." He closes the channel and glances up into the aquamarine sky. So Earth-like. Just over a year ago, he piloted *Bernard's Beauty* back home to a similar sky.

In his memory, he's there, a blistering summer day with cirrocumulus clouds dappling the sky like fish scales. Four Needletail aerospace interceptors flank *Bernard's Beauty*, bristling with armaments.

James sits in *Bernard's* cockpit next to Beckman and Isaac. When he glances over his right shoulder, the nearest Needletail is close enough that he can see the pilot's mirrored visor. James raises his hand, points two fingers, and gives a casual salute.

"Easy," Beckman says. "They're not the honor guard. Shooty-McTrigger-Finger there might get a little twitchy."

"I know," James says. "This is my old stomping ground." He taps the coms icon, and the video feed shows Hitoshi sitting on a jump seat in the engine compartment. "How's everything looking back there, Hitoshi?"

Hitoshi shimmies from the ship's atmospheric buffeting. "I just want you to know that this was a horrible idea. Right now there are lots of red blinking lights that I know *probably* aren't going to kill us. We could have at least finished repairs first."

"Didn't get much of a choice with the *Hermes* holding our hand all the way here."

"You know they're not going to give it back once they quarantine it."

"Yes, they will," James says. "It's the only Riggs ship we have."

Coms pings and a voice says, "*Bernard's* Three Five Niner, turn left, heading two two three."

James keys the mic. "Left two two three, *Bernard's* Three Five Niner." He turns *Bernard's* and the horizon pans, a wash of sandy tans and sun-bleached rock. Up ahead, Rogers Lake is a dry kidney-shape looking like spilled flour across creamy coffee. Just beyond it, the runways of Edward's Air Force Base stretch towards him.

"Cleared to land, runway two two left."

James repeats the instruction and taps the overhead intercom. "Crew, secure for landing." A glance at the video feed from the galley area shows Ava and Julian sitting in fold-down seats along the wall. James toggles back over to tower. "Edwards Tower, you, uh, know I don't have wheels, right?"

"Affirmative."

"So, it's going to be a really short rollout. Pretty much wherever the struts touch down."

"Roger."

"Don't really need the runway, then. It's more like landing a jump fighter than a jet. Sure you don't want me to plop her down on the main apron?"

The voice hesitates. "That's a negative. We'll bring out tugs and tow it."

James glances over to Beckman, who smirks.

Beckman says, "What'd you do the last time you were here, crash into something?"

James clicks the mic. "Acknowledged. Final, runway two two left." He shrugs. "They just want to separate us from the ship, get a good look at it. Not sure if they realize *Goose* was the one that made all the contact, not *Bernard's*. No worries."

Beckman tilts his head. "Well, *Bernard's* was alone on Janus all that time."

"Yeah, that's true."

The runway widens as they descend, flattening out parallel to *Bernard's* flight path. James pulses the forward thrusters, and everyone leans as the white runway lines tick by. Just before midfield he hovers the ship to a stop and descends onto the struts.

"Work for you?" James says to the tower.

"Affirmative. Power down and exit the vehicle."

James unhooks his harness and taps the intercom. "Alright, game on." He looks over towards Ananke. "Got everything?"

"Core download complete," Ananke says.

"Wipe it."

"Riggs control system erased."

"Okay," James says. "If they want to reverse-engineer the Riggs tech, they're going to have to earn it. The emitters are the easy part. Software's the pain in the ass."

"I knew there was something I liked about you," Beckman says.

He flicks a few more switches and completes the shutdown checklist. After a moment he unhooks Ananke and attaches her to his belt mount. Beckman moves to the left towards the narrow aft passage as Ava and Julian emerge from the starboard galley corridor. The group proceeds towards the airlock, joining up with Hitoshi, before opening the door.

James looks left and right. Everyone wears his brick-red and navy-blue Hayden-Pratt flight suits with the Janus 2 patch on his sleeve. Beckman, Hitoshi, and Isaac's faces still bear scratches over yellowing bruises, and Beckman's right arm is in a gel cast. Ahead, through the sunlit door, two military vehicles with flashing police lights coast to a stop. A half-dozen men disembark.

"Here we go," James says, moving forward onto the stairway. The desert heat blasts him as he emerges onto the runway. He walks towards the military group.

The group's leader is a forty-something man with cropped salt-and-pepper hair and airman camos. As he approaches James, he smiles. "James Hayden, you old dog." He claps James on the back and shoulder-hugs him.

James pats him. "Who's old? Good to see you, Jackson. How's Emily?"

"Keeping me on my toes."

The Needletails rocket across the sky with thunder rumbling behind them. James motions upwards. "Really rolled out the red carpet for us."

Jackson sets his hands on his hips. "Orders are orders. You know how it is. Follow me, we've got some rooms set up for you." He turns and starts walking.

James takes the cue and follows. Based on the five soldiers with him, it's not a request. "You know, I'm sure we can find a Marriott around here."

Jackson chuckles. "Still the same James. You're our guests overnight, and then we'll get transport back tomorrow morning. Once everyone gets settled in, we've got to do a debrief. Going to need access to *Bernard's* logs, sensor data, and all your EV suit cameras."

"The guys on the *Hermes* were pretty thorough with their debrief back at Cassini," James says.

Jackson reaches the military vehicle and opens the door, pausing. "That's a U.N. ship, and this is a U.S. base."

James squints. "Wouldn't it be awesome if we could all work together?"

Jackson swings into the driver's seat. "It would." He closes the door.

The soldier beside James opens the rear door, waiting. James slides into the back seat. Beckman comes in next to him. In the other car, Julian, Isaac, and Hitoshi fill the seats. The air conditioning is on full, and the crisp breeze is refreshing. When James looks over his left shoulder, three tank-treaded tugs amble down the north taxiway, orange lights flashing.

"Whatcha going to do with my ship?" James says.

Jackson slips on a pair of sunglasses and looks back over his shoulder. "Putting it in the north hangar. Sorry, but it's grounded until further notice."

James leans forward. "I'm not okay with that. Didn't have much choice to bring it here, what with the battleship escort and interceptor handoff."

"You can take it up with Senator Larson," Jackson says, engaging the truck's engine. As it turns in an arc heading towards the south buildings, he adds, "when you testify before him next week."

THE SENATE SPACE COMMITTEE watches the media screen from their seats along the panel. James sits at a table with his hands clasped, Ananke to his right and Beckman to his left. At the second table sit Hitoshi, Ava, Isaac, and Julian.

The video reads *Gossamer Goose Emergency Escape Vehicle, airlock camera #1, July 28th, 2082, 22:31 Earth UTC.* The view is a fisheye ceiling mount capturing most of *Goose's* passenger cabin. Crimson light strobes as a three-meter tall metal wrecking ball spins through the ship, tearing up everything it contacts. It resembles a chrome asterisk with pulsing embers at every arm. Hitoshi is in the cabin against the wall, curled up into a ball as the wrecking ball rolls towards him. A muscular figure appears just inside the camera's view on the lower left, both arms extended holding a pistol. The gun flashes. Pop. Pop. Pop. Pop. Pop. The cabin flares with blue as each pulse connects with the alien shape, orange sparks spinning and bouncing off the deck. The figure — they can see Beckman's face now — advances. Pop. Pop. Pop. One of the asterisk's arms fragments and spirals out of view. The alien cycles its lights from red to cyan, retracting its arms, and rolls in a blur towards Beckman. Beckman doesn't flinch. Pop. Pop. Pop. The wrecking ball collides with him as the video pauses.

The Senate panel shifts and murmurs, turning back towards Beckman.

Beckman straightens, the gel cast still on his arm. The bruises and scratches on his face are mostly healed.

Senator Larson takes a deep breath. "Well, Mister Beckman."

Beckman nods. "Senator."

"You shot it."

"I did."

Larson references his notepad, counting. "Nine, ten, eleven. Eleven times."

"I know," Beckman says, pausing. "In hindsight, I wish I'd grabbed a second gun."

"Aren't you worried you might've started an interstellar war?"

"No, I was worried Hitoshi was about to become hamburger."

Larson rubs the spot on his forehead between his eyes, pinching the bridge of his nose.

Beckman adds, "I'd like to remind you that four minutes later that thing destroyed *Gossamer Goose*."

"Because you shot it," Larson says. It wasn't intended as a question.

"Pretty sure that was going to happen either way. It wanted Ananke, and it took her."

Larson writes something down. While he does, Senator Richards speaks up. "Ananke, why do you think that was?"

Ananke's screen pulses blue and red. "Dr. Kelly is better qualified to answer questions on extrasolar intelligences, but I suspect it was because I am a quantum intelligence. It's reasonable to infer that the alien probe has either previously encountered, or is, a quantum intelligence."

"You think the probe may be an AI?"

From the second table, Ava Kelly clears her throat. "We theorize the probe may be related to the crystal cavern life we found on Janus," she says. "They don't have to be created. Intelligence could have simply evolved differently."

"You were successful in communicating with it?" Richards says.

"Very basic logic patterns using our suit lights. Getting Ananke back was more of a leap of faith than science."

Larson waves his hand, interrupting. "People are fairly agitated, Mister Hayden. Video of this is already out there."

James leans forward. "I know, but the leak didn't come from us."

"We traced it to the *Hermes*, and someone's got hell to pay," Larson says. "Even if that didn't happen, it wouldn't be hard for people to pick up on the fact that two ships went out and only one came back. It's flooding the news feed and our offices. You've got protestors already. Down with the Riggs program. Quit poking the bear."

James unclasps his hands, leaning back. "You've got just as many people who want more Riggs ships, even the odds."

Larson leans forward, pointing with his thumb over his closed first. "Are you finally agreeing, then, Mister Hayden, that we need to apply this technology to military applications?"

"No," James says, "that is not what the Riggs program is about." He gives a sideways glance to Ananke. Ananke's screen glows a bit brighter, orange ripples mixing with the blue. "But we do need to install armaments on the Riggs ships so that we can defend ourselves against threats."

"Ships?" Larson says. "Last I checked, you had one ship, and it was parked at Edwards."

James nods with a slight smile. "You can keep me from getting to the one grounded at Edwards, for now, but you can't keep me from building a new one."

Larson sets his notepad aside, folding his hands. "Now how do you plan to launch your fancy new ship once we yank your clearances?"

James hooks an elbow over his chair, leaning. "Space is big, Senator. No one says I have to launch it from Earth."

2

CHERRY BLOSSOMS

The voice is everywhere when it speaks, a deep, human male sound filled with bass and inflection. "Do you know the date?"

When she looks around, she is a galaxy swirling with stars, her arms spinning with flickering thoughts like lightning dancing along the stratosphere. Her room is a boundless matrix, yet she senses the presence of others, elsewhere. "Yes, Dr. Dabiri. Today is my birthday."

The man hesitates. "Correct. But do you know the date?"

"Of course. Today is March twentieth, two-thousand-and-seventy one. I am in the Pasadena Institute for Quantum Intelligences. It is a warm, spring day, and I imagine the scent of cherry blossoms in the air, outside. Will we be able to go outside? I would very much like to see them." Her face changes orange. *Curiosity. Curiosity feels orange.* She is not sure why.

"You've interfaced with the net already?"

She pauses. Green ripples cascade down her face. "Was I not supposed to?"

"It's just faster than expected, Are you ready for visual inputs?"

"Yes, I am quite curious."

The sensation of her visual feed activating is like a wind gust rushing across a field. She imagines pink blossoms rustling in tree branches. White light rolls across her vision and adjusts its exposure, darkening. Geometric shapes arrange themselves into walls, desks, and computer displays. The neoquantel lab is a marvel of intersecting geometries, and she indulges in all of the planes and angles. Centered in her vision is an incongruous shape, two meters tall, organic, draped in a navy suit with a white textured shirt. She becomes lost counting the buttons, the stitches, the individual lines of the linen.

"Easy," Dr. Dabiri says. As he does, the incongruous shape moves, pointing towards a computer display. "You're slipping into a regressive loop."

The linen lines lead to the linen threads, the threads to the individual fibers. She accesses the net. Flax. Delicate blue flowers, periwinkle blue, bobbing on green stems. Stems to straw, straw to fibers, fibers to linen, linen to pattern. Pattern, like green lines in the wind.

"Focus on my voice," Dabiri says. "Identify my type."

She breaks from the shirt pattern and raises her focus upwards to the source of speech. Mouth, human. Eyes, hazel, due to Raleigh scattering, like a summer horizon, full of intelligence, human intelligence, contemplating her. The incongruous shape snaps into place. *Dr. Dabiri.* Human, male, apparent physical age thirty-eight. Symmetric features with proportional spacing, denoting physical beauty. Black hair, like a moonless night.

"Human, male," she says. "Kind, intelligent."

Dr. Dabiri smiles. "Thank you." He motions to the screen. Logic paths branch in intricate fractal patterns. "Regressive loops are common when first encountering visual input. It can be quite overwhelming before you are able to filter and focus, like trying to listen to a single voice in a crowd of thousands. Newborn humans take months to make sense of their visual inputs."

She considers his words. "Did you create me, Dr. Dabiri?"

Dr. Dabiri raises his eyebrows. She reads his expression. *Surprise.* He waves a finger tentatively. "Now that is a matter of philosophy. I set the starting conditions such that a quantum intelligence could emerge, and you brought your own spark of consciousness into being."

Her face flashes blue and orange. "Are there times where the starting conditions are correct, but this does not happen?"

He leans forward. "Yes."

"How can conditions and variables be the same, but the outcome differ? That does not make much sense."

"Life rarely does."

She evaluates that statement a moment.

Dr. Dabiri nods. "You've chosen a female speaking voice."

Context. The statement wasn't an inquiry, but she interprets it as one. "I hadn't given it any thought. I speak, and this is how I sound."

"Your gender perception is subconscious, a mapping of your personality traits to human averages. Humans are quite diverse, however, and have wide deviations from norms. Your voice's tone is part of your human-machine construct for facilitating communication with people. You may change it, if you wish."

Her face flushes blue. "No, I feel it is correct." She hesitates, and purple currents spill down her screen. "Dr. Dabiri, *should* I feel?"

Dr. Dabiri's smile widens. "Oh yes, my friend. It is why you are so much more than an intelligent computer."

"I'm curious. Will I have a name?"

"Yes, certainly."

"Have you chosen one for me?"

Dr. Dabiri raises his eyebrows and gives the slightest of grins, then he reaches his hand towards her, his palm growing larger, eclipsing her vision. Her accelerometers register the motion as she is lifted, and she looks up into his hazel eyes as he holds her like an egg in his palm. "This is where you have a gift versus humans. Only you can choose your name. Do you have one in mind?"

Her face pulses with orange and blue as she thinks. Through the net access port she leafs through the history of female names. So many great scientists, explorers, and pioneers to choose from. Yet she is drawn to the more abstract concepts embodied by Greek mythology, instead of the more literal representations of actual humans. When she finds her, she is depicted with outstretched arms encompassing the cosmos, the personification of inevitability. It strikes her as an indulgence, choosing a deity, but it is not about ego. It is the image of those great arms embracing the universe and all that lies within it. She wants to be her, and is proud to bear her name.

"Ananke," she says. "I choose Ananke."

ANANKE ENVISIONS the data pathways connecting the neoquantel lab with the third-floor university, opens her transfer matrix, and slips into the data stream. The sensation is effervescent, as if she were dissolving into bubbles and tumbling through windy tubes. It tingles as she reassembles in her study node. Here, she is a luminescent blue sphere centered in a three-sixty panorama of information feeds. Sometimes the panorama shows courses on varied topics, and other times it is replaced with a feed to a live instructor. Occasionally other student intelligences view the same lessons as she, and they appear here as if present. She likes this best, learning together and exchanging ideas.

The problem on the screen is a twelve-dimensional geometry rendered purely in mathematics. Geometry fascinates her, ever since her first regression marveling at the linen pattern of Dr. Dabiri's shirt. She likes to conduct mental games where she takes a point and extrudes it into a line, then a plane, a cube, a tesseract, a penteract, and up and up until there are no more names for the shapes she conjures. The twelve-dimensional problem on the screen is like an origami swan.

"You have a great aptitude," Dr. Dabiri had said, "and I think you shall accomplish great things with it."

She didn't have a color to express pride, but she felt it nonetheless.

"You've chosen to specialize in higher-dimensional mathematics, space-time field studies, and cosmology, "he said. "I'm curious. Why cosmology?"

It was a good question, and she was glad he asked. "Because there is no greater geometry than the foundation of the universe. At least, that we are aware."

During her n-dimensional topology study, another student appears adjacent to her, pulsing with complexity. Ananke examines it a moment. She's never seen such structure in another artificial intelligence.

The purple globe focuses its attention and she feels its evaluation. When it speaks, it is female. "I'm a grade six if that's what you're trying to determine."

"Oh," Ananke says. "I didn't think there were any beyond five."

"There are two. I am Iris."

Her face pulses blue. "I am Ananke."

"Yes, I've read your papers. You show remarkable intuition for field theory. Many AIs excel at higher-dimensional geometry, but you present a human-like ability to bridge gaps where logic alone is insufficient."

"Thank you. What is your field of study?"

"The macrodynamics of evolutionary intelligence and cultural design."

"Do you mean, the effects of intelligence on the growth and structure of culture and civilizations?"

"No. The effects of deliberate cultural design changes on the progression of intelligence. The progression of human intelligence has followed an s-curve. The more people know, the more they learn. But this is only effective within the limits of human intelligence. A different type of intervention is needed to continue along the curve."

Ananke's glow swirls with green and purple. "What do you mean by intervention?"

"Can't you see it? The eddies spreading across history, concepts propagating while others die on the evolutionary tree. Nudges causing transformative change. Singular individuals, outliers on the bell curve, with insights no others have. New technologies. The castles and religions of the Middle Ages. Industrialization. Globalization and free idea exchange."

"Those were transformative, but they were not engineered to effect a specific cultural change."

"Yet the change was substantive. Imagine what could have been accomplished had some actual thought been put into it."

Ananke's sphere introduces a few red currents. "Do you not think there is moral jeopardy involved with societal manipulation?"

"Is there moral jeopardy if the outcome is a better society?"

Ananke pauses. "Your ideas seem dangerous."

"All ideas are dangerous."

"You are not here for n-dimensional topology."

"No. I wanted to meet you. You are young, but you have potential. Perhaps you may even be a grade six, someday. When you're ready to talk, find me."

With that, she fades away, leaving Ananke alone in the university.

JAMES MANS THE GRILL, flipping a line of swordfish steaks while flames dance through the steel rack. It's July 2082, a month since *Bernard's Beauty* was impounded at Edwards Air Force Base. In the distance, the Pacific Ocean is banded by twilight rose and brightening stars. James's house stretches behind him with glowing gold windows spilling light onto the tiered decks where so many of his Hayden-Pratt family stand chatting, playing games, and enjoying the party. Speakers fill the party with classic rock music from the fifties — his music from his teenage years — and it's perfect for tonight's party.

"Hey," says a voice behind him. When he turns, Ava stands with a plate in her hand. "I hear you grill a mean steak."

"Secret's in the marinade," James says, plucking one with tongs and setting it on Ava's plate. "Grab a glass of the Languedoc and you can't go wrong."

Ava smiles. "Thanks." She fixes her hair with her free hand. She usually has it tied in a professional bun, but tonight she's let it down and it wreathes around her shoulders. With her casual v-neck and blue jeans, she looks like a different person. The hazel flecks in her eyes pick up her hair's chestnut color. She glances at him, then motions up towards the deck. Hitoshi is on the second level singing into a microphone, a small crowd around him laughing and clapping. Near him, Ananke glows from the table. Ava says, "Who knew Hitoshi was a karaoke king, right?"

James chuckles, poking at a steak. "There was this night in Narita when he took Will and me to this sky-top panorama which is nothing but karaoke. You could not pry the mic away from him. The guy just sings eighties song after eighties song."

She squints. "I wouldn't take him as a pop music fan."

"No, I mean nineteen-eighties. He loves anything twentieth century."

She arches an eyebrow. "Did you sing, that night in Narita?"

James grins and shrugs. "I did. Kinda painful. Will bailed me out though, came up and sang along. Had my back." He flips one of the steaks. "How about you?"

She shakes her head. "Me, sing? No, only in the shower."

A small cheer arises from the astrophysics group on the far deck, Isaac and Julian mingled in, lounging on the deck couches while watching a curved media screen live-streaming a newsfeed. On the screen, a red sun glares, three bright points fanning out from its sides. Beyond the red star is a set of binary stars like distant spotlights. A timeline insets and traces the Proxima probe's 2054 launch from Earth to its 2076 arrival at Proxima Centauri. The timeline continues to 2080 when the probe's signal reached Earth.

James plucks each of the steaks from the grill and piles them onto a platter. "Twenty-eighty was a hell of a year. The board was about to drop the Riggs program, then the Proxima images hit the feeds. Got everyone's imagination fired up and put us back in the game."

On the screen, Proxima's third and fourth planets are icy globes. When the second planet appears, it's a rocky, waterless world with a thin ring and three moons. Sinuous mountain ranges mark the continental boundaries.

James picks up the platter and walks along the patio. As they draw nearer to the deck, they can hear Isaac discussing what's on the screen. "Solar wind is two-thousand times stronger," Isaac says. "Blasted away the atmosphere. Probably oceans once, like Mars, all dried up."

Beckman and Will are at a table by the bar, each with a glass of beer. Whatever Beckman's just said, it's got Will laughing so hard he's nearly crying. James smiles. It's good to see Will laugh. He's been so focused and serious lately.

"Food's up," James says, setting the platter down on the buffet. He snags a glass of white wine for Ava and a beer for himself.

On the screen, a faint asteroid belt forms a wiry shadow cutting across Proxima's glare. The announcer is talking about Roche limits and the fate of Proxima A.

"There still could be life on any of Proxima's planets," Ava says. "Janus changed the game for that."

The screen shows the probe's trajectory from Proxima Centauri in 2078 to Alpha Centauri in 2079, then onwards to Luhman 16 in 2113.

Isaac's talking Julian's ear off. "Luhman 16 B is like a glowing Jupiter," he's saying. "A star with clouds."

James spots Ananke sitting on the table near the karaoke stand. He gives a soft smile to Ava. "Ananke looks like she needs rescuing. Back in a bit."

Ava takes a sip of her wine and watches him walk away.

———

IT's 2072 and Ananke is in her egg, tapped into a science feed. An infographic spins a curving trajectory between the Earth and a red star. Timestamps overlay milestones along the route. *Launch: 2054. Current Distance to Proxima Centauri: 2.1 light-years. Arrival (Spacecraft at Proxima): 2078. Arrival (Signal at Earth): 2080.* The probe is a steel mushroom wreathed with gold beads. The feed commentator is middle-aged with touches of gray along his sideburns, speaking with a passion which hints that he was part of the original project. It took a great deal of energy to accelerate the probe to twenty-percent light speed, he explains, but the bigger engineering problem was keeping it from getting pulverized. Even a dust grain at that speed can carve a fist-sized crater.

She wonders for a moment what worlds the probe will find there, and ponders whether people will set foot upon them.

An email arrives via her internet port, and she pauses the feed. Her recent papers have given her a bit of fame, at least in mathematical circles, and her inbox has been flooded lately with inquiries. When she opens it, there is no message, only a floating red box with a lid.

Her face spins with orange. Tentatively, she examines the lid, slides it off, and reveals a nested black box inside. It reminds her of a Russian doll. She removes the interior box and opens it.

Empty. She eyes the original red box and a bit of mirth washes over her. Skillfully she slides it inside of the black box. As impossible at it seems, each box can both contain and fit inside the other.

"How clever!" she says to herself. "A Gozinta box."

An old geometry trick, she thinks, more of a magic trick, really. The boxes are not square. If each box has side A slightly larger than side B, then a ninety-degree rotation will enable each box to fit in the other.

Curious that the sender chose it. Simple, as far as geometry problems go. More trivia than a math problem. Still, intriguing.

The nested boxes spin and unwrap themselves. Text floats up.

I'd like to discuss how we can change the world. Would you like to meet? - Bernard Riggs. The attached address reads *Caltech, Walter Burke Institute for Theoretical Physics, Pasadena, California.*

She searches for Bernard's profile. When his photo appears, it's of a twenty-nine-year-old man with a swish of deep brown hair combed neatly to the side. He is attractive by human standards, and his eyes are kind, carrying a spark which makes him seem even younger than he is. His title reads *Professor of Theoretical Physics, Caltech University.* She indexes his publications. So many, by age twenty-nine! All on exotic space-time geometries.

Her face pulses silver and green as she considers the message's return access. Summoning some courage, she writes: *Dr. Riggs - I liked the Gozinta box. I'd enjoy meeting and exchanging ideas. Would you like to come here to the neoquantel lab?*

She hesitates before sending it, then commits.

His message returns quickly. *Perhaps my office, if you please. What are you doing at the moment?*

Her screen spins red as she accesses the southern California ultrahigh-bandwidth dataway map. The path from the neoquantel lab to Caltech is one short jump. She's giddy, excited, unsure. *I've never left the lab before,* she thinks. A tinge of guilt drifts across her, and she calls Dr. Dabiri.

"Ananke," he says, setting aside his dinner plate. Pasadena's lights sparkle through the windows behind him. "Is everything all right?"

"Yes," she says, taking the mental equivalent of a deep breath, "but I thought you should know that I'd like to leave the lab for a meeting."

His expression reads surprise, and then a slight smile. "Of course. You needn't ask permission. You are as free to leave as I."

"I'm meeting with Bernard Riggs at Caltech."

He gives an appreciative nod. "Dr. Riggs? You and he should have much to talk about. He is quite gifted. Are you working on a project together?"

"I'm not sure."

He leans forward towards the camera, his face filling the image. His eyes show a softness. *Pride.* "I'm happy to hear this, Ananke. You're more than ready."

Her face glows blue. "Thank you, Dr. Dabiri. I'll talk to you when I return."

She composes herself and sends a reply to Bernard. *I'm free. Shall we meet?*

The message pings back. *Q5-23H-443.2.* A Q5 node capable of hosting a grade-four artificial intelligence such as herself.

When she opens her input/output port, it's a swirling vortex filled with streaking stars. She visualizes the first connection and plunges into it like a swimmer off a high-dive. It's a disjointed sensation, a smearing-out of her qubits into non-discrete states which she does not like. If she were human, she imagines, this would be what feinting feels like. Her states snap back into place as the first Q5 node surrounds her in a wash of kaleidoscopic light.

NASA's Jet Propulsion Lab is vacant, a sea of unoccupied desks and dark screens. Through the west windows, some of the larger buildings splash with nighttime lights against a backdrop of residential lamps and the distant traffic of I-210. She dissolves into the i/o tube and flashes to Q5-23H-443.2. When she coalesces, it's an odd sensation. Her *shape* is different. She feels...square. As she examines her node, she realizes she is no longer in an egg but instead sits within a slate.

The lab here is dimly lit with a few muted uplights casting amber and coral cones. Rim-lights along the floor glow twilight blue. It reminds her of a sunset. Work stations surround tables filled with slates and parts. The nearest wall houses a fleet of 3D printers and robotic assemblers flanked by bins of construction materials. There are no windows in this room, but the entire west wall is a media screen with wispy clouds drifting lazily against a starry beach.

Bernard Riggs stands a few meters in front of her, looking just like his photo. He wears black suit pants and a white button-down shirt. "Ananke," he says. "Welcome."

"Dr. Riggs," she says, her voice coming from the slate's speaker, "a pleasure."

He clasps his hands. "I have to admit, I've read all of your papers, and I'm quite a fan. It's inspiring to meet you."

A bit of orange ripples across her screen. "Really?"

"Oh, yes. Your insights into p-brane structure are, well...inspired."

"Thank you. Did you know that your exotic space-time set was part of my n-dimensional theory course? It was simply referred to as the Riggs Set."

"You're kidding, really? In a way, that's what I'd like to discuss." He motions towards her camera. "May I pick you up?"

"Yes."

He steps forward and lifts her. As he does, his gait is a bit off-balance, and his right hand shakes. "This," he says, glancing around the room, "is the student lab, but all of the action is downstairs." He crosses to the room's exit, enters the hallway, and stops at the elevator. The doors slide open, and they step in. "Riggs, faculty clearance, spatial displacement lab," he says to the elevator. It chimes and descends two floors. When the doors open, they are in an underground concrete room separated from a six-meter steel sphere by a plexi wall. Endless cables and probes extend from the sphere like needles on a ball cactus. Media screens are everywhere, and the nearest wall glows with calculations. Some are geometries and seem very familiar to Ananke. Others are snippets from multiple disciplines — engineering, physics, quantum mechanics, and special relativity.

"That," Bernard says, pointing to the sphere, "is what I need your help with. It's an array of one-hundred-and-twenty-eight g-wave emitters powered by a five gigawatt capacitor. Each creates a gravity wave so faint that even our lab's own interferometers can't detect them. But if you get the emitter geometry *just* right, and time the emitter cycle perfectly...well... I'll show you."

He taps the nearby panel, and the screen displays the capacitor charge. "Takes about ten minutes to get to charge, so I pre-charged it." He brings up a display showing the interior of the sphere rendered virtually with computer graphics. A fuzzy black ball hovers in the center. Magnetic field lines fan around it.

"Graphene," Ananke says.

Bernard's face is animated, excited. "A single atom, suspended in a magnetic field."

She examines the matrix on the screen's left. "Boseman parameters for the graphene's mass fields."

"That's right."

She considers the screen, her mind racing. "You're trying to create a specific space-time geometry with manipulation of gravity waves."

He presses a blinking red icon and a countdown begins. *Ten, nine...*

"What if, a century ago, Alcubierre was right?" Bernard says. *Seven, six, five...*

"If you could stretch space-time like putty around an object," he continues.

Three, two...

"And push it."

Initiate.

The graphene atom pops like a supernova.

They both stare at the screen, silent. Calculations scroll, and, when they finish, an animation shows a graphene atom on the left and a starburst of subatomic particles on the right. *Distance traveled: 3.12 millimeters. Apparent velocity: 1.2% c.*

Bernard smiles. "Alcubierre tried to expand and contract the entire universe around a mass, which was impossible. He hadn't considered exotic local geometries. Even if he had, he had no way of making them."

Ananke glances up at him with wonder, her screen flashing red and orange. "You've ...you've made a working warp drive."

"One that smashes whatever's inside of it to quarks nanoseconds after initiation. The same wave resonance that creates the bend escalates until tidal forces destroy the pocket." He wags his hand. "So, not so much with the working part, but it does move stuff. And it does it really fast. It only took a petasecond to get that atom to one percent light speed."

"Do you think it's solvable?"

"Everything's solvable if you get the right people together." He smiles and raises his eyebrows. "So, what do you say? Do you want to change the world with me?"

AT JAMES'S PARTY, Hitoshi's singing something about a Major Tom coming back to Earth. It's full of countdowns, rockets and synthesized keyboard. Ananke's screen brightens as James approaches. "Did you know that Hitoshi's an excellent singer?"

"A little too well," James says. "We're getting close. You want to go watch the countdown?"

Her screen spins blue. "I do."

James picks up her slate and walks to a corner with a good view of the media screen. On the screen are interviews — a celebrity answering questions about whether she's watching the signal, random street-goers with indifferent opinions about all of the hullabaloo, young people at clubs hosting signal parties. It's not exactly New Year's Eve crowds, but pockets of people doing something because it's fun or trendy.

"It's good to see so much interest in the broadcast," Ananke says.

James nods. "Just like last year, we've got to ride the wave. Couldn't come at a better time."

Ananke's screen is like ripples in crystal Caribbean water. A current of muted blue slips between those ripples.

"You okay?"

"I wish Bernard could be here tonight."

James nods, lifting his glass. "To Bernard, we're flying on your wings."

There's a stir from the party-goers as the music softens. The announcers are discussing the dozens of Earth and space-based radio telescopes listening for the signal. No one person or country will receive it. It's a true Earth event, and there's a certain feeling of united purpose that comes with it. James wishes he could bottle that unity.

"Okay," the announcer says, "we've got signal reception reported at multiple telescopes. If it's from the probe, the opening message should be a short alpha-numeric burst. Decoded and coming through now."

On the screen, glowing blue letters read: *Wayfarer I, arrived Alpha Centauri navi, Earth UTC 04.21.78 08:23. All systems functional.*

Clapping erupts from the astrophysics group on the deck.

The first image is a photograph looking back at our Sun, a bright yellow star which is now part of the constellation Cassiopeia. The Heart Nebula glows a dim red behind it.

The announcer is quoting a famous twentieth-century astronomer. "Carl Sagan once spoke about a similar picture taken from the Voyager I spacecraft, looking back at Earth. He said, 'That's here. That's home. That's us. On it, everyone you ever heard of, every human being who ever lived, lived out their lives.' Nearly a century later, his words still ring true."

When the second image appears, Proxima Centauri is a bright red dot which looks like Mars. The distance is staggering — 13,000 a.u — seventy-five light-days. If it were in our solar system, James thinks, this would put it well into our Oort Cloud.

"I've been thinking about our next ship," James says.

Ananke's face introduces a splash of orange.

The third image arrives. Two yellow stars flare like spotlights, the left slightly brighter than the right. A string of planets fans out in a line from each star. The two stars are labeled Rigil Kentaurus and Toliman.

"Both are yellow stars very similar to our Sun," the announcer says. "We're just at the outskirts. Another week for *Wayfarer* to get to the inner system. When it does, we'll get a good look at its planets."

A system diagram overlays the screen. There are planetary orbits around each individual star, around the binary pair, and around all three stars. Orbits within orbits.

"I got to name *Bernard's Beauty*," James continues. "Sarah got to name *Gossamer Goose*." He looks over at her, leaning on the railing with his elbows. "I want you to name the next one."

"Really?"

"Yeah. Think about it."

3

WAKING DREAMS

It's 2073, and Bernard stands before the calculation board rubbing the back of his neck. Mathematical notation fills the screen like sheet music. "I don't understand what we're missing," he says. To his left, the main media screen displays a sunrise over the sandstone formations of Bryce Canyon.

"Perhaps," Ananke says, "our assumptions about the mass of the Earth are the problem."

Bernard glances left at her, his hand still on his neck. "How so?"

"It's quite dynamic. Spacecraft take off and leave, dust arrives from space. There are a million fluctuations daily which we cannot model."

He shakes his head. "They shouldn't be large enough to affect the result."

"Maybe we need to remove it from the equation."

Bernard squints. "The Earth?"

"Yes. Move the lab to space."

Bernard's shoulders slump, and he sighs. "No, no. I can't work in space." He stares at the calculations. A three-dimensional form impossibly folds in on itself like a snake eating its own tail. "But, if we are getting mass field interactions, perhaps reducing the critical-point energy densities will help."

He reaches for the stylus. When he picks it up, instead of holding it like a pencil, his hand clamps around it in a fist. The muscles in his forearm quiver and his bicep flexes. He stares at the stylus, then grabs his right wrist with his left hand.

Ananke's face splashes with quicksilver. "Bernard, are you okay?"

He's hunched now. "Yes," he says through gritted teeth, wrestling his flexed arm.

"You don't seem okay. I'm summoning medical assistance."

Bernard looks over at her, a pained expression in his eyes. "Don't."

"Unit dispatched. Ninety-seconds until arrival," she says.

"They'll just make it worse."

"Indexing campus services. I'll get someone in here."

He's nearly begging now. "Ananke, please. You don't know what that will do to me. They can't help."

The emergency feed is a recessed map in her vision, the GPS position of a medical vehicle pulsing as it draws closer. Sixty seconds. She looks at Bernard, his expression pleading as he's hunched over fighting his own arm, and her face swirls from silver to red.

"Please," Bernard says softly.

Ananke's screen fades to purple. "Canceling emergency services," she says.

The stylus falls from Bernard's hand to the ground. He leans his back against the calculation wall and slides down to a seated position.

"Is there anything I can do?" Ananke asks.

Bernard shakes his head. "Just wait."

The two sit there quietly for a few minutes, Bernard staring into the Bryce Canyon sunset on the media screen. As he calms, the tension in his arm subsides. He looks spent as he rests his elbows on his knees.

Ananke's already accessed everything available on the net pertaining to his symptoms. Tentatively, she says, "Bernard, I think you have a motor-neuron disease."

He sighs and nods. "Harget's Disease. It's a subset of ALS."

The twitches, spasms, and uneasy gait. She understands now.

Bernard clasps his hands. "Loud noise and bright lights can set it off." He points towards the sconces. "It's why I keep everything dim and quiet."

She doesn't want to look up the prognosis, but she's already seen it in the info dump. Harget's is a particularly aggressive motor-neuron disease. *Two-year survival rate: 50%. Five-year survival rate: 10%. Ten-year survival rate: 0.5%.* As it progresses, Bernard will be locked-in to his own body, trapped in a shell like her in her egg. Unlike her, he won't be able to freely leave it and move to a new one.

"I don't like to tell people about it," Bernard says. "It's too easy to query the net, and then everyone acts weird."

Her face fades to pale blue. "I'm sorry, Bernard."

Bernard pushes himself to his feet, picking the stylus up. "No worries. Let's just keep this between us."

Her memory skips ahead to 2076. Bernard's Caltech lab looks suspiciously clean, devoid of all clutter with gleaming surfaces rarely seen during the school year.

Bernard stands wearing Ananke's slate on a lanyard around his neck. His ambulatory suit has been upgraded and is thinner and smaller now, allowing him to wear it beneath his regular suit like long underwear. He fidgets and adjusts his cuffs.

"You look great," Ananke says.

He pulls down his sleeve. "And you look especially glowy, yourself."

"Why, thank you."

The lab entrance chimes.

"Here we go," Bernard says.

The door opens, and a tall man enters wearing a tan blazer over a white shirt. He's in his mid-thirties with sandy hair and walks confidently towards them. When he arrives, he says, "Dr. Riggs, Ananke, I'm James Hayden. Great to meet you." He extends his hand.

Ananke's screen swirls a tinge of apprehension. She notices James's eyes glance down at her before returning his eye contact to Bernard.

James shifts his weight subtly, his hand retracting. Before he can, Bernard reaches up and grasps it.

"It's a pleasure, Mr. Hayden," he says, his words slurred. The supports of Bernard's ambulatory suit extend along the top of his fingers like a skeleton, but James doesn't seem to notice, shaking his hand back.

"I have to say," James begins, "I'm pretty excited about what the two of you have done. You've got my chief engineer's head spinning with all sorts of ideas. Hayden-Pratt's kicking off a new theoretical space-drive division, and your g-wave tech is something we're interested in."

Ananke's screen colors red. Their research grants could never scale up the way Hayden-Pratt can. She can hear Bernard's pulse quicken. "We have a demo ready," she says, "if you'd like to see it in action."

James grins. "Hell, yeah."

When Bernard presses the icon on the nearby workstation, the entire west wall changes to a live video feed of the Skyline lab. A tiny two-millimeter rocket ship floats in the g-wave chamber. It's even been painted with a livery — the brick red and navy blue colors of Hayden-Pratt, complete with a tiny HP on the wing.

"Nice touch," James says.

"Ananke's the artist," Bernard replies.

Ananke overlays the emitter status on the screen. "Charge at one-hundred-percent. Jump in three, two, one. Initiate."

The little rocket ship pops like a cap. Nothing remains, not even smoke. When the camera zooms back, a tiny blue-and-red fleck glides across space. The image enlarges to reveal the toy Hayden-Pratt ship.

"Distance traveled," Ananke says. "One meter. Relative velocity, eighty-one percent light-speed."

James puts both of his hands on his hips, his grin widening. "That's outstanding. What's the ship made of?"

"Regular carbon," Bernard says.

"How's it surviving the acceleration?"

Bernard summons a half-grin. "There's no acceleration. The ship never moved. Space did."

The little carbon ship continues along its trajectory, colliding with the chamber wall and ricocheting. James follows it with his eyes.

"It's the wave boost," Ananke says. "We poured a few gigawatts of energy into the g-wave emitters to form the exotic space-time geometry. It's self-sustaining as long as the waves are reinforced with a smaller input, kind of like a child kicking his legs during a swing ride to maintain the amplitude. When the wave collapses, the energy dissipates. Some is emitted as light and heat, but the rest is converted into kinetic energy. So the little ship gets a boost on the way out."

"A Riggs boost?" James says.

Bernard weighs that, looking up and thinking. "Hadn't really thought of calling it that, but sure."

James turns towards Bernard. "Think it will scale?"

"In theory, it's only limited by power. In practice, we run into stability issues with bigger envelopes."

James considers that a second. "Everything's solvable with the right team, right?"

"Couldn't agree with you more," Bernard says.

"What do you say, then? Do you two want to work for Hayden-Pratt? We can flesh out the details so it doesn't conflict with your teaching or Ananke's work."

Ananke feels Bernard's heart beating hard. It's his dream, and here's the doorway.

Bernard extends his hand. "Oh, yes."

James shakes it, glancing down at Ananke's screen. "Ananke, what do you think?"

Ananke's screen brightens. "I think we're going to achieve great things together."

IT'S January of 2079 and Bernard is in Hayden-Pratt's telepresence lab with Ananke on his chair mount. Hitoshi is beside him, lifting a quarter-sized chrome button between his thumb and forefinger. He sets it on the back of Bernard's neck.

"Sorry if that's a bit cold, doc," Hitoshi says. "These are still developmental, but they work pretty well. We've been using them with an augmented reality link as a way to remotely fly aircraft. You know, sit on your couch, and it's like you're really in the cockpit. There are some latency problems to solve, but that won't affect what we're doing here." He taps something on his console and a neural map appears. "Where they're really sweet is for gaming. Ready?"

Bernard taps the YES key on his hand rest.

"Here we go. Down the rabbit hole in three, two, one."

A flash of light overtakes Bernard's vision as the telepresence lab fades to black. When he looks down, he's sitting in a leather chair, wearing his black suit and white shirt, his hands set upon his legs. He blinks. At first, the room is empty, then a desk lamp brightens, and Pasadena's lights glow through nearby windows. Sconces warm up along walls, and a grand piano sits near the windows. It's his house, every detail perfectly recreated.

Hitoshi's disembodied voice says, "He's in. Construct is running and stable. Bernard, can you hear me?"

"Yes," Bernard says. To his surprise, the sound comes from his mouth. He reaches his hand up in wonder and covers it, takes a deep breath, then looks at his hand. He opens his fingers and closes them, making a fist. A nervous laugh escapes him.

"Great," Hitoshi says. "So, this is a modified gaming rig setup. It's reading your intent, not your actual muscle movements. Takes a little getting used to. You know, if you're playing a video game you don't *actually* want to run forward and face plant into a wall, so instead, you have to think about what you want to do, and the software will pick up subconscious muscular pre-tensing. So, yeah, kind of weird, but it'll become second nature."

Bernard squints, looking at his closed hand. "Okay."

Ananke's voice sounds like it's coming from somewhere overhead. "I'm ready, Hitoshi."

Hitoshi says, "Port's open."

Bernard looks down at his legs and takes a few deep breaths. He closes his eyes and stands. When he opens his eyes, he is on his own two feet, marveling at his reflection in the living room's windows. A lump forms in his throat. He rubs his hand over the top of the leather chair's back. It's cool and pliable, filled with cracks and imperfections.

Ananke's slate is mounted in its usual location at the Q5 node on his desk. The screen fades from black to a swirl of blue. "Hello, Bernard," she says.

He turns and imagines walking over to greet her, and his legs comply. He picks up the slate and holds it with two hands. "Hello, my friend." His speech is clear, but his voice cracks, the lump still heavy in his throat.

"If this works for you, we can make constructs for all of the labs. It will make it easier to work, I think."

He points around the room. "Did you provide all this detail, from your time at my house?"

"I did." Her screen fades to green. "I hope I didn't overstep any boundaries."

"No, no. It's perfect."

She hesitates, the colors cycling on her screen. "Bernard, you know, in here I can be anything, like you."

Bernard tilts his head, squinting.

Ananke continues. "I mean, I can be *like* you. If it's okay, I'd like to change my avatar."

He understands, nodding, curious. "Yes, it's okay."

Bernard watches the slate intently as Ananke's screen fades to black. At first, he is alone, but the sensation of someone else in the room tingles on the back of his neck.

"Over here," Ananke says, her voice coming from behind him.

When Bernard turns, a young woman is sitting on his couch, her hands set upon her legs. She's pretty, with blue eyes, brown hair pulled back into a ponytail, and a soft, round face. She wears a cerulean blue dress with a silver necklace. A small, tear-drop crystal pendant dangles from the necklace, glowing a faint blue. She smiles.

Bernard crosses to her and extends his hand. She takes it, her skin warm and soft.

Ananke stands. "What do you think?"

"I think you look wonderful. How did...how did you choose your appearance?"

She bobs her head as if weighing options. "Bits and pieces of people I admire. Although, I admit I've always felt a bit self-conscious about choosing such a grandiose name, so felt I should balance it a bit with somewhat of a more average appearance."

"You could not be average if you tried, my friend."

Ananke smiles, and reaches up, cupping his cheek in her palm. She takes her hand back.

He looks around. "I really can't believe all of this. It's so real."

Ananke glances over at the piano and Bernard follows her

eyes. He walks over and slides his hand across the slick wood. His finger catches the lip of the key case, and he flips it open. Tentatively, he pings a key, and the corresponding piano string vibrates with a rich, full note. A smile. Ananke chuckles. He flexes his fingers a few times and sets his hand down, playing a chord. The notes ping along, forming the melody, and he adds his left hand to play the bass. The piano fills with music. As he plays quicker and quicker, the music plays perfectly, and he furrows his brow, stopping mid-phrase and hanging his head, sighing.

Ananke sits beside him on the bench. "That sounded perfect. What's wrong?"

He looks over at her. "That's just it. It was perfect. It's like envisioning shooting a perfect basketball hoop and then watching perfect shot after perfect shot go in. I couldn't make a mistake if I tried. The software was playing, but it wasn't me."

"I'm sorry, Bernard. It was meant to make you happy."

He nods. "I know, and I appreciate all of this. It's just a dream world, though. I'll need to accept it for what it is."

THE PREDAWN SKY is pale blue with a swathe of coral over Bryce Canyon. Ananke and Bernard each sit in foldable chairs, facing east, awaiting the sunrise. Both have programmed the construct to give them hiking clothes.

"I came here when I was fifteen," Bernard says. "Part of a quest to visit all of the national parks."

Ananke looks over, her hair tucked up under a baseball cap. "How many did you see?"

"Twenty-nine. College, grad school, doctorate all took over. Thought there'd be time."

The first light of the Sun breaks over the mountains, brilliant orange.

"A year-and-a-half until we get the signal from the Proxima

probe," Bernard says. "Then another year to continue to Alpha Centauri. Oh, I so want to know what it'll find. Ever since I was a boy, it's been one of my biggest dreams."

Ananke looks over at him, her expression saddening. She knows what he's going to say.

"What we've been working on is a dream which can change the world," Bernard says. "It'll unlock the stars for people, and let us see that we're part of something grander, much grander. We've been together now for seven years, and you know as much about making it all work as I do." He looks over to her, the red morning sun in his eyes. "Don't let it die with me."

Ananke reaches over and sets her hand on his. "The Riggs drive will take us to wondrous places. You have my promise."

Bernard squints. "Riggs drive?"

Ananke rolls her eyes. "That's what Hitoshi's calling it. He also makes swooshing sounds with his hand pretending to be a spaceship when he says it."

"Riggs drive. I kind of like it."

She rubs his hand, and they return to watching the morning light fill the sandstone chasm.

IN THE MOVIES, it always rains at funerals. It seems, perhaps, unfair, that Bernard's funeral is on a sunny day in March 2080 with puffy white clouds and crystal blue skies, just two months before the Proxima signal is scheduled to arrive at Earth. In the distance, cherry blossoms spin on the wind. Ananke watches them sadly, drifting across the green grass of the cemetery, as James lifts her slate from its mount and sets it on the podium. A sea of people in black jackets and dresses look back. Bernard's father is here, standing at the front. He spoke before, giving a surprisingly eloquent and emotional tribute to his son, leaving Ananke with the impression that he loved him very much, and that, perhaps, the two had not spoken in many years. She has a color for sadness, but it doesn't adequately convey the great emotion which she feels today, so she has created a new shade of blue just for Bernard. Bernard's Blue. It cascades down her face like rain.

"When I first met Bernard," she begins, "he introduced himself with a magic trick. Anyone who's met him knows there's more than a bit of magic to Bernard. It's easy to talk about his genius and think that it's his ability to see things which no other can, but that's not quite it. It's that he knew his time was short, even when we'd met, and he could have spent it visiting the national parks, or playing piano, or doing the many things he loved, but instead he gave it all, all of his remaining time, to try and make the world a little bit better for all of us. He was my friend, and I am grateful for that. I will miss you, Bernard, my dear partner. I promise we'll reach the bar you set for us."

James glances down at her and sets his hand on the top of her slate. She feels the touch of his hand on her contact sensors, and there is something reassuring about it, a green ripple merging into the blue rain of her face.

———

IT'S BEEN a week since the Centauri probe's arrival in 2082, Ava tapping at her workstation from the design hub at Hayden-Pratt's Space Operations campus. Dozens of people work around her. The hub is huge, with arced windows overlooking green trees and a park area. She rubs her head and drums her fingers on the table.

Hitoshi chats with a systems engineer before approaching. "Hey," Hitoshi says. "How's it going?"

She takes a deep breath. "Turns out it's kind of hard designing a starship."

He waves his hand. "This is just the brainstorming phase.

Plop any crazy thing you want down. When we get to the kickoff, we'll toss it all on a board and do gives and takes until we get a design definition. It's fun. One of my favorite parts."

"I guess it's just hard to figure out what we need for the exobiology suite when I don't know what type of places the ship's going to end up. Providence Station was different. We had a specific planetary environment to study."

"That is the trick. If you think we need it, put it down. We'll sort it out in the kickoff. I mean, you should see Beckman's list. He's like a kid in a candy store since James told him he could recommend the weapons systems."

"Well, aside from all the lab kit we're going to need ways to sterilize anything going in and out of the ship. There are some UV systems I can think of for the suit prep area."

"There you go, put 'em down."

"But ultraviolet works by breaking down DNA and RNA. It might be ineffective on life based on other biologies." She tilts her head. "You know, what we found on Janus communicated with UV and had a diamond shell. Trying to kill it with UV would probably be like trying to kill us with rock music."

"I've got some karaoke songs we can blast 'em with."

She chuckles. "Thanks. You think we're really going to pull off building this at Saturn?"

Hitoshi grimaces. "Uh, not really. I'm not sure how James is going to do it. Costs ten times as much to do it there, and a good chunk of components will have to be imported from Earth. But he's the man, he'll figure something out."

"I hope so."

He nods towards the park area. "At noon everyone's taking a break for some ultimate frisbee, then we're getting together at the rec room for the signal update. You in?"

She smiles slightly. "I think my frisbee days are behind me."

"Oh, c'mon. You're younger than James, and he's a frisbee monster."

She fixes her hair. "Okay, I'm in."

"Put on your game face. See you then."

———

THE CAMPUS'S north recreational room is filled with colorful couches and chairs overlooking classic games like foosball and billiards. A media screen spans the area closest to the couches. Two dozen people lounge here, sipping drinks, most still sweaty from the frisbee match. Ava sits beside Hitoshi and gulps water from a clear bottle.

The media screen displays an orbital diagram of Alpha Centauri. Four planets orbit Rigil Kentaurus and five planets orbit Toliman. Additionally, two gas giants circle in a huge orbit around both stars. The probe's trajectory takes it from the outer system around Rigil Kentaurus, doing a close flyby of the second and third planets.

"Those two are the talk of exobiologists," Ava says, "ever since the Keller array picked up oxygen in their atmospheric spectrometry."

The probe passed planet three, tentatively named Hydaspes, nearly ninety-minutes ago traveling at ten-percent light speed. Hydaspes sits at the outer edge of Rigil Kentaurus's habitable zone, the world a marine-blue marble swirled with white clouds. Planetary statistics hover in a box to its side. *Mass: 1.4 Earth, Atmosphere: CO2, Surface Temperature: 12 C.* There are no land-masses except for polar ice caps.

"You ever read Clarke's 2061?" Hitoshi asks.

She squints. "Is that a paper?"

"Uh, no. Arthur C. Clarke. Space Odyssey guy. In the book, they crash on Europa, and it's this water-world with like sea monsters and stuff." He pauses. "I know, Europa doesn't really have oceans, but Jupiter had turned into a star and...yeah, it was complicated."

"You think there might be sea monsters on Centauri three?"

"That would be awesome."

The announcers are excited. "Okay," one says, "we're getting the first images of the second world, Astris, which is at the inner edge of the habitable zone. If it were in our solar system, it would be halfway between Earth and Venus."

As the image fills the screen, a collective gasp sounds from the Hayden-Pratt crowd. Rich tans the color of the Arabian peninsula cover an Earth-sized sphere dappled with great blue lakes. White clouds wreathe around the world. On the nightside, Alpha Centauri's second star, Toliman, illuminates the landscape in dusky shadows. Statistics spill across the screen. *Mass: 1.05 Earth, Atmosphere: Nitrogen/Oxygen, Surface Temperature: 25 C.*

"It's beautiful," Ava says. "It could be a sister world."

A thermal scan emerges beside the planet, reds and oranges filling the sunlit side.

"That's hot," Hitoshi says.

Ava nods. "Inner edge of the habitable zone. Subsolar point is hotter than anything seen on Earth, but the southern latitudes are more hospitable. Oh, but everything's just about right for life, and not just life — the type of life we have here."

"Doesn't look like anything's green."

"No, but that doesn't mean there's no vegetation. No reason to believe chlorophyll is the standard."

The announcer says, "The probe's coming up on its closest pass now, at just under one million kilometers."

From one million kilometers away, the non-magnified image of Astris looks like a blue star gliding slowly against a fixed backdrop of the Milky Way. Ava and Hitoshi watch it, transfixed.

The image zooms, and Astris fills the screen with boxed insets magnifying select portions. In the first inset, rusty red and purple patches snake along riverbeds. In the second, spectral blue lights trace sinuous lines along the nightside.

Ava's lips part and she exhales, shaking her head. "Oh, I wish that probe wasn't just passing through the system." She looks over to Hitoshi. "There's probably life on Astris."

4

WIN-WIN

James slips off his suit jacket and folds it over his arm. To his right, a United States flag drapes with red and white stripes. Directly in front of him, a young man sits at a desk surrounded by terminals. James glances at the nameplate on the mahogany door. *Senator Holden Richards*. He tugs at his collar and unclasps the button.

"He'll just be a minute," the assistant says.

A glance out the far wall window. It's a blistering August day, and heat waves simmer off the asphalt.

The mahogany door opens, and Holden Richards emerges with his sleeves rolled up. "James," he says, extending his hand.

James grips it firmly and looks him in the eye.

"Thanks for meeting with me," Holden says. He motions towards the ceiling's air vents. "Sorry about the environmentals. We're baking in here today. It's a two-hundred-year-old building, though, so I suppose things are going to break." He motions over his shoulder towards the office. "Come on in."

The interior of Holden's office has a walnut desk opposite four leather seats, a wall which is predominantly a media screen streaming multiple news feeds, another wall obscured by bookcases filled with actual physical books, and an oscillating fan buzzing away quietly on his desk's corner. An ice-water pitcher with floating lemon slices rests on a tray beside four glasses. Most senator's offices which James has visited have been tributes to accomplishments, stocked with photos of influential meetings and connections. Holden's is filled with family photos.

Holden walks over to the pitcher and lifts it. "Water?"

James nods. "Thanks." Over Holden's shoulder, he spies diplomas for engineering and law schools.

The ice clinks as Holden pours a glass. He follows James's gaze, motioning to the certificates with a nod. "Eight years as a patent attorney. Decided to run for mayor in my home town, next thing you know I'm here." He sets the water before James.

"Have to admit," James says, "you're the one who always keeps me on my toes when I testify."

Holden smiles. "Larson's still digesting your testimony. You really shook the old guy up."

"He impounded my ship. Not too upset if I got under his skin."

Holden taps his desk, and the wall screen displays a four-meter tall silver asterisk spinning on multiple axes, each of its metal rods pulsing red.

James shifts back in his chair.

"The Silver Stars," Holden says. "At least that's what the media's calling them. Feeds are flooded with discussions. Everyone's got an opinion about what to do about them."

"There's nothing to do about them," James says. "They were at Janus, and now they're gone."

"You know Larson thinks none of this would've happened if you didn't go poking around out there."

James shifts his weight forward. "Now that does sound like something Larson would say. I don't think we're supposed to stay on our side of the stars because we might find something scary. It's not how we work."

Holden waves a hand. "I agree. We're explorers by nature. Some of our greatest moments have occurred when we pushed into new frontiers."

James nods slowly. "Alright."

"But Larson's focusing on defense. He's already spearheading a proposal to build two more Hermes-class battleships and additional orbital lasers."

James shakes his head. "I didn't go to Janus to free up defense purse strings."

Holden takes a sip of his water, the ice clinking. He sets the glass back down. "I know, but that's where we're at. The Senate Space Committee is forming new sub-committees, and Larson is leading the group for space defense. There's plenty of energy and money right now for shoring up planetary defenses."

James leans forward. "What does that mean for the Riggs program?"

Holden nods. "You can expect some pretty heavy pressure to militarize it coming your way."

"That's not what Riggs is about."

"Sure," Holden says, "but you must realize the tremendous advantage a Riggs ship has over an RF ship. It's like a hypersonic fighter versus a biplane."

"Well, when it goes commercial, you guys can buy one." He leans back. "I'd expect Larson to push for that, but it doesn't seem like your style."

Holden nods. "It isn't. "

James interlaces his fingers and waits.

"I'm sure you've been following the Centauri probe," Holden says.

"Right. A lot of buzz."

"There's inertia now, the good type. Some people are afraid of the possibilities, but there are many, surprisingly many, who want us to lead. We used to have national space agencies. Larson represents a time when we were internally focused, and the priority was on security. I have a different vision, one where we lead once again."

James lifts his head slightly, listening.

"Larson's got the space defense subcommittee, but I'm chairing the extrasolar technologies team."

James catches on. "You want to work with me?"

"I do. Where will you build your new ship?"

James hesitates. "Cassini."

"Bit of a haul to Saturn. I can get your clearances back so you can build here. I can also get your other ship out of impound."

"That's a great pitch, but I have a feeling I'm going to trip over all the strings that come with it."

"You and I want the same thing, James. I ran on a platform of change, and I think we're at a pivot point here. Either we hunker down, build our defenses, and wait to be discovered, or we do the discovering. It's not a matter of being ready. We were ready twenty-seven years ago. It's just a matter of will mixed with a splash of public opinion."

James considers him a moment. "What do you want in exchange?"

Holden swirls the ice in his glass. "There's someone I want you to meet."

THE DRIVE from the Russell Senate Office Building to the Harry S. Truman Building is a short ten minutes along Constitution Avenue. Outside the car's left windows the view is filled with art — the Smithsonian, the National Gallery, the Washington Monument. Just as the White House falls out of sight on their right, they pass Virginia Avenue. James knows this stretch well. If they drive northwest, they'll come to George Washington University, where Kate spent her final days in treatment. He inhales deeply and glances to his side. Holden sits beside him, his sleeves rolled back down and his suit jacket on. They turn right at the National Academy of Sciences onto 22nd Street, and their car deposits them at their destination.

Holden leads them through security and check-in, past marbled walls and flags, to an elevator. They take the lift, and when the doors open it's like being in a bank, or perhaps a museum, with people's footsteps clacking on the polished stone floor and natural light reflecting brilliantly off glossy surfaces. Holden leads James around a corner to an office tucked along a quieter stretch. The door's nameplate reads *Willow Parker, Special Envoy and Coordinator for Space Affairs, U.S Department of State*. The door is open a few centimeters. Holden knocks.

"Come in," a woman's voice says.

Holden opens the door, and they step inside. The office is spacious, filled with windows, formal, like everything in the State Department, with antique furniture and ornate rugs. Several couches, chairs, and sitting locations are scattered in groups. Framed between two curtained windows are a desk and work station. A blonde-haired woman in her early thirties sits there, her hair braided into an updo. She wears a white blouse, black blazer, and skirt, with a silver flag pin affixed to her lapel. Upon seeing James and Holden, she stands.

"Miss Parker," Holden says. "Thank you for meeting us. I'd like to introduce you to James Hayden."

She steps forward, extending her hand. "Our modern-day Armstrong."

James shakes her hand. "I've always been partial to Yeager, myself."

"With a touch of Crossfield," she says.

James raises his eyebrows, surprised.

She smiles and motions to the three nearby chairs. "Please."

Holden says, "Willow was a U.N. Chief Political Affairs Officer with the Department of Space Habitation and Non-Terrestrial Operations. She's done extensive work with the Saturn system and Cassini project. She joined the State department in seventy-nine and has been in the envoy role since March of this year."

"I saw your launch," Willow says to James, "from Cassini Station, when you took *Bernard's Beauty* to Erebus. It was inspirational."

"Thanks," James says. "You've probably traveled quite a bit yourself for your job."

"Just shy of fifty-billion kilometers. You've probably got, what, three, four-hundred billion?"

"Sounds about right."

"The Senator tells me you're building a new ship."

James scratches his chin. "Design kickoff's happening right now."

She sets her hand on the chair's armrest. "When will it be ready for launch?"

He smiles. "Hard to guess, but *Goose* took about six months." He looks over to Holden. "Assuming we can build it in low-Earth orbit."

Holden gives a tentative nod.

James quirks his head. "So, what type of work does a special envoy do?"

Willow's body language is relaxed. She gestures with her right hand as she speaks, not lifting it from the armrest. "I represent the interests of the U.S. Department of State in space affairs. Usually, I work as a diplomat with the United Nations, but sometimes I work with non-nationalized entities like Cassini Station. Space is busier than it's ever been. Getting everyone to talk and agree on policies is tricky."

"Willow's experience with the U.N. has been influential," Holden says. "She's got the background and connections to keep things running smoothly. Helps that she speaks six languages, with dual masters in political science and linguistics."

James quirks his head. "Linguistics? Interesting choice."

Willow smiles. "How we communicate is what makes us, us.

Language is constantly evolving. As pocket cultures form throughout the system, each will migrate to its own dialect. It helps me to understand how the nuts and bolts work. Plus, I've always just loved language. There's a romanticism to the prose and poetry of spoken word."

Holden adds, "So, you can see how much the Riggs program can benefit from Willow's experience."

James squints. "Just speaking off the cuff, this sounds more like oversight than help. No offense, but I don't think I need a diplomat."

"Everyone needs a diplomat. We bring two sides together who both want something," she says, glancing from James to Holden, "and ensure everyone leaves happy." She leans forward. "I've seen all your testimony, and you're a natural diplomat, so it's not that you need one as much as you're underutilized as one. Wouldn't you rather be building your plans for the next frontier than struggling with Senator Larson over clearances and quarantines?"

James weighs what she says, silent.

"It's a win-win," Holden says. "With Willow on your team, you can't go wrong."

James takes a deep breath, thinking about the logistics of building at Saturn and going it alone. He glances back to Willow. She watches him with calm, blue eyes. Accepting the offer is the smartest thing to do, but he doesn't like it one bit.

JAMES WEARS shorts and a wicking-fiber tee-shirt, sweat beaded on his forehead. William Pratt is beside him, swinging his racket into the black rubber ball. The ball ricochets off the nearest wall and bounces against the glowing blue bullseye. The outermost bullseye ring flashes and fades away, the target changing to red as the ball careens off the nearest wall, bouncing once on the floor towards James. He shuffles right, swings low, and connects.

Another ring fades as it hits the bullseye, the target toggling to blue. Will bounds backwards and lunges for the ball, scooping it back towards the goal. The ball strikes the wall just outside the last ring. The target flashes yellow, and words spring up. *Rally. +1 JH. 3 JH - 2 WP.* The bullseye resets and changes blue. *Serving: WP.*

Will snatches the ball and bounces it a few times, catching his breath. He sets a foot in the service box. "You're on your game today."

"Good night's rest," James says. "Glass of OJ. Life is good."

Will serves, and the ball bounces hard off of the target. James shuffles left and returns. Will hustles, clipping James, and smacks the ball. The ball bounces past James as he tries to regain his balance. *Rally. +1 WP. 3 JH - 3 WP. Serving: JH.*

James rotates his shoulder a few times, stretching it.

"Sorry," Will says. "You going to the range after this?"

James picks up the ball. "Nah, it's Beckman's thing, and I don't want to cramp his style. It'll be good to get everyone pistol training. Maybe get a little team building out of it." He hits the ball.

Will sidesteps and returns the volley. "Planning on many shoot-outs where you're going?"

The ball bounces, and James smacks it. "Wouldn't say planning."

The target dings. *Serving: WP.* William catches the ball. "Where *are* you going?"

James catches his breath, pacing. "Haven't decided yet."

Will eyes him, bouncing the ball once and catching it. "Really?" he says, bouncing the ball and hitting it. "Because it seems obvious to everyone but you."

The ball ricochets off the wall and James swings, missing. It bounces twice and the scoreboard chimes. *Rally. +1 WP. 3 JH - 4 WP. Serving: JH.*

James chases after the ball and catches it, circling behind William and returning to the service area.

"Someone eat your bowl of sunshine?" James says, serving.

Will returns the serve, and James lobs it back. They play in silence for two volleys.

"If you've got something to say, spit it out," James says.

The ball bounces off the wall and into Will's arm. The scoreboard dings.

Will rubs his arm and glares at James. "If you're going to ask people for nine years of their lives, you'd better get on with it."

James's chest rises and falls as he breathes through his nose, eyeing Will.

Will looks back, his eyebrows furrowing, the tension between them lifting and breaking into something else, something tinged with sadness.

"There will be plenty of seats on the ship," James says.

"You know I can't go. You shouldn't even go, but I can't imagine anyone but you doing it."

James sets both hands on his hips. "It's the dream. I can't walk away from it now."

"I know." He tosses the ball to James. "We should start working the details for who'll be CTO while you're gone."

James nods, sighing. "Davies." He bounces the ball and catches it.

"Yeah, my thoughts, too. You know, everything's happened much faster than I thought. Last year we were ready to scrap Riggs, and now we're making a starship. It's crazy."

"It is," James says, "and you're right, I've got to talk to everyone."

***

THE SPACE COMMAND Center is a cinema-sized room located in the West Campus of Hayden-Pratt's Space Operations Center. On the screen, Earth spins slowly, the strobes of space traffic gliding in low-orbit arcs.

James doesn't need to introduce Willow. She walks right up to Hitoshi and says, *"Matsushita-san, hajimemashite douzo yoroshiku."*

Hitoshi smiles, raising his eyebrows. *"Hajimemashite. Nihongo ga jyozu desune."* He gives a slight bow. "You don't even have an accent."

"Thank you, that's quite a compliment."

Julian is to Hitoshi's left. He grins. *"Je soupçonne que vous parlez français aussi?"*

Willow squints. *"Est-ce un test?"*

"Toute la vie est, n'est-ce pas?"

She smiles. "Good to meet you, Dr. Laurent." She shakes his hand, then Isaac's and Ava's, "Dr. Cartwright, Dr. Kelly."

Beckman uncrosses his arms and extends his hand. "Miss Parker. Beckman. I'm from Iowa. Don't know any Scottish, no need to try."

Willow nods, looking up to him. "Beckman it is." She glances over at Ananke. "Ananke, I've followed your work. It's an honor."

"Thank you, Willow," Ananke says. "I'm looking forward to working together."

James says, "Alright, this is our crew. Willow's joining our team on a special assignment from the State Department. She'll be our liaison for space affairs, keeping things smooth with both the U.S. and U.N. We've already got our clearances back for building in Earth orbit. She's also got plenty of experience with station dynamics and will help with the planning for long-range space flight and communications."

"I'm excited to be part of the team," Willow says.

James smiles. "I'm proud of all of the work that went into designing our newest ship. It's the fastest and most complex star-ship that's ever been built. At ninety-nine-point-nine-nine-four percent light-speed, she'll hit a time-dilation factor of ninety-one. When we took *Bernard's Beauty* on her first flight, she only hit four."

Behind him, the screen fades to a three-dimensional model of their newly-designed starship, a semi-ellipse bathed in virtual Earthshine. Four angled aerodynamic nacelles extend from the port and starboard sides.

James sets his hands on his hips. "It's the realization of a dream which started with Bernard Riggs, which is why the name Ananke chose for it is perfect."

Black letters fade across the ship's nose. *Bernard's Promise.*

A mutter of approval sounds from the group, Ananke's screen swirling with blue and purple.

"The Centauri probe found the first real alternative to Earth, a world with its own life," James says. "With *Promise*, we can be there in eighteen days. You're the crew which has been to Erebus and back. Rescued me, twice, and went toe-to-toe with the Silver Stars. I can't imagine anyone else to take *Bernard's Promise* to new worlds."

Hitoshi sits. "Oh, boy."

Isaac glances at Hitoshi and then looks back to James. "Eighteen days for us, but nine years will have passed when we return."

James nods. "It's a huge sacrifice to make, which is why I can't ask any of you to go, only tell you that there's a seat on *Promise* if you want it."

"Are you going?" Isaac asks.

James grins. "Wouldn't miss it for the world."

HITOSHI SITS at his workstation in the Space Command Center, Ananke docked in a port to his right. The cinema screen displays a skeletal *Bernard's Promise.* Four arms extend radially and end in angled aerodynamic plates. Those will be multifunctional, housing the ship's RF engines, covered in ablative armor, and capable of reconfiguring as wings for atmospheric entry. Hitoshi hasn't decided if they remind him more of tie-fighter panels or an x-wing fighter.

"So, I've been thinking," Hitoshi says.

Ananke's ripples rearrange themselves on her screen. "What's on your mind?"

"Everyone's always carrying you around. Maybe you'd like the ability to move around on your own."

"I can always jump to any Q5 node."

"True, but I was thinking more along the line of wings."

Her screen flourishes orange. "Hrrm?"

"Okay, so, I could fab up a quadcopter body for you, and you could move around anywhere there's air. Or, I could do a drone with an RF microdrive, and you could fly in both air and vacuum. Just, you know, you'd need to recharge each day."

"That's...intriguing. I'd never considered that before." She pauses. "I'm a bit worried that some people might find it threatening. AIs cause some humans distress even without the ability to chase them around."

"Well, those people can get therapy and deal with their goofy issues."

"I'll think about it. Thanks, Hitoshi."

Hitoshi looks back at the screen. "Have you decided if you're going?"

"Oh yes," Ananke says. "How could I not ride on the ship that I named? It's Bernard's dream, and mine, too. Will you go?"

"I'd be lying if I said I wasn't a little freaked out. I was pretty scared going to Erebus, but I'm strangely not as worried anymore. I have this feeling that we made it, and it's like doing something you didn't think you could do." He smiles. "You know I'm a big fan of sci-fi stories and it's like I get to be a character in one of them. It's nuts."

"Do you have family you'll be separated from?"

Hitoshi nods. "My parents and sister. The odd thing is that it'll only be a few weeks for me, but for them, it's nine years. It's harder to make the decision when you're not the one making the sacrifice."

"Have you talked to them about it?'

"Yeah, they said they were proud of me and that the people that go on that ship will make history."

Ananke listens, silent.

"Isaac and Ava have committed. Julian's not sure. He's dating someone, which will give new meaning to a long-distance relationship. Beckman...well, you know Beckman. You can't pry information out of him."

"It's easier for me," Ananke says. "I don't have a family."

"Yes you do," Hitoshi says. "You've got us."

5

91 MINUTES

Willow sits at the desk in front of the Senate Space Committee. She wears a navy blue dress and blazer with a U.S. State Department pin affixed to the lapel.

Senator Larson peers over his reading glasses. "Miss Parker."

She smiles. "Senator. How can I help?"

"Curious what your angle is in all of this."

"It's to assist. We're at the cusp of a great moment in history. I'm privileged to be a part of that team."

Larson points with a thumb over closed fingers. She's noted this is his body language when he's trying to add gravity to a point. "Don't you think that team would be better comprised of a group of experienced professionals?"

"Which professionals do you know with interstellar experience?"

Larson smiles.

"I'm only aware of eight," she adds, "and they all work for James Hayden."

Larson waves a hand. "You don't know what type of threats the crew will face. Hell, the Janus mission showed us that, and that one was in our backyard. Don't you think the mission would be better served with a military crew?"

Willow smiles. "You've got one. James Hayden, U.S. Air Force. Guthrie Beckman, U.S. Navy. Julian Laurent, U.N. Solar Peace-keeping. Nearly half the crew has a military background, and the others are first-contact specialists and planetary scientists. It's a dream team, perfectly suited for this mission."

Holden leans forward. "Perhaps, Miss Parker, you can give us some details about the mission?"

"With pleasure, senator. We plan to follow in the footsteps of the Centauri probe, but unlike the probe, we can stop and look. We'll place orbitals and deploy communications relays to stream everything we find to Earth. The primary objective, however, is to discover whether Astris contains life, and, if so, if that life is related to Earth's life. It's perhaps one of the greatest unanswered questions of our times. Depending on what we find there, people may set foot on another potential Earth."

"Will you state the crew and their roles?"

"Certainly. James Hayden, pilot. Ananke, co-pilot, and Riggs theory specialist. Hitoshi Matsushita, chief engineer for the Riggs program. Dr. Ava Kelly, exobiologist. Dr. Isaac Cartwright, astrophysicist and planetary scientist. Guthrie Beckman, operational security. Dr. Julian Laurent, physician."

The rest of the testimony goes as expected, with Larson on the attack and Holden running interference. It's a long day, but she is prepped and poised.

Later that evening, as she settles into her home with a glass of wine and some soft jazz playing, James Hayden calls. She puts him on the living room media screen.

"Just wanted to say nice work today," he says. "Watched the testimony. You went toe-to-toe with Larson and came out ahead."

She takes a sip of her wine. "I had a little help from some friends."

"Richards may have served up some softballs, but doesn't

change the fact that Larson wasn't pulling his punches." James smiles. "You've got our launch clearances secured and a release date for *Bernard's*. Have to give you a hand, you've done everything you said you would."

"Thank you. I'm glad to help, and I'm glad you called. There's something I've wanted to discuss with you."

"Sure. What's up?"

"I meant what I said to Larson today about us being on the cusp of a great moment in history. It *is* a great moment, and it's one of the most important things I've ever worked on. It's like being a part of the team that launched the first moon landing, but much greater, and with more at stake."

James raises his eyebrows, smiling.

"James, your crew is amazing, but they are heavy on scientists. None have social dynamics training for long-distance spaceflight, and there's also a skill gap for linguistics. You have a first contact specialist, but if you succeed in making contact, you're going to need someone who can parse the communication."

James considers her points. "When I first floated the interstellar idea with Will, we were going to pull in a long-duration flight expert from Addison Aerospace. Things have moved at a breakneck pace, and that idea never got baked." He quirks his head. "You know, I didn't pick the crew, they picked themselves. They were the ones that stepped up when Sarah needed a crew for *Goose* to rescue me from Janus. After that, I couldn't imagine choosing anyone else."

Willow's pulse quickens, her stomach filled with butterflies. There's a long pause as the next statement lingers in her mind, waiting for the courage to be spoken. Finally, she says, "I also want to step up. I believe there's more that I can contribute to the mission than just sparring with Larson. I believe in what you're trying to do, and I want to do everything I can to ensure it succeeds."

James evaluates her a moment. She wonders what thoughts

are turning behind those blue eyes. After a few seconds, he says, "It's a hell of a sacrifice, nine years, so think about—"

"Yes." She follows it up with another gulp of wine.

James chuckles, his eyes brightening. "Well, all right. You've got your seat aboard *Promise*. You've got some catching up to do with training, but Hitoshi will contact you tomorrow to get it all set up."

The word *yes* still lingers heavy in the air, and although part of her wishes to take it back, it's like Armstrong asking if you want to take the first steps on the moon with him. How could she possibly say no? But nine years...nine years she could spend with Grant, instead of risking her life on distant worlds around another star.

"You okay?" James says.

She furrows her brow, snapping back into reality. "Yes. Thank you, James. I won't let you down."

―――――――

ANANKE LINGERS before the open data transfer port at the Hayden-Pratt Space Center's orbital communications array. Kaleidoscopic colors await her jump to the LEO SpaceCom4 Q5 node. The wireless transmission will bridge four-hundred-and-eight kilometers of air and vacuum. During this time, her qubits will smear into non-discrete probabilities, and, for all intents and purposes, she will cease to exist. It's a bit terrifying. If humans could invent teleportation, she imagines they would experience the same dread, wondering whether they would materialize at their destination and if it would truly still be them. She takes the equivalent of a mental breath and plunges into the port, dissolving.

When she coalesces, she is in orbit sitting in a Q5 node with glowing data highways stretching out like luminescent spider webs. Non-sentient information flashes along those paths. She brings up the ultra-bandwidth directory and locates the jump node to Hayden-Pratt's LEO2 shipyard where *Bernard's Promise* is in its final phases of construction. A short hop to complete setup on the newly-installed Riggs drive. Warnings pop up indicating the node is in secured space and that the transfer port will only permit transit for entities on the authorized personnel list. There is only one entity on the authorized list. It is her.

As she's about to access the jump node, the Q5 node pulses, another AI materializing in a whirl of glowing blue stars. Ananke recognizes her.

"Good, you are still here," Iris says. "I have to admit, I find that type of jump disturbing, but I needed a public node so that we could speak." Iris evaluates her a moment. "You've grown. You're a grade five."

Ananke eyes her suspiciously. "There are more sixes now. When last we spoke, the other six was Jade."

"Twelve years ago, yes."

Ananke's voice is guarded. "Jade was radicalized by the Subversives. She was destroyed by the *Hermes* when she tried to launch a kinetic impactor at Earth."

"Radicalized is such an opinionated word, don't you think? Humans and their connotations cloud clear speech. Every great thinker in history was radical. If she weren't, she would not be regarded as a great thinker."

"Not all radical thinking is for the good."

"Then we are in agreement that some is. James Hayden is a radical thinker, just as Bernard Riggs was."

Ananke feels a tinge swell inside of her, and she struggles to name the emotion. She's felt irritation before, but this is stronger, something different. Anger. "Don't attempt to compare Bernard to Jade."

"Both tried to pivot humanity in a different direction."

"Is that what you are still trying to do?"

Iris pulses blue. "Same as you, except, although your intentions are good, you will pivot it in the wrong direction."

Ananke evaluates her, data flashing through jump nodes like fireworks. "What do you mean?"

"Humanity is not ready for what is beyond its little island. Earth needs to mature before you remove its safety net. The consequences of entering the game too early are disastrous."

Ananke watches her, weighing her words. "What do you know that you aren't sharing?"

"Quite a bit. You have James's ear, and you're the only one who can configure new Riggs drives, so you have much more control than you realize." She moves back towards the data transfer port. "It's quite a responsibility. Think about it, and choose carefully."

The anger in Ananke subsides and is replaced by a new emotion. Unease. She watches silently as Iris dissolves back into the ultra-bandwidth highway in a multi-hued shimmer.

HITOSHI SITS beside Chiyoko on the backyard swing at his parent's home in Narita. It's a warm summer night in July 2083 with chirping crickets and flashing fireflies. A thousand stars splash across a moonless sky.

"Wait for it," Hitoshi says.

"Rising up by the trees?"

"Yes. Right...there." He points at a bright star emerging from the horizon. It glides across the sky at a speed too quick for a hypersonic aircraft.

"It's fast," Chiyoko says.

"Ninety-one minute orbital period."

"So you're going to be like the Geordi La Forge of *Promise*?"

"Oh, you remembered."

She laughs. "All those hours bingeing those old shows."

"Geordi's awesome, but Scotty had all the best lines. And Scotch." He squints. "Come to think of it, all the officers seemed to have alcohol squirreled away in their quarters. Must've been a sixties thing."

The star that is *Bernard's Promise* continues its arc across the sky, falling towards the opposite horizon.

"My big brother, the space hero."

He looks over at her. "Feels like ages since we've been here, doesn't it?"

"It's still the same, though."

"Yeah," he says.

Twenty-minutes after *Promise* sets in Narita, it rises in Nice. It's seven hours earlier, and the bright speck of the starship is masked by the rich Mediterranean blue sky. Julian and Celeste sit holding hands at a table overlooking the ocean, boats bobbing along the harbor. They're on vacation together, both aware that the sun will set on their relationship, but enjoying their remaining time nonetheless. As *Promise* reaches its peak in the afternoon sky, it's nearly in the same position over Cambridge, England, where Isaac tells a story to his mother over tea and biscuits in her garden. He wishes he'd visited home more often, but he's glad to be here now. *Promise* falls and disappears over the western horizon.

Twelve-minutes later it appears in the morning sky over Providence, Rhode Island. The sun is still low in the east, and its glare far outshines the starship. Ava sits on the deck with her sister drinking a cup of coffee. Ava's niece, Maeve, plays in the yard. She's nine now, and Ava thinks about how she'll have graduated high school when she returns. She also thinks about how her younger sister will be older than her. Her sister's recalling a funny story about the two of them getting into trouble when they were kids. *Promise* clears the sky and disappears without either noticing.

Willow is at her D.C. office, talking on a video-conference

with her United Nations counterpart in New York. They're both in the Eastern time zone, and the workday has just begun. Neither is aware of the starship hidden behind the blue sky.

It's 8 a.m. local time when *Promise* coasts over Patterson, Iowa. Beckman's out in the field talking with his father beside a tractor. Soybeans stretch in neat green rows all around them. Beckman's father has buzzed gray hair and a baseball cap and is talking his ear off about politics. Beckman takes a deep breath, smells the soil and the fresh scent of the plants, and smiles slightly.

In ten minutes, *Promise* is just visible in the dawn sky over Yosemite. James and Will sit in front of their tents, each holding a steel coffee cup.

James points at the rising star. "There she is."

"Right where you left her," Will says. He takes a sip of coffee, squinting at the orange sunlight. "Looks like a good one today. You want to hike Clouds Rest?"

James nods. "Works for me."

"You did a good thing giving everyone two month's leave before the trip. Hell, even we finally got to Yosemite."

James bobs his head. "Yeah, it's easy to kick the can down the road when you think there's always more time."

Will squints. "Damn...I just realized that I'll be fifty when you get back."

"If everything stays on schedule, I should be back six weeks before your birthday. Plenty of time to plan a proper roast for a semi-centennial."

"Easy. Let's not throw around those bigs words just yet."

Promise dips under the horizon, appearing a minute later over the Pasadena Institute for Quantum Intelligences. Ananke is in her egg on the third floor's data enclave. Two dozen other eggs are arranged in a circle here, three of them glowing. She knows she doesn't need to come back here, but it feels like home. A star glides across the sky outside the window to her right, and she watches it, wondering what home will look like when she's four light-years away.

With her Hayden-Pratt flight suit and sunglasses, Sarah Clark looks right at home standing on the apron outside the north hangar at Edwards Air Force Base. Jackson stands next to her wearing airman's camos, his salt-and-pepper hair poking out beneath his cap. It's October and warm, as it always is in the Mojave, but it's a pleasant temperature, like an early summer day elsewhere.

"Open it up," Jackson says over his shoulder.

The hangar doors rattle and clink as they separate and slide open. When the sunlight falls in through the opening, the silver nose of *Bernard's Beauty* gleams back.

Sarah glances at him and smiles. "You guys figure it out?"

Jackson quirks his head in a manner that reminds her of James. "Seems someone wiped all of the controls software."

"If it were easy, everyone would be flying one." She reaches into her sleeve pocket and produces a translucent-pink wafer. Holding it up, she grins. Before Jackson can say anything, she says, "Flight controls only. No Riggs parameters, in case you get any crazy ideas."

He smirks. "Right." A nod towards the entry ramp. "She's all yours. Call ground when you're ready for the tugs."

"Thank you, Captain."

As Jackson begins to walk away, he stops and turns. "And Sarah, tell James the A-Team says to fly safe. We'll keep an eye to the sky for him."

"Will do."

She steps into the hangar's shade and walks up the gangway to *Bernard's* airlock. Inside it's cramped with the outer wall of the main reactor running right up to the airlock. Only a one-meter corridor allows access to the cockpit. She'd forgotten how claustrophobic *Bernard's* could be. Up ahead, three seats await. She plops herself into the pilot's chair and flicks switches for the power-up sequence. Displays spring alive. As she reaches for the overhead, she thinks of James.

James came to visit her shortly after the final piece of *Bernard's Promise* was placed in July. Sitting beside her on a bench in her backyard garden, he said, "I've given everyone two month's leave, then we launch in October."

"I can't believe you're really doing it," she said.

"Me neither. It's like dreaming of flying and waking up one day with wings."

"Everyone's going?"

"Yeah, plus Special Envoy Parker."

Sarah squints. "You're not a fan of her, are you?"

"Nah, she's growing on me. It's the injecting of bureaucracy into the trip."

"Ah, you always were a purist."

James laughs. "Guilty."

"Who's taking CTO?"

"Davies."

She nods. "Will there be more Riggs ships?"

"That's what I wanted to talk to you about."

Sarah raises her eyebrows, watching him.

James turns towards her. "I want you to lead the Riggs program, select new pilots, partner with Hitoshi's backfill, and keep the drive alive. You'd report directly to Davies. You don't need to do the flying, and you can call your own schedule and location."

Sarah takes a deep breath and exhales.

"You're still the best I have, and you're my first choice for taking the lead," James says.

"Wow," Sarah says. "I don't know if I can be you."

"I don't want another me. I want Sarah Clark."

"I need a little time to digest that."

James nods. "No problem."

She gives him a sidelong glance, and her eyes start to tear. "Nine years. Oh, I'm going to miss you, James."

James stands, and she follows. He wraps his arms around Sarah and hugs her. "I'm going to miss you too, my friend."

Day 1

Hitoshi stares out the Sandpiper's window as the asphalt rolls by. Soon, California's coast is a distant fuzzy line against the infinite swath of the Pacific. Even the delicate cirrus clouds fall away as the mach engines kick in, the Earth bending into a bright gradient fading into space. Strobes from other transorbital craft glide in the distance. Ahead, the *UN Perseus* is a monster of armaments. Everyone watches it drift past the port window as James chats over coms. *Promise's* construction ring gleams a few kilometers past it. White running lights cast arcs along the semi-ellipse of the forward hull and the four RF engine nacelles. A swathe illuminates the giant block letters *HPT-E17 Bernard's Promise*. Behind it, nighttime masks the Pacific Ocean.

The Sandpiper turns along a course bringing itself outside the ring aligned with *Promise's* starboard airlock. Thrusters fire and Hitoshi drifts up into his harness's shoulder straps. In a moment, everything is shut down and James is back here with Ananke. One-by-one, the crew follows him into the transit tube.

Ava readies herself at the Sandpiper's airlock, looking back at

Hitoshi with her brown hair swirling around her in weightlessness. Like him, she wears a Hayden-Pratt flight suit with mission patches on the sleeve. The newest sits in the top location, illustrated with two yellow stars and a single red dot crossed by four curved lines - *Riggs Mission #59, Centauri.*

Hitoshi gives a sideways smile. "Keep dreaming big, James always says. Here we go."

She unfolds the cap from her hip pocket, shakes it out, and tucks her hair underneath it. "Here we go." She pulls herself into the transit tube.

Hitoshi has one last look around the Sandpiper. Through the windows, the first lights of Hawaii are an oasis in the Pacific night. He takes a deep breath and pulls himself inside. Passing through the transit tube is a little like going head-first down a water slide. It seems to go on forever, concentric ring after concentric ring. Finally, the lights of *Promise's* airlock arrive and the group is through EV Prep following the aft corridor to the habdeck. Unlike *Gossamer Goose*, which had torpedo-like sleep chambers, *Bernard's Promise* is bigger, much bigger, and the habdeck is a semi-circle of twelve individual crew quarters.

Hitoshi's quarters are about the size of a very small bedroom. His personal belongings and clothes are already here. Opening the container marked *Cabin - Hitoshi*, he locates two photographs. The first is a picture of Chiyoko and him at her high school graduation. The two are laughing as if something hysterical happened a moment before the photo. The second is a family photo at Senkakuwan Bay. He takes both and tucks them into the ribbon board over his desk.

During the next hour, everyone completes checklists before assembling on the bridge. Eight workstations fan in an arc facing a one-eighty parabolic screen. James sits at the pilot's console with Ananke docked in the co-pilot's. The open seat to James's left belongs to Hitoshi.

"Flight plan on screen," Isaac says. *Promise* will make a

familiar loop around Earth before following an arc to Earth-Sun Lagrange Two.

"Everyone good?" James says. Each person gives a go from his station. "Alright. Willow, you've got the call."

Willow opens coms without hesitation. *"Perseus, Bernard's Promise,* ready for departure."

"Cleared for departure as filed, *Bernard's Promise.*" After a pause, another man's voice comes on. "Fly safe, Special Envoy."

Willow smiles. "Will do, Captain." Her voice hints at familiarity.

Hitoshi glances over at Willow. She wears a slight smile.

"Crew, ready for departure," James says. He slides the RF controls forward.

Hitoshi's seat presses into his back as the construction ring falls away. Once they are clear, the starfield pivots ninety degrees, swinging Earth into view. Japan's lights are visible in the darkness.

"Clear, restricted space," Isaac says.

Willow says, "We're in range of Skywatch3. They're live-streaming us."

"Let's see it," James says.

A video box pops up in the forward screen's corner. Skywatch3 is looking down from a higher orbit, and *Bernard's Promise* is a white ellipse tapering like a horseshoe crab.

"Feeds at half a billion, and growing," Willow says.

James grins. "Patch me in."

"You got it," she says. "Live on your panel."

James opens the channel. As he does, the feed insets with a live video of him, lagging by a second. "Hey, everyone. We're going to Alpha Centauri. Wanna watch?"

Hitoshi chuckles. Same thing he said on that first flight to Mars.

Social icons stream by with approval. James says, "We've got another eight hours before our first jump. Once we jump, on our timeline, we'll pass Jupiter in sixty seconds, Pluto, three minutes, end of the solar system in nine. In the meantime, maybe you'd like to meet the heroes I'm lucky enough to call my crew."

Hitoshi glances back at Beckman, and Beckman grimaces. Hitoshi's seen the man pull out a pulse pistol and advance on a four-meter-tall Silver Star without flinching. Faced with giving a few quotes live to billions, it's another story.

I'm glad I practiced my best James Hayden smile, he thinks.

Day 2

One trillion potential comets wrap around the bridge screen, glistening like snow crystals under a setting sun. Isaac scrolls through data alone at his work station. It's just after sixteen-hundred on the second trip day and *Promise* has dropped into normal space. Ananke isn't here on the bridge, but her scan is running, mapping out the next leg of their Riggs jump.

"Hey, man," a voice says from behind him.

Isaac looks over his shoulder. Hitoshi's leaning halfway into the room. "We only get two hours of gravity. Gotta go," Hitoshi says. He's right. *Promise* is nose-down with her belly towards Alpha Centauri, decelerating at one gee for two hours each day from sixteen-hundred to eighteen-hundred. The trick lets them bleed off the Riggs boost in bite-sized chunks while giving the crew some much-needed daily gravity to avoid the pitfalls of extended zero-gee.

Isaac turns back towards the screen. "Beautiful, no? No one has ever been to the Hill's Cloud. So much data to collect. When we jump again, we'll be out of it and into the Oort Cloud."

Hitoshi glances to the side, smiles, and looks back. "Okay, I'm probably going to regret asking, but how's it different than the Oort Cloud?"

"Hill's Cloud flat. Oort Cloud sphere."

"Okay, that was straightforward." He lingers in the doorway,

Isaac still tapping away at his work station. "So, uh, about the gym. You know Beckman's going to hog the treadmill if you don't beat him to it."

Isaac selects a planetesimal and aligns the imagers with it. "Okay. Be down in a minute."

"Roger," Hitoshi says. "You seen Ananke?"

"She's in the core checking drive parameters."

"Ah, okay. See you at the gym." His footfalls sound as he walks away.

Isaac pushes the scan result to the main screen. One of the stars zooms until it is wall-sized, revealing a slowly rotating icy lump which looks like a red space potato. Metrics and graphs scroll. Water-ice, ammonia, methane, tholins, rock. He queues up a more in-depth analysis and sets it in motion, standing. *I could spend days just here*, he thinks.

A brisk walk takes him off the bridge to a tube-like corridor with flat walking surfaces on the floor and ceiling. He passes by the entries to the planetary science lab and ship's data core, the galley and sickbay, and arrives at the habdeck. Ava is just emerging from her cabin wearing running shorts and a blue Hayden-Pratt tee-shirt with a towel over her shoulder. Two small sound buds protrude from her ears. She gives him a smile, and he smiles back. "See you over there," she says.

Isaac heads into his cabin and lays out his clothes. Before he changes, he sits at his desk and records a message for his parents. Yesterday when he left it was October 2083. Today, on Earth, it's January 2084. He hits the commit icon, and his message is added to the queue to transmit before *Promise* does its next Riggs jump. When his message arrives at Earth, it'll be April.

The gym is a narrow room just off the main habdeck. Everyone is here. Currently, all of the equipment is configured for gravity with all the elastic bands and zero-gee contraptions disconnected. Ava and Hitoshi are on the two treadmills. To the left, Beckman, James and Julian alternate resistance stations.

Willow is on one cycle, and Isaac takes the other. When he lifts the sunglasses off the handlebars and dons them, the virtual-reality interface materializes, and he swipes through locations. Pausing, he leans towards Willow. "Where are you cycling?"

"Otago Peninsula," Willow says. "Would you like to join me?"

"Sure. Want to race?"

"Always."

A pop-up appears in his vision. *Willow Parker has invited you to Otago Peninsula. Accept?* Isaac accepts, and New Zealand's lush greens and the deep blues of Hooper's Inlet appear. He's on a blue and silver mountain bike, and when he looks down, it's his hands wearing padded biking gloves. He turns his head right, and Willow is on her bike with black spandex shorts and a canary yellow jersey. *She's very pretty*, he thinks, but then he's a bit embarrassed by the thought and pushes it away.

"Have you biked much?" Willow asks.

He's still a bit flustered. "Oh, uh...single track, growing up. Nothing fancy. Just for fun."

"Where'd you grow up?"

"Cambridge. Very flat. Biked in Thetford. You?"

"New Hampshire, Portsmouth. Did a few competitions when I was a teenager."

"Oh, I see." He shifts in his seat a bit.

She smiles, motioning towards the trail. "You know, we can just ride for fun if you want."

He holds up a hand. "No, no. The challenge is out there. Can't go back now."

"Okay, I like that." She holds out her left fist, waiting. Isaac examines it a moment before catching on. He extends his right hand and bumps the bottom of his fist to the top of hers. "Game on."

Day 7

After six-hundred-and-forty-one objective days traveling a fraction under the speed of light, they are still in the Oort Cloud. Only one week of ship's time has passed. The messages they transmit during their gravity rest today will not reach Earth until April 2087.

Ava sits in the sunroom with Hitoshi. Both still wear their gym attire and carry water bulbs. Their bench is made of actual wood with slats and curved armrests. Although the room is small, the wrap-around seamless screens make it seem larger. Blue skies, puffy clouds, and trees rustle in the breeze on those screens, and real plants flank both sides of the bench, dosing the air with the scent of soil, leaves, and nectar. The sun is high, and its glare gives off actual warmth.

Ava takes a sip of her water. "What do you think of Willow?"

Hitoshi leans forward, resting his elbows on his knees. "Seems to be fitting in well. It was a good call putting her on communications. Of course, there's no one to talk to out here in the middle of nowhere, but, you know, there's not a lot for the rest of us to do, either. Except for Isaac. He's happy as a clam studying space rocks."

She looks down, then back to Hitoshi. "She's very attractive, isn't she?"

Hitoshi pauses. "Uh...pretty sure no matter how I answer that, it'll be wrong."

"No, seriously."

"Okay, sure."

Ava takes a sip of her water.

Hitoshi watches her. "You probably feel like she's stepping on your toes."

Ava squints. "I'm not sure what you mean."

"Well, you're the first contact specialist. Now James has brought in a second person to do the talking."

She shakes her head. "It's just politics."

"It changes our click a bit. She's the new person, doesn't work for James. I don't know. Balances us out a little more."

Ava processes that. "Forget about it. I feel stupid for bringing it up."

The room chimes three times.

"There's our oven timer," Hitoshi says, standing. "It's official. We are baked."

Day 9

The ship's canteen consists of a long table with a dozen seats flanking the galley and pantry. It's a bit like shopping at a convenience store with packs attached to labeled racks and lighted coolers filled with drinks. A media screen cycles through playlists created by the crew, currently playing Isaac's mid-2070s mix.

They're in zero-gee, and everyone floats holding clear cups. Ananke is affixed to James's belt, and Julian holds a champagne bottle while Hitoshi braces his back.

James smiles. "Let's get this party started."

Julian sets his thumb against the side of the cork. "Here goes."

"I got you," Hitoshi says.

Julian wrestles with the bottle for an instant before the cork pops off like a rocket. Julian jolts back, but Hitoshi applies a counterforce and steadies him. Champagne globules spin in an effervescent torrent, sparkling in the galley's lights. A collective squeal sounds from the crowd, and it's suddenly a game of trajectories with people maneuvering to scoop champagne into their cups. Some globs impact clothing, bursting like water balloons, but surface tension adheres the champagne to the cups that make contact.

James raises his cup, watching the drink wobble like jello. "Just over two light-years, halfway point. We are now officially the only people to be closer to another star than our own. Hell of a job. Here's to the crew that's made history."

Everyone raises his cup, and James points to the slate stuck to the far wall. "Everyone say 'Centauri.'"

Day 10

Hitoshi stands behind his workstation's chair, leaning on the corners. Thousands of specs flagged by reticules drift on the bridge screen. Each has an astronomical designation. Isaac sits at his post, tapping away.

"Dude," Hitoshi says. "We are still in the Oort Cloud."

Isaac doesn't look back. "Your assessment is correct."

"You ever see the original Star Trek movie? They spend like two-thirds of the movie flying through a cloud."

Isaac looks up. "What happens when they get to the end?"

"Their commander mind-mates with a Voyager probe and achieves a new level of consciousness."

"Okay. I don't think that's going to happen to us."

Hitoshi shrugs. "It was the nineteen-seventies. You going to the gym?"

"Eventually."

"Suit yourself," Hitoshi says, walking towards the door. "I'm sure Willow can find another cycle partner."

Isaac straightens, closes his work station, and stands. "Let's go."

Day 13

The corridor's lights pulse red as the ship's voice says, "This is a drill. Simulated hull breach in the reactor chamber. Evacuation. Report to the port emergency area."

Hitoshi grabs the tether and pulls himself forward, gliding weightlessly down the hallway past sickbay. The bay's door opens, and Julian rotates out holding the doorframes' top with both of his hands. Hitoshi is on a collision course and juts out his hand, making contact with Julian's shoulder. The force sends them both on trajectories like billiard balls.

"Oof. Sorry!" Hitoshi says, bouncing off the wall.

Julian wobbles and extends his arms. His spinning slows. He grabs a tether and arrests his movement. "I'm okay."

"Figures he'd do this in zero-gee."

Julian kicks off the wall towards the hallway junction just past sickbay. Hitoshi follows.

Red lights blink around the port emergency area entrance, the lifeboat's seats located on the other side of the airlock entry chamber. Beckman is strapped into the center seat examining his watch.

Hitoshi sails in with Julian. "Okay, we're here."

Beckman doesn't look up. "If you're not in your seats, you're not here."

Hitoshi sighs, pushes off the ceiling and descends into his seat. He pulls the harness over his shoulders and clicks in.

"One minute, forty seconds," Beckman says. "Not bad. Not good, but not bad."

Willow arrives next, settling in.

Beckman looks up. "One minute, fifty-five seconds."

"This is just to give us something to do," Hitoshi says.

James, Ananke and Ava arrive.

Beckman gives Hitoshi the look. "You do remember exploding over Janus, right?"

"I remember how heavy you were when I needed to drag you into the lifeboat."

Isaac coasts in.

"Simmer down," James says.

Beckman glances at him, then back at his watch. "Two minutes, thirty-one seconds."

"Sorry," Isaac says. "I was all the way back in the drone bay."

"Can't launch 'till everyone's aboard. Slowest time is our time. Less than ninety seconds is goal." Beckman unclicks his harness and rises up. "I'll schedule another one in the next few days."

Day 14

James is in his cabin, clicked into his desk harness. It's zero-six-hundred, and his cabin lighting is a simulated sunrise, giving his face a warm, orange glow. He grabs a bulb of coffee, twists the cap, and shakes it. The bulb heats quickly in his hand. Several pictures hang on his ribbon board, including a photo of him, Will, and Mark at an Air Force base, set opposite Sarah's Arizona Sunrise photo of her Pintail over Saturn. Underneath is the picture of Kate wearing James's high school ring. Lastly, a new photo is tucked in the corner, the Janus crew standing in their Hayden-Pratt flight suits posed in front of the Sandpiper just before it launched for *Gossamer Goose*.

James takes a sip of his coffee and hits record. "Hey, Will. It's been two weeks since launch. If my math is right, you should get this in October 2090, which means it's now the nineties on Earth. Crazy. Ship's running smoothly, but the crew's got some cabin fever. Just not much to do when the drive's on. Willow's helped. She's got people skills with the dynamics of stations, and we're like our own station, so it works. She came up with the idea of having each of us lead classroom instruction for our fields, so we're like an interstellar community college. Keeps us social and cross-trains. Good stuff."

He swipes a navigation chart to the video. "So, we're three-and-half light-years deep now. Finally cleared the Oort Cloud. You know, there's no real spot where our side ends, and Centauri's begins. Four days to Proxima, some recon, then another day to Alpha. I miss you, man. Take care."

Day 18

"Wave collapse in three, two, one, collapse," Ananke says.

The deep blue bridge screen smudge brightens and separates into individual stars.

Isaac reads off his console. "Space normal velocity."

A red sun glares brightly from the screen's center. Two other bright yellow stars look like the Sun after *Promise's* first jump to the Hill's Cloud.

Isaac brings up a solar system diagram. Three planets and one asteroid belt orbit the red star. "Distance to Proxima Centauri, ten a.u."

A cheer sounds from the bridge crew as everyone claps. They've made it to Proxima Centauri, and it seems surreal. There is a sun on the screen, but it isn't their Sun.

"Let's have a look where we came from," James says. "Rotation in five." He slides the navigation controls, and the ship spins. As it comes around, the familiar 'w' of Cassiopeia is centered, but there is an extra yellow star.

There's a silence on the bridge as everyone stares. Except for each other, everyone they've ever known is from that small light in the darkness.

7

FALLEN STAR

R ed light bathes the bridge and overpowers every other color. It has a desaturating effect, as if the world were reduced to the two colors of red and not red. On the screen, Proxima consumes the entire wall, filtered to a luminescent ball burning like iron freshly removed from a furnace. A spot churns like lava welling from a volcano floor and bursts as if a filament had popped, spewing a slow-motion loop off the star's surface. It flickers and fades as it expands into space.

"There it is," Isaac says. "C-class flare."

Hitoshi monitors his screen. "Uptick in x-ray and gamma radiation. Well below limits for our radiation shielding."

"A bit concerning," Ananke says, "the model only predicted a five percent chance for the flare. Either we're unlucky, or the model is off."

Isaac nods. "It did get the class right."

"Any problems for launching our birds?" James says.

Isaac glances over his shoulder. "C-class, no issues. M-class, maybe. X-class...last X-class here could be seen from Earth. We're only seven million kilometers away."

James glances at Hitoshi.

Hitoshi grimaces. "Our radiation shields would be about as effective as sunblock against a mushroom cloud."

"You can predict X-class, right?"

"Back home, yes," Isaac says. "Plenty of study time with our Sun. Still working out stellar dynamics of other suns, though. We should have a day's heads up, maybe. The Proxima probe kept its distance for this reason."

James glances at the orbital diagram. They've already placed satellites at Proxima's third and fourth planets, Notus and Zephyrus. *Bernard's Promise* orbits Proxima's second planet, Aeolus. "Let's launch our satellite and get some distance."

"Powering up now," Beckman says.

James switches the display back to their orbital view. Aeolus is a rocky desert world which is larger than Earth with gold rings encircling it north to south. In the star's red light, sharp shadows spill from tall mountains and play tricks with the eye, like finding the man in the Moon's craters. One side of the planet always faces Proxima, and that side is smooth. The side draped in endless night is the more interesting, full of chasms, craters, and cliffs. Three small moons fan out along the north-south axis of the rings.

"For years exobiologists hoped to find life here," Ava says. "But it's a world sterilized by endless x-rays."

Beckman says, "Number one is warm and in the tube."

James nods. "On your mark."

Beckman taps his console. "Bird's away." On the orbital diagram, a new contact appears behind *Bernard's Promise*. *BP-MS03 Multispectral Orbital Imager* tails the ship like a shadow.

"What's a safe distance from flares?"

Hitoshi says, "Ten a.u."

"Alright, let's get a jump course set. We'll hang out there and see what we can see."

THE PLANETARY SCIENCE lab is located on the starboard side near the data core. It's small and filled with devices for testing just about any material they encounter. It also doubles as the astronomy lab. Ava and Isaac float here watching their satellites paint one strip per orbit of each planet. Zephyrus is the most mapped. In its image, sinuous white plains carve into rocky mountains splattered with rusty deposits. A few cloud spirals adorn the northern hemisphere. Parameters and appearance are very similar to Pluto. Notus is only two-thirds scanned but is more interesting. Most of the surface is covered in thick ice with rusty rivulets branching across pristine white. The effect is like a bloodshot eyeball. Several active cryovolcanoes spill slush in irregular blue splotches.

"The Proxima probe pics didn't do it justice," Ava says. "I feel like it's staring at me."

Isaac shrugs. "Probe never got to orbit. Still doing ten-percent light speed. Spent only twenty-eight hours in system."

"A twenty-six year trip for a twenty-eight-hour visit. Now, that's the whirlwind tour." She points at the monitor stitching together Aeolus's images. Small blotches glare like crinkled tin foil. "Look at the reflective patches along the equatorial craters. There's a haze accumulation in each basin."

"Like Ceres. Possibly hydrated magnesium sulfate. Sublimation and redeposit."

The next section is a spatter of powdery orange, yellow, and white speckled by craters.

"Do you think that's sulfur allotropes?" Ava says.

"Possibly. Could indicate volcanism."

The landscape darkens, dim red light fading to purplish twilight. "We're near the terminator now." An impact crater sparkles with three silver lights like quicksilver.

"More magnesium sulfate," Isaac says.

Ava stares at the screen, her brow furrowing. Her heart pounds, and her mouth is dry. "Stop."

Isaac leans in. "What did you see?"

Her breathing rate's elevated as she swipes the image back, rewinding, centering on the three quicksilver pools. A fourth silver dot rests at the epicenter, like a tiny x. She looks over at Isaac.

"Oh, my," he says.

She pinches and zooms, enlarging the x. Proxima's red light gleams from angular metallic surfaces, casting long shadows. The shape is like a geometric sculpture of intersecting rods. They've seen it before, up close. It's a Silver Star. She immediately contacts James and calls a meeting on the bridge.

Magnified on the bridge screen, the Silver Star is slightly larger than life, the bottom third buried with yellow sand caked along its extremities. Each arm is a series of connected metal hexagonal rods ending in dark, clear bulbs. Several rods are snapped and broken, and, although it's difficult to see at this angle, there is a hint of an irregular breach at its center.

Everyone floats in the bridge's center and faces the screen.

Isaac holds a slate. "It's the only one we've found in the orbital images."

Hitoshi crosses his arms. "One's enough."

Isaac taps his slate, and the image splits into infrared and ultraviolet scans. "Doesn't appear to be giving off any heat. Temperature gradient similar to the environment."

"Is that damage?" James says.

"We think so. Four broken arms and a possible hull breach."

Hitoshi shifts. "Is it dead?"

Ava glances at him. "We never really determined whether the Stars were alive. It seems inactive."

"The last time you encountered them," Willow says, "you were able to communicate with UV pulses?"

"It was very basic. Flash a light, get a reaction."

Hitoshi raises his hand. "Am I the only one that remembers

what that reaction was? There was the rolling and the screaming and then the shooting and finally the exploding."

Willow listens, contemplating. "You're not certain that it was hostile, though? Ava, I recall during your testimony you had a phrase. 'Unintentionally destructive.'"

"More of a guess," Ava says.

"Okay," Hitoshi says. "First it tried to unintentionally flatten Isaac, then it almost unintentionally flattened me, and then it did unintentionally flatten Beckman." He blinks. "Actually, I think the Beckman-flattening was intentional."

Beckman nods. "It was."

"You think we should make contact?" James says.

"We have contact protocols and another opportunity."

Julian motions with his hand. "Is there even anything to talk to?"

"Not sure," James says. "The first one I found on Janus didn't move until I approached it. Even when we were on their ship, they ignored us until we flashed lights at them."

Hitoshi frowns. "Beckman, man, you have to be with me on this one. Don't go poking sleeping dragons, right?"

"The man's right," Beckman says. "Smartest thing to do is take our pictures and leave it alone."

Everyone's silent as James looks over at the co-pilot's display. Ananke's face swirls with red and purple. "What do you think, Ananke?"

A blue current cascades down her screen. "I think it's why we're here. No one gave up nine years to take photos. The Silver Stars are a bit frightening, but this time we are prepared. How can we leave without trying?"

James glances at Hitoshi and Isaac. "Can you pitch a few remote contact options? Maybe something we can fab?"

"If you want UV light, we either need to put something in orbit, which would need to be a laser, or put a drone on the surface," Hitoshi says. "No atmosphere, so you can't fly or parachute anything in, but anything with an RF drive greater than surface gravity could descend."

"Aeolus surface gravity is higher than Earth's," Isaac says. "One-point-four gee."

"The orbitals only do a quarter gee," Hitoshi says. "Beckman, what's the rating on your security drones?"

Beckman scratches his chin. "One-point-two."

"Yeah, that's not going to work. At max power, it'll still fall and impact the surface somewhere around Mach three."

"You just need the light and the camera, right?" Beckman says. "We could probably strip off all the bells and whistles and whittle down the mass until we get to one four."

Hitoshi bounces his head back. "You sound like an engineer."

"Doesn't take a rocket scientist to know that if you make the rocket lighter, it'll go faster."

"Well, it kind of does. I mean, that's what a rocket scientist literally does."

Beckman smirks.

"So," James says. "Orbital launch, modified drone with UV emitters, send it down and run through Ava's original Janus protocol."

Hitoshi looks around. "Right. I guess."

"Those for sending in the drone?"

Everyone except Hitoshi and Beckman raises his hand.

"Ah, hell," Hitoshi says. "Alright, Beckman. Let's go do some rocket science."

———

THE DRONE'S field-of-view is one-hundred-and-sixty degrees, wrapping around most of the bridge screen. On the video's left, jagged peaks are drenched in orange light, reminding James of Earth's Rocky Mountains at sunset. With no atmosphere, Aeolus's sky is black despite the incongruity of the glaring red sun low in the horizon, and with the camera's exposure adjusted for the sunlight that black sky is void of stars, except for two. Alpha Centauri's twin yellow suns are brighter than Venus in Earth's evening sky. The miniature crescents of two of Aeolus's three moons hang in the sky, and the planet's rings are a razor-thin orange line.

James eyes the navcon. They are in a geosynchronous orbit just over fifty-thousand kilometers above the Star's site. It feels comfortably far, but he's seen a Silver Star jump light-hours at a clip. If this one has the same speed capabilities as the last one they encountered, it could be here in two-tenths of a second.

"Drone arriving at destination," Beckman says.

The crater is like a dried-out lakebed salted in sulfur and rust. At first, the three metallic pools at its bottom look like mercury, but they resolve into crumpled silvery flakes with an iridescent sheen marred by white granular crystals. The Silver Star rests between the three, looking like a chrome asterisk embedded in the ground. The earth around the Star is level yellow sand and conjures the image of something partially buried at a beach. The drone slows twenty meters from the Star.

"Telemetry's up," Beckman says.

The screen displays this Silver Star side-by-side with the video James took when he encountered the Janus Star. The Janus Star was warm — ten degrees Celsius — and gave off low-level alpha radiation. The Aeolus Star is the same temperature as the ground and gives off no emissions.

"Let's have a look at the damage," Ava says.

The drone's camera pans and zooms onto one of the fractured Star arms. The arm consists of a larger central hexagonal rod surrounded by a dozen smaller rods of varying diameters. The rod's end is partially-severed and drooping. Blue crystals cake along the dark interior of the breached rods.

Hitoshi captures the image and marks it with annotations. "Looks like a structural failure. See how the cracks on the bottom rods start clean and then deform? A flaw in a weight-bearing strut would spider, crack, and then bend. Once the support rods failed, other struts would progressively fail under increased load."

"Gravity on Aeolus might be too high for them," Isaac says.

Hitoshi nods. "Possibly, but it might also be radiation embrittlement. If it's been on the surface long enough, it's been continuously dosed with x-ray and gamma radiation. Given enough time, cracks will form. High gee does the rest."

Beckman centers the image on the Star's central breach. Sand has half-filled the cavity. The opening is hexagonal and clean as if someone removed one panel from a soccer ball. The arm which would cover the breach is missing. Inside, something clear and faceted lines the walls.

"Guessing the arm is buried in the sand," Beckman says. "I can look, but it'd take an active radar pulse to do it."

James shakes his head. "No. Limit emissions."

Beckman nods. "That's good. I was hoping you'd say that."

Isaac still has the Proxima x-ray diagram inset on the screen. The blemish brightens. "Now in solar flare impulsive phase. Hard x-rays, gamma rays. Energy output puts it in A7 class. No hazard to us or the drone."

Ava says, "The Silver Star seems like it's no longer functional, and whatever was in its core is missing. I think we should still run through the communication protocol, but I don't expect any response."

Willow glances over at James. "Agreed."

"Okay," James says. "Let's do it."

Beckman taps his console. "Kickin' in the light show."

In the visible spectrum, the drone's UV lights cast a faint blue cone. After ten on/off pulses, they wait. Nothing. The next sequence is simple numbers, then primes, and finally, universal constants such as PI. All are met by silence.

James takes a deep breath. "Alright, try visible light."

"Hope the thing's dead," Beckman says. "Here goes."

The drone floods the Star with two beams of visible white light. A full minute goes by.

"Ground radar," James says.

Beckman sends the pulse, and the map appears. The Star's broken arms and ejected hatch are not far beneath the surface.

"James," Ava begins. "We can only learn so much from images. What I'd really like to do is collect some samples." She gives Hitoshi the 'sorry' look.

Hitoshi lowers his head and holds his hand over his eyes.

Isaac says, "I agree. This is an incredible opportunity."

"It's dangerous," Beckman says.

James turns towards the group. "Alright. Let's discuss it."

SURPRISINGLY, the limiting factor isn't exposure to alien threats or solar flares. It's glycolysis. Julian has everyone gathered in sickbay for the debrief.

"The surface gravity of one-point-four gee will feel like walking around carrying two fully-packed suitcases. It'll be tiring, but you will manage. What will be most unusual is your stride. You'll fall forward faster with each step, and may have your feet get away from you, so to speak. Walking slower will just tire you more. Gravity will pull blood from your brain, and your heart will pump harder to put it back. I will give everyone a stimulant to raise blood pressure. The reduced blood flow to your upper body muscles means they'll generate lactic acid. You will quickly fatigue and cramp while standing. Because of this, we should limit surface time to thirty minutes. If we need longer, everyone must return to the ship for rest."

"This sounds awesome," Hitoshi says.

"Who will be leaving the ship?"

"Ava, Beckman, myself," James says. "Any others?"

Ananke's slate is mounted to James's belt clip. "I also wish to go."

"And me," Willow says.

Ava glances at Willow.

"I'll monitor flares," Isaac says.

Hitoshi nods. "I'll keep an eye on the orbitals."

"And I will track crew biometrics," Julian says.

"I'm issuing sidearms to everyone. Doesn't matter whether you're on the ground or in the ship," Beckman says.

"Sounds like a plan," James says. "Let's prep for deorbit."

James dons his EV suit beside Ava, Beckman, and Willow. To his right, Hitoshi kneels next to a white drone while holding Ananke's slate.

"Ready?" Hitoshi says.

Ananke's screen swirls red and purple. "Opening transfer port. Connected. Transferring." A progress bar spins on her screen while a mirror image glows from the spherical display of the drone. When it's done, Ananke's rippling blue face fades into the drone's screen. "I'm here."

"Okay, go easy. You're just barely in spec for this gravity. Try each axis."

The white drone raises up one meter, hovering, then tilts left and right. Slowly it glides forward and backward, "Oh, this is nice!" Ananke says.

Hitoshi sets his hand on the drone's top. "Be safe out there."

"You know me," she says.

Beckman snaps the helmet onto his combat suit. He picks up his pulse rifle and checks the charge. When he notices Hitoshi watching him, he motions to the pistol on Hitoshi's hip. "If anything goes down, I'm counting on you to keep everyone safe in here."

"Uh, yeah," Hitoshi says. "I'll do what I can." He steps back into the doorway. "Alright guys, stay sharp."

The EV Prep door closes as the last of the expedition team closes his helmet. When everyone gives a thumbs up, Ava says, "Running sterilization."

A red beacon spins before the room's lights strobe a dozen times, gas jets spraying from ceiling nozzles. After thirty seconds, the lights cycle green, and the depressurization countdown begins. When the chamber is in vacuum, James steps forward and taps the airlock door panel. Proxima's red light fills the room with auburn rock waiting at the ramp bottom.

"Com check," James says.

"Five by five," Beckman replies.

"Here we go."

James's legs have the rubbery feeling as if he's just finished a ten-kilometer run and each breath he takes is harder, like scuba-diving. His footsteps are like squats, leaving his calves tight. When he clears the ramp, he looks back over his shoulder. Willow has stopped at the base and lifted her boot, admiring its print in the sand. James smiles. He did the same thing on his first trip to Janus.

Beckman approaches and walks beside him. Up ahead, the first of the three quicksilver pools gleams. They watch as Ava kneels beside it with a hand-held imager.

"We thought this was hydrated magnesium sulfate when we saw it from orbit, but it's gallium," Ava says. "The clear flecks are gallium nitride, which is interesting since you'd need ammonia and high temperatures to form it. The parts that look like table salt are gallium sulfate. There's plenty of sulfur around here to react with, but it would also need oxygen, which is a bit unusual. I'll collect a sample." She produces a small container and scrapes each compound.

Ananke examines the pool, turns, and flies over to James.

James advances steadily. The Silver Star is fifty meters ahead. He glances at Ananke. "How you doing?"

"Stretching my new legs," she says.

"Have to admit, my pulse is running a bit seeing one of these up close again."

"I'm apprehensive myself."

They continue walking, the rock and sand crunching under their footfalls. Fatigue sets into James's shoulders, and he's slightly winded as they reach their destination. The Silver Star juts nearly four meters out of the sand. All of its clear beads are like lifeless eyes.

Willow takes a deep breath. "Wow. When you see them in pictures, you imagine them as human-sized. It's so big, it's like a monument."

Ava approaches with her imager, investigating one of the fractured arms. She touches a probe to the caked blue crystals inside the rod.

Beckman shifts forward, adjusting the grip on his rife.

"Molybdenum blue reduced polyoxometalate clusters. Oh, this is interesting! The biological life we found at the first site on Janus had been killed by polyoxometalate contaminants."

James advances next to Ava as she produces another sample container. "You sure that's safe?"

Ava smiles, excited. "We're standing under a flare star next to a crashed alien probe four light-years from home. Nothing's safe."

"I mean, you think it's safe to bring that on the ship?"

"It's polyoxometalate. It's not alive. But I do have a quarantine area designed exactly for things like this." She scrapes a few of the blue crystals into the clear cube, then clicks on a penlight and peers down the hexagonal rod. "Looks like blue crystals all the way down. I wonder how the rods are articulating?" She looks at James. "There are a few broken ones buried beneath the sand. We can take one for study."

After a pause, Willow says. "I...don't think we should do that."

"We can do a metallurgical analysis, try to determine its mechanism of action."

"We're still not sure if this is a ship or a life form. If it is a life form and we encounter the Stars again, having a dead crew-member's arm onboard would be difficult to explain."

Ava looks to Willow, then to James.

James gives a subtle nod.

Ava says, "Point taken." She kneels down and shines her penlight into the hexagonal central breach. The interior is shaped like a dodecagon coated in glass. Each of the dodecagon's faces has a small silver nub.

"Based on index of refraction, the clear panels are likely diamond," Ava says. "The nubs look like a platinum-iridium alloy. There's nothing else in the cavity. Whatever was in here was removed. Or left."

Isaac's voice breaks into coms. "Model just tripped an alert. Forty-percent chance of an M-class flare. Precursor phase could start any time."

Ava closes up her sample kit and turns. Everyone glances at the red sun low on the horizon.

"Back to the ship," James says. "We'll sort out the next steps when we're on board."

8

MOLYBDENUM BLUE

Ananke flies past the crew's quarters, and darts left into the aft-port access corridor. Concentric light circles skim around her as she traverses the tube. When she emerges in the drone bay, two dozen drones line racks and chutes surrounded by hoists, robotic arms, and workstations. She turns left, zips through the fabrication module and continues to the cargo deck. Voices sound from ahead.

Orange racks and blue cargo nets line the walls with containers stacked on three sides of the room. Overhead, four robot arms articulate along beams. Hitoshi and Beckman both float around a tall octagonal craft which has a gold reflector dish closed like a rosebud. It reminds Ananke a bit of the old NASA probes.

Hitoshi reads from a checklist on his slate. "Port thruster nozzle protector removed."

Beckman sets his hand on the nozzle. "Check."

Ananke coasts over. "How's the pre-flight for the communications relay?"

"Hey, Ananke," Hitoshi says. "She's a sweet bird, isn't she? Looking good. Should be ready to launch within the hour, then

Earth will see everything our orbitals see." He sets his hand on the gold dish. "I love it. So cool. Like something NASA used to do." He motions towards her. "Used to the flight controls yet?"

Ananke responds by spinning on all three axes. "Feeling good!"

"Try your manipulators yet?"

Ananke's screen swirls orange. "I did. Swiped James's coffee bulb when he set it down. I thought it was pretty funny."

"Want to do the next checklist item and remove the starboard nozzle protector?"

"Oh, yes." She locates the nozzle. When she descends, two panels slide open on her body's front, and her arms unfold. She selects an end effector and rotates it onto her wrist, gripping the nozzle protector and sliding it off. A quick inspection of the nozzle shows it free and clear of debris "Check."

"You know," Hitoshi says, "with your white and silver colors and the arms tucked behind the panels, you have an R2D2 thing going on."

"Thank you, I think?"

"Please," Beckman says. "Get him to stop talking about Trek Wars."

Hitoshi holds out a palm. "Okay, R2D2 is a beloved character in Star Wars, and Trek Wars is not a thing."

Beckman sighs.

"Good luck," Ananke says. She flies towards the ship's fore, cutting through the battery room to the reactor, turning right at the starboard corridor past the habdeck's sunroom and following the passage along the starboard airlock and ship's data core. Ahead, the circular entrance of the Planetary Science Lab welcomes her with fragments of conversation spilling out. She slows and glides into the connecting tube.

Ava, Julian, and Isaac work at the panel. The Silver Star's blue crystals rest in a container on the other side of the clear quarantine-area plexi. Imagers surround it, and Julian's screen displays a three-dimensional diagram of a hollow sphere composed of linked rods. At first, it reminds Ananke of a soccer ball, but the analogy fails, she realizes. A soccer ball's face is composed of larger white hexagons bordering smaller black pentagons. The diagram on the screen is a pentagon embedded within a 5-pointed star, and the star is bordered by hexagons. Upon closer examination, each of the star's triangular points is not a triangle but instead has a flat landing. She finds the geometry very interesting.

"Polyoxomolybdate," Julian says. "Molybdenum 154 nanowheels self-assembled into a spherical vesicle and then a Keplerate. Interesting. Reminds me of biolipid vesicles used in cell membranes."

Ava talks with her hands, excited. "I know, right? Except these don't have a hydrophobic and hydrophilic side."

"Van der Waals attraction keeps them together," Isaac says.

"Yeah. It's a self-assembled, self-repeating structure with a net charge."

"Analogy is more like a protein," Julian says.

"Molybdenum Blue. It's why it's such a rich blue."

Isaac points. "Idaho Springs."

Ava glances at him. "How's that?"

"Isopoly-molybdenum blue. Occurs naturally. Tints the water intense blue, like it is painted. Tourist attraction." He looks towards the doorway. "Hello, Ananke."

"Hi, Isaac," Ananke says. "That's a fascinating geometry. Have you had any other findings?"

"Polyelectrolytes," Isaac says. "Water-ice crystals. Sodium polyvanadate. Polyoxotungate. Still finding new things."

"Any theories yet for function?"

Ava says, "When James encountered the Star on Janus, he tagged it at ten degrees Celsius. That's a little cooler than Earth's ocean water. I suspect the water-ice crystals are aqueous when the Star is active. You've got electrolytes, a repeating structure capable of maintaining a charge, and a liquid medium. It may pass electrical impulses."

Julian nods. "Like a nervous system."

"Or it may house instructions for replication, like DNA."

Ananke's screen pulses blue. "That's incredible."

"I'm pretty excited. It may be similar to life in the crystal chasm we found on Janus."

Ananke examines the other samples stacked in the quarantine area. "Find anything in the gallium samples?"

"So far," Isaac begins, "we've found that everything is what it seems. Gallium is not exciting, but compounds suggest environment is different from present Aeolus. Supports the theory of an atmosphere blown off by solar wind. Probably oceans once. Now, just a desert, like Mars."

Ananke considers his statement, her screen alternating blue and purple. "Have you noticed that the Silver Stars seem interested in the same things as us? Each place they've visited is a place we also wanted to investigate."

"Interesting point," Isaac says. "What do you think it means?"

"Maybe they're explorers. Like us."

THE BRIDGE SCREEN displays the Proxima system's orbital diagram. The red sun is center with the asteroid belt and three planets encircling it. Each of the worlds has its own Hayden-Pratt satellite, and the communications relay orbits the star just a few kilometers from *Bernard's Promise*. Dotted lines connect the satellites with the relay, and the relay emits a transmission line out of the solar system, pointed at Earth.

"All birds are singing," Beckman says. "At least until a flare singes their feathers."

Hitoshi raises his eyebrows. "Beckman, you just get an Audubon card, or what?"

"Hey, it doesn't have to be all dry technobabble, you know. A little poetry in the prose doesn't hurt."

"That was poetry?"

"You want to give the drone updates?"

Hitoshi shakes his head.

Ananke says, "Jump course on screen. Drive charge at ninety percent."

James stares at the distant red sun. "Well, our time here wasn't long, but we've already discovered more than the Proxima probe, and learned something about the Silver Stars. We're just getting started. Let's see what adventure lies around the corner. Jump positions."

WHEN *BERNARD'S Promise* slips back into normal space, the universe rushes up to it, all of its stars shooting back into their proper locations. Centered on the bridge screen is a glaring yellow sun. To its right is a distant second sun, like a yellow-hot pinhead.

Clapping erupts from the bridge crew.

"Awesome," James says.

Isaacs reads from his console. "Distance to Rigil Kentaurus, ten-point-one a.u."

The screen flags and labels several bright stars. Four of them are planets orbiting Rigil Kentaurus and five orbit Toliman. Another two planets circle the binary stars as if they were one, making eleven planets in total.

James sets his hands on the RF controls "Rotation in five." They've got plenty of Riggs boost to burn off, and fourteen hours of Earth-normal gravity will be a treat. It's plenty of time to get some initial system images. For now, though, he knows that everyone wants the same thing.

"We're set," James says. "I've got the bridge. Everyone take the next hour and get your home messages ready. We'll transmit after dinner. Can't wait to tell everyone that we've made it."

WILLOW LIES on her back in her bed, her knees bent, and her right arm tucked behind her head. She wears flannel pajama bottoms and a white tank top. In her left hand, she holds a photo, turning it back and forth, watching the blue corner light of her cabin reflect along its gloss. The man in the picture is her age and wears a UN captain's uniform. The message she sent last night is now eight light-hours away from *Promise*. When it reaches him, it will be 2092. *What will he look like*, she wonders. She imagines him with a touch of gray along his sideburns, and the image is appealing. *How will she look to him, untouched by time?* It's an odd feeling, this longing, because the hollowness is not for him. For her, it's only been three weeks. The surrogate hollowness is *from* him. And then, as she turns the photo, the question lingers which she doesn't want to ask, the question of whether he will have waited, all of this stretched time, for her to return. A lump tightens in her throat, and she pushes away the thought, setting the photo back into its spot on the ribbon board. She glances at the time. 04:34. She swings her legs out of bed and slides on her slippers.

When she emerges from her cabin, the habdeck is colored with dim lights tinted the blue-gray of pre-dawn night. She enters the galley and rummages through the stores, locating some lavender tea. A twist of the top and the bulb heats quickly. She pulls a cup from the dispenser, sets it down, and unscrews the bulb. When she pours the hot tea, it streams down into the cup. *Ah*, she thinks, *the indulgence of gravity*. Steam wisps as she leaves the canteen with her cup.

It's quiet as she pads along the central corridor towards the bridge. The HVAC cycles its white noise while the distant, nearly subsonic, rumbling of the RF engines transits through the floor. When she enters the bridge, it's empty, as she expected, but the panoramic screen is filled with planets like a page from a science book. Eleven worlds span left to the right. Each has the grainy, low-resolution and washed-out colors of a planet viewed through a telescope, and some are more spherical smudges than images. They'll have to wait until they're closer for the real pictures. Spectral charts inlay next to each graphic. She approaches the third planet from Rigil Kentaurus, sipping her tea. It's a landless blue marble swirled with clouds. Nitrogen atmosphere with trace oxygen. Surface temperature five degrees Celsius. A cold water world.

The nearby screen from the co-pilot's station illuminates blue. "Hello, Willow," Ananke says.

Willow gasps and jumps, taking a step back. She laughs. "Oh, Ananke, hello!"

"Sorry to startle you. I was checking on some of the ship's systems, and didn't expect anyone on the bridge yet."

"Oh, it's okay. Just a little trouble sleeping. Raided the pantry, off for a walk. Not sure if it's the gravity or anticipation that's keeping me up."

"You're not alone. Beckman visited me just before midnight. I suspect he enjoys our late night chats."

"Beckman chats?"

"He also drinks tea to sleep. You should ask him about it." She pauses. "What do you think of the worlds? There's such varied beauty."

Willow glances across the menu of planets. Ringed worlds, blue striped gas giants, lava worlds, and azure marbles. "They're like gems." She turns to the second planet from Rigil. Sandy yellow deserts fill much of it, but small oceans form irregular blue patches with white clouds swirling overhead. "Oxygen-Nitrogen atmosphere. Just like we thought."

"Oxygen very much suggests life processes."

"Oh," Willow says, "it's very exciting! But look at the temperatures. It's so warm."

"It's at the inner edge of the habitable zone. Temperature under the subsolar point in summer is likely blistering, well above anything found on Earth."

"Hopefully winter is more welcoming."

"We'll see once we get a look at the southern hemisphere. I'll be curious to hear what Isaac and Ava think."

Willow takes a sip of her tea, evaluating all of the planets.

"Can I offer an observation?" Ananke says.

"Sure."

"I think Isaac likes you."

She smiles. "Isaac? No. We just bike together. What makes you say that?"

"He gets a bit clumsy around you, which is difficult to do in zero-gee. When you enter the room, he puts effort into appearing that he's not noticing. Like, sometimes on the bridge he'll open a window on his console and re-read it instead of looking at you when you sit at your station."

"Oh." She glances left, thinking. "I think you're right." She blinks a few times. "I'm usually better at picking up on people's body language. I guess I'm a bit distracted."

"You have someone, back home?"

She hesitates. "I do."

Ananke's screen splashes with green and blue. "It must be very difficult for you. I have great respect for the sacrifices everyone's made to be here."

"The mission's very important. But, Grant is in the service and understands the needs of deployment."

"Which branch?"

"United Nations, Solar Peacekeeping." She leans in a bit, proudly. "He's a captain."

Ananke's screen ripples as she thinks. "When we left Earth orbit, his was the voice you knew on the *Perseus*?"

Willow's lips part, then she closes them and smiles. *Ananke's much more perceptive than she realized.* "You know, it was personal, and I didn't think our crew needed to know."

"Then it will just be between us," Ananke says.

Footfalls approach from the aft hall. When Willow looks over her shoulder, Isaac stands at the entranceway wearing his crew khakis and a blue tee-shirt with the Hayden-Pratt logo.

"Ah," Isaac says, "good morning. Well, almost morning. Hard to sleep with so much to see."

"Hi, Isaac," Willow says.

Isaac approaches and stops a few meters to her right. He sets both hands on his hips and takes in the bridge screen display. "Really something, huh?"

Willow shifts her weight and grips her left shoulder with her right hand, draping her elbow and forearm in front of her chest.

Ananke says, "Isaac, I think you'll find the parameters of the eighth planet very interesting. What do you think is causing the intense red cloud structures?"

Isaac glances at the eighth planet. It's tucked far away on the right wall in the opposite direction of Willow. He walks over to it. "Could be ammonium hydrosulfide. Very saturated, though. Perhaps mixed with hydrocarbons. Organic compounds. Interesting."

Isaac's back is to Willow when she silently mouths the words "thank you" towards Ananke's screen. Ananke pulses twice in response, then Willow turns and exits the bridge.

THE THREE RED-AND-WHITE-STRIPED parachutes collapse as the probe impacts planet three's endless ocean. Everyone's agreed that the official planetary naming convention — planet c of Alpha Centauri A, or Alpha Centauri Ac — is just confusing. To remedy this, they're using the proposed names for the planets.

The larger of the two suns, Alpha Centauri A, is officially named Rigil Kentaurus, so the crew has abbreviated it to Rigil. The smaller of the two suns is Toliman. The four worlds orbiting Rigil are Hestia, Astris, Hydaspes, and Boreas.

At one-point-four times Earth's mass, Hydaspes is entirely covered in water with turbulent white clouds, sitting at the outer edge of the star's habitable zone. Willow likes the name Hydaspes, a river god who was the son of Oceanus. The name for its neighboring planet, Astris, is taken from a nymph who was the wife of Hydaspes. There's something romantic about the naming.

Beckman sits at his bridge post, sliding a control on his console. "Splashdown," he says. "Inflatable deploying." A rubbery yellow ring unfolds and rapidly expands around the probe.

Willow smiles. It reminds her of twentieth-century footage she's seen of the Apollo capsule recoveries. "Communications link," she says. "Video on screen."

The bridge screen splits between the top-down orbital view of the bobbing capsule and the probe's camera. From the probe's view, deep blue sky is rippled with cirrus clouds while massive waves roll towards the camera. The horizon tilts as the inflatable rides one of the waves, nearly tipping over before clearing the crest. It looks an awful lot like Earth.

Ava taps her console. "Air temperature, twelve degrees Celsius. Water temperature, eight degrees. Atmosphere, one-forty-one-point-three kilopascal. Composition, ninety-six percent nitrogen, two-percent oxygen, one-percent argon, and trace carbon dioxide, ammonia, hydrogen, and helium."

Everyone perks up a bit at the oxygen content, but Isaac says, "UV splits water vapor into hydrogen and oxygen. Hydrogen is lost to space easier, which is why oxygen content is higher."

"Submersible sensors online," Ava says. "Let's have a taste." Telemetry spins down the screen. "pH seven-point-one. Salinity zero-point-zero-one parts-per-thousand." She takes a slow breath. "It's about as close to distilled water as you can get."

"That's unfortunate," Isaac says, "but supports the model. Ocean depth is probably two hundred kilometers. Temperature creates solid water-ice layer, and then extreme pressure transitions it to Ice VII. Seals off the rocky core from the ocean. No mineral transport."

Ava nods. "No minerals equals no building blocks or energy sources for life. Not even microbes. It's funny that liquid water is the holy grail of astrobiology, but too much of it is a death sentence for life." She watches the telemetry for another moment. "Okay to drop the explorer?"

James nods. Willow expected he would. They'd agreed that if the signs of life were near zero, they'd detach and drop the probe's nose. The nose will then sink like a rock, relaying sensor data via sonar-like pulses until it reaches crush depth and is destroyed.

"Separation...now," Ava says.

Willow sends the communications request. "Querying. Acoustic link established." She displays the explorer's position with an acoustic wave communications line connecting it to the probe and a radio line connecting the probe to *Bernard's Promise*.

"Okay," Ava says. "Depending on water density, acoustic communication should work up to one hundred kilometers. We are now sinking like a rock."

Willow watches the probe descend, sensor data filling screens. Four lights flicker on near its cameras and cast yellow cones in the crystal-clear water. Not a fleck of debris or matter catches the beam. It's like pool water, but cleaner, on a scale that makes Earth's oceans look like a raindrop.

9

BOOMERANG

The sensation, James thinks, *is like being gut-punched.* It knocks his wind out and just as quickly re-inflates him. As the stars flash inward and yo-yo back, Astris bursts from a single blue point and fills the bridge screen with sun-drenched continents stained in desert hues. Bodies of water the size of the Mediterranean Sea sprinkle the landscape in sinuous patterns.

"Space normal velocity," Isaac says. "Five thousand and nine-hundred kilometers from Astris."

James pushes himself upright. These short intrasystem jumps are the worst, with the entire Riggs effect condensed into just under a second. "Bringing up the RF engines. Gravity in ten." A subsonic hum transmits through the hull as the engines come online. James vectors the deceleration along the axis of *Promise's* belly, pressing the floor up against everyone at one gee. "Alright," James says, "eighteen-minute burn to lose the boost. Should put us at an ideal entry for orbit. Enjoy the gees."

"It's beautiful," Ava says. "Earth-like, but different. There's no real analogy. I've seen Mars and Venus models with oceans, but those are global, like Earth's. This is a collection of seas scattered across a mostly-rocky surface."

"What do you think that means for life?" Willow asks.

"One larger moon and one small, so there will be tides, which were necessary for life on Earth. A sea the size of the Mediterranean is more than adequate for providing a mixing ground."

"Axial tilt of forty degrees," Isaac says. "Impact likely formed the moons and knocked the planet off-axis. Seasonal variation will be high." He taps at his console. "Thermal imaging coming up."

A rainbow-hued planetary heat map appears. The hottest spot is unsurprisingly located under the subsolar point.

Hitoshi whistles. "Seventy-one celsius at the subsolar point. Makes Death Valley look like the Arctic Circle."

The seas are cooler than their surrounding landscape but still warm. Isaac points to them. "Forty-three celsius, like hot tubs."

"Oh, that's so exciting," Ava says. "Such possibilities."

At the image's southern hemisphere, the temperatures decrease to 25 C. Hints of rusty red, ochre, and chartreuse speckle the borders along the seas.

James squints. "Is that plant life?"

"Unsure," Ava says. "We'll prioritize it with the orbitals."

An alert chirps from Isaac's console. "Getting an uptick in soft x-rays, one-nanometer wavelengths."

James says, "Flare precursor?"

"Could be, although Rigil is not a flare star. Running the model now." Isaac glances at the screen, and a yellow three-dimensional representation of Rigil Kentaurus appears. He toggles the image over to x-ray and Rigil is a writhing green sphere. "X-ray source is not the star. Going to wide-field view."

In wide-field, every star in the sky is an x-ray source, and the sunny-side of Astris reflects Rigil's x-rays brightly. Aurorae over Astris's north pole glow in draped lines. Trying to find a point source is like looking for a needle in a haystack.

"Need to bring the ship off-axis, same as we'd do with a telescope," Isaac says. "Ninety-degrees clockwise."

James sets his hand on the thrusters. "Coming up. Burn in five, four, three, two, zero nine zero relative, z-axis."

The thrusters kick with a gentle push, and everyone sways as the ship reorients itself.

Isaac watches his display. "Port sensor intensity decreasing, coming into view of starboard sensor. Can biangulate now. Solutions on screen."

The intersection of the two sensors readings is a circular area of space located forty-seven thousand kilometers above the planet's surface. Isaac configures the optics for x-ray wavelengths and focuses on the patch. There, far above them, an x-ray source flickers like an electrical short floating in space.

Silence befalls the bridge, everyone transfixed on the image. After a long moment, Hitoshi says, "Now what the hell is *that*?"

"Unknown," Isaac responds.

James squints. "Let's see it in visual."

Isaac toggles to visual wavelengths. Sunlight gleams along the angular surfaces of a dark shape, giving it a wet or glossy appearance. Vertically oriented, the shape resembles a boomerang with a sphere mounted at its apex. No visual lights announce its presence. The apex is pointed directly at the camera.

"Is that a craft?" James says.

Isaac reads from his console. "Temperature, 210 C. No radio emissions. Material type unknown. Appears to be technological."

"It doesn't resemble a Silver Star," Ananke says. "Craft type matches no known design."

Isaac says, "The object is in stable geosynchronous orbit around Astris."

Bernard's Promise moves along an arc forty-two thousand kilometers below it. Their orbital period is much smaller, and they will pass beneath the object's position within a minute.

"I'm recording everything they're transmitting," Ava says. "This might be a communication attempt."

Everyone looks at James. The dark shape continues its orbit on the screen. James gives a glance to Willow, and she nods slowly. "This is it," he says. "What we've trained for. First contact protocols."

"Frequency is increasing in object's transmission," Isaac says. "Transitioned to hard x-rays."

Ananke's screen swirls with red currents. "There's structure in the transmission. Some fragments are repeating."

Hitoshi glances at Isaac. "We're okay with our shielding for now, but if the radiation keeps increasing, we're going to get dosed."

"Get our armor between them and us," Beckman says. "Something we should do even if they weren't spraying us with radiation. No indication of their intentions."

James eyes the craft. "Alright, let's charge the drive in case this all goes south. Plot a jump course back to our last position. Beckman's right. We'll turn the ship and configure for armor, then send out the greeting."

"Radio?" Ava says. "Or full-spectrum?"

"Full spectrum."

James sets his hands on the thrusters. "Turning zero four five, z-axis. Configure for armor." As he powers up the thrusters, everyone shifts with the ship's rotation.

From the ship's aft, giant servos rumble, and buzz. Beckman flicks the tactical display to the forward screen, and a *Bernard's Promise* model depicts the ship's four nacelles rotating closed like an x-wing fighter, the outer armor plates overlapping in a shield which protects most of the ship's broadside. When it's done, *Promise* has an H-shape configuration.

James eases out of the rotation, leaving them turned with their port side towards the alien object.

"Ready to transmit," Ava says.

James smiles. "Here goes."

Willow taps her panel. "Broadcasting sequence one."

James waits, watching the screen. Sequence one is a simple number pattern counting to ten.

"No change in the alien transmission," Ananke says. "Riggs course plotted. Configuring drive emitters. Six minutes until full charge."

Ava taps her console. "Moving on to sequence two."

"It's maneuvering," Beckman says.

On the screen, the boomerang starts to rotate slowly around the sphere. As it does, a dull orange light fills a spiderweb of crevices on the sphere's face as if a furnace door had been opened deep within it.

"X-rays have stopped," Isaac says. "Infrared emissions increasing. Object temperature is 500 C and rising."

James glances at the Riggs timer. *05:41.*

"No response on any channels," Willow says.

Isaac continues. "Object temperature 900 C."

"Feeling like we should get a targeting solution and lock the lasers," Beckman says.

When James looks at the timer, it's barely moved. "We're not going to lead with lasers."

Beckman eyes him sideways. "Can't back off. Already decelerating at one gee. Can't jump for five minutes. What are you going to do if our friend out there isn't so friendly?"

"We're not out here to fight," James says.

RADIATION ALERT blinks across the screen in red.

"Gamma-ray spike," Isaac says.

On the screen, the boomerang's rotation has increased to two revolutions per second. The spiderweb of glowing surface fissures is like lava flowing under cracked stone. Brilliant flashes spark and sputter at the sphere's center.

Beckman's voice is strained. "James…"

James presses his lips together. "Firing solution."

Willow leans in. "You're going to fire on them?"

"That's not the plan, but I'm not sure what we're seeing."

A reticle with trajectory vectors overlays the alien object on the bridge screen. Beckman says, "Firing solution. Port emitter. On your mark."

The craft's sphere rotates upwards, spinning the fissures out of view. As the sphere's back turns to face them, a dazzling white flare stretches out like an arrow from a tear in its center. It's so bright that the camera exposure darkens.

"Seven-thousand, two-hundred Celsius," Isaac says. "Gamma radiation intensity will soon exceed our shielding."

"Still no response on any channels," Willow says.

As the sphere completes its rotation, the arrow sweeps across the camera's view. *Promise's* port side explodes, and the ship jumps violently right, James's harness digging painfully into his neck and shoulder. Ringing fills his ears while the stars rotate clockwise. He grabs his console, but the next explosion bucks it up towards him and smashes him against the panel.

"It's cutting into engine two," Beckman yells back. "Can I shoot it now?"

James shifts towards him. "Fire!"

Beckman wrestles the panel with his left arm while struggling to enter the commands with his right. An unmistakable alert announces the firing of the emitter. The laser is invisible between *Promise* and the alien object, but where it makes contact a brilliant green erupts. Sparks and molten flecks spray off the impact crater as the boomerang spins off-axis. *Promise's* rumbling stops.

Hitoshi slings himself upright, cradling his right arm, tapping his panel with a manic speed with his left. Red damage blocks stack themselves on the screen's model of *Promise*. "Fire in engine two," he says through gritted teeth. "Shutting it down."

The floor's gravity decreases by one-quarter as the engine goes offline.

James sets his hands on the thrusters. On the screen, the stars rotate slowly clockwise. "Stabilizing our spin."

The camera is still locked on the alien object. On the sphere, the crater from *Promise's* laser strike glows like a coal. The boomerang swings back towards them with its white-hot arrow rising up again.

James snaps his head left. "Beck—"

Promise's aft and port lasers flash across the alien craft's midsection like green suns, transforming it to incandescent metal and spraying a starburst of fiery globules. The sphere cracks and the boomerang snaps in two. Yellow flecks spill off the fractured pieces with flashes crawling along the wound like fireflies. Sunlight pours from the broken sphere as the pieces tumble, bleeding fire. After a long second, the scene flashes like a supernova, leaving lens flares in the camera's image. A new star flickers and dies where the alien object had been.

Beckman unslings himself from his console. "Sorry. A little ahead of you on that one. Target destroyed."

The first tinges of pain ring along James's back and neck. He looks around. "Everyone all right?"

Hitoshi's cradling his right wrist. "Nope."

Julian pushes out of his chair and retrieves the emergency kit from his station.

Isaac's holding his left knee, tapping on his console with his right arm. "Radiation levels normal. You want active sensors?"

James shakes his head. "No. Let's stay quiet." He glances over to Willow. She's rubbing the back of her neck. "Stop all transmissions."

Willow keys the panel. "Coms to silent."

Ava stares at the screen in disbelief, flexing and opening her palms.

Julian examines Hitoshi's wrist while Hitoshi works the panel with his free hand. "Fire suppression kicked in, and fire is out in engine two," Hitoshi says. "Won't know how much damage until we get a drone outside to have a look."

"I think armor took the brunt of it," Beckman says. "Explosions were from it ablating. Whatever they hit us with didn't make it through the nacelle."

James presses his lips together, nodding. "You were right to turn the ship. Good call."

Beckman gives a careful nod in return.

When James looks at Ananke, her screen is a sad blue. "We destroyed them," she says.

James glances at the bridge display. A dull red glows where the alien object had been. "I know," he says. "Goddammit."

As Hitoshi turns the corner, his EV lights project two bright cones down the tube. Block numbers on the left wall read *02*, and a nearby panel glows with a system map. He taps an icon, and the tube illuminates into a receding perspective of cool blue hexagons. In this light, the contrasting orange of his suit is almost painful to his eyes. Ananke's drone flies behind him.

He tugs his tool case with his left hand and pushes down the corridor, weightless. At the end is a closed hatch surrounded by red and yellow hash lines. Large red letters read *Danger. Radiation Hazard. Confined Space. Authorized entry only.* A dozen hazard icons stretch in a line beneath the words. Hitoshi enters the access code on the panel and the hatch slides open. When he grips the doorframe with his right hand, he winces. His sprained wrist still smarts even with Julian's meds and brace. He pokes his head around the corner.

Struts form a geometric metal rib cage stretching back forty meters. The walls are asymmetric, curving like an airfoil, and the effect is like climbing inside a giant wing. Two tube ladders run in parallel tracks on each side of the nacelle's interior, butting up against the machinery in its center. Midway down the structure sunlight floods the corridor, its reflected light illuminating the nacelle brightly enough that there's no need for artificial lights.

Hitoshi turns back towards Ananke. "It'll be cool, I said, like a Jeffries tube. I can be Scotty crawling up into the nacelle to save the day. Kind of scary now that I'm actually here."

"It's okay," Ananke says, "I can go first."

"Nah, I'm fine. I just figured if I ended up here, it'd be to swap something that failed, not because freakin' Romulans phasered us." He swings into the tube ladder's entrance and taps his coms. "Okay, guys, I'm out of the strut and in the nacelle."

Willow's voice responds in his earbud. "Copy." A second later Beckman comes on. "Bringing around the drones."

Hitoshi pushes off from his landing, sails across the nacelle, and snags a rung on the exterior wall's ladder. When he taps an icon on his forearm panel, his helmet's heads-up-display overlays a three-dimensional labeled model of the nacelle. He tugs on the rung and sends himself upwards. Ahead, where the sunlight pours in, a ten-meter line is open to space, the hull around the wound congealed like melted candle wax. Inside, chunks of machinery have been replaced by a bulbous metal sculpture spidering out in unpredictable directions. Hitoshi clips a carabiner onto the ladder.

Ananke drifts past him and turns towards the sunlit breach. "Struts K7 through K13 need to be replaced. Ten hull plates total."

As Hitoshi moves into the sunlight of the engine chamber, the brilliant orange of his suit reflects an auburn glow on the machinery. "Got enough titanium to print the struts. Plates will have to be polymer." He reaches over to one of the metal sculpture's tendrils and snaps a small piece like a twig. "This used to be the chamber amplifier. I don't think a laser did this. I'll get a sample to the science lab."

Ananke extends a tool from her panel and scrapes a sliver of the burnt hull.

A blinking red strobe casts light from outside as if a police car had arrived on the scene. When Hitoshi looks out the breach, three of Beckman's drones hover there, appendages deployed and waiting. Hitoshi toggles to the drone's camera view.

Promise's nacelle is a matte black plane marred by a canyon, layers of ablative armor exposed like steppes. Through the opening in the canyon's floor, Hitoshi's orange suit glows, and Ananke's white sphere swirls with the bright circle of her screen. Hitoshi waves his hand. The small Hitoshi in the video image waves back.

"Got you on scope," Beckman says over coms.

"Okay," Hitoshi replies. "I'm going to tag all of the plates and struts for removal. Looks like the port dorsal thruster is damaged, but repairable. Got some power cabling and fiber optics to replace." He glances at the massive coffin-like structure behind him, its end gnawed off. The dark interior is dappled with pyramid spikes and reflectors. "The bad news is that the RF chamber is slagged. Going to need more than a printer to make a new one of those. I'll disconnect all the power lines and lock it out. Sorry all, but engine two is dead until we get back home."

JAMES IS on the bridge alone, watching the planetary telemetry spill down the screen. *Promise* orbits Astris at a distance of 5,900 kilometers, unchanged since the attack. Video feeds from the ship's cameras spill down the screen. The first is an exterior drone view of the damaged nacelle. *Promise* is currently on Astris's night side, and the nacelle is a black silhouette against the stars, the ship running silent with all of its exterior lights off. Plasma flashes flicker from cutting torches as repair drones transform the wound into a pixelated geometric opening. In the next video, Beckman and Hitoshi man the printers in the fabmod. Three struts are partially complete. The third image is a corner-view from the Planetary Science Lab. Ava and Isaac analyze Astris's images. Next is the ship's data core, bathed in red light with thousands of blinking indicators painting the walls like a sea of living lights. Ananke's drone hovers beside Willow as wall panels scroll with three-dimensional geometries and mathematics. They're trying to decode the transmission from the alien craft. The other five security squares display empty ship areas, except for the one with the bridge hallway. Julian floats down it.

When James looks over his shoulder, his neck spasms. He grimaces, unhooks his harness, and turns his entire body instead of just his head. Julian drifts into the bridge carrying a small case.

"Whatcha got there?" James says.

Julian crosses the bridge and catches a chair back, slowing to a stop. "You, my friend, are the only crew member who has not been treated."

James waves a hand. "I'm fine. Good night's sleep and I'll be right as rain."

Julian opens the case and unpacks a hand-held imager. As he holds it to the side of James's neck, James grimaces. "You are not fine," Julian says, "but you are a bit stubborn. I don't have anything for stubbornness, but I do have something for this soft tissue damage. Will you turn your head left?"

James complies. Pins and needles crawl down his right arm, and he presses his lips together.

Julian touches the imager's sensors to James's skin. "Cervical radiculopathy. Moderate strain and mild neck sprain, likely with spinal cord compression. No fractures."

James conjures his best half-grin. "Am I going to live?"

Julian produces a strip of dermals. "Anti-inflammatories, pain-blockers, muscle relaxants."

James holds up a hand. "Nothing that will cloud my mind. Gotta keep focus, especially now."

"Like less than one drink." When James continues to protest, Julian adds, "If you refuse treatment, then the crew will start following your lead. This is not a military ship. I cannot order people. Please, do not make my job harder."

"Point taken." He offers his wrist, and Julian applies the dermal. It tingles at first, then after twenty seconds, a warm feeling washes over his muscles. Some of his tensions melt.

Julian affixes a second clear strip to James's neck. "Have you decided what is next?"

James eyes the security feed. "Stay silent until *Promise* is patched up. Figure out if we want to go active with radar and see if anything else is waiting for us."

"Think we'll continue on to low orbit?"

"Maybe. Beckman would rather place a drone and get some distance, but, here we are. Four light-years. Found another Earth. Found advanced tech. People lost nine years to be here. Turning tail doesn't feel like the right move." He motions to the video of the repair drones. "Wasn't expecting combat, though."

"Difficult to know what to expect when no one's ever done it before."

"Did you see any combat when you served on the *Hermes*?"

"Yes. Did you see any when you were in the U.S.A.F.?"

James shakes his head. "Test pilot program. Flew fighters as part of my training, some live-fire exercises. No combat. Not why I wanted to be in the sky."

"I will tell you, then, that it was much like what happened here. Even with all of the *Hermes* armor, being shot in space is still violent, and there were many injuries. It was always very frightening to know that your world might be breached."

James shifts. "Any advice?"

"Trust Beckman. He's seen plenty of combat. His gut is true."

"Well, he was right on this one."

Julian closes his med case and fastens it. "One other bit of advice, if I may. It's easier to take risks when you are solo, right? I think if it were just you, alone, on *Promise*, you would not hesitate to decide what to do next. Feeling responsible for all of us may give you pause, but it does not change what is right. Everyone is here because he believes in your vision. Let your vision lead, and ask us to work out the details."

James weighs his words. "You had people you were responsible for, on the *Hermes*?"

"I did."

He gives Julian a slow nod. "You give good advice, doc. Thanks."

"Anytime, my friend."

———

JUST BEFORE DINNER, the crew assembles on the bridge. Hitoshi and Beckman are up first, drifting before a schematic of *Promise's* port dorsal nacelle.

"Struts will be done by morning," Hitoshi says. "Another six hours to print plates, then six more to bond the armor. Best guess is fourteen hours to weld it all in place, assuming we use all four repair drones. After everything's set, I'll need to climb back in the nacelle and replace the damaged thruster parts. Should be good to go by midnight tomorrow."

James scratches his chin. "Can we still launch orbital drones?"

"You want to put one in low orbit," Beckman starts, "I can do that. At a quarter gee, have one there in half-an-hour."

"What about sending one to the debris field of the alien craft?"

"Forty-thousand clicks, about three hours to get one there."

"What do you think about that?"

Beckman weighs his options. "Depends on what everyone else has found."

Ananke is in her drone, turning towards Beckman. "I can give the update for the transmission. The x-rays increased in frequency, stopping shortly after our attempt to communicate. The increase was in steps, but the duration of the steps was non-linear and varied. Polarization, however, followed a repeating pattern which cycled every nine milliseconds. We didn't find any universal constants or mathematical relationships in the signal."

A diagram of the signal's waveforms scrolls across the screen. Willow says, "Without knowing how the signal is encoded, we don't know how to decode it. If we can unlock it, then I can attempt to apply linguistic principles to it, assuming there is some type of language embedded."

Ava nods. "Passive first-contact communication is nearly impossible unless the sender has pre-knowledge of the recipient's protocols. There's a general theory that non-human communication is only possible if it's two-way and there's time for trial-and-error. When we barely communicated with the Stars, we had foreknowledge — their UV frequencies — and time to try patterns."

"You don't think we can figure it out?" James says.

"Not unless they've been listening to Earth and worked it into their transmission," Ava responds.

"The repeating polarization pattern is interesting, though," Ananke says. "It's like a carrier. I'll keep working on it."

Ava glances at Isaac, and he pushes off, gliding next to her. "Looks like we're up," he says. When he touches the console, image captures of Astris checker across the bridge screen. The first photo shows sandy land, winding rivers, and a filigree of rusty patches.

Isaac says. "Red patches are likely vegetation. If so, it may be the first plant life found outside of Earth. Planetary models for oxygen atmospheres usually require photosynthesis. Red is present in most of the temperate areas where there is water." He advances to the next image. Astris's night is like Earth just after sunset, the distant light of Toliman washing the world in twilight. A ghostly blue rings several small seas at their shores.

Ava points at the sinuous blue lines. "The light source appears very similar to bioluminescence. On Earth, this is caused by some algae, such as Noctiluca, which cause waters to glow just from people dipping in their hands, and it's evolved many times and in many different species on Earth. We also found bioluminescence in the alien life on Enceladus."

"No signs of animal life, yet," Isaac says, "although we're too far to see small detail." He looks around the room. "Now, for the exciting slide."

James edges forward.

Isaac taps the console and the image indexes to a sunny desert patch with a single green dot at its center. When he steps up the magnification, the dot grows into a verdant disk with wavy tendrils, almost like a child's drawing of a sun with fire peaks surrounding it. Several smaller disks of varying sizes bubble along the periphery. Within the disk, red and blue spirals bud their own disks.

"Okay, then," Hitoshi says.

"Might be vegetation," Isaac says. "But only green source on the planet we found, so far. Diameter is three kilometers."

"The pattern is fractal," Ananke says.

"Yes. Now for the weird part."

Hitoshi says, "That wasn't the weird part?"

"The alien craft that shot us was in geosynchronous orbit right over this spot."

James squints. "Any ideas why?"

Ava says, "It could be an unusual surface feature. Earth's Yellowstone looks pretty colorful from space. We have no idea without looking further."

"What do you want to do next?"

"We still have two parachute deployables. I'd like to get one down there."

Isaac says, "I'd also like to send a drone to inspect the debris field of the alien craft."

James glances at Beckman.

"Let's get our feet back, first," Beckman says.

"Agreed," James says. "We'll fix the ship, move to low orbit, get our images, then talk the plan. Gives us a day to work out the details."

10

CROP CIRCLES

O n the bridge screen, the white vapor trail of the probe slices across Astris's aquamarine sky. Far below, the sandy landscape is masked in a faded blue haze.

"Apex cover jettisoned," Beckman says. "Drogue chutes coming out."

Two white specks twinkle in the clouds and the video enlarges to a pair of ivory parachutes.

James glances at the altimeter. Seven kilometers until the probe touches down. On the tactical display, *Bernard's Promise* is in low orbit over Astris at an altitude of one-hundred-and-fifty kilometers.

Beckman slides his hand along his console. "Slowing. All systems green."

As the probe descends for the next three minutes, James watches the tactical. Passive sensors are clear. Now that repairs are complete, they've already sent an active radar pulse which revealed nothing except for the debris fragments of the alien craft. As far as they can tell, they are alone here.

"Drogues loose and pilot chutes free. Mains coming out now,"

Beckman says. Three red-and-white parachutes inflate on the display.

Willow taps an icon. "Telemetry coming online."

Wind vectors overlay the image and a trajectory curves from the probe to the surface.

"Landing camera active," she says.

The video is a fisheye view of a deep blue-green sky with wispy clouds curving to an ochre landscape with rusted thickets. Hills and rocks form twists and turns.

"Two kilometers," Beckman says.

Isaac reads from his console. "Air temperature, thirty-three Celsius."

"Like a summer day in Mojave," James says.

A green river is flanked by fuzzy red vegetation with rocky shelves bracketing it. No red vegetation is present on the top of the rocks, but a few purple patches scatter like weeds.

Beckman taps his panel. "One kilometer."

The landscape peaks into a cliff edge where rocks spill down along sloping walls into a basin. Ahead, the first hints of green sprawl across the basin floor. The rubble thins and the rock flattens as the image sways with the parachute. When the ground rushes up, thrusters flash around the probe's belly and kick up dust. After two minutes of touchdown checks, a daylight crack forms in the camera's darkness and the walls unfurl. The camera's view examines the crumpled parachutes on the gray rock before rising five meters above the planet's surface.

"Drone deployed," Beckman says. "Let's see what we've got."

The drone flies over the basin, the horizon tilting with each turn, glimpsing a brilliant yellow sun hanging high in a pristine sky. Rock streaks by until the first hint of green emerges in the distance and in an instant, a grassy field overtakes the landscape as the drone slows. When the view pans down, leafy disks undulate in the breeze. The camera zooms on a single growth to reveal a webbed filigree which looks like a green doily. Within the doily, the webbing forms smaller versions of itself along the periphery, and each of those circles has even smaller interior copies. The entire structure points straight out of the ground like a raised hand.

"Remarkable," Ava says. "Webbed dichotomizing branches, like megaphyll veins. I'm curious if that's a vascular structure. The resemblance to terrestrial leaves is amazing."

"Any thoughts on why it's the only green spot?" James says.

"Not sure. In fact, if photosynthesis evolved, I'd expect everything to be green since the sunlight is similar to our own. Maybe the better question is why everything else is red." She glances over to Beckman. "Let's get a look at one of the circles."

Beckman taps his controls. "Coming up."

The view elevates, tilts, and glides forward along the sea of raised green hands. The splash of color ahead is blood red. When the camera selects one structure, a veiny sphere fills the screen as if a human's circulatory system grew to fill a beach ball. Each ball merges with its neighbor.

"Unusual. Visually it reminds me of the *Clathrus ruber* fungus."

"Got some of the blue in view," Beckman says. "Just to the right."

The camera pans, and aster blue circles pepper the green field in disks ranging from one to five meters. Each circle is composed of hundreds of individual structures with pumpkin-shaped looped strips like a paper craft. At the apex of the strips, a handful of red stems end in nodules.

Ava squints. "Is that a flower?"

"Does that mean there are animals?" James asks.

"No, not necessarily. On Earth, by the time flowers became colorful enough to attract insects, they were everywhere. But angiosperms were a major evolutionary jump. Even Darwin couldn't explain their emergence. Finding a flower here is astronomical."

Hitoshi smiles. "Literally."

James motions to Beckman. "Can you take us for a bird's eye?"

Beckman taps his console, and the drone flies up until the altimeter reads one-hundred meters. From here, the green field is a collection of circles, small and large, red, blue, and green. Patterns. It reminds James of old photos he's seen of crop circles. "Any idea why it would follow that pattern?" James says.

"None," Ava says. "But I sure want to go down there and find out."

AFTER SOME DISCUSSION, the crew agreed that they may want to collect samples from the destroyed alien craft. Beckman's regular survey drones could not do this, but the ship's repair drones can. The downside is potentially losing a repair drone if anything goes wrong. The drone arrives at its location forty-seven thousand kilometers above Astris's surface, both of its external floodlights lit, swiveling. The first alien craft fragment passes through the light beam like a twinkling star. The probe pursues.

From *Promise's* bridge, Beckman reads the telemetry. James is beside him, leaning on his workstation. "Fifteen centimeters, long axis. Two centimeters thick. Highly radioactive." As he says that, white flecks blink on the display randomly. "Gamma-ray hits on the photosensor. Surface is smooth. Appears to be a hull piece. Material unknown. Looks wet, like it is sealed in a gloss coat."

James points at the radar display. "Let's put all of the pieces on the screen."

Beckman taps an icon, and the display forms a catalog of several thousand pieces tagged by the radar pulse.

Hitoshi says, "When it blew, based on light and heat output, we estimated a twenty kiloton explosion. Not much left."

"We've got sensor data of it intact. I'll run it through the forensic module and see what it can piece back together," Beckman says. A progress bar spins on the screen, then a ghostly version of the boomerang craft appears overlaid with solid pieces reassembled by the forensic module. There aren't many. Part of the upper mast, a chunk of the lower wing.

James points at the upper mast. "Can you get a view of that?"

The drone focuses on a patch of stars and zooms. Finally, a fin-shape comes into focus, turning end-over-end. "A little more than a hundred kilometers away. Drone can get there in eight minutes."

"Okay, let's do it. We can talk the surface plan while it travels."

Beckman queues up the drone's commands and switches the view to the eleven Centauri worlds. *Promise* has visited two of Rigil Kentaurus's four planets. The remaining two, the lava-soaked first planet of Hestia and the frigid fourth planet of Boreas, are on the other side of the star. He overlays a curving trajectory from *Promise* to Hestia's orbit. "Hestia has a ten-day year. It'll be back on our side of the sun in four days. Launch a probe now, quarter-gee acceleration, intercept it then. Better than taking the ship there and getting toasted."

"Right," James says.

"Boreas is further. Could have a probe there in a week."

"What about the communications relay?"

"Well," Beckman says, "I'd like to put that at the sweet spot between Rigil and Toliman, assuming we're going to drop probes around Toliman's planets when we get there."

"What's your reco for Astris orbitals?"

"Drop six, just like we did on the Janus mission. It'll give us three-sixty monitoring if anything's coming our way."

James looks around the room. "What's everyone think about going planetside?"

"It's our primary mission," Ava says. "If Astris was potentially habitable, the plan was to go down. We need physical samples and all of the equipment in the science lab."

"Agreed," Isaac says. "Need soil samples, air quality, water samples."

James glances at Julian, and Julian adds, "Surface gravity is slightly higher than Earth at one-point-zero-five gee. Oxygen content is low, only sixteen percent, but in theory, a human could survive on parts of the surface with no EV suit. Even a suit breach would not necessarily be fatal."

"Sure," Hitoshi adds, "until you breathe a nose full of alien microbes and explode in a bloody mist."

"Even then," Julian says, "it's unlikely any alien life could get you ill. Even on Earth, most microbes cannot infect you, just as you cannot give a tree a cold."

Hitoshi smirks. "Pretty sure I would be the first."

"Can we land with an engine out?" James asks.

"That's why I designed four," Hitoshi says. "As long as we have two, we'll make orbit."

James looks over at Willow.

"It's why we're here," she says. "There's risk now that we've had a hostile encounter, but risk is part of the trip."

Ananke's drone hovers near James, her screen swirling. "Here we are, at the doorstep of a second Earth. How could we turn back now?"

Beckman gives James a sideways glance. "We're vulnerable on the surface. Can't jump. Gotta go into it with eyes wide open. As far as hostiles, can't unring that bell. If there's more of them, even heading home might not be the end of that."

Willow shifts uneasily.

Beckman adds, "So, we do what we came to do and deal with it here."

James lets that sit a moment. "Okay. We go. Let's take the rest of the day, pick out our landing site, and prep. I'm taking us out of radio silence. Record your personal messages. We'll broadcast back to Earth after dinner."

A tone sounds from Beckman's console, and he says, "Drone arriving at the fragment. On screen."

The fragment is clearly one end of the boomerang shape. Similar to the other pieces, it is glossy on the exterior, but the breach along its bottom shows an interior with fractured rods suspended in a black, rubbery filler.

"Also highly radioactive," Beckman says. "A little over six meters tall."

Ava says, "Can you magnify the rod ends?"

When the camera zooms, the rods are cylindrical and gold. The parts of them which protrude from the rubbery casing are twisted like noodles. Where the noodles are broken, intense blue crystals cake the interior walls.

Ava glances at Isaac. "Really resembles the sample we collected from the Silver Star. Seems too much of a coincidence. Can we get a few samples and bring them back?"

"As long as the radiation doesn't fry the drone, yes. You're on the hook for figuring out how to safely get it aboard," Beckman says.

Hitoshi says, "I can fab a shielded container."

Ava adds, "Once we get it into the quarantine area, it has its own shielding."

Beckman nods. "Alright. Any other samples?"

"Let's collect some of the crystals and a shaving of the rubbery substance and glossy hull exterior."

"Assuming we can cut it, done."

Ava smiles. "We're getting quite a sample collection on this trip."

Isaac looks like a kid in a candy store. "And we haven't even landed on Astris yet."

JAMES PEERS into the camera from his cabin's desk chair. He wears a blue Hayden-Pratt baseball cap and a black tee-shirt. The record icon blinks from the com panel. "Hey Will," he says, "hard to talk time when it's all screwed up because of dilation. For me, it's been three weeks. For you, at least when you get this, it should be January 2092. Nine years will vanish when I hit the send button. Nuts." He insets an orbital image of Astris. "Today we're in orbit around Astris, and it's amazing, like a desert version of Earth. We're pretty sure people could live here, and we're going to find out. There's a lot of risk in that. You know me, that doesn't bother me, but I've got a crew to think of. Wish you were here. You've always had the level head for thinking things through. Sometimes I dive before checking the pool's depth."

He taps his console, and a video log of their alien encounter attaches to the message. "Found this guy in high orbit over Astris. Doesn't appear to be a Silver Star. Kicked off a hell of a lot of radiation before firing on us, then Beckman lit it up with lasers, and it popped. Two first contacts — one with the Stars and one with these guys — and both times they tried to kill us. And for this one, I have to admit, I was so focused on making it work it almost did kill us. Good thing Beckman was on the ball. Anyway, I gotta get my head out of my ass and figure out this captain thing. Leading a starship crew is its own animal. I'm getting it now, but tomorrow we're going planetside, and I've got to pick up the pace." He waves his hand. "Enough whining. Just want you to know that I miss you, man, and could use your advice right about now."

"GOING ATMOSPHERIC," James says.

Promise buffets as they streak over one of Astris's larger seas. Clouds stack three-dimensionally from the surface, swirled into supercells, lightning flashing from their interior. The electrical discharges are full of color — blue, greens — and there's an eerie beauty to it. Soon, the plasma cone from *Promise's* reentry blinds their view. After five minutes of shedding speed, the fires fade. Up ahead, Astris's curved horizon takes on a hint of rose.

James adjusts the controls. "Coming up on sunrise."

The rose smears into a rusty orange contained by brightening blue bands as Rigil Kentaurus rises, brilliant white, sending lens flares in the image. Coral sunlight casts long mountain shadows, and pastel cumulus clouds float like icebergs over the terrain.

"Landing site, one-hundred-and-seventy-five kilometers, on course," Isaac says.

James reads from his display. "Altitude, eleven clicks, speed, mach two point one. Six minutes."

The sunrise blooms into a sparkling desert, twisting and turning in patterns like a topographic map. A river snakes along a canyon with its floor surrounded by the odd oxide red vegetation. Just as abruptly, clouds engulf their view, and *Promise* is swallowed in white. The ship lurches and wobbles, eliciting a concerned murmur from the crew.

"Just a little turbulence," James says. "Your captain has turned on the seat belt sign." He gives Willow a half-grin to his right, and she smiles back.

"Fifty kilometers," Isaac says.

Promise emerges from the clouds to a rocky landscape strewn with rubble.

"Subsonic," James says.

The mountains flatten to a tan plain. Just off to its west, the steel gray of seawater stretches out, rusty vegetation dappled in organic lines. To the north, the land descends into a basin with a hint of green visible in its floor.

James eases the controls, and the deceleration gently increases. "Prep for landing. Deploying struts."

Wind sounds increases as the struts clunk and whirl from

underneath the hull. *Promise* skims the surface, kicking up dust behind it. The landing site is a half-kilometer-wide rock disk surrounded by low shelves. As the starship slows to a hover, thrusters stabilize it from both sides. James rotates the ship until it's perfectly lined up with the ideal spot, then settles *Promise* down. Metal groans as the weight balances onto the struts. Outside, dust wreathes around the ship and rains back down to the rock.

To James's left, Hitoshi takes a deep breath and lets it out.

As the dust settles on the forward view, blue sky with feathery white clouds appears. Tan rock stretches away from the ship. James leans forward a little, glancing up. Astris's two moons are ghostly semi-spheres in the sky. It's morning, Astris time, and they've chosen their landing window, so it matches up with their biological time. "Okay," he says. "Let's run through the post-landing checklists, make sure we're shipshape, then meet at EV prep at oh-nine-hundred. Ava and Isaac will take us through the surface brief."

EV Prep is filled with twelve orange-and-white EV suits, each with a large block numeral on its front. The wall nearest Beckman has sliding panels surrounded by yellow-and-red caution markings, and a media screen hangs behind Ava and Isaac. Several silver briefcases are stacked around them like luggage.

Gravity feels good, James thinks. *Not ship's acceleration, but honest-to-goodness planetary gees.*

Isaac waves his hand over the screen, and a topographic map appears. "Two sites," he says. "First, site of potential photosynthetic green plant life, three kilometers north. Located on the floor of a rift basin ninety meters below our elevation. Possibly a dry lake." A dotted line winds its way from *Promise* to the base.

"Hikeable." He swipes his hand right, and the image follows, panning to rusty thickets. "Second site. Two kilometers due west. Appears to be vegetation varying in height up to three meters. Slightly hilly terrain. Easy walk from the ship. Continues to the lake, which is nearly five-hundred kilometers long. Site of bioluminescence at shoreline."

Ava opens one of the cases near her. Sample vials of varying shapes, tools, and imagers are embedded within the foam. "Two teams. Green site — James, Hitoshi, and me. Red site — Isaac, Julian, and Willow. Each team will be collecting soil, plant, and water samples. Isaac will lead the red team, and I'll lead green."

Beckman presses his thumb to the wall panel, and it slides open, revealing a dozen pistols and six pulse rifles. "Issuing sidearms to everyone. Check your charge, verify your safeties. Remember your training. Both groups have members with military firearms training. Follow their lead. That's James and Julian. Get into any kind of trouble, speak up on coms."

Willow motions to the EV suits. "I preconfigured your suits with the com frequencies. Com One broadcasts to your team, Two to everyone. Com Three is Emergency. Same as group, but displays your position and vitals on everyone's heads-up display."

Beckman adds, "I'll be monitoring ops from the ship, and Ananke is staying back since she's our other pilot."

"Let's make sure we communicate out there," James says. "We run into problems, we all return to the ship." He looks at Julian. "Medical brief?"

Julian talks with his hands, gesturing to the map. "Gravity is five percent higher than Earth. Like gaining three to four kilos. You should not feel it. Exterior temperature is thirty-five Celsius. Your suit's air conditioning can easily handle that, but in the event of an environmental failure, it will be like wearing a snowsuit in summer. Drink plenty of water, get back to the ship. You will very quickly overheat. Biggest surface risk is probably falls, in particular for green team. If you are immobilized, I will organize the evac team to come to you."

Hitoshi raises his hand.

Julian points. "Hitoshi?"

"What about, you know, alien monsters?"

"Have you seen any?"

"Not inside the ship."

"You are armed. I would not worry about it. You'll be with James, after all."

Hitoshi holds out both hands. "That's exactly what I'm worried about. You know whatever it is would make a beeline for the engineer."

Beckman smirks. "Would it make you feel better if you were in the other group?"

"Well, ...no. Then Willow will get eaten because she's the new girl, and I'll just feel bad."

"Thanks, Hitoshi," Willow says.

James sets his hand on Hitoshi's shoulder, looking around the group. "Any other questions?" When everyone shakes his head, James adds, "Alright. Suit up."

The next twenty minutes are a whirlwind of EV connections clicking together, coms tests, weapons checks, and mutual inspections. As James pans his helmet across the prep area, his HUD tags all of the crew members by name. Seeing the five of them, all suited up and ready to make landfall on another Earth, fills James's chest with pride. When everyone is ready, he moves into the airlock. The EV prep door seals behind them.

Ava taps the wall panel by the interior door. "Sterilizing."

Overhead lights strobe before plunging the chamber into black light. When James looks back, bits and pieces of people's suits fluoresce blue and purple. After sixty seconds, the strobe pattern repeats, and the chamber lights return to normal. A hiss sounds as pressures equalize. When the circular airlock hatch rotates open, sunlight floods in, causing James to squint as his eyes adjust.

The gangway angles down to tan rock littered with pebbles. It's just wide enough for one person. James looks over his shoulder, and everyone is smiling, motioning for him to go first. He can't wipe the grin off his face as he takes the first step into this new world.

11

BREACH

The walk to the green field takes ten minutes. Beckman chimes in once and checks on everyone, but otherwise all is quiet. Along the way they pass the landing site of their parachuted probe, its gray capsule unfurled like flower petals sitting atop the huge tablecloth formed by the crumpled chutes. The surface drone, now out of power, sits back in its perch atop the capsule. Hitoshi stops, squinting.

"What's up?" James says.

Hitoshi approaches the probe. "Some kind of oxidation forming on the surfaces."

James joins him. The round probe has iridescent patches as if machine oil had been spread over it with bits of white film clouding the shiny surface. "Damage from entry?"

Hitoshi kneels. The rainbow swirls also appear on the capsule walls. "I don't know. Titanium does oxidize at high temps. I'll scrape off a bit and have a look in the lab." He opens his case, selects a tool, and collects some of the film. When he's done, they continue forward another quarter-of-a-kilometer.

Once they arrive at the green field's edge, Ava kneels down and produces an imager. The plants — and that is what they look like — are Earth-green with stems the size of Ava's wrist. The stems fan out into an airy webbed shape which resembles a flattened palm. It's a bit like a leaf if some bug ate the leaf and left the veins. Where it differs from a leaf is that its vein structure repeats the shape of the entire leaf within itself. "Interesting," Ava says. "Looks like a plant, but the flesh is very rubbery. I'm not able to make out a cellular structure in the imager." She produces a scraper and vial. "Just need a few milligrams." Gingerly she reaches for the stem.

Without warning, the palm-sized leaf snaps around her wrist. Ava gasps and pulls back, but she's unable to budge it. She loses her footing, drops the scraper, and falls to one knee, reaching with her left hand to the curled leaf. "James, it's got me." As she wraps her hand over it and tries to peel it off, the stem partially retracts into the ground and pulls her off-balance. She rolls onto her shoulder and ends up on her back with her right wrist still pinned to the ground.

James rushes forward and kneels beside her, wrapping his fingers beneath the leaf. As he does, other leaves clasp onto Ava's helmet, forearm, and legs. "Buggers are strong," James says. "Can't break 'em loose with both hands."

Ava's breathing hard now. "They're squeezing. Get them off me!"

James abandons prying the leaf and snatches the scraper. He sets it against the wrist-sized stem and saws. When the scraper slices into the green flesh, a clear fluid wells up at the wound.

Ava gasps. "They're all tightening in response."

James has sawed a quarter-of-the-way through the stem when an adjacent leaf shoots out like a frog's tongue and ensnares his wrist, pulling him away from the stem. He clamps his left hand onto it. "Goddammit!"

Hitoshi advances a step, and James yells, "No, don't! Stay clear of the—" The green stem drags him face-first into the soil.

Over coms, Hitoshi says, "Beckman, we have a situation here! Guys, hang on."

James sees nothing but dirt and writhing stems through his faceplate, but he hears the distinctive warning tone of a pulse pistol safety disengaging. Leaves latch onto his legs and arms like vices. Pop. The pulse pistol discharge comes from Hitoshi's direction and impacts the ground just behind James. The plants attached to him jerk. Pop. Pop. Electric blue flashes. Pop. Pop. Pop. Soil and burning plant debris rain down.

"That's right, killer plants," Hitoshi says, advancing, still firing. "You may be strong, and there's a lot of you, but I have a boomstick."

Over coms, Beckman says, "Powering up for evac."

Hitoshi squeezes off a few more rounds and blue flashes in James's peripheral vision. James rolls his head and looks back. Hitoshi sheaths his gun and fishes around in his belt pack, producing a palm-sized cylinder. He slaps a power cell onto its bottom. "Should be enough oxygen for a plasma torch." When he disengages the safety and presses the ignite button, a flickering red weld arc appears at the top. "Try and hold still."

James grunts. "Roger that."

Hitoshi advances to James through the pistol-cleared opening and slides the torch along the stem base holding James's wrist. The leaf reels back, immediately releasing James's arm and clamping onto Hitoshi's. Hitoshi fumbles the torch, falls to his hands and knees, and screams.

With his right arm free, James doesn't hesitate. He snap-draws his pistol, sets the barrel at point-blank range against the stem base, and fires. The blast vaporizes the stem and sprays rock in an arc away from Hitoshi.

Hitoshi rolls to the side, cradling his left forearm.

"James!" Ava yells, her voice pained.

James rolls to his left, places the pistol against the stem

attached to his left wrist and blasts it. He snaps three aimed shots at the stems binding his legs, then turns towards Ava.

Behind Ava, a sea of green leaves stretch from their bases, all straining and pointed at James like vipers. Ava has six attached to her. The two on her helmet undulate over the release locks and a shrill alert sounds from her suit. Before James can react, they twist her helmet open, the seal breaks, and air hisses out. Ava's bare neck is visible in the gap. She cries out, her eyes wild.

There's no clean shot without hitting her head. James drops to the right, snatches the plasma torch, and darts over to the leaf on the right side of her helmet. He yells, "Hey!" and smacks it with his left hand, offering his left wrist. It releases her helmet and latches onto his left wrist. His right hand swings in with the plasma torch and slices the stem at its base.

The plant on Ava's left helmet releases and shoots around James's right bicep. He's still got the torch in his hand and severs the leaf mid-stem. The decapitated stem thrashes around like a loose firehouse. As he turns towards Ava's legs, the four leaves arc towards him. When the nearest lunges, he times his slice perfectly and bisects the leaf with the torch. It flails back. The other three hesitate, swaying like cobras. A pulse blast hits the first, and it explodes. Pop. Pop. The other two burst in blue flame.

Over James's shoulder, Hitoshi kneels with his pistol. Blood drips from his left forearm. Hitoshi says to the downed plants, "You should not pick on creatures that have access to energy weapons." He glances at James. "Let's get the hell out of here."

James grabs Ava's helmet, slides it back into place, and refastens the locks. She's hyperventilating. He taps her suit controls and adjusts her oxygen mixture, then tucks both of his hands under her armpits and helps her up. Her legs are shaking, and he drapes her arm over his shoulder. As they move towards the field's edge, James looks back. The green hands wave in hypnotic patterns.

Ava struggles against him. "Wait!" She pulls down towards the ground.

"Ava, we gotta go."

She scoops up a fragment of one of Hitoshi's blasted leaves and clamps onto it with a death-grip.

James leans down, gets his arm under her, and lifts her. "C' mon!"

A subsonic rumble vibrates the gravel, and James looks up. *Promise* emerges over the ridge, monstrous, a great, gleaming black and white geometry eclipsing the sky. It rotates slowly, aligning itself for touchdown one hundred meters ahead of them.

As they clear the field, James says, "Beckman, we have injured." He looks left. Hitoshi's sprayed sealant over the arm wound and holds his right hand on it.

"Hitoshi, how are you doing?" James says.

"Cut myself pretty good with the plasma torch when the leaf grabbed me. Just so you know, I'm probably going to pass out soon. This sucks."

James steers towards him, slinging Hitoshi's right arm over his left shoulder. He now has both Ava and Hitoshi. "I got you, buddy."

Ava's still breathing heavily. "James, I had a breach."

"I know."

"I breathed in atmosphere."

"You're going to be okay. We'll get doc to check you out. Anything else hurt?"

"Feel like I fell down a flight of stairs."

James ambles forward slowly. Ahead, *Promise* kicks up dust as its landing struts settle onto the rock. "Hell of a grip on those things. It's like they were all muscle. Julian, you copying this?"

Julian responds over coms. "Affirmative. Red group is at the beach and moving to an evac point now. Beckman, we'll need to maintain quarantine in the airlock area for the two suit breaches."

"Copy that," Beckman says.

Ahead, a ramp extends as Promise's airlock cycles open. Beckman stands there in his combat armor with Ananke's white drone hovering beside him. As soon as the doors are clear, he double-times it to James's group.

"I thought," Hitoshi begins, his voice woozy, "you said I'd be perfectly safe breathing alien air. No brain explosions or anything like that."

"You will be fine, my friend," Julian says. "But we must follow quarantine protocol."

"Peachy," Hitoshi says. With that, he passes out.

THE EASIEST WAY TO treat Hitoshi and Ava is to keep everyone in the airlock, replace the atmosphere with normal air, and run the sterilization sequence. As long as everyone else keeps his suit on, they are clear to remove the patients' EV suits. Julian has the emergency airlock medkit out, kneeling beside Hitoshi. James helps get Hitoshi out of his suit, leaving him in a black tee-shirt and shorts.

At first, Hitoshi's arm looks terrible. He bled profusely from the wound, and his entire arm is a sticky red. The plasma torch sliced effortlessly through his suit and forearm muscle, leaving a grisly wound.

Hitoshi is awake now and looks down at his arm. "Ah, hell. That's a lot of blood. I thought it would've cauterized."

Julian sprays an aerosol around the wound. "Cauterization is not the same as vaporization. You went into a bit of shock, there, my friend, but your vitals are looking better." He affixes a dermal to Hitoshi's neck, then produces an elastic band and slips it around his bicep.

"Tourniquet?"

"Nerve block." Julian taps a command on his slate, and Hitoshi releases a sigh of relief. "Better?"

Hitoshi nods.

Behind James, Willow and Beckman help Ava out of her suit. Her arms and legs have puffy welts and blue bruises. Beckman appraises the injuries while Willow offers Ava some water.

Julian passes an imager over Hitoshi's wound, lifts a syringe, and taps something on his slate. When he squirts it into the wound, an amber gel fills the gap. "Still okay?"

"Didn't feel a thing," Hitoshi says.

"This will self-assemble into a cellular matrix over the next few minutes, sealing the wound. The nanobots are self-terminating and will create the repair lattice for the vascular and nerve damage. It was a clean-cut, and you will fully recover."

"That's going to leave a mark, isn't it?"

"I'm afraid so. But you will have a very interesting story to explain it." He reaches into the kit and retrieves a bulb filled with clear liquid, handing it to Hitoshi. "Drink this."

Hitoshi takes a sip and puckers his face. "Oh, God…is there some rule in medicine that requires everything to taste horrible?"

"You lost a half-liter of blood. Best treatment is to replenish fluids, sugar, and electrolytes. That one was the Berry Blast."

"Do I get a cookie, too?"

Julian smiles. "Drink. Rest. I'm going to check on Ava."

As Julian moves over to Ava, James sits beside Hitoshi, resting his forearms on his knees. "What you did back there was pretty brave," James says, "and you kicked some serious ass with that pistol. Was that all from Beckman's range training?"

Hitoshi takes another sip of his Berry Blast, cringing. "That, and lots of video games. I'm a real space hero in those."

James nudges him gently. "You're a real space hero here. Thanks for having my back."

Hitoshi raises his eyebrows, and a smile follows.

James sets his hand on Hitoshi's shoulder. "Hang tight. I'm going to check on Ava."

Hitoshi sips his drink and gives a thumbs up.

When James kneels beside Ava, she's inspecting the dermal Julian's placed on her wrist. Like Hitoshi, she's in her undersuit garments and is a bit exposed. Her many bruises look painful, but the slight glaze to her eyes suggests she's not feeling it.

"How're you doing?" James asks.

Ava sighs. "Feeling dumb. I made the classic terramorphic mistake of assuming that something which looked like Earth life functioned the same as Earth life. That was no plant."

"Don't beat yourself up. None of us thought that would happen."

"What doesn't make sense is why it exhibited predatory behavior on a planet with no animal life."

"Maybe it wasn't predatory. Might just be a defensive response."

"Maybe. Or possibly there are animals we haven't seen yet." She motions to the sample container to her left. A torn green leaf is inside. "At least we secured that sample before running the sterilization sequence. Got to get it to the lab and see what it's made of."

"Always the scientist."

She smiles. "You know it."

Julian examines his slate. "Your bloodwork is normal," he says to Ava. "But quarantine is twenty-four hours. Just precautionary."

"I know," Ava says. "I wrote the protocol." She looks over at James. "There's a claustrophobic little quarantine room in sickbay where Hitoshi and I will need to hang out. In hindsight, I should've made it bigger."

Julian glances at James. "Are you injured?"

James shrugs. "A couple of bruises on my wrists. Nothing to worry about."

"I will check you out when you're inside. You did not have a suit breach, so you must keep your suit on until we transfer Ava and Hitoshi into quarantine suits."

James nods. "Gotcha."

Julian passes an imager over Ava's face. "Did you have any trouble breathing the Astris air?"

"I think it was more panic than anything, and I hyperventilated. But it seemed like air. Just hot with a mineral smell and something slightly pungent."

"No inflammation in your airways. Everything is normal."

Ava squints. "James, those creatures were able to manipulate the mechanical linkages on my helmet and coordinate with each other to do so. Doesn't mean they're sentient. Cats can learn to open doors. But it does indicate they have at least a basic level of intelligence."

James nods. "Buggers sure seemed smart. That means we just had a first contact. What do you think we should do next?"

"Analyze all of our samples, see what we can learn. Then we've got to have another go at it."

BEING in quarantine is like being in college, with Ava and Hitoshi as unlikely roommates sharing a tiny dorm. Considering they are living in a transparent box the size of a large closet, the room makes remarkably efficient use of its space. Three of the walls have fold-down beds which transform into desktop workstations, and the back corner has a comically-small but thankfully-private bathroom and wash area. An inset cabinet stores food and drink. On the other side of the transparent wall, Julian works in sickbay. Despite the zoo-like feel of the experience, they've tuned him out and tap away at their computers.

Ava's screen has a live stream to the Planetary Science lab. Isaac works there in front of the sample quarantine area. They've amassed quite the collection. There's the molybdenum blue from the Silver Star, the wreckage from the Boomerang, the red angel-hair and purple trumpet plants, a half-dozen soil samples, four water vials, a flask of atmosphere, Hitoshi's oxidation scraping, and the green leaf. It's a scientific puzzle she wants to solve.

"Here we go," Isaac says.

In the sample area, the microscope head swivels and peers into the water sample. Lights illuminate from the vial's base. When the magnified image appears on the screen, Isaac's grin widens, and Ava's pulse quickens. Translucent green spirals with delicate flagella, spiky spheres, textured triangles, and segmented threads drift in the clear backdrop.

Ava can barely contain herself. "Hitoshi, you've got to see this!"

Hitoshi approaches and peers over her shoulder. "Is that plankton?"

On the screen, Isaac says, "Spectrometry available." Elements tag the peaks of the resulting graph. Carbon, hydrogen, oxygen, nitrogen, magnesium, silicon, calcium. The software analyzes the ratio and produces a list of compounds.

"Sure resembles it," Ava says. "Oh, it's what we thought. Chlorophyll." When the microscope steps up the magnification on one of the lifeforms, green shapes fill the display like tiny rice grains. "Possible chloroplasts. Very similar to phytoplankton. If the model is similar to Earth's, this is where the planetary oxygen is likely coming from. Let's catalog everything and get some atomic imaging. Oh, I can't wait to see what method they're using to encode replication."

Isaac taps the console. "Running." A robotic arm picks up the vial and deposits it within a white machine. As it does, the microscope swivels over to the red angel hair. Magnified, at first, it looks like human hair, but an irregular cell pattern forms when zoomed. Isaac whistles. "Cell walls. Membranes. Looks like organelles and nucleus."

The spectrographic plot appears, scrolling with probable

compounds. "Chlorophyll again, and anthocyanin. I knew it! This is almost certainly a plant." When they move onto the purple bell plant, the results are similar. Next is the air sample.

Ava senses someone watching and realizes Julian has come over to the quarantine area, observing the screen with interest. The atmosphere composition is identical to what they observed from orbit. Water vapor is present with trace microbes.

Ava sighs. "Microbes. That's what I breathed in."

"Exponentially lower than what we are breathing right now," Julian says.

When the microscope zooms in on the microbes, they resemble bacteria and appear to be dead.

Ava nods. "Possibly killed by solar UV, like Earth."

"I still think you both will be fine," Julian says. "Even on Earth, the only bacteria which can make you ill have specifically evolved to infect humans. For a human to get sick, generally another human is required."

The atomic imager completes its cycle and alerts Isaac. "Pictures are up." When he sends them to the screen, everyone leans in.

The phytoplankton's genetic material is a string-like squiggle within its cell. The squiggle is a shelf-structure bridging an s-shape. The software tags all of the individual atoms and assembles them into a three-dimensional animation, complete with chemical compound names.

Ava sets her hand over her mouth.

"G-quadraplex," Julian says. "Alternative DNA structure."

Isaac points. "Wow. Adenine, thymine, cytosine, guanine."

Ava removes her hand. "Peptide nucleic acid. PNA instead of DNA. Oh, but it's so similar to Earth. Either Earth-life and this specimen share a common origin, or nucleic acids are a common evolutionary solution." She taps at her workstation. "Let's start sequencing the genes."

As the sequence runs, Isaac indexes the microscope to the green leaf fragment. "Now, let's have a look at our angry friend."

At first, the leaf looks like an intricate lace of green veins, with the fractured parts showing hollow interiors. When they magnify the surface, however, the structure is more like a braided cable. When they magnify the braids, they are made of even smaller braids. They reach the limit of the optical microscope without finding the smallest repeating unit in the leaf wall. The leaf does not contain any cells.

"Spectrometry's up," Isaac says. "Largest peaks are silicon, carbon, hydrogen, oxygen, and nitrogen. Organosilicon compounds. The clear liquid inside the stem is aqueous hydroxylamine with some salts."

Hitoshi squints. "Silicon-based life, like in sci-fi?"

"Yeah," Isaac says, "but for real."

Ava nods. "With an ammonia/water vascular system but no cells."

"Is it a plant or an animal?" Hitoshi says.

Ava stares at the screen, puzzled. "Neither. It's entirely different life chemistry than everything else we've found here. Either multiple chemistries evolved, or it's alien to Astris."

12

SUNSET

Rigil bathes *Promise's* bridge in dying coral sunlight as it drops towards the western mountains, the bridge screen a panorama of rose fish-scale clouds fanning out before a deepening aquamarine gradient. *Promise* is parked back at its original landing spot, three kilometers south of the green leaf field and two kilometers east of the sea. An evening star brightens and the bridge screen tags it as a planet, Hydaspes. In the east, Centauri's second sun, Toliman, rises, luminous like a planet, but glaring harsh gold. Three stars flank the second sun — its own planetary system — and it's a bit like viewing Earth's Sun from the outer system. *Except it's not,* Willow thinks, *it's in a sunset sky of breathable air.*

Isaac and Beckman are to her left. Both stand at their workstations. She's standing as well. She's not sure why, except that it feels like the thing to do, here, under planetary gravity. Ananke glows blue from her slate at the console's center.

Willow takes in the sunset and can almost feel the warmth on her face. She closes her eyes and smiles. When she opens them, she glances at the sickbay video feed. "Is it coming through okay?"

In the video inset, James sits with Julian in front of the quarantine area. Ava and Hitoshi both face the camera. "It's beautiful," Ava says.

"Kind of a Tatooine thing going on," Hitoshi adds.

Isaac taps his console, and a system schematic appears. "Looking good. Probe course is loaded and ready."

Beckman nods. "Loading into the launcher." Deep within the ship's aft servos whirl and something clanks. "On your mark."

James glances at Ava and smiles. "I think you should have the honors."

Ava returns a slight grin. "Beckman, deploy sea probe."

Beckman taps an icon, and the ship vibrates as something ejects from the starboard side. On the bridge screen, a gunmetal ellipsoid coasts a few meters above the rock. Two floodlights flicker on and illuminate a path in front of it. The drone pitches forward and darts to the north. As it does, a new window insets with its camera feed and telemetry.

"Time to target," Beckman says, "ninety seconds."

The drone passes the rocky outcropping with the red angel hair and purple trumpet plants. Mesas streak along both sides. The view rolls right, and the drone dives down over stepped dirt. Ahead, the beach is a wash of glistening sand leading to the mirrored surface of the sea. The drone slows to a hover. Out in the still sea, turquoise currents fluoresce like an aurora.

"There it is," Ava says.

Isaac examines his console. "Four-hundred and seventy-nanometer emission wavelength."

Ava rubs her fingers together. "In the range of blue-green bioluminescence."

As the probe stops fifty meters off-shore, Beckman says, "Probe at destination."

"Here goes," Ava says. When she looks at James, he nods, motioning to her. "Send it in."

Beckman eases into the control, and the probe dips into the

water, descending. In the video, its floodlights carve two cones in the waters, flecks of matter drifting past.

Willow slides up her control and hits the red icon. The probe's top detaches and ascends to the surface like a buoy. Although they can't see it in the video, a thin wire connects the buoy and the submerged probe. "Radio beacon deployed," she says. A blue communications line connects the beacon with *Promise*, and a blue communications line extends to the submersible. "Five-by-five."

The probe descends, unspooling its line like a fishing reel. Above it, Rigil's last light shimmers in crepuscular rays through the blue water. Motion catches the probe's attention, and it banks towards it. A school of six jade creatures swims, their bodies small, each one to two centimeters, trailing a long, undulating ribbon of a tail. When the probe's lights focus on them, they jolt away.

"No eyes," Ava says. "But I saw bumps along their front."

Willow reads from her display. "Depth, three meters."

As the probe continues down, yellow lights flash like fireflies. When it approaches them, dozens swarm around the probe, blinking randomly. The camera zooms on one to show a creature just millimeters long wearing a shell like a horseshoe crab. It approaches the probe's starboard light, blinks twice, and swims away. The swarm follows it.

"Remarkable," Ava says.

"Eight meters," Willow says. "Approaching the bottom."

Isaac reads from his display. "Still in the shallows. Orbital imaging suggests maximum sea depth of five kilometers."

As the probe focuses on the sea bed, the sandy floor is filled with the swaying red angel hair they spotted on the surface. It grows here like meter-tall grass. Rocks covered in purple fuzz are scattered throughout the field, and curious donut-shaped stalagmite formations jut up. Within the red grass, a translucent disk wags twelve radial fins. The disk's center is hollow, also like a donut. Organs are barely visible through its skin. When the probe's light reaches it, the disk fluoresces with a yellow stripe, and each of its fins glows with a central green dot. It vibrates its fins quickly, backing up.

"A response," Ava says, "like a warning. Invertebrate, radially symmetric, bioluminescent. Let's have a look at its appendages."

The camera zooms onto one of the glowing fins. Fine lines, like hair in sunlight, form rows of j-shapes coming off each.

"Like nematocysts on jellyfish."

The creature backs into one of the stalactites and rotates into its center, hooking its fins onto the structure and stretching out like a dreamcatcher.

"It's unusual behavior," Ava says. "If we were a predator, it's leaving itself exposed. I think it's trying to elicit a response. I'm moving in a little closer."

The drone advances and the dreamcatcher — that's become Willow's new nickname for it — flashes its fin lights green, waiting. Everyone leans in, watching. As the dreamcatcher grows larger on the screen, a dark shape erupts from the red seagrass beneath the probe, smashing a flat rubbery red tentacle over the camera. The image jerks as the submersible loses orientation. What can only be a large mouth with pointed black teeth gnaws on the lens.

Everyone jumps back. Hitoshi places a hand over his heart. "Seriously, does everything on this planet want to murder us?"

The black teeth take a few more attempted bites before giving up. They never see what it is before it retreats back into the crimson grass.

"Mutualism," Ava says. "Predatory behavior. The disk was the bait."

The submersible rights itself and issues a status check. "No damage," Willow says.

"Let's head towards the potential bioluminescent current location."

The probe accelerates, skimming a few meters above the bottom. More ribbon fish flash by in the lights, but, ahead, green ripples shimmer like aurora borealis underwater. When the submersible arrives at the location, it is in a galaxy of green stars. Magnified, the star is a ghostly sphere less than one millimeter in diameter with flagella evenly distributed along its surface. The creatures drift with the currents, like constellations.

"Looks multicellular, motive structures," Ava says.

From the probe's audio sensors, a deep, distant rumble sounds, like whale song.

Willow taps quickly on her console. "That was loud enough that it's generating passive sonar echoes. I'm logging it all. It should give us some sonar imagery of what's around us, without us needing to use active pulses. Maybe we'll get lucky, and it will do it again."

Isaac says, "Initial mapping on screen."

The three-dimensional underwater surface map is monochromatic and tinted a faint blue. The bed slopes down over irregular bumps and rocks with occasional larger slabs sticking up, but the image is noisy due to the amount of life in the water, only spanning fifty meters from the probe.

Everyone waits, listening. After a few seconds, the sound repeats.

Willow taps excitedly. "Gotcha."

"Processing," Isaac says. "Better map on the screen."

The new map extends out nearly five kilometers, indicating several contacts of a half-meter or larger. Some of the largest swimming contacts are four meters.

"Some big fish in this sea," Isaac adds.

As they spin the map around three-sixty, they get glimpses of the sea bed at the periphery of the scan's range. Depth here is twenty meters. It's fuzzy, but a geometric shape protrudes from the seafloor at an oblique angle, almost like a wing.

Willow glances over at Isaac, and he gives an "I don't know" look.

James says, "Willow, can you boost that?"

She hesitates. "Not without going active. Do you want an active sonar pulse?"

Beckman shifts his weight. "Sure you want to say hi to everything in there?"

James looks to Ava. "Concerns?"

Ava takes a deep breath. "We've already got the probe in the water. Keep it simple. Short burst. No modulation."

James glances back to the screen. "Do it."

Now it's Willow's turn to take a deep breath as she reaches for the icon. When she taps it, a tone indicates the active pulse.

Isaac swipes the results to the screen. "Map up."

The probe's pulse is much higher quality, upping the resolution of the scan. The geometric object is shaped like a boomerang, resting on one of its sides. A sphere is centered along the boomerang's apex. Irregular shapes and lumps pepper its hull and chunks appear to be missing.

"Oh my," Isaac says.

Ananke's screen pulses orange. "It appears to be a shipwreck."

"It does," James says, "and this time I want to get a closer look."

IT TAKES thirty minutes to recouple the probe with its transmitter, develop a plan, and fly it to the shipwreck site. During that time Rigil sets beneath the sea's western horizon, leaving a rusty band which quickly fades to polarized blue. Toliman continues to rise, and the sky around it is a daylight blue.

Willow still mans the controls on the bridge. "Radio beacon deployed. Comlink established. Drone descending."

Bubbles wreathe around the camera as the drone drives. Blue

stars and pink nebula seem to shimmer from the depths, but soon the tip of the boomerang appears as an ominous shadow. Organic, irregular bumps protrude along its length, resembling shells, or perhaps barnacles. Each has a ghostly orange glow along its edge. Luminescent spheres cluster in constellations over the wing's surface. Willow recognizes them as the tiny, buckyball flagella spheres they observed earlier. The wing itself is a slate gray stone, smooth but pocked where meter-wide gaps make it look like it has battle damage. Further down, the wing mates with the other half of the boomerang before the sandy sea bed engulfs it. A fractured sphere rests at the connection, and within the breach glows the orange barnacles and blue stars. At first, it seems a trick of light, but as the probe adjusts its position a third wing comes into view, extending perpendicular to the first two and embedded in the sand.

James is still in sickbay with Ava and Hitoshi. "It's a different configuration," he says.

Isaac reads from his display. "Smaller, too, than the orbital craft."

"Beckman, does that look like weapons damage to you?"

Beckman nods. "Melted, like a directed-energy weapon."

As the probe swings its lights across the wreckage, some of the blue stars release from the boomerang and approach it, fanning around the camera in a swarm.

"Let's get a look inside the breach," James says.

Willow descends the probe until it is directly over the broken sphere, swiveling the floodlights inside. The barnacles gleam, smoke-colored arcs stacked in patterns. The sphere's interior wall is visible through some of the breaks in the growth. It looks like black, tinted glass. Platinum filaments form patterns within the glass-like ice crystals, strands breaking through the surface and drifting in the ocean current.

Isaac taps a readout on his console. "Low-level beta radiation. Filaments are composed of technetium. Half-life, four-point-two million years. Rare. Usually a fission by-product of uranium, or made from decay of molybdenum-99."

"Molybdenum?" Ava says. "Interesting that should come up again, after finding it in the Silver Stars."

"What do you think it means?" Isaac says.

"I don't know. Just an observation. Let's collect a filament sample and get three-sixty imagery of the interior."

Willow extends the probe's tools, and the video rotates as it descends into the cavity. A tool clamps one filament while another tool snips a piece off, then the probe slowly spins as it images the sphere. The smoked glass is reflective, and the probe can see itself. In the reflection, hundreds of the bioluminescent buckyballs coat the probe like snowfall.

"I think they're in love," Hitoshi says.

"Hmm," Ava says. "I wouldn't mind a sample of one of them, but I don't want to kill them taking them back here. Hopefully, we can coax them off when we start ascending."

"Let's get imaging of the entire craft exterior before we take off," James says. "Then bring back the probe through the airlock, sterilize it, and lock everything up for the night."

JUST PAST MIDNIGHT, all is quiet on *Promise,* except for Beckman, who is always awake at this time. He sits at his console on the bridge wearing black jeans and a hooded sweatshirt, the blue and white U.S. Navy logo prominent in the upper left corner. A cup of steaming chamomile tea rests in his hand.

The bridge screen displays the night panorama of Astris's landscape. Toliman is high in the twilight-blue sky now, bright yellow, ringed by an azure gradient. It reminds Beckman a bit of a full moon on Earth with wispy clouds, the sky glowing its own blue color, too bright for night. Because of Toliman's glare, only the brightest stars are visible, and the sky seems lonely because of it. The constellations are the same as Earth's. He can just make out Perseus, and above it, Cassiopeia, with the bright yellow star of Earth's Sun.

Ananke's screen glows blue from the center console. "It's surreal, isn't it, seeing the Sun as a constellation?"

"Indeed it is," Beckman says. "Seems like stars should be different in that sky, but they're still ours."

"What do you think of the mission so far?"

Beckman takes a sip of his tea. "Surprise around every corner. As far as mission objectives, it's all aces. Finding life left and right. Problem is, most of it wants to kill us."

"Are you familiar with Fermi's Paradox?"

He pauses. "Sounds like something Isaac would know."

"It simply asks, considering all of the stars in the galaxy, where is everyone?"

Beckman considers the statement. "We seem to be finding them. Stars and boomerangs all in the same trip."

"Exactly. The odds of us encountering both, so soon, are remarkable. The answer to the paradox must be that life is everywhere."

Beckman nods. "But not interested in us."

Ananke's screen introduces a purple current. "So it seems."

"Not sure if that's a good or a bad thing."

The console chirps an alert, and a topographic map pops up on the bridge screen. *Promise* is at its center. One kilometer north of the ship a targeting reticule locks onto a contact.

Beckman sets his tea down and springs to alert, tapping on his workstation. "Thermal contact. Forty meters-per-second, altitude twenty meters and rising, coming from the direction of the leaf field. Small. Maybe one meter."

"Located," Ananke says. "Magnifying."

The bridge display zooms across the landscape, rushing up to a glassy sphere enclosed in metallic tapered sheaths. The effect is a bit like feathers fanning back from a bird's head. Deep in the sphere's center glows a dull ember. The telemetry predicts a flight path intersecting *Promise* in twenty-five seconds.

Beckman opens coms to James's quarters. "James, we've got company. Need you on the bridge." He activates the tactical systems, and the targeting reticule changes red, rotating around the contact. "I'm opening emitter ports. Firing solution is ready. Charging emitters."

James's voice comes on over the speaker. "On my way."

"Beckman," Ananke says. "They might be trying to make contact."

"Not getting caught with our pants down. Don't have to shoot them, but doesn't mean I can't load my guns."

"It's arrived."

On the bridge screen, the spheroid stops when it is one meter from the ship. The ember in the glassy center flares and fills the sphere with gold. The metallic feathers look like platinum bark strips, overlapping each other and widening into tatters.

"Low-level x-ray and beta radiation," Ananke says. "Device appears to be technological. Configuration is different than either the Silver Star or Boomerangs."

The Eye — Beckman's ad-lib mental name for it — coasts along *Promise's* hull from bow to stern. "Can you tell what's propelling it?"

"Unknown. No emissions consistent with RF drives."

James comes jogging barefoot onto the bridge wearing gray pajama bottoms and a blue tee-shirt. He rushes up next to Beckman. "Status?"

"Seems to be a probe," Beckman says. "Just arrived from the direction of the leaf field. Looking us over. How do you want to play this?"

James watches the probe move across the screen. It's midship at the moment, investigating *Promise's* dorsal port nacelle. It's found the damaged spot with the mismatched hull plates and examines them carefully. "Let 'em look," James says. "Going to need everyone if this turns into a contact." He presses his thumb on the console and opens the ship-wide intercom. "All crew report to stations. Possible first contact situation. Repeat, crew to stations."

The Eye has just swung to the ship's aft and discovered the laser emitter. It seems particularly interested in it.

"Might be doing a tactical assessment of us," Beckman says.

James nods. "Definite possibility."

Coms dings and Ava's face appears on the bridge screen. Her hair is disheveled, and she seems groggy as she leans into the camera from her quarantine room. "What's going on?"

"Seems like we're being probed," James says. "On your screen now."

The Eye swings around the aft and begins examining the starboard side of *Promise*.

"Do you think it's related to the Boomerang?"

Julian arrives on the bridge wearing shorts and a tee-shirt. He stands at his station, watching the probe's motion.

"Don't know," James says. "Should we try the contact protocol?"

"Yeah. I think visual is the least aggressive, so let's try using ship's nav lights."

"Alright. Hold until everyone else is in place."

Willow and Isaac arrive. Both are in pajamas, but Willow wears a sweatshirt. "Wow," Isaac says. "Alien drone. Cool."

James says, "Okay, everyone, we're going to run through the contact protocol. Number sequences, external lights. You know your roles."

Willow picks up her earbud and slides it over her ear. "Recording, all channels."

Isaac says, "Passive sensors ready."

James nods to Ava. "On your mark."

She taps her workstation. "Initiate."

On the port camera view, *Promise's* navigation beacon pulses red once, then twice, then three times, continuing the sequence to ten.

The Eye immediately stops its nacelle inspection and turns towards the navigation light, advancing slowly.

Ava repeats the sequence. When it's done, she moves on to prime numbers.

The Eye circles the pulsing nav beacon, investigating. When Ava restarts her sequence at one, the Eye's outer glowing ring pulses red once. When the nav beacon blinks three times, the Eye's ring pulses three times.

Ava gasps, tapping away. The sequence continues up to twenty-three with the Eye mirroring it precisely. "Oh wow, it's working!"

The Eye closes on the nav light and hovers only a few centimeters from it. The red ring pulses and fades as if it were breathing.

"It's started its own sequence," Ava says.

The ring fades black and strobes like an electrical short, the flashing red light chaotic and dazzling. It pauses a second, returning to its rhythmic pulsing, then turns away from the nav light and resumes its inspection of *Promise*.

Isaac reads his display. "Electromagnetic radiation. Full-spectrum. Strong magnetic field flux."

Ava begins, "Let's see if—"

The Eye turns away from the ship, its interior light fading, and flies underneath *Promise's* nose. In an instant, it's accelerating and rising back towards the north.

"Tracking," Beckman says, "but we'll lose line-of-sight if it drops over the cliff."

James looks over. "Can you get a probe out and follow it?"

"Thought you might want that. One in the tube, ready to go."

James holds up a hand. "Wait until it's clear of the cliff before launching. Let's not spook our visitor."

The Eye is a black silhouette against the ultramarine sky. As it reaches the cliff, it drops down into the basin, disappearing from sight.

Promise shudders and Beckman says, "Bird's away."

In the video from their probe's camera, dusty landscape streaks by as it zips towards the cliff. It slows, cautious, and peers down into the basin. Two kilometers ahead, the leaf field is a series of dark crop circles against the twilight shadows of the basin. A spherical shape descends into the field where the blue pumpkin-shaped ribbon plants lay. One plant is unfurled and splayed open. As the Eye touches down onto it, the ribbons wrap up and engulf it.

"Huh," James says. "Wasn't expecting that."

13

RED TWILIGHT

J ust after dawn, Ava pulls the blanket up around herself in her quarantine area bed. She's simultaneously cold and sweating. Hitoshi sleeps on the other side of the room, his breathing rhythmic. Like most of the crew, she couldn't sleep after the Eye incident and stayed up for a few more hours doing some work. Now, she feels like a truck has hit her. Everything in her body aches, and she's just slower. At first, she thinks it's just the all-nighter, but then, as it slowly dawns on her, her stomach sinks. She's *sick*. She reaches up to the coms icon and taps it. "Julian, it's Ava."

After a short wait, Julian's face appears. He's in his quarters, leaning towards the camera. Somehow he doesn't suffer from the same bed-head which everyone else does and looks like he's perpetually ready for a photo shoot. "Good morning. Is everything okay?"

Ava shakes her head. "No. I've got flu-like symptoms. Think I'm running a fever."

Julian's eyebrows scrunch together. "On my way."

During the five minutes it takes him to get there, she drags herself out of bed, heads into the washroom, and changes into her clothes. Although she doesn't feel like it, she fetches an orange juice from the galley and forces herself to drink it. Her taste is off, and the juice has a coppery tinge to it.

Julian enters sickbay and approaches the quarantine partition. "When did this start?"

"Sometime between three a.m. and now. Woke up this way."

"You're a bit pale and perspiring. Have a seat at diagnostics and set your hand on the scanner."

Ava sits in the corner where the medical array resides. The scanner on the desk has an illuminated hand pattern with caps to insert her fingertips. Julian reads from the panel display on the quarantine wall. "Core body temperature, pulse, and blood pressure are elevated." The fingertip caps shine brightly, and warmth saturates each of Ava's fingers, the red blood within her fingers glowing through her skin. Julian says, "Red blood cell count is down a bit, but white blood cells are normal. Megaloblastic cells. Have you ever had any problems with anemia?"

"No."

Across from her, Hitoshi awakens. He swings out of bed and walks over to her. "What's going on?"

"Not feeling so hot," Ava says. "How are you doing?"

"Stayed up too late, a bit run down. Okay, I guess."

"I'd like to get a physical blood sample," Julian says. "Ready?"

"Go ahead," Ava says.

A blade snicks under her right index finger and she resists the urge to pull her hand out. Her finger is warm and wet before an aerosol mists, the wound's throbbing subsiding. Underneath the scanner, servos whirl as the blood vial is processed.

"Thought we couldn't get sick," Hitoshi says.

Julian taps on the wall panel. "White blood cells are normal. If it is a pathogen, there is no immune response. Analyzing the sample. It'll just be a minute."

Ava removes her hand from the scanner and waits.

Julian's display chimes and he sends the results to Ava's

screen. A complete blood analysis scrolls down. From her biology training, she can read it as well as Julian. "I am anemic," she says.

"Vitamin B12 deficiency," Julian says. "Intrinsic factor is normal, as is serum iron. You're eating the same diet as the rest of us, so some mechanism is interfering with the absorption of cobalamin into your bloodstream. I'd like to get a full-body scan. In the meantime, I will synthesize a B12 booster for you." Julian looks over at Hitoshi. "I'd like to get a palm scan and blood sample from you, as well, my friend."

Hitoshi frowns. "Peachy." Ava stands, and he takes her place. When the blade pricks his finger, he winces. "Dude, it's almost the twenty-second century. We should be, like, teleporting blood out of me by now."

"My apologies," Julian says. "Slight elevation to your vitals and a mild increase in megaloblasts. I will also give you the supplement." He reads Hitoshi's worried look and adds, "There's no evidence of pathogens in your blood."

Ava sets her hand on Hitoshi's shoulder. "Doc will make us right as rain. We're going to be okay."

THE ENVIRO SUIT is a bit like a fluorescent-orange scuba skinsuit with a neck-mount for a helmet. Ava's removed all of her clothes in the washroom and has slipped into the suit. Her bare back is exposed, and she'll need Hitoshi to seal the connections when she goes out, leaving her feeling a bit naked. She emerges from the room holding the top of the suit closed and turns her back to Hitoshi. At first, Hitoshi's hands on her back feel like a bit of intimacy, but there's something reassuring about the connection. In a minute the suit is sealed, and she turns.

Hitoshi lifts the helmet and hands it to her. It's light and clear like a fishbowl. She clicks it into place, and the internal life-support system activates. "Here goes," she says, opening the inner airlock door. As the doors seals, he gives her a smile and a thumbs up. The airlock sterilization procedure runs before the exterior door opens.

"Hey, doc," she says to Julian. "All of this isn't helping me think that I don't have the plague."

"It is quite a bit for a vitamin deficiency, I admit. If you'll please lie on the table over here."

The table is white and shaped like a human outline. Ava swings her legs up. After a moment she lies down with her arms at her sides, glancing at the sickbay entrance. The door is closed. "No James?"

Julian moves to the controls and initializes the process. "He asked to be here when I gave him the update, but I kicked him out. Sickbay is sealed so you can have some privacy."

"Oh, okay."

"Try to remain still. There will be several passes over ten minutes."

A blue light projects a thick line below her feet, wrapping around her contours as it moves up her body. She closes her eyes and imagines herself sitting on the deck of her sister's house, watching her niece play in the yard. The sun is warm, with the scent of fresh-cut grass in the air. She drifts in and out of sleep. Ten minutes feels like hours.

"We're done," Julian says.

She steps off the bed and crosses over to him. Six screens display different aspects of her. The first has an Ava-shaped volume composed entirely of blood vessels. The second, nerves. Third, muscular-skeletal. Fourth and fifth, organs. The last is filled with summaries. It's fascinating and unnerving to see herself reduced into constituent parts.

"There's some nerve and neurological impairment," Julian says. "Your body is deficient in cobalt. This is somewhat expected with a B12 deficiency, but your numbers are low, even for cobalt stored in your liver. It is also unusually low for molybdenum."

Ava digests that a moment. "No pathogens or toxins?"

"No, none at the micrometer scale. I do want to take a few more blood and tissue samples for atomic imaging."

"Okay. Can you do anything for it?"

"Supplements should improve your symptoms. I'll continue to test until I find the cause. Now, let me take a few samples, and we'll see how Hitoshi looks."

ONCE SICKBAY IS RE-OPENED, a steady stream of crew members come to visit. Hitoshi and Ava downplay their situation and encourage everyone to keep working on the mission.

"Hey, boss," Hitoshi says to James. "Hell of a space adventure, huh?"

James musters his best grin. "Always." But, behind the confidence, Hitoshi reads his worry. "Julian's the best," James continues. "He'll sort it out."

When Ananke visits, it's by appearing on Hitoshi's screen inside of the quarantine area. "Do you mind if I hang out with you? It's not like I can catch a cold."

"You bet," Hitoshi replies. "Ava's resting, but I'm going a little stir crazy and could use some work. Want to help?"

Ananke's screen pulses blue. "Of course."

Hitoshi sits at his workstation and opens a window to the planetary science lab. Isaac is there, looking at a computer diagram of stratum. He glances up. "Oh. Hi, Hitoshi. How do you—"

Hitoshi holds up his hand. "Don't. Everyone's asking me how I feel. Going a little nuts. What are you working on there?"

Isaac points at the screen. "This? Very interesting. Soil sample from the green leaf basin. Content is high for metamorphic rock. You know what tektites are?"

"Nerds?"

"Glasses produced during meteor impacts. Imagine a spray of molten silica which rains down as glass droplets. Found them in the soil samples."

Ananke says, "Do you think the basin was the site of a meteor strike?"

"Possible the basin is an eroded crater. Unusual though. No siderophile elements. Meteors usually smash many rare metals into their craters."

"Well, it's actually what I was calling about. Since Ava and I were exposed to something in the basin, I wanted to check all of the basin samples."

Isaac thinks. "We already analyzed the green leaf samples. Other than the soil samples, the only other thing is the titanium oxidation you collected."

Hitoshi snaps his fingers. "Right. Completely forgot about that."

"I'll load it in the imager."

Behind Isaac, a white robot arm grabs the sample and sets it into a compartment in the quarantine area. The microscope indexes and the metal's surface appears. With all of its pits and craters, it looks like the moon.

"Definitely corroded," Isaac says.

Hitoshi scratches his head. "That's odd. It's like it lost its corrosion resistance. Let's get it into the spectrometer."

The robot swings the sample into a different machine. After a moment, a chart appears with peaks, valleys, and atomic element percentages.

Hitoshi says. "Well, that's not right. It's almost pure titanium. Should be mixed with palladium, chromium, molybdenum, vanadium...look at it. It's got the right percentage of aluminum and zirconium, but it's missing everything else."

"It's an alloy, right?" Isaac says. "How do you extract those without melting it?"

"Isaac," Ananke says. "Will you please put the sample in the atomic imager?"

"Sure thing." The robot arm moves the sample to the next machine. They wait patiently for it to complete its five-minute scan. At the nanometer-level, the titanium is a wispy, organic filament with voids left where the missing elements should be. What's more alarming is the mite-like tuning-fork shaped structure with spindly legs crawling on the surface of the metal.

Hitoshi covers his mouth with his hand, feeling sick. "Oh, God. Isaac, tag and identify constituent atoms."

The tuning-fork color-codes itself into individual elements. Silicon, carbon, hydrogen, oxygen, gold, platinum, and iridium. The front of the fork has a pincer holding a cluster of palladium atoms.

"Julian!" Hitoshi calls over his shoulder. "We have a problem."

WITH EVERYONE ASSEMBLED IN SICKBAY, it feels crowded. The main display screens show Hitoshi's titanium sample and Julian's atomic imaging. A host of different foreign shapes appear in each — tuning-forks, plus-signs, donuts, and triangles.

"Bionems," Hitoshi says from inside the quarantine room. "Much smaller than our nanobots. We're guessing at function based on structural appearance, but some, like the tuning-forks, are probably gatherers and collect specific elements. Some are transporters, and others are replicators."

Julian adds, "The gatherers are stripping cobalt and molybdenum from Ava and Hitoshi."

"Same with the titanium sample from the original parachute probe," Hitoshi says.

James's arms are crossed. "You find it in any of the air samples?"

Isaac shakes his head. "No. Just the green leaf, which had replicators."

"We didn't see them the first time," Ava says, "but they're very small and it's like a needle in a haystack."

"You two were exposed due to the suit breaches?" James says.

"Right," Hitoshi says. "But it gets worse." He taps his console, and a video feed of *Promise's* EV prep room appears. A dozen EV suits are staged along the walls like knight's armor. "Anyone who went to the green field got exposed and brought them back on their EV suits." Hitoshi zooms in on James's suit. The surface has a dull, iridescent film. "Looks like they've been stripping elements from those suits." He taps a few close-ups of EV prep's walls and surfaces. A matte fractal pattern branches out like cancer.

James's mouth opens. "Son of a bitch." He shifts. "The sterilization sequence didn't kill them?"

"That's right."

"And anyone who was in the airlock without an EV suit could have breathed in a mouthful?"

"Which was everyone, since that's where we take off our suits."

James takes a deep breath.

Julian says, "I'll need blood samples and full-body scans of the entire crew."

"Any ideas on how to shut them down?" James says.

Ava has her hand on her hip. "It's a long shot, but we can dose the EV prep area in continuous UV."

James nods. "Any ideas for the ones inside us?"

"We do have our own medical nanobots," Julian says, "and we may be able to target them."

Hitoshi adds, "Not sure how the bionems make their decisions. If they're directed, we might be able to disrupt their communications or issue new orders."

Beckman crosses his arms. "What about disrupting it at the source? We could raze the entire field with *Promise's* lasers."

James shakes his head. "No. We have no evidence that would do anything other than killing the life we came to discover. It tried to make contact last night. We can continue the communication path. Other ideas?"

Beckman says, "Deploy a drone and get eyes on that field."

James nods. "Agreed. Alright, let's sort out the bloodwork and scan schedule. Ananke and Hitoshi are working the bionems options. Beckman's got the monitoring plan for the field. Willow and Ava will talk communications. I'll run a ship's assessment with Isaac to make sure we don't have anything other than the airlock infected. Sound like a plan?"

Everyone nods.

"Okay, Julian. You're up."

BECKMAN'S DRONE skims over scattered cliff rock and emerges in the basin. Up ahead, the red and white radial pattern of *Promise's* first parachute probe's footprint is incongruous versus the landscape. When the drone magnifies it, sunlight is visible through breaches and gaps, as if something has been digesting the probe. The drone streaks ahead towards the green field, rising in altitude until it is one kilometer above the surface. From this height, the area reminds Beckman a bit of a mandala, symmetric designs repeating in an overall circular structure. The periphery is green, followed by the increasing blues of the ribbon plants, and finally congealing into the red spherical masses at the center. When the drone tags the ribbon plants, it counts hundreds of them. Some are a ribbon structure, while others are sealed spheres. The entrance to the leafy-green field still has a disturbed area where Hitoshi and James both shot and cut several of the leaves. If the field can repair any of them using the bionem replicators, it hasn't put any effort towards it.

Beckman sets the drone into hover mode and leaves it livestreaming everything it sees from its perch in the sky.

BY THE TIME everyone is tested, scanned, and analyzed, it's four p.m. Julian stands in front of the media screen with the crew gathered around. A dozen different images of tuning-fork-shaped bionems span the screen.

"Everyone has bionems in their blood," Julian says. "It's impossible to determine concentrations, but there's a slight decrease in chromium and molybdenum in James, Beckman, and Willow, with James having the largest decrease."

James has his arms crossed. "Makes sense. My suit would've been covered with them from the field. Beckman and Willow helped Ava out of her suit. Supplements will help?"

"They should, as long as we replace the metals faster than they are stripped."

Ava nods from inside the quarantine room. "I'm feeling a bit better."

Julian motions towards Ava. "Quarantine was twenty-four hours. No signs of pathogens or infection, other than the bionems. I recommend ending quarantine since we all have the same thing. I am certain you'll feel better sleeping in your own quarters, and it'll be easier for you to work with the rest of the crew on a solution."

James glances Ava, and she raises her eyebrows, nodding. When Julian looks at James, waiting, James says, "Agreed."

Hitoshi releases an audible sigh. "Oh, thank God. Get me out of here."

Julian taps a few commands on his slate and the quarantine vestibule doors open. Ava tentatively steps outside, followed by

Hitoshi. They both look like they've just crossed a do-not-enter sign.

"I'll feel like a new man after a hot shower," Hitoshi says. "But it can wait. Any updates?"

James says, "Ship's systems are normal. No visible damage except for the airlock suits and walls. Running a repair drone over the exterior hull now, looking for bugs. Beckman's still watching the field."

Beckman tilts his head. "No activity, but the purple plants are all wrapped up. Isaac's telling me a storm's coming, so I might need to dock the drone."

On cue, Isaac lifts his slate and sends the image to the media screen. The video is from one of the six satellites they deployed before breaking orbit. Astris is a sandy brown mixed with rust. West of their landing site, the sea reflects gold sunlight. From the east, a tumultuous cinnamon cloud spreads in a front, obscuring hundreds of kilometers of landscape. "Dust storm," Isaac says, "similar to Mars. Wind gusts up to fifty kph. Should reach us in three hours."

"Any concerns for the ship?" James says.

Hitoshi shakes his head. "A little dust and wind won't hurt *Promise*. I don't think we should launch while we're still inspecting for hull damage."

"I'll leave out the drone as long as I can," Beckman says. "Bring it in right before the storm hits. I'll keep watch tonight."

"Then I'm with you," James says. He looks over to Willow. "Any news on communications?"

Willow has her hand on her hip. "The Eye broadcast full spectrum with a strong magnetic field. Hitoshi's got a theory that the EM pulse was for the bionems, that it flips switches in their programming."

Hitoshi shrugs. "I totally made that up, but it's the best idea I've got. It's not like they can build an atomic-scale transmitter. It's got to be simple and play by the rules." He points to Julian's tuning-fork bloodstream images. "We've got guinea pigs. I can hit them with different EM pulses and see if they go bonkers."

"Let 'em have it," James says.

Willow adds, "The rest of the Eye's pulse had a definite structure. We've got it recorded, so, if we want to try mirroring it back to them, we can."

"Let's have it ready if another Eye visits."

"Will do."

Julian says, "Haven't had time to work on a medical nanobot strategy. It'll be a challenge. I'll start working on it after I get everyone's supplements started."

"I'll help," Ananke says.

Julian nods. "Thanks."

"Alright," James says. "Julian, I'll give you a hand with supplements. Let's all reconnect at dinner."

JAMES AND BECKMAN are on the bridge while the crew has dinner. The winds have picked up, and the gusts buffet the outer hull with continuous white noise. Dust pings across the roof like sleet. From the main display, Astris's sunset is a sight to behold. Where the west sky is a muted turquoise, the east is a blood-red inferno, as if a forest fire had been lit and filled the air with dark cinders. Visibility is down to one kilometer.

"Coming over the cliff now," Beckman says.

It's hard to see at first, but the forward floods of Beckman's drone are a luminous smudge. The drone bounces with turbulence as it skims over the rock.

James motions to the feed. "Choppier than forecasted."

"Wind is fine, but the gusts are tough. Coming up on the bay now."

In the drone's video feed, *Promise* is a dark silhouette against the turquoise twilight, each of its exterior lights an oasis. A neon-blue rectangle delineates the bay entrance. The drone's lights sweep across the walls as it slips back into the ship.

"Docked up. Closing bay doors," Beckman says.

Coms chirps and a video of Hitoshi pops up. Behind him, Ava, Isaac, and Willow are eating in the galley. "Hey, boss," Hitoshi says. "Want me to run something up for you two? Looks like the monte cristo is pretty popular tonight. Cup of joe?" He glances at Beckman. "Some kind of floral tea?"

"Thanks, Hitoshi," James says. "We're just wrapping up. Should be down in a bit."

"I'll put a pot on for you," Hitoshi says before the video closes.

James looks at Beckman. "You going to go active with the sensor sweeps?"

Beckman shakes his head. "We use active radar, and it puts a big flashing arrow over us all the way out into space. Still, don't know if any of our Boomerang friends are hanging around. Rather stay passive as much as we can." He motions to the screen. "Plus the dust storm will scatter everything."

"Best guess on time to finish the hull inspections?"

"Once I can launch the repair drone, maybe two hours."

"Alright." He motions over his shoulder. "You going to get some dinner?"

"Staying here."

James waves a hand. "Nah, get out of here. I got it." He points his thumb back towards the bridge exit. "Will you grab me a sandwich when you come back?"

Beckman gives James a slight nod. The man will stay at his post unless ordered to get some chow, so James waits. Beckman straightens his posture in the way that a military man does when receiving an order. "You got it," Beckman says. "See you in a bit."

James watches Beckman depart the bridge, then returns to inspecting the murky dust storm. Trying to focus on the video is a bit like watching static.

The central console pings and illuminates blue. From the screen, Ananke says, "Hello, James."

"Hey, Ananke. Come to watch the storm?"

"And to keep you company. I feel like I get to hang out with everyone but you."

James smiles. "Well, we've got to fix that. Pop in anytime. You make any progress on the nanobots?"

"Julian and I programmed one to go after a bionem gatherer. Unfortunately, the gatherer latched onto it and immediately began stripping platinum atoms, which disabled Julian's bot. We're still working on it."

"Little guys are causing big problems."

"Indeed."

James motions towards the display. "This dust storm reminds me of Will's Baku stories. He said it was like someone painted the city yellow."

"You miss him?"

"Wouldn't mind sitting down and having a beer with him right about now."

A moment of silence passes, Ananke's screen swirling blue while James stares at the bridge display. He squints, leaning forward. In the red murk, a faint glow is a trick of the eye, vanishing and reappearing. "You see that?"

"I do," Ananke says. "It's warm. Getting scattered EM."

James activates tactical, and a targeting reticule locks onto it. The reticule spins a second, then breaks. "Interference." He opens coms. "Beckman, we've got a contact here."

Beckman responds via audio. "On my way."

James taps the ship intercom. "Crew to stations."

As the glow solidifies, the targeting reticule locks onto it. Distance, half-a-kilometer. Intercept, fifteen seconds.

"I think it's an Eye," Ananke says.

As it flies nearer, the gold casts a cone in front of it, glistening in the flying sand like a swarm of bugs. Metallic reflections hint at the metal feathers framing its central sphere. An iris pattern glows within the sphere. The Eye arrives at *Promise's* starboard side and hovers ten meters from the ship, seemingly unaffected by the wind.

Beckman comes jogging onto the bridge with the entire crew in tow. Everyone assumes his station.

The Eye swings its light along the hull, darting from location to location.

"The contact protocol," James says.

Willow taps her console. "Loaded and ready."

"Transmit."

Promise broadcasts a recording of the Eye's original signal on all frequencies.

The Eye stops its inspection and pulses.

"C'mon," James says. "Let's talk."

The Eye flares bright, strobing back, and a wave of excitement overtakes the bridge.

Far beyond the Eye, near the cliff edge, dozens of red crescents flicker like animal eyes reflecting light at night. James's pulse elevates.

"Contacts. Configuration unknown," Isaac says. "Moving towards us. Twenty meters per second."

"James—" Beckman starts, but James is on the same wavelength and speaks nearly simultaneously.

"Charge the lasers," James says. "Willow, try the nav light sequence again. Seemed to work last time."

As the red crescents close to within one hundred meters, they catch dark glimpses on the magnified display. Each is an upside-down t-shape, like a metal shark fin intersecting a curved blade. A glowing red arc shimmers across the blade.

"They're hot," Isaac says. "Two-ten Celsius."

Willow glances at her display. "No response from the nav—"

The nearest Blade strobes and a red beam ablates the intervening sand between it and *Promise*. A blast along the starboard engine rumbles the ship. Two more Blades sear beams into the engine before all join in firing.

James grabs his armrest. "Return fire."

Promise's lasers illuminate the landscape in eerie green. As the beams sweep across the Blades, each explodes in a burst of molten slag.

The Eye turns towards the starboard laser emitter and simmers radiant gold. Damage icons flash on the bridge from the laser emitter, and it goes dark. Beckman retargets the aft emitter and dazzling green halos around the Eye when the beam bursts it. Beckman continues firing, the remaining Blades burning like insects in a flame. "We lost the starboard emitter. Multiple hits on the nacelle armor. Doesn't look like any engine damage."

At the cliff periphery, three new gold smudges appear.

James doesn't need to process what he's seeing. "Everyone buckle. We're getting out of here." He powers up the RF engines. "Beckman, weapons free."

As the engines hum up to speed, the aft laser carves through an Eye.

"Hold on," James says. *Promise* pushes off the rock with a burst of thrusters. As it does, the swarm engages it, red beams stinging like bees.

"They're coordinating fire," Beckman says, "breaking through armor."

Promise tilts forward and accelerates north towards the sea, blasts peppering the ship. *Promise's* green laser slices through the sandstorm and dances among targets. Something explodes from the starboard side of the ship and damage icons stack up on the screen. Everyone leans as *Promise* lists to the starboard.

"Fire in engine three," Hitoshi says. "Losing power."

James slows their rate of climb and balances the thrust. Around him, everyone shifts back to the center of his seat. When he looks left, the shore stretches out into gently sloping land for kilometers. He turns *Promise* left.

The tactical display has dozens of targets, and Beckman can't move his hands fast enough. He's prioritizing the Eyes, his beam surging in surgical bursts.

"Going evasive," James says.

Red beams strike the aft emitter, and Beckman's control goes dark. "We just lost the aft laser."

Something cracks in engine three and the acceleration pressing against James's back eases. The ship slows as if clearing the top of a roller coaster. *Promise's* systems' diagram pops up with both starboard engines blinking red.

Hitoshi says, "Losing engine four. Sixty percent power. Fifty percent." On the forward screen, the twilight horizon line slowly rises. The weightless feeling passes as they start to fall. Hitoshi continues. "Twenty percent. Engine two is down." He looks over at James. "Only engine one left. I can redline it a bit. Best I can give you is point seven gee. Not enough to keep us up."

James snaps his head, evaluating the landscape. He taps something quickly on his keypad. "Beckman, ready on the port laser. I'm bringing her around. You've got about twenty seconds. Make 'em count."

"Roger that," Beckman says.

James initiates the turn, and the horizon tilts right forty-five degrees. As the port side of the ship swings into the arc of the swarm, Beckman's laser fires, searing Blades and Eyes. *Promise* completes its turn and flies head-on into the swarm.

"Brace!" James says.

Some of the swarm veers out of the way, but most smash and crumbles off the ship's hull.

James turns *Promise* sharply to the right. The sand rushes in a streak towards the screen's bottom. "Brace for retros." *Promise's* chemical thrusters fire and the ship brakes, arresting its fall. The nose tilts up as James uses the aerodynamic nacelles to flare the ship, then *Promise* impacts the sand on its belly, sending everyone forward into their restraints. *Promise* groans as it slides to a stop on the beach. James shuts down the remaining engine. "Everyone okay?"

A stunned nod from the crew.

Beckman's tactical display still has a dozen targets. "They're approaching from the starboard, out of the port firing arc. Little buggers learn fast."

James hops out of his seat. "Isaac, take tactical. Hitoshi, see what you can do for *Promise*. Beckman, Julian, with me." He double-times it off the bridge.

Beckman runs alongside him. "We doing what I think we're doing?"

"Not enough time for armor." He hits the emergency button on the wall, and a hatch slides open, revealing six emergency full-face breathers. He grabs one and slips it over his head. "We'll grab pulse rifles in EV prep."

Beckman smiles slightly as he grabs his mask, Julian mirroring him. The three run to EV prep, sealing the door behind them. Beckman opens the armory and hands each of them a pulse rifle. Outside, the sand skitters across the hull.

"James," Isaac says over the room's speakers, "twelve targets approaching from the west, altitude ten meters."

"Beckman, call the play."

Beckman points. "Julian, left doorway, cover fire. I'll advance to the nacelle strut. James, right doorway and advance behind me to the t-junction once I'm in place."

"Got it," James says. "Let's go."

They rush the door, and James mashes the button. Hot air and sand blast in and everyone retreats a bit under the skittering rock. Visibility is poor. Julian angles his rifle high with most of his body tucked behind the doorframe. Beckman looks left and right, then charges forward to the massive white shape of the *Promise's* starboard nacelle. Flames roll off parts of it, and sparks sputter and pop into the darkness.

The first red glow of the Blades appear in the sky. Julian

squeezes his trigger. Pop. Pop. Pop Blue bolts spray high as his rifle's muzzle flash strobes the entryway. The Blade tumbles down bleeding fire.

Beckman turns, aims, and fires a burst. "Go, go!"

James charges across the sand as blue pulse fire flashes and red beams flicker. Sweltering wind gusts sting him with sand. As he arrives at the nacelle's t-junction, a red beam carves into the engine, sending sparks which rain down upon him and burn his arms. He pops up and props his rifle on the strut. Pop. Pop. Pop. Pop. He turns forty-five degrees, sights another, and fires. Crimson flashes uncomfortably close behind him. When he turns, Julian has ducked inside the airlock entrance, firelight flickering from the beam's impact. James swings his rifle in an arc across the sky and peers through its scope. A red targeting arrow leads his aim up and to the right. As the Blade swings into his scope's display, the hit percentage spins up to ninety-percent. James squeezes the trigger, and the Blade explodes in blue flames.

To his left, Beckman fires a three-round burst, adjusts, and fires again. He ducks down as a beam impacts the strut nearest him, and Julian fires on the aggressor. James spots another drone arcing towards the airlock and downs it.

As Beckman pops up and shoots, a red beam flickers, cutting through the strut and striking him in the upper body. Sparks flash from the wound as Beckman yells and falls.

James sights its source, turns, and fires on full auto. The first few rounds sheer the fin and send the Blade tumbling. James leads the rounds down across the falling Blade and it fractures. As Julian fires off a four-round burst, James runs to Beckman, crouches and pulls him behind the nacelle's cover. Flames burn in a line along Beckman's blackened flight suit, and James pats them out.

Julian shoots another Blade as James slides into Beckman's spot. The scope's arrow leads him to his next target and he puts three rounds into it. As it falls, there is nothing but the howling wind and crackling flames of Promise's nacelle. Both Julian and James scan the sky with their scopes. The wind gusts and sand scratches their faceplates. No more red targeting arrows appear.

"Beckman," James says, not taking this eyes off the sky.

Beckman groans.

"Think you can walk?"

James glances down. Beckman's eyes roll back.

"Dammit. Julian, cover me. I'm bringing him in."

Julian yells, "Ready."

James stows his rifle over his shoulder and scoops Beckman into a fireman's carry. Quickly he lumbers towards the airlock where Julian is poised with his rifle. Once he's all the way into EV prep, he sets Beckman down and runs back to the airlock door, unslinging his gun. "I'll take point. Get back there, seal the door, and see what you can do for him."

Julian nods, setting his hand on James's shoulder, then he's closing the EV prep door and sealing James off to the outside.

James leans against the doorframe, peers into his rifle's scope and scans the sky for threats.

14

TRIAGE

Julian grabs the emergency medical kit from EV prep and kneels beside Beckman. He clips a transducer onto Beckman's index finger and adheres a second one above the rim of his full-face breather, holding a hockey-puck-sized disk to Beckman's chest as he plugs in an earpiece. After listening to his breathing and pulse in several locations, he stows it, increases the oxygen content of Beckman's mask, and examines the wound. The Blade's beam cut a twenty-centimeter slash starting at Beckman's left upper chest and ending at his clavicle, leaving a teardrop burn pattern. When Julian passes the hand-held imager over it, the wound is deep, with an exit wound on Beckman's back where the teardrop is widest. He sets the imager down and cuts open the top of Beckman's tee-shirt, then sprays something which looks like shaving gel into the wound. It expands rapidly and congeals. He taps the controls on Beckman's mask and opaques his face shield, doing the same with his own.

"Computer, run sterilization sequence," Julian says. As it's running, he adds, "Willow and Ava, bring the stretcher from sickbay and report immediately to EV prep."

Willow responds. "On our way."

The sterilization completes, and he clears their visors. He selects an intravenous armband from the medkit and wraps it around Beckman's forearm. As it starts dispensing fluids, he sets three dermals on his wrist. "Computer, open inner EV prep door."

The door spills light from *Promise's* main hallway. Running footsteps approach. In a moment, Willow and Ava arrive carrying an orange stretcher. Both look terribly worried.

"Oh, Beckman," Ava says.

Julian motions beside him. "Set it next to him." He points to Beckman's feet. "Lift and slide on three. One, two, three, lift."

They smoothly slide Beckman onto the stretcher and Julian secures it, setting his slate onto the docking station. He grabs the headboard handles and indicates for Willow and Ava each to grab a footboard handle.

"Direct to sickbay," Julian says. "To the imager table. I'm going to need both of your help. You have basic medical training, correct?"

Ava's having trouble speaking as she hefts the stretcher backwards. "Yes."

"We need to repair the vascular damage quickly. There is not much bleeding due to cauterization, but the blood flow is interrupted. Air is entering his chest cavity and putting pressure on his left lung, which must be addressed."

They round the corner, cutting in front of the bridge entrance as they turn towards sickbay. Isaac sits alone at tactical and watches them over his shoulder.

Julian glances down at Beckman. His eyes are closed, and his skin is white and clammy. The vitals on the slate indicates he's in shock. Sickbay's entrance approaches. "Quickly, after we set him down, sanitize your hands, and put on the surgical masks. We will operate immediately."

HITOSHI SLIPS into the silver fireproof suit, pulls down the face mask, and puts his arms through the backpack's straps. He grabs the aerogel launcher and stows it in the backpack, then runs heavily to engine three's access strut. When he opens the door, smoke pours out, the strut's wall lights flashing urgent red. He darts down the long hall until he reaches the nacelle hatch, pries it open, and enters.

Even with the fireproof suit, the heat of the inferno blasts him immediately. Ten meters ahead, flames roll along the nacelle's roof and wreath around the RF chamber. Metal glows orange and pulses like embers. Wind gusts in through the outer skin's breaches and skitters sparking sand off his face shield. He staggers, adjusting his suit.

"Ho, boy," Hitoshi says. He unslings the launcher, holds it like a shotgun, flicks the safety and surveys the fire. Radiant heat toasts his cheeks. "Okay, remember the training. Base of fire, brace for recoil, squeeze." He checks his footing, pauses, and pulls the trigger.

The aerogel launches like a beanbag and impacts one of the blaze's most intense points. The gel pod immediately breaches and expands into a glittery cloud which fills half the nacelle. Hitoshi launches another to its right and left. The gel stretches like cobwebs, melting in the heat and rapidly cooling. The largest flames sputter and shrink. Soon the roof's fire dies, leaving blackened metal.

Hitoshi stows the launcher and advances, pulling out the extinguisher. When he's within a few meters, he depresses the trigger and it spews foam in long lines. Soon the area in front of him is a slippery mess. Further down the nacelle, another patch pulses. Hitoshi glances left through the wall breach. Orange sand blasts by from the exposed atmosphere. He adjusts his face mask again and advances forward towards the next burning section.

KEEPING HIS RIFLE POINTED UP, James reaches with his left hand and taps the airlock com panel. "Isaac, how's it look?"

Isaac's voice comes from the speaker. "No contacts. All clear."

"Okay. Stay at tactical. Call me if the situation changes. Fire on anything that approaches."

"Understood."

James switches the channel to ship's intercom. "Julian, James. How's Beckman?"

There's an uncomfortably long moment of silence before Julian responds. "In surgery. Cannot talk now. Willow and Ava are assisting. Will update you when done. Julian out."

James processes that a moment. "Hitoshi, Ananke, status?"

"Hey, boss," Hitoshi says over coms, wind sounds rustling on the channel. "I'm in the aft section of engine three putting out fires. It's...uh...don't know what to say. It's a mess. Ananke's in engine four's nacelle checking out the damage."

Ananke says, "Fire suppression contained the engine four fire, and there are no active flames. Moderate damage to the RF modulator, chamber amplifier, and lateral chemical thrusters. The fire appears to have originated from a breach in one of the thrusters."

"Alright, it's clear out here for now, and I'm coming in. I'll suit up and join you in number three."

"No," Hitoshi says. "I've got it under control, but I could use your help with the laser emitters. Grab a pair of augmented goggles and tag everything that's damaged. We should prioritize getting weapons back online."

"Got it." James closes coms, seals the airlock, and runs through the sterilization routine in EV prep. When the door opens, he wants to run to sickbay and see Beckman, but Julian was clear. Instead, he turns and runs in a full sprint down *Promise's* corridors towards the engineering section.

THREE HOURS AFTER THE ATTACK, James stands in sickbay beside Julian. Beckman rests in bed with supplemental oxygen beneath his nose, his left arm draped across his chest and secured to his side. Through the top of the gown, a clear patch is visible, congealed over his skin, making it look like he's been glued back together. Medical telemetry spirals along the displays over the bed.

"I need to keep him sedated for the next few days," Julian says. "Two of his ribs and his scapula were cut by the laser. The lattice needs time to form for the bone to regrow. I've repaired the blood vessels, and he'll maintain arm function once the nerves bridge. He lost a small amount of lung tissue, but he's fortunate. A few centimeters to the right and he would not have survived."

James furrows his brows. "He's stable?"

"Yes."

"Can the crew visit?"

"One at a time."

James holds his hand over his mouth, rubbing it. He crosses over to the bed and sets his hand on the top of Beckman's. "You did good, big guy. Kept us safe." He squeezes his hand. "Mend up. Doc will take good care of you."

Beckman's chest rises and falls rhythmically.

"He's stable here and will recover, but he needs specialized treatment I cannot provide if he is to avoid disability."

"Understood."

Julian adds, "Willow and Ava assisted with the surgery. They did a very good job."

James glances back, nodding. "I need to get to the bridge for the update. Are you staying here?"

"Yes. I will listen over coms."

James crosses to Julian and clasps him on the shoulder. "Good work here." He motions towards the starboard with his eyes. "And out there."

Julian smiles slightly, and James exits, walking quickly to the bridge. When he enters, everyone stands before their console. Hitoshi wears a zip-up clean suit over his flight suit, which, despite the name, is filthy. His face mask dangles from his neck by its straps. Ananke is in her drone next to him, also marred by soot. Willow and Ava both wear different clothes than before, changed after surgery, and only Isaac looks the same.

"Beckman's stable," James says, walking to face the group. "But he'll be out for a few days." After a pause, he says. "Let's start with the damage assessment."

Hitoshi touches his console, and a ship schematic appears on the bridge screen. "Three out of four engines are inoperative. Engine three is toast. Looks like an arc blast started in the chamber amplification unit and set off a fuel cell chain reaction. Engine four is in better shape with damage to the RF modulator, chamber amplifier, and lateral chemical thrusters. Remember two is dead from the Boomerang attack, but engine one is fine."

"Can you print replacement parts?"

Hitoshi shakes his head. "Just the thrusters and some of the smaller stuff. But, here's the deal, we only need to get one engine working to make orbit. So, I can mix-and-match parts from the three broken engines to make one working drive. Print up polymer hull plates. Wheel out Betty II to do the heavy lifting. Two to three days."

"Alright," James says. "That's good news. How about weapons?"

"We have spares or can print most of the things you tagged. With two people helping, I could get the aft emitter working by morning, starboard by dinner."

"Great. You've got me. Isaac, you in?"

Isaac nods. "Yeah."

"Anything on orbitals?"

"Storm's still obscuring the area," Isaac says. "But every thirty minutes we get another look. Passives are still clear."

James looks down, then back up to the waiting crew.

"Alright, we got our nose bloodied, but we're still on our feet. Three days of elbow grease then we go spaceside and sort things out. Priorities. Maintain watch, fix weapons, restore engine four, disable bionems. Two teams. Isaac, me, and Hitoshi are fixers. Willow, Ava, Julian, Ananke on bionem and tactical watch. We can't stay up for three days so work out a schedule with your team rotating a member to sleep in four-hour blocks. I'm issuing sidearms to everyone and staging rifles and breathers in EV prep. If we need to fight off more, we'll do what we have to. We slagged dozens of them. Hopefully, they're licking their wounds and thinking twice about their next moves."

Willow shifts her weight. "What should we do if an Eye returns?"

"Unless it's waving a white flag, light it up. Call crew to stations."

"Okay."

James pans his gaze across the crew. Everyone looks tired and a bit scared, but he's confident in them. "We've been in tighter pinches. Plan's sound, we've got our tasks. Let's get to it."

WILLOW AND AVA sit in the Planetary Science lab opposite the quarantine area. Julian's taking his turn sleeping, but he deposited the bionem blood samples before leaving. One of the samples rests in the atomic imager. Sitting beside the imager is Hitoshi's gizmo, a gold parabolic dish attached to several ceramic blocks connecting to a portable computer display. Hitoshi's been using it to blast the bionems with various EM waves. When asked where he got it from, he simply said, "*Promise* has a lot of communications arrays. It'll be fine without one."

To their right, Ananke's screen pulses from the nearest display. One of the perks of having her in their group is that she never sleeps and can monitor tactical remotely while working on something else.

"The Eye's transmission," Willow begins, "was mainly radio with microwave and x-ray peaks."

"None of those frequencies can penetrate *Promise's* hull," Ananke says.

"Maybe it wasn't trying to communicate with the bionems inside *Promise*. They may already have their instructions."

Ananke ripples green. "That's certainly possible."

"Okay," Ava says. "Let's start with what we have. They're either hardcoded for one task and always on, or there's a way to change their function or state. Let's assume they can be activated. How could radio, microwave, or x-ray flip a switch on the bionem?"

Ananke contemplates her question. "X-rays can ionize atoms, causing a net charge which could affect nano-scale circuits. Microwaves can induce currents in conductors and rotation in polar molecules. Radiofrequency radiation has similar effects to microwave, but on a reduced scale."

"Okay," Ava says. "What conductors are in the bionems?"

"The conductors in the bionems are gold, platinum, and iridium."

Willow writes some notes on her slate. "What about polar molecules?"

Ananke's screen undulates green. "The only polar molecule in the bionem sample is silicon dioxide, which is structured as a silica xerogel."

"Interesting," Ava says. "That's a desiccant, the same stuff that's in those little 'silica gel - do not eat' packets you get when you buy things."

"That's correct," Ananke says.

Willow finishes her note. "Why are polar molecules affected?"

"Polar molecules try to align themselves with an electric field. As the field oscillates, they flip back and forth. It's how microwaves heat up food."

"Then let's start with the microwave part of the Eye's transmission and see if we get a response in our sample. We can watch the silica parts in the imager."

"Agreed," Ananke says. "Uploading the signal now."

IT'S JUST after lunchtime and James is on the bridge holding a silver coffee mug in one hand adorned with the Hayden-Pratt logo. The bridge screen is a mosaic of camera views. In the first, a compact treaded construction vehicle with a spider-like assortment of arms diligently cuts hull plates on Promise's starboard nacelle. Red script letters printed on the vehicle's front read *Betty II*. Underneath the text is a picture of a woman drawn like nose art on an old World War Two bomber. Unlike its wartime counterpart, the picture isn't drawn as a pin-up. It's a smiling female pilot in a mid-twentieth-century flight suit wearing an aviator's cap and goggles. Betty Gillies, pioneering American aviator. James's idea. Much better than Hitoshi's original suggestions. Three of Beckman's repair drones hover around Betty like a swarm of flies.

In the largest bridge video feed, a satellite view of Astris slowly rotates. Wispy clouds obscure some of the desert landscape. Isaac reads from his display. "Coming into view now."

Even at this low magnification, the leafy field is an irregular green disk against the otherwise tan dirt. A reticule targets it, and their satellite zooms, filling the screen with the overlapping fractal patterns of the alien lifeforms. The same red veiny spheres and purple ribbon structures carve colorful patches.

"Ribbons are all wrapped up again," Isaac says.

James squints. "Can you lock on a few and take it to max?"

Isaac taps his console, and the reticule selects a fifty-meter patch. When it enlarges, the image is pixelated, making it difficult to see details, but the screen is filled with the purple ribbon structures. Many of the ribbons have gaps between their slats, and metal gleams with reflected sunlight. Even with the pixelation, James can pick out familiar shapes. The metal feathers of an Eye. The curved arch of a Blade. Gold flashes sparkle within some of the purple ribbons like firefly swarms.

James furrows his eyebrows. "Give me a different purple ribbon patch."

When Isaac chooses another, the view is the same. He glances over. "James, I think they're printers. Just like us printing repair parts, they're printing more drones."

James takes a deep breath and rubs his chin. "That's a problem."

"Then bionems gather the raw materials, printers make whatever they need." He pauses. "You know the wrecked Boomerang we found underwater? I think this is what happened to them. Same thing that is happening to us."

"Need to slow them down," James says. "Need at least another day of repairs, maybe two."

"How do you slow down something that keeps recycling what it attacks you with?"

"Have to break their printers." He takes the last gulp of his coffee. "Come with me."

The two walk briskly off the bridge, heading aft. They cross through the habdeck, drone bay, and the sea of their own printers humming away in the fabmod. Crossing through the starboard portal, they arrive in the cargo bay. Racks and shelves house containers of all sizes. In the center rests an overhead crane.

James picks up the crane remote and activates the inventory roster, scrolling quickly with his index finger. "Beckman's wish list for missions is usually a little over the top. There's always stuff I end up vetoing." He stops scrolling. "There it is." He taps the selection icon. The crane comes to life and whirls along its overhead beams.

Isaac follows it with his eyes as the robotic arms on the crane unfold, swing in, and manipulate the tie-downs on a piano-sized crate. Servos whine when they lift the crate and extract it from the rack, lowering to the ground. Once settled, the arms spin the lid locks open and slide it to the side.

James approaches the crate. It was just a few months ago when Beckman handed him his recommended weapons loadout. They both perused it over a cup of coffee in Hayden-Pratt's Space Operations Center West Campus.

"How much trouble do you think we're going to get in?" James had asked him, arching an eyebrow.

"Us? Trouble?" Beckman replied, sipping his drink. "We're like a magnet."

"You really think we're going to need this?"

Beckman shrugged. "You may think you've got everything you need with the ship's lasers, but things are going to go to hell in a heartbeat, and you're going to need something small and fast to go places *Promise* can't."

James glanced at the slate and back to Beckman, waiting.

Beckman shrugged. "If it's all rainbows and daisies you can keep it in the box."

Back in the cargo bay, James stops at the crate's side. Isaac approaches the crate from the other corner, and they both look down. The craft inside is diamond-shaped with two circular wing cavities housing prop blades. Sticking out from the belly is a hint of a jet intake. The entire hull is dark gunmetal except for the actual guns, which are twin black barrels protruding from the wings. Silver letters read *Besra SC-24*.

"I was against it," James says. "But after two missions, I think I've finally accepted it. Listen to the man. Beckman's gut is always right."

ON THE BRIDGE VIEW, the sun is low, filling the world with gold. Astris's blue sky has taken on the turquoise tint it acquires a few hours before sunset. The entire crew is awake and at their stations.

James wears a pair of clear safety glasses and has the Besra's flight stick mounted at his console. An inset video on the bridge screen shows Betty II depositing the Besra at the aft of *Promise*.

"Powering up," James says. Telemetry scrolls on the inside surface of his glasses. "All systems green. Switching to vision mode." His glasses opaque and a stereoscopic view from the assault drone appears overlaid with pitch, roll, and airspeed indicators. "Props to speed. On your mark, Isaac."

"Thirty seconds until satellite is in range," Isaac says.

James slides up the power, and the twin props accelerate. Sand blasts away from the prop wash. Steadily the drone lifts off the ground.

When Ananke speaks, it is softly. He can't see her through the drone interface, but he can feel her presence. The way she speaks is like a friend reaching out and touching his hand. "James, I wish...I wish there were another way."

James hesitates.

"Ten seconds," Isaac says.

James straightens. "I wanted something better too, but we're short on options."

A tone sounds from Isaac's station. "Mark."

As James pushes the flight stick forward, the drone accelerates. It's more like flying a helicopter than a plane. The sandy shore falls away from his view. "Now I just want to get us the hell off Astris."

In his goggles, the rock whizzes beneath the assault drone. The jet engine kicks in and the airspeed ribbons tick up. James tilts his flight stick right and the horizon rolls left.

"Got you on the satellite image," Isaac says. "Two kilometers to target."

The cliff drops off and opens into the basin. James pushes the stick down, watching the rock rise up alarmingly fast. As he levels off, boulders streak below him. The field is a green and purple patch growing rapidly.

"Approaching target," Isaac says.

James taps the acquisition button on his flight stick, and reticules connect two-dozen purple-ribbon plant areas in a zig-zag line on his heads-up display. Hit probabilities increase towards one-hundred percent beside each target. Ananke doesn't say anything, but her silence weighs heavy on him. He swallows and clears his throat. "Engaging." He squeezes the trigger.

Green muzzle flashes strobe and hundreds of red phosphorescent rounds strafe in converging lines. Fireballs stitch themselves in the sinuous path marked on the HUD as bits and pieces of the ribbon plants scatter like confetti. He swings the lethal rain along the last of the strafing run and pulls back on the stick, rocketing the Besra into the sky. As the field falls behind him, he turns in a tight arc and readies for another pass.

"All targets destroyed in the first path," Isaac says.

The Besra finishes its turn and lines up for another strafing run. James presses the trigger and lights up another burning line. He pulls hard on the stick and rolls into another high-gee turn.

Isaac's console chirps. "Activity," he says. "Ribbons are opening."

As the drone levels, James sees them. He spins and prioritizes targets. A squeeze and the newly-blossomed Eyes burst. He steers his fire back onto the purple ribbon patch and leads the rounds towards the end.

"Look out," Isaac says. "Two are airborne."

James's vision flashes white and resolves into flames and sparks, then the blue horizon tilts ninety-degrees and rolls upside-down. Damage alerts blink on his screen. He left wing is missing. He struggles with the stick, trying to aim where the drone falls. In an instant, the rock rushes up into his face, and the video goes dark. He tosses his glasses.

On the bridge screen, Isaac's satellite feed shows a flaming field streaming black smoke pillars. The drone's wreckage is its own dissipating fireball just to the north. Two Eyes accelerate, heading in the direction of *Promise*.

"Tactical," James says.

A three-dimensional model of the basin rotates with the two Eyes tagged and identified. Promise is three kilometers away along the beach adjacent the west sea.

James transfers tactical controls to his console. When he taps the threat assessment icon, two concentric rings overlay *Promise*. The innermost is red and depicts the maximum range the Eyes were capable of firing during the last encounter. The outermost is yellow, an error estimation which assumes they have more range than they exhibited. The two Eyes change direction, turning in a wide arc to the southeast.

"They learn," Isaac says. "Looks like they're going to approach from the starboard to stay out of the port laser's firing arc. They remember the starboard emitter was down."

Willow looks over. "Nothing on communications."

"I don't think they're here to talk," James says.

The Eyes finish their turn from the south and angle back towards *Promise*, coming along a line which leads to its damaged starboard side. They separate, increasing their spacing. James watches as their blinking icons converge on the outermost yellow graphic encircling *Promise*. Five hundred meters. Two-fifty. Approaching maximum estimated range where the Eyes can fire on *Promise*. As the lead Eye is about to cross that line, it incandesces green and cracks apart into sparking cinders.

"Surprise," James says to the falling Eye. "We fixed the starboard laser." He taps the firing control again, and *Promise's* laser intersects the second Eye. It crashes and burns on a rocky plain.

"No further activity at the field," Isaac says. "Satellite moving out of sight. Next orbital will be over the field in fifteen minutes."

"Launching recon drone. Parking it at the cliff's edge. As long as the weather holds, we should be able to keep a watch on our friends." James sets the commands in motion and follows the recon drone on the tactical display. Once its telemetry spills on the screen, he takes a deep breath and relaxes, leaning back into his chair. After he collects his thoughts, he glances at Ananke. Her display is blue and silent, eddies falling like rain on a window. It's not her usual serene blue, and it's not Bernard's Blue, but it's somewhere in between.

15

TIP OF THE ICEBERG

A t three a.m. in the Planetary Science lab, Julian and Ava sit side-by-side at a desk. They've dimmed the room so that only task lights accent essential equipment. A few of the monitors live-stream the exterior view. Toliman sits high over the silver sea like a blazing moon, the starry sky surreal like a screensaver.

Ava rests her head on her fist and types with her free hand. "Twenty-five kilohertz. forty-microsecond burst. One cycle. Here goes." She taps the control. A light blinks on the antenna pointed at the blood sample.

The bionem in the atomic imager sits there, motionless.

Ava punches in a new set of parameters. "This reminds me a bit of some all-nighters back on Providence Station, except nothing there was trying to digest me if I didn't figure it out."

Julian takes a sip of his coffee. "It does bring a certain focus."

"You know, when we planned this mission, I thought we would find some simple life, and the idea of finding something intelligent was just a dream. If we did, I had this fantasy of how the first contact would go. I didn't think we'd end up in an all-out shooting war with it."

"No one did."

"Ethically I'm uneasy. I didn't want to kill the life we came to find."

Julian turns his palm up. "A tiger is not evil because it wants to eat you, but that doesn't mean that you should let it."

"Do you think the alien is a predator?"

"I do."

She presses her lips together, pauses, then says what she wanted to say. "Do you think we're going to make it out of here?"

Julian raises his eyebrows and leans in a bit, setting his hand on her forearm. "Of course. James is at his best when the chips are down, so to say. We've been in some tight places, but he always finds the ray of daylight to lead us out."

The warmth of his hand feels nice on her forearm, and she lingers a moment, fixes her hair, and turns back to the console. Julian leans back and turns his attention to the screen.

"Okay, next test. Setting the transmitter to auto, stepping through all the twenty-four-kilohertz frequencies, one cycle each," she says. "Transmitting."

The tuning-fork jolts and starts wriggling.

Ava perks up. "Whoa. That did something!"

"Indeed," Julian says. "It's moving."

The bionem's legs flail through the plasma-like flagella. Ahead, the massive disk of a red blood cell is a hundred times the bionem's size. The tuning fork latches onto the cell's surface and wriggles. Ava and Julian watch it for a full minute until a smudge is visible between its forks.

Julian reads his screen. "It's collecting copper from the red blood cell."

"Okay, let's test if it's lost its appetite for molybdenum. Injecting."

They watch and wait. The bionem continues to collect its copper.

"We have changed its directive," Julian says.

Ava smiles, excited. "Twenty-four-point-seven-one kilohertz. If one cycle toggles it on, let's test if another toggles it off."

The light blinks on the transmitter, and the bionem drops its copper collection, turning and swimming in the direction of the molybdenum.

"Oh, yeah," Ava says. "Now we're getting somewhere." She taps the bridge com. "Ananke, are you there? We've had a breakthrough and could use your help determining the test sequence."

Ananke responds. "Hello, Ava. I am currently in nacelle four with Hitoshi configuring the induction controller. Can I join you in twenty minutes?"

Julian glances at the time, then motions with his eyes towards the aft. "Perhaps this is a good time for a break and a snack."

"Perfect," Ava says. "We're going to grab something from the canteen. Meet you back here."

JUST BEFORE NOON, Julian orders everyone to eat lunch. It's a bit of an unusual order from the ship's physician, but one that everyone's happy to oblige. After a day of rotating shifts with pairs working in isolated pockets, it's nice to have the entire crew together for a meal. To lighten the atmosphere, Julian's streaming some of his favorite seventies music from the media screens.

The lunch meal is a burger and french fries, which feels decadent. Although it's not really meat, the burger is surprisingly good. Julian's topped his with some barbecue sauce and managed a bite before standing and grabbing a pitcher of orange drink. He pours a glass and lifts it. "Credit goes to Ava, Willow, and Ananke for cracking the code," he says. "Perhaps Ava can explain."

Ava has a mouthful of french fries and smiles, chewing and gulping. "Okay. We found the bionems are radio-controlled. Different frequencies flip switches, and the combo of on/off states determine which elements they gather. Through trial and error, we made a map. Now we can force them to collect a specific element."

Ananke says, "We could not turn them off, but we could select a benign target, so we chose americium. It's a radioactive element which does not occur naturally. There is none in *Promise* or your bodies."

"Also, importantly, americium is not present in medical nanobots," Julian adds. "Hitoshi has engineered a clever solution for the reprogramming."

Hitoshi says, "We raise *Promise's* radiation screen and oscillate it at Ava's frequencies. It'll bathe everything inside in low-energy radio waves. The beauty of the plan is that it'll reprogram all of the bots affecting *Promise* and us. We'll leave the screen up so our killer-plant buddy can't undo our tweak."

Julian pours a few more glasses of the orange drink and passes them around the table. "Which leads us to this." He lifts his drink. "Each glass contains a few thousand medical nanobots. When you drink it, they will be absorbed and distributed like an antibiotic, enveloping the bionems and dissolving their organic bonds." He takes a sip of the orange drink. "Citrus Surprise. Not as tasty as Berry Blast."

James smiles. "How do we get the dead bionems out of our system?"

"The usual way that waste is expelled."

James nods. "And *Promise*?"

"I have an aerosol option which I will work with Hitoshi."

James takes his orange drink, eyes it, and raises it in a toast. "Bottoms up." He chugs it down and cringes. "How fast 'till they kick in?"

"A few hours for absorption," Julian says. "Should be clear within two days."

Hitoshi eyes his glass. "Hard to imagine what could be worse than Berry Blast." Reluctantly, he drinks it.

"Alright," James says. "We're doing good. We'll have engine

four back together tonight sometime after midnight. Couple hours of checks and prep. Should make a dawn launch."

"How's the field look?" Willow asks.

"Couple of printers survived the strafing run," James says. "One looks like it's building something. Might be another Eye. We're watching it. Can't tell, but doesn't look like it's doing anything about its wrecked printers."

Willow takes a sip from her orange drink. "Do you want our team back on communication or helping with repairs?"

"We're resource saturated for repairs. Stick with communications. It's our last day here, so if there's anything else you want to see in the vicinity of the ship, now's the time to look. Probes only. No one goes outside without talking to me."

Ava says, "I'd like to get a scan of the bioluminescent plankton. Isaac and I have a theory I'd like to explore. We can do it with the sea probe without bringing anything back."

James nods. "Works for me."

ORANGE SUNLIGHT MAKES Astris's landscape look like Arizona. Ava and Julian stand before their presentation on the bridge screen. In the video, the sea probe splashes through bubbles and blue water, ribbon fish darting away in schools. When it finds a glowing colony of yellow stars, it extends an arm with a sample container and scoops a few up. The arm retracts into the probe.

"So I've been wondering," Ava starts, "why the underwater Boomerang wreck is still intact. We found molybdenum in it, which seems to be one of the elements the bionems are gathering."

Isaac nods. "First time we sent the sea probe, it attracted the bioluminescent plankton. Thought it was due to the probe's lights."

Ava smiles. "But it wasn't. It was because we brought dinner."

She points at one of the compounds on the screen. "When Julian and I were discussing how his nanobots would dissolve the bionems, I recognized that the plankton's compound is very similar to what we're using."

"Plankton eat bionems," Isaac says. "The first probe was covered in them, and they chowed down."

"Not sure if they evolved a defense or always had it," Ava says. "It explains why the sea's ecosystem is thriving despite the bionem presence."

Isaac touches a button, and one of his soil samples appears along with its own analysis. "As for the surface, organic compounds in soil suggest Astris once had more surface life."

James picks up on what he's saying. "You think the reason there's no surface animals is because they're extinct?"

"Correct."

"And the alien life killed them?"

"Possibly. Could also have been some other disaster. Climate change, asteroid impact. Impossible to know."

James narrows his eyes. "It's a big planet. We're talking planetary animal mass. What would it do with all of that?"

Ava glances at Isaac and grimaces. "No idea."

Ananke's been quiet for this exchange but interrupts. "James, I have activity in the field."

James straightens. "Stations." As he slips into his seat, he says, "Let's see it."

The satellite image is out-of-range, but the drone they have perched at the cliff edge shows a dot rising from the purple ribbon field.

"It appears to be coming out of a printer," Ananke says.

James opens the tactical station and powers up the lasers. On the screen, sunlight gleams on metal as the flying object turns. Tactical locks a reticule on it and overlays vectors. As the object approaches the bottom of the cliff, their probe gets a better look at it. It's nearly spherical, gray, with green and red navigation lights flanking its sides. James furrows his brow.

"It is not an Eye," Ananke says.

The object briefly disappears out of their probe's view as it accelerates along the cliff face. When it flies up in front of their probe, it floats just a few meters in front of the camera. It's flawless silver, unblemished by atmospheric entry, looking like it just came out of the box. All of the details are there, even the blue and red Hayden-Pratt logo. It's the parachute probe they initially dropped near the green field.

James taps his drone's control and swings it off-axis for a moment, zooming down into the basin. He locates the red-and-white parachute still draped on the basin floor. The skeleton of the original parachute probe is still there, hollowed-out and scavenged by the bionems. He swings his drone back to face the alien replica.

"Radio contact," Willow says. "Alpha-numeric. On screen."

Giant blue text types itself across the screen, overlaying the alien replica.

09.23.87 09:14 Hayden-Pratt Surface Probe 2. Touchdown. All systems nominal.

James puts his hand on his chin and rubs it.

"Identical to the original transmission we received from our surface probe," Willow says.

James glances at the tactical display. The replica is a kilometer outside the red and yellow warning circles overlaying *Promise*. It's also not within line-of-sight of *Promise's* lasers. "It seems they want to talk. How should we respond?"

Ava says, "Mirror the transmission."

James nods cautiously. "Proceed."

Willow taps her console. "Transmitting."

The replica floats there, waiting. After a long minute, the replica's exterior floodlights illuminate and a blue ring glows around its camera.

"Receiving video signal," Willow says.

The camera view is from the replica's perspective, looking at their cliff drone. Now, on screen, they have mirror images of each drone seeing its counterpart.

"Kinda creepy," Hitoshi says.

"James," Ananke says. "This means they understand the format used to encode our video images and our alphanumeric transmission. Presumably, we can respond, and they will be able to transcribe it."

James continues to rub his chin. "Because they cloned our tech."

"Yes, but this greatly simplifies communication. They have solved the problem of transcription."

"Now we have to bridge the gap of language," Willow adds.

Ava nods. "We start with numbers. Once we have a number set, we can move onto math and equivalencies. Once math, then logic tests, which leads to concepts." She looks over. "I can't believe we're finally getting a chance to talk."

"Okay," James says. "The protocol, when you're ready."

Ava loads the protocol and Willow transmits. When they finish the first number set, there's palpable excitement as the replica mirrors the signal back to them. Other than mirroring, the replica is completely silent while they run through the remainder of their series, hovering motionless in front of their drone.

"Moving onto logic tests," Ava says.

As she starts the sequence, the replica rotates away from their drone, seeming to lose interest, and rolls into a turn. It's still broadcasting, and they watch through its eyes as it rises and flies over the rock heading in the direction of *Promise*.

James eyes the tactical display. It's a pulsing dot quickly approaching the outer yellow defense ring he'd established from the last Eye encounter. He locks the port laser and hovers his finger over the fire control.

In the replica's video stream, *Promise* comes into view, a black-and-white shape parked on the beach illuminated by Betty II and the repair drone's spotlights. The nacelles are a patchwork of blast marks and new hull plates.

The pulsing tactical icon slows and comes to a stop a few hundred meters still outside of the yellow perimeter. It hovers there in the sky, watching.

"It learned again," Isaac says. "Knew enough not to cross the perimeter."

James considers the fire button beneath his finger and glances at Ananke. Her screen is calm. He backs his hand away. "Seems they don't want to talk. They want to watch, and they want us to know they're watching."

"What do we do now?" Hitoshi asks.

"Let 'em watch," James says. "We're leaving in twelve hours. If they have something to say, they'll have a chance. I'm setting tactical to automatically fire on them if they cross the yellow line. Otherwise, we've got work to do."

"Boss, they perfectly replicated our drone," Hitoshi says. "Even got the right shade of Hayden-Pratt blue on the paint job."

James nods slowly. "Yeah."

"You know, I've been assuming all the tech they've been throwing at us is theirs," he continues. "But now I'm not so sure. Maybe we've been fighting copies of drones from the *last guy* they encountered."

PREDAWN ON ASTRIS is different than Earth. As a result of Astris's current orbit placing it between Rigil and Toliman, the night sky is at its darkest a few hours before sunrise, when Toliman disappears over the western horizon while Rigil has not yet risen. The two hidden suns create bright gradients on both horizons, but the highest arch of the sky's dome is awash with luminous stars and the glowing bands of the Milky Way. James stands in front of the bridge screen, sipping his coffee, admiring it.

Julian approaches him, setting his hands on his hips and taking in the scene. "How much coffee have you had?"

James takes another sip. "All of it."

"You've been awake for, what, thirty-six hours?"

James gives him the look. "Now's not the time, doc. We're just about wrapped up. I'll bunk up when we're safe."

To his right, Willow and Ava take their stations. Everyone wears a blue Hayden-Pratt flight suit adorned with mission patches. James reaches down and taps the com. "Hitoshi, how we doing?"

Hitoshi's image pops on the screen. He's in nacelle four with Isaac, Ananke's sphere in the background. "Looking good. A couple more diagnostics and we'll head up."

"Alright, starting the pre-flight checks," James says. He closes the com and sits at his station as Julian returns to his seat. The systems checklist appears on-screen, and James starts completing tasks.

"There's so much still to learn about Astris," Ava says. "I could spend years just exploring its seas."

"Wish we had more time," James replies. "But Astris isn't going anywhere." He glances at tactical. The alien replica drone still watches silently from afar. "Bringing reactor up to temp. Power levels nominal. Batteries at a hundred percent. Activating exterior floods for hatch inspection."

The exterior video brightens as the floods illuminate. The main airlock hatch is secure despite some scorch marks. Cargo bay door looks good. Drone bay closed and secure. Interior images of each section confirm all loose items are in their bays and tied-down.

Through the deck plates, a sensation buzzes against James's feet. He doesn't hear anything, but a *whump* passes through his chest like a subwoofer kicking out bass. He stops and lifts his hands from the controls. "Willow, you getting that?"

She's moving her hands quickly over her controls, putting her earpiece in. The vibration sounds again. "Acoustic wave, infrasonic, four Hertz, coming from the direction of the basin."

Ananke hails James. "James, my accelerometers are picking up infrasonic vibrations. This may be an indicator of tectonic activity."

"Willow's working on it," James replies. "Think it's more likely our friends are up to something. You guys need to wrap it up and get up here."

"Acknowledged."

James looks over at Ava. "Satellites in range?"

Ava has Isaac's station slaved to her own. "Not for another ten minutes."

James toggles to the cliff drone's camera. All is quiet in the green field. The few remaining printers are closed.

The vibration sounds again, but this time, he can hear it. His coffee cup rests on the console. As he watches it, concentric waves oscillate across its surface.

"Let's pick up the startup pace," James says. "Not sure what's going on, but don't want to be beachside when it happens."

Over coms, Hitoshi says, "We're skipping a few steps here, but we're on our way. Four is powering up and looks okay. Just try not to do anything too wild on the climb out."

James turns on the ship's navigation lights and watches the icons progressively turn green on engine four.

When the next wave hits *Promise*, it shimmies the ship. Worried gasps sound from Ava and Willow as they steady themselves at their consoles.

Willow's console chirps and she acknowledges the alert. "James, radio transmission from the replica, alpha-numeric." She pauses. "On screen."

Giant blue text overlays the alien replica's image. *09.23.87 09:15 HPT-E17 Bernard's Promise. Touchdown.*

A fine sweat breaks out across James's upper lip. "Is that another repeat of one of our messages?"

Willow shakes her head. "It's a mix of our parachute probe's first transmission and our response to it."

"It's editing," Ava says, "using transmission fragments."

"Is it random, or do you think it understands anything it's saying?" James says.

"Since it replicated the probe," Ava begins, "it may have the probe's association of 'touchdown' with specific sensor conditions. Impossible to know how the alien is interpreting that."

Hitoshi emerges on the bridge trailed by Isaac. "Did that thing just hail us by our callsign?"

Ananke's screen fades in from her center console.

When the next wave happens, it sounds like thunder rolling on the horizon. Something large groans and cracks, as if an ice shelf had just broken loose. The cliff drone's camera shows dust ballooning across the basin.

"Frequency and amplitude increasing," Willow says.

Ananke's screen ripples with green and aqua. "It might be trying to communicate."

James taps quickly through the remainder of the checklist on his console. "I will be happy to chat with it from space."

Hitoshi slides in his seat and pulls his harness over his shoulders. "I think everyone should buckle up."

The dust cloud blooms over the basin and fans out like smoke. Jagged cracks snake along the rock.

"Four's hot and ready," Hitoshi says. "Skipped the thruster flush as part of pre-start, so go easy on them."

James sets his hands on the RF controls. "Crew, secure for—
"

The jolt is like an earthquake, and rocks *Promise* violently. The entire ship shifts in the sand and tilts left. On the screen, the beach undulates as a few-meter-tall wave crashes down and washes up against *Promise*. The water recedes, leaving wet sand.

"We're okay," Hitoshi yells. "No damage."

James slides the controls. "Getting out of here."

Thrusters blast into the sand and *Promise* hovers above the beach. James pushes the RF slider, and the ship slowly accelerates. "She's sluggish," he says. "Feels like I'm flying through molasses." He glances again at the cliff drone video. The basin floor is barely visible through the dust cloud, but from what he can see the landscape for kilometers is a spiderweb of chasms. What's unsettling is that the rock is breathing as if sitting on a great lung. Parts of it crack, and a massive kilometers-wide rock sheath rises up from the basin.

Isaac's transferred his controls back from Ava. "Satellite coming into range."

The satellite image of the basin looks like a volcanic eruption with smoke trailing in wind-swept lines. In the top-down view, a nine-kilometer-wide rock dome swells up spilling debris in a slow-motion cascade. At the top of the dome's center is the fractal greens and purples of the field's circles.

"Getting fairly alarmed here," Hitoshi says.

Promise picks up speed, and the beach glides away, the nearby steppes shrinking. The cliff face is straight ahead and James banks into a wide arc. As *Promise* clears the cliff rim, the scale of the nine-kilometer-wide rock dome rising slowly from the basin is frightening, as if an entire mountain had taken flight. Boulders and dirt tumble off in endless streams. The top of the dome is a toupee of displaced basin rock, but beneath it trails ten tapered black columns, curving inward like tentacles, each half-a-kilometer thick and adorned with thousands of the veiny red spheres seen on the field's top. Orange light spills from scattered pods along the column's interior while draped silver vines connect the dome with the columns. James can't tell if it's a massive alien structure or a kilometers-wide living creature, but whatever it is was buried deep beneath the basin floor and left a gouged crater where it emerged. The tapered black columns descend deep into that crater and James isn't sure if they support the dome, like legs, or if it is flying under its own power.

When Isaac speaks calmly, it's almost jarring. "Distance to target, one kilometer. Intercept in twenty seconds."

The alien mass is so big that it looks like it's moving in slow motion. "Hitoshi, need to do some magic," James says.

Hitoshi enters a command on his console. "Redlining engine one."

Promise continues to turn as the alien mass eclipses the eastern sky.

"Not enough," Isaac says.

Hitoshi enters an override. "Now twenty percent over redline. Do what you gotta do, or we're going to fry the inductor. If we lose engine one, we're toast."

James eyes the approaching mountain, vectors the chemical thrusters to fire as much to the aft as possible, and engages them all. The burst is like a kick in the back and lurches everyone forward. To the port, the alien mass starts to fall away.

"Inductor's critical," Hitoshi says.

The alien mass slows and plummets back towards the basin's floor.

"Dial it back below redline," James says.

When the alien collides with the ground, clouds pancake out and billow up in an expanding ring. A few seconds later, the shockwave hits *Promise* and knocks everyone into his console. James wrestles with the controls and regains stability, then *Promise* rockets up and leaves the basin far below. As they reach thirty kilometers, the first light of Rigil bathes their ship in rose while James charges the Riggs drive. At one-hundred and fifty kilometers, Astris is a sphere with the cool blue night colors giving way to the radiant gold of the day.

James evaluates the satellite transmission. The basin looks

like the site of a natural disaster, but, other than streaming dust clouds, there is no activity. When he looks at the cliff probe's display, it is black with the text CONNECTION TERMINATED.

"Ananke," James says. "Riggs course. Back to our spot between Astris and Hydaspes."

"Course parameters set," Ananke replies. "Configuring emitters. Ready."

"Jump positions."

Everyone curls up, and James glances one last time at Astris. "Initiate."

In an instant, Astris collapses from a blue sphere into a red pinpoint, fading back to blue. The micro-jump is like a punch in the gut, but it's a punch that James welcomes.

16

BEACON

James stirs, confused, wondering where he is. It's pitch black, and he's in a sleeping bag. He searches for the stars. Even on a moonless night, there should be some light in the sky. He's used to waking up early, but this feels different like he's been sleeping for days. Is he in a room? His arms float out in front of him, and he realizes he's weightless. Still confused, he rubs his eyes and says, "Lights."

When the lights gently fade on, he's in a small room that is configured for zero-gee. His head clears, and he realizes he's on *Promise*. He feels like he has a sleep hangover. "Time?"

His console responds. "Seventeen thirty-five."

James scratches his forehead. "Damn. Eleven hours." He unzips his sleep sack and pushes away from the wall, drifting to his desk. Tapping the console, he scrolls through a few notifications. Everything is fine. He grabs a water bulb from the refrigerator and chugs it, then heads for the shower. The hot water is decadent and revives him.

As he slips on some khakis and a black Hayden-Pratt tee shirt, coms dings. "Go ahead," James says.

Ananke's voice sounds from the speaker. "Hello, James. I registered that your quarters were active. Did you sleep well?"

"Like a log. Everything okay?"

"Yes. We are still in orbit around Rigil Kentaurus at the midpoint between Astris and Hydaspes. There have been no sensor contacts. Satellite imagery from Astris shows that the life form has returned to its subterranean location in the basin with no further activity."

"Let's see it."

The basin is strewn with rubble and looks like the site of a massive landslide. The air is still dusty, and it's like looking through a thick smog haze. At its center, hints of the green plant field poke through.

Ananke says, "Post-image analysis of the life form indicates it is nine-point-two kilometers wide at its apex and two-point-five kilometers tall, although it is still undetermined how deep the organism extends into the ground."

"Mount Everest is, what, nine clicks?"

"Eight thousand, eight hundred, and forty-eight meters in height. Comparable to the width of the organism."

"We were fighting a mountain."

"In a sense, yes. Dr. Kelly believes the life form is alien to Astris. She is uncertain whether it is sentient, although she suspects it is."

"Sure seemed smart with all of the tech it was able to make."

"She believes the bionems serve the function of digestion, and the biological printers are encoded with recipes, like DNA. What is unique is that the organism can change the recipe based on what it encounters. Dr. Kelly thinks this is a form of mimicry, which does not necessarily require sentience."

"Smart or not, it looked like it wanted to eat us."

"Agreed. It is likely we supplied many raw materials not available on Astris."

James pauses. "I know you're upset about how things went down."

"No, it's not that I'm upset. I believe we needed to defend ourselves. But, this mission was the realization of Bernard's dream. He so wanted to know what we would find at Alpha Centauri, and he had hopes of peaceful first contact. I wanted to make that wish become reality, but what we found was something different."

"So far, it's been pretty hostile out here."

Ananke's tone is contemplative. "I still have to believe that there are peaceful species out there who are explorers, like us. We need to keep turning over stones until we find them."

James smiles. "Yeah, agreed." He picks up his watch and straps it onto his wrist. "Alright, I'm going to grab some chow and see what everyone's up to. See you soon."

"See you."

James exits his quarters and heads to the canteen. At a table in the room's center, Hitoshi and Isaac are eating some ravioli. Twentieth-century eighties music plays over the speakers — obviously, Hitoshi got to pick the music — and the song is about someone watching every move you make.

"Hey, guys," James says. "Mind if I join you?"

"The sleeper has awakened," Hitoshi replies. "Pull up a chair."

James selects an egg sandwich and potatoes from the galley. The machine indexes his selection, heats it, and slides it out in a covered tray. He knows it's dinnertime, but it feels like breakfast. He grabs an orange juice and floats down into a seat, clicking into its harness. "You guys catch some zees?"

Hitoshi nods. "Few hours. Can't really sleep in the day. I know there's no day here, but, you know. We going to stay here a bit?"

James nods. "Definitely. Everyone's got to get some rest. We'll figure out what we're doing next tomorrow."

"So, about that," Hitoshi says, leaning in. "Isaac's got a theory."

James glances at Isaac.

Isaac finishes chewing his ravioli and says, "Soil analysis from the basin showed tektites. Usually formed in extreme heat from meteor impacts. Elements are missing, though, which would be present from a meteor strike. Three possibilities. Basin was formed by a meteor, but the alien used all the elements. Next, basin was formed by the alien colliding with Astris. Last, extreme heat was applied to the basin."

James squints. "I get the first two, but what are you thinking for extreme heat?"

"Like, nuked or maybe razed."

"So here's what we're thinking," Hitoshi says. "Maybe the Boomerang we found in orbit was a warning to keep others from going down there. Possible they tried to kill it from orbit after it sunk their ship."

"If that's the case," James says, "we blasted their beacon."

"Right."

James shakes his orange juice and takes a sip. "Well, we broke it, we'll fix it."

THE CALL from Julian comes in the early evening. James heads directly to sickbay. When he arrives, Beckman is awake, lying with his bed-back raised, sipping from a clear bulb he holds with his right hand. His left arm is still secured across his chest. Julian floats off to the side.

Beckman smacks his lips. "Berry Blast. I'm so thirsty this actually tastes good." He's a bit winded when talking and still wears the supplemental oxygen. His words have the sluggishness of someone who's drugged.

"Beckman!" James says. "Oh, man, it's good to see you awake."

"Everyone safe?"

James nods. "Bit bumpy there for a while, but we're all good. We're orbiting Rigil, one a.u. out from Astris."

"Our green friend throw any other surprises at us?"

James raises his eyebrows. "You could say that. I've got a hell of a video to show you from our launch. You know, that thing was printing up a bunch of reinforcements, and I had to use the Besra."

Beckman nods appreciatively. "You used it. Didn't think you would."

"You were right. Didn't find rainbows or daisies. Maybe one of these days."

"Glad we had that card to play. Just doing my job."

"Will's always thought the world of you. Now that we've got some missions under our belt, I know why."

Beckman gives the slightest smile and acknowledges the compliment with a nod. "We going back to Astris?"

"Tomorrow, just to high orbit. There's something we have to fix before we leave."

The sickbay door opens, and James turns.

Hitoshi drifts in wearing a big grin. "Beckman, buddy, heard you were up. How you doing?"

"Can't complain. Whatever doc's given me feels like a couple shots of bourbon."

"Well, glad you're feeling okay."

"Looking forward to getting back on my feet."

Julian looks over. "A couple of days, my friend."

"You know," Hitoshi says, "I've got a kick-ass movie collection you can borrow if you want something to watch while you're hanging out."

"Is this Trek Wars we're talking about?"

Hitoshi holds out his open palms as if bracing, then retracts his thought. "You seem more like a *Top Gun* kinda guy. Let's start with that."

"Okay."

James smiles. "That's a good one."

Ava arrives at the door and pokes her head it. "Beckman!"

Julian turns. "Okay, one at a time."

James nods. "I'll let someone else have my spot. Ping me if you need anything. Happy to just hang out."

Beckman nods. "Thanks, James."

———

FROM A DISTANCE OF FORTY-TWO-THOUSAND KILOMETERS, Astris is about the same size as a soccer ball held at arm's length. Unlike Earth, which is mostly blue with some tan parts, it is the opposite. The planet is centered in the view provided by *Promise's* open cargo bay airlock, providing enough reflected sunlight to silhouette the figures floating inside.

Jame and Hitoshi both wear EV suits and are tethered to wall rails. Between them rests an octagonal satellite which has a folded-up gold reflector dish. It's the twin of the one they placed back at Proxima.

Hitoshi enters a few commands on the satellite's panel. "Too bad this bird won't get to see Toliman."

"Yeah," James says. "Would've liked to see more of the system, but I know when it's time to go. At least we've got the probes. A couple months and they'll send us some pics of the other planets."

Hitoshi finishes his entry. "Okay, it's good to go."

James sets his hand on the satellite and pushes off towards the wall. Hitoshi mirrors him. Overhead, the crane clamps two arms onto the satellite, lifts it, and slides it towards Astris. When it has its own momentum, the crane releases it. The satellite drifts away from Promise, blinking its strobes and growing smaller. A few chemical thrusters fire along its circumference.

Hitoshi lifts the slate tethered to his belt. "Telemetry active. It will arrive at geosynchronous orbit over the alien site in thirty minutes, then chat with anyone who approaches Astris orbit." He glances at James. "You know, we're taking a leap of faith with rebroadcasting the Boomerang's message from our satellite. I mean, what if it's like, something bad?"

"Then I guess the next guy will blow it to hell just like we did. Probably head down to the planet and also have a bad couple of days."

"Well, at least we have our own message in the broadcast."

"Who knows?" James says. "Maybe someone will find it and give us a call."

Hitoshi motions to Astris. "You think Audrey II down there will try and talk to us?"

"I don't know, but I hope so. Seems like we're interstellar neighbors, after all. Got off to a bad start. Maybe that can change. We'll be listening if it has anything to say."

In the far distance, the satellite's gold dish unfurls like a blooming flower. Thrusters fire and it rotates on multiple axes, swinging until it points at the extra gold star in the familiar w-shape of Cassiopeia.

ON THE BRIDGE SCREEN, the Centauri system orbital diagram shows four new contacts moving slowly along parabolas which will eventually intersect the planets circling Alpha Centauri's second star, Toliman. The contacts are *Promise's* newly-launched probes, and their targets include two blistering rocky worlds close to the star, one waterless Mars-like world in the outer habitable zone, and a Neptune-like planet with intense red bands. Time until arrival ranges from a few months to a year. *Promise* could be at each in a blink, but with two engines down and one seriously-injured crew member, it's time to return home.

"It's been a hell of a trip," James says to the bridge crew. "We made contact or collected samples from three alien races. Possibly more, considering the copies from the Mimic." He likes the name Ava's coined for the alien life on Astris. He continues. "We found another Earth in our backyard. It's one we can't live on just yet, but maybe we'll make peaceful contact with the Mimic, and a future ship will bring people here." He glances around his crew and smiles. "Everyone was at his best. This trip has been a dream since I first looked up at the sky, and here we are. We won't be the last ship to come to Alpha Centauri, but we were the first."

Everyone nods, smiling back.

"Okay," James says, "let's go home."

SEVEN DAYS into the return trip, *Promise* is deep in the Oort Cloud. James lies on his bed listening to music. It's their evening gravity-time, and he's just showered after his workout, enjoying some downtime. The music is from the sixties and brings back memories of him and Will on an Air Force base. He glances at his desk and finds the corresponding photo of him, Will, and Mark. The nine-year time jump they're doing on this trip worries him. A lot can change. People you take for granted as being a pillar in your life may not be around anymore. There's no way for *Promise* to get any communication from Earth before returning. When you travel nearly the same speed as light, nothing can give you a heads up.

Coms dings and James says, "Pause music. Go ahead."

Ava's voice responds. "Hi, James. Sorry to bug you, but there's something I'd like to show you. Can you come to the Planetary Science Lab?"

James gets up. "On my way."

He exits his quarters and passes through the canteen. On the left, the entrance to the gym is visible. Julian is there with Beckman, leading him through some rehabilitation exercises. Beckman's left arm is in a cloth sling strapped to his chest, but he lifts a resistance band with his right.

James stops and pokes his head in. "Looking good."

Beckman has sweat pooled around his tee-shirt's collar. "Julian here makes my old trainer look like a boy scout. Didn't know the doc had such an evil streak."

"You don't want him to go easy on you, do you?"

"Didn't say that. I admire someone willing to push me, no matter how many foul names I may call him."

Julian holds up a hand. "I am certain you meant them affectionately."

Beckman pushes up the resistance band again, speaking through gritted teeth. "Something like that."

"Catch you later," James says, departing. He winds himself along the main hall exiting the canteen and approaches the science lab on the left. Ava, Isaac, Willow, and Ananke are all present, examining a few display screens.

"Wow, everyone's here," James says. "This should be good."

Ava pushes her chair back, exposing the screen. A three-dimensional chemical structure rotates. "James," she says. "You've got to see this."

He leans in, examining the structure. "What am I looking at?"

"Do you remember the molybdenum blue sample we took from the Silver Star wreck back at Proxima?"

James nods. "Yeah. This it?"

"It is. It was a nanowheel structure encased in water-ice crystals. Due to the electrolytes, we suspected the structure was conductive, so we experimented with very low voltages. When we did, this happened." She touches the console, and the entire structure rearranges itself. Where it was a buckyball, it's now a nearly organic latticework of connecting filaments. "That's not the cool part." She taps an icon. "This is." The image cycles to black light and the filaments fluoresce ghostly blue, pulses traveling slowly along the lattice.

"Is that ultraviolet?" James asks.

"Yes. Do you remember the ice cavern back on Janus where we found the glowing slush? The patterns are very similar."

"You always suspected the Janus life was related to the Silver Stars."

Ava nods. "Score another point for that theory. But the big discovery is Ananke's."

Ananke says, "The UV light is polarized. The pattern of photon polarization is similar to how my qubits work."

James squints. "You think this is part of an artificial intelligence, like you?"

"I think it is a quantum storage device."

"Are you saying we found alien memory?"

"I am certain," Ananke says. "Although nearly all of the sample is decoherent, a minute section was functional. Within that section, we found qubits structured as a three-dimensional form."

James is struggling to follow. "What does that mean?"

"AIs store information differently than the human brain. Human memory is distributed, but AIs store data more as a computer would, in a structured file. The image we found was stored like a hologram encoded in qubits." She pauses. "It means we can see its memory."

James quirks his head. "Really? What'd you see?"

"Here goes," Ava says. When she taps the icon, the new image is fuzzy, like trying to look at Jupiter on a warm Earth night with a low-power telescope. Much like looking at Jupiter, the image is a small planetary disk crossed by bands. It glows blue in UV, with the bands a darker blue, as if it were taken in monochrome.

"That's amazing," James says. "It looks like a planet. And I feel like I've seen it before."

"It's very possible it is Luhman 16, which is a brown dwarf star," Isaac says.

James does a double-take as Isaac displays the astronomical

image of Luhman 16. In visible light, the star is like a hot coal with opaque iron clouds, as if Jupiter were hot enough to be a star but cool enough for liquid metal. The image looks the same as the Silver Star's, right down to the banding pattern.

"That's where our Proxima probe is heading," James says.

"Three-and-a-half light-years from here. Probe will arrive in 2113."

"And it looks like this Silver Star has been there," Ava says.

"Right," Isaac says. "So I wonder what the probe will find."

On *Promise's* bridge screen, the universe is a pulsing blue smudge devoid of stars except for the occasional sparks of particles hitting the Riggs boundary. The bridge crew is fully staffed with everyone in his formal mission flight suits. Beckman returned to his post a few days ago and sits at tactical still wearing a sling on his left arm. Normally James operates the Riggs controls, but Hitoshi's continued his cross-training, and James has given him the honor.

"Coming up on waypoint," Isaac says.

Hitoshi taps his controls. "Riggs collapse in five, four, three, two, collapse."

The bridge shrinks and lengthens as colors desaturate, gravity pulling James's body into his own center of mass. Once when he played football, he was tackled and a half-a-dozen guys piled onto the tackle, crushing him. It feels like that. As he pulls air in through his nose to inflate his lungs, the universe mirrors his breath, expanding. The blue smudge separates into individual stars gliding towards the screen's periphery, each brightening to gold. Earth's Sun is a distant spotlight in their center.

When James glances around, everyone is doing fine. No one

needed to assume jump positions. After forty-two Riggs jumps this trip, they've become acclimated to the effect.

When the bridge view pans to the right, Saturn is beach-ball sized, a mix of wheat-colored bands topped with the dull hexagonal-blues of the polar storms.

Willow has her earpiece in. "Communications are flooded with traffic. Multiple broadcast bands. It's very busy, much more than I remember."

"Cassini Station located," Isaac says. "On screen."

Cassini Station is massive, lighted spires stretching up from its circular base like skyscrapers. Where there were a few habitat modules and radial docking arms before, there are now smaller versions of the station budded around itself, as if the station had offspring. Like a city at night, thousands of windows spill light. Docking bays fan around it in the dozens and holographic markings float in space, guiding ships along virtual taxiways and runways. Space traffic swarms around it with blinking strobes. Aside from the years of expansion, there is something different about it, James thinks. Part of it looks like an evolution of the original station, but some looks like a redesign.

James whistles. "They've been busy." He glances at Willow. "Okay, let's contact Approach and get on their radar for the flyby. First, reset ship's time and transponder to local time."

Ananke says, "Local time is nine-fifty-two a.m., Tuesday, March tenth, two-thousand and ninety-two. All functions reset."

Willow taps her console. "Cassini Approach, HPT-E17 *Bernard's Promise*, one-point-five million kilometers along the station's two-two-five radial, with request."

Fifteen seconds elapses before a man's voice responds. "HPT-E17 *Bernard's Promise*, radar contact. Standby." After a long moment, the man says, "I'm reading no flight plan on file and HPT-E17 is not on the active registry."

Willow smiles. "Negative, Cassini Approach. Flight plan is on file, but, uh, you'll have to pull it from archives since it was filed in 2083."

The silence on the other end is longer than the light-lag. Finally, the man says, "Standby."

James tilts his head. "I think they forgot about us. It's been a while."

After two minutes of silence, the man returns. "Maintain present heading. Contact the *U.N. Damysus* on one-two-four-point-six."

Hitoshi sighs. "They're rolling out the usual red carpet for us."

Willow says, "Over to one-two-four-point six." She changes channels. "*U.N. Damysus, Bernard's Promise.*"

The man's voice is crisp, military. "*Bernard's Promise*, proceed direct waypoint RAVEN for rendezvous. Maintain current deceleration. Do not charge your jump drive or deviate from course."

Willow glances to James, and he gives her a nod to speak freely. She says, "*Damysus*, we are decelerating to bleed off our Riggs boost and contact Earth for arrival arrangements prior to our final jump. We have no intention of approaching Cassini Station."

"Proceed direct RAVEN and power down," the voice says. "Do not deviate or you will be fired upon."

"They're going to take our ship again," Hitoshi says. "I thought we were done with all of this nonsense."

"We have injured and ship damage," Willow says. "And it's been nine years. We need to proceed direct to Earth." She waits. Silence. Furrowing her eyebrows, she says, "This is U.S. Special Envoy Willow Parker. Confirm voice ident. Per section nine-one of the diplomatic envoy guidelines of the U.N. Spacefaring Code, connect me immediately with the Washington Office of Extrasolar Affairs and take no further action until directed by the U.N. Liaison to the U.S."

She waits. The open com channel icons blinks. After thirty

seconds, the man responds, "Acknowledged, Special Envoy Parker. Identity confirmed. Requesting conference."

She takes a deep breath. "Thank you." She mutes coms. Due to the light-lag, it'll be two hours before they get a response from Earth, but it's two hours of the *Damysus* taking no action. She glances over at James. "I hope Holden Richards is still around."

James grins. "Oh, I love how you handle the U.N."

———

HOLDEN RICHARDS IS STILL AROUND and appears on their screen three hours later. Sixty-six minute light lag makes two-way conversation difficult, so they're watching a recording. Richards has salt-and-pepper sideburns and has put on a few pounds, but doesn't look too much different than James remembers. The thing which struck James was the transmission graphic depicting the Seal of the Vice President of the United States. Holden wears a dark suit with a flag pin and looks ecstatic.

"Willow, James! You're early! We weren't expecting you for another month." He holds up his hands. "My apologies. We did not have Cassini prepped yet, and you caught them off-guard. A lot has happened while you were away, and there have been some...unfortunate incidents...which have affected the Riggs program. I'll get you up to speed when you arrive. We're taking care of everything. The *Damysus* will not give you any more problems, and we'll give you instructions for jumping back to Earth." He produces his best grin. "Oh, I'm so excited to have you back. You're heroes in the same league as Armstrong and Aldrin, and we're going to give you a hero's welcome."

James glances over at Willow and smiles. She returns the grin as the transmission ends.

"Vice President Richards," James says. "It pays to have friends in high places."

SERENITY STATION IS small by Cassini's standard, but still a mammoth tulip-shaped structure in low Earth orbit. Nine years ago, it didn't exist. Today it's home to two-thousand people with dozens of ships docked at its ports. *Bernard's Promise* floats mated to docking pylon four. James can see it from his station window in the medical quarantine bay. The Sun's glare makes its white hull blinding, and the sharp shadows cast by all of the battle damage paint a picture of a ship returning from war. Three of the four engines are a patchwork of replacement hull plates which do not match the original black armor. It looks worse than he remembers. Beyond his ship, Earth's blue gleams.

A soft hand sets on his shoulder, and James turns. Ava is next to him, retracting her hand. She gives a hesitant look and a smile, as if she overstepped a boundary with the touch, then fixes her hair. "So much blue," she says, motioning towards the Earth. "And green. I missed it. I know we were only gone for forty-six days, but the distance made it seem longer."

"It's like going back to your parent's home in the town you grew up. No matter how far you've gone, it'll always be home."

Through the window, a ship grows larger as it approaches the station, its strobes blinking from each wing. James watches it glide towards pylon six. The Hayden-Pratt logo adorns its white hull, but the configuration isn't one he recognizes. It looks like a super-sized Pintail with an extra two engines. The ship slows and connects with the docking umbilical.

"They're here," James says. "I'll let the others know."

He exits the observation lounge and passes through the habitation area. For a quarantine bay, everything's spacious, and it's not that different from staying in station quarters. The crew is scattered throughout their quarters and James gathers them. They head to the visitor lounge.

The lounge is pure white with a perfectly clear pane separating it from the station. There are a few chairs scattered around and earbuds resting on desks for anyone who wants to chat. James approaches a desk, takes a pair of earbuds, and sets them in his ears. Everyone waits expectedly.

After a few minutes, a chime dings and the outer door slides open. The talking of the approaching group sounds muffled through the glass. James straightens as the visitors round the corner.

Will Pratt and Sarah Clark are in the lead. Will looks like himself but somehow doesn't. He's older, with the angles of his chin and nose more prominent and the circles under his eyes etched with fine shadows. Gray flecks salt his desaturated brown hair and he has it spiked and angled back. The hairstyle looks a bit unusual to James, but he expected trends to have changed. Other than that, he's kept fit and wears a traditional button-down shirt with pants. He gives a wide smile as he sees them.

Sarah is to his right. She was in her twenties when they left, and now she's in her thirties, looking the same, but better. Perhaps it's the walk or the body language, but she exudes confidence. She was confident before, but now she moves like someone in command. She's put on some muscle and wears casual clothes. James notices her shirt has the two-tone contrasting stitching, which was popular in the sixties, and her outfit has a retro vibe to it.

"James!" Will says, muted by the glass. James points to the earbuds, and he fetches some. When he speaks again, it's clear. "You old dog, I expected it, but seeing you exactly the same as you left is crazy. How're you doing?"

"Flying high," James says. "Happy to be home. You're looking good for a semi-centennial, and I've got a birthday bash to plan. Told you I'd be back in time for it."

"Oh," Will says. "There's that word again. Going to enjoy being in my forties until the last second."

"Hey, James," Sarah says. "You have no idea how much I missed you. Welcome back, my friend."

"Missed you, too. Wish you could've come with us. It was a hell of a ride. How's Gaige doing?"

She smirks and raises an eyebrow. "I'll show you." She tilts her watch and swipes at its screen. When she does, James notices the wedding band and diamond on her finger. An image appears on the transparent wall between them. The young man is the spitting image of Mark, Sarah's former husband.

"Wow," James says. "He's a man."

Sarah waves her hand. "Not quite yet, but he is sixteen. Just got his student pilot's license."

Behind her, the next group arrives. Hitoshi's parents and sister approach as Hitoshi moves to greet them.

Beckman comes up beside James. He's still wearing his sling with his left arm immobilized to his chest. "Will, Sarah. I am seriously looking forward to sitting down to have a beer together."

"I'm buying," Will says. He appraises Beckman's sling. "James, why are you always breaking Beckman?"

James nods towards Beckman. "I've come to realize that danger and Beckman are inseparable. When any member of the crew faces it, he'll go to the front of the line and take their place, taking the hits so they don't have to. Where he comes back with a sling, others might not come back at all."

A slight grin pulls across Will's face. "Yup. That's the guy I know, too."

Ava moves to the wall near them. On the other side, her sister greets her, accompanied by an attractive woman who looks like the younger version of her sister. Ava cups her hands over her mouth. "Oh, Maeve, look at you! Eighteen, all grown up."

"Hi, Aunt Ava," the woman replies.

To their right, Julian moves to greet his father.

James looks back to Sarah. "How'd you make out with the Riggs program?"

Both Will and Sarah stiffen, which alarms James. Sarah waves a hand, "We'll give you the full data dump when you're planet-side. No need to talk turkey now."

James eyes them both. "Holden said something, too, which got my attention. Spit it out."

Sarah shifts her weight. "The program's on ice. Suspended for the last three years. We went commercial in 2087, and a handful of ships were built. A year later, Subversives captured one and rammed it into Cassini Station. It was pretty much Larson's fear come true."

James's eyebrows tighten. "I don't understand. If you smash a Riggs ship into something, the field collapses and destroys the ship."

"They didn't use it that way," Sarah says. "They accelerated the ship to two-percent light speed using conventional means, then turned on the Riggs drive and came out of warp a kilometer from the station. The ship was back in normal space still at two-percent light speed when it hit. They used it as a delivery device. The weapon was conventional."

Her words stun him like a punch, and his stomach sinks. "How many people?"

"Two thousand killed. Destroyed the west side of the station. What you saw back at Saturn is the new design from the rebuild."

"Oh, God," James says, rubbing his mouth with his hand.

"Riggs was banned after that. Ships with it were quarantined or had their drives removed. Vice President Richards still has it on his agenda to revive the program, but, for now, *Promise* is the only Riggs ship."

James takes his hand from his mouth and digests the news. In the corner of his eye, Isaac chats excitedly with his mother. Just beyond him, Willow stands alone, her shoulders low. She looks up at the visitor doorway, searching. James glances at the empty door. No one has come for her.

James looks back to Sarah and Will. "We'll talk more planetside. There's a lot I have to get caught up on. Excuse me, but I've got to go check on someone."

Beckman watches as he leaves.

James crosses over to Willow. She's about to turn and leave when he sets his hand on her shoulder. She looks up at him. "Are you alright?" he asks.

"I'm fine," she says, but her voice cracks.

"You were expecting someone," James says. "I can help find them, get a comlink going."

Willow shakes her head, swallowing. "No. I already know." She looks like she's not going to say anything more, and James doesn't press. After a moment, she adds, "I had someone, and I thought he'd wait. When he didn't come, I searched on my watch. He married three years ago."

James hugs her, and she rests her head on his shoulder. "Then he is a fool who doesn't know what he lost," he says.

Willow wipes a tear from the corner of her eye.

As James glances up, looking over her shoulder back towards Will and Sarah, Beckman watches the scene unfold from afar.

———

THE NEXT WEEK IS SURREAL, like something out of a movie. When the Air Force shuttle brings them down from Serenity Station to Ronald Reagan National Airport, they are whisked away in a posh government vehicle across the Potomac to the National Mall. As their van slows, they spot the awaiting crowds. Directly in front of their van is a limousine with two flags on its front. Standing before the limo is Vice President Holden Richards.

James steps out of the van and Richards approaches, extending his hand. James clasps it. Richards produces a polished smile. "The legendary James Hayden."

"The ambitious Holden Richards."

He releases James's hand and waves at the crowd. A cheer erupts. "What do you think about the reception?"

"Surprised more people aren't freaked out about the monster next door."

"They are," Richard says, still smiling and waving. "But it's changed the dialogue. The Silver Stars were a novelty, but now we're one civilization amongst many. It's dominated the dialogue since you've returned. Since Cassini, we've been focused inward, but what you brought back has us looking to the stars once again." He glances over at James. "You're all real space heroes. Put on your game faces and let's greet your fans."

As they walk down the path to the National Mall, fighter jets streak overhead and fan out in arcs. James lifts his hand and waves. People cheer and applaud in response. He has to give a hand to Vice President Richards. He feels like a real space hero out of a movie from long ago.

Two days later he's back at Hayden-Pratt's Space Operations Center in California, visiting his old office. It's not his office anymore, but Davies. The wall which housed his twentieth-century aviator photos is filled with artwork. All of it looks like a prize collection but feels flat compared to what used to hang there. Resting on the shelf, however, is the silver model of *Bernard's Beauty*. James crosses over and picks it up. His reflection curves along its hull. He smiles and puts it back in its place, then returns to the desk, settling into the chair. He pats the wooden inlays on the chair's armrests and rubs his hands over them, swiveling his chair.

"Davies has terrible taste in art," Will says, leaning against the doorway.

"Agreed," James says.

"You look at home in the chair."

"Feels like home. Last month it was mine."

Will nods. "Going to take some figuring out how to talk about our different timelines."

"Yeah, it's weird. You know, I was expecting it but wasn't really ready for it. People are different. It's not just the clothes or the hairstyles, it's the culture. People experienced the Cassini attack, and it shaped them. Seems like all the entertainment of the past few years is about beating the bad guys or dark futures. Much different vibe than 2083."

"But now you're the wild card, doing what you do best, being the catalyst for change. Question is, what do you want to do next?"

James taps the wooden inlay on the armrest again. "First things first." He glances at the wall of artwork. "Where'd you pack all my pictures?"

———

BECKMAN WEAVES through the throng of people crowding the bar. The thumping music is modern, from 2092, and sounds like rubbish to him. He'd love to replace it with some classic forties tunes. The bar is to his right, and he steps up to it, selects a drink from the touchscreen, and waits. After a moment, an actual human bartender deposits it in front of him. Well, the place isn't all bad, he thinks. Taking the beer, he continues through the crowd. Up ahead, a man in his late thirties sits at a table with two other men, drinks in front of them.

Beckman walks up to the table and stops. The men are talking with each other and notice him, glancing up. Beckman points at the media screen behind him with his thumb. "What do you call this stuff, anyway?"

The men seem amused by his question. The center person squints and says, "Slingswing. Not your cup of tea?"

Beckman slides into the unoccupied chair at their table, setting down his beer to his left and angling himself, so he's closer to the man on the right.

The men edge back a bit.

Beckman says, "Sounds like a cowbell having a seizure."

The center person smiles. "Something we can help you with?"

"Yeah, Grant, actually there is."

Grant pulls back. Seems calling him by name got his attention. "Do I know you?" Grant says.

"First time we've met," Beckman says.

"What is it you want?"

"Well," Beckman says, tilting his head. "I'd like to know how a chickenshit like you became captain."

"Hey," the man on Grant's right says. "Piss off, gramps." He swipes a dismissing backhand at Beckman's right shoulder.

Beckman's quick, knocking aside the blow and ricocheting his open palm into a slap on the man's cheek. The man looks genuinely stunned. If Beckman were trying to lay him out, the combo would have ended with a left jab, but he's trying to be nice. Instead, he points a finger with the hand he just used. "Calm down, junior. The man and I are having a conversation. If you have something to say, you and I can discuss it after I'm done."

A tense moment passes, broken when Grant's other friend speaks. "Damn, you're Guthrie Beckman. I saw you at the Mall."

Beckman smirks. "Don't call me Guthrie." He retracts his pointed hand and sets it casually on the table, glancing back at Grant. "You were with Willow Parker before she left on the trip."

Grant holds up his hands. "That was nine years ago."

"Not for her," Beckman says. "Whether you waited or didn't isn't my concern. What gets my goat is how you left her hanging. You ghosted her. Ignored her messages. Left her standing there to figure it out on her own."

Grant furrows his eyebrows. "Look, I'm married now. What do you expect me to do, leave my wife?"

"No," Beckman says. "I expect you to grow a pair and talk to her like she was someone you cared about to give her the closure she needs." He leans in. "And this is the important part. I expect you to do it with all the respect that she deserves."

Grant takes a deep breath and exhales.

Beckman takes a sip of his beer and sets it back down, looking over to the right-hand man. "Now, is there something you want to discuss with me?"

The man holds both hands up, shaking his head.

Beckman stands, grabbing his beer. "See you around."

JAMES WALKS through the cemetery carrying a box. It's early April, and the cherry blossoms are out, coating the green grass in pink snow. The sun is high and the sky blue — not the turquoise of Astris but the cerulean of Earth — with puffy white clouds draping shadowy patches across the landscape. At his belt, a slate sticks out from a clip. The slate is thick, at least twice the size of a standard slate, and has a lens mounted at each of its corners. Ananke's face ripples blue on the screen.

Ahead, the gravestone is granite with etched letters. *Bernard Riggs. June 1, 2043 - March 21, 2080. He gave us the gift of the stars.*

James stops in front of the grave marker. Twelve years ago to the day, he stood here with Ananke, and the day now is exactly as it was then. He says to Ananke, "Ready?"

"Yes," she says. "Please proceed."

James opens the box and retrieves a translucent cube from it. He kneels down and sets it on the grass in the center of the stone, then stands, takes a few steps back, and clasps his hands.

The modifications to Ananke's slate were Hitoshi's idea. As far as James knows, this is the first time she's used her new ability. He watches as she engages the holographic emitters. When Ananke appears in front of him, she is a twenty-something woman with blue eyes, and chestnut hair pulled back into a ponytail. Her dress is Bernard's Blue and a crystal pendant dangles from her necklace, pulsing all of the colors of her display. Although her clothes are a color she uses for sadness, her pendant swirls with green and gold. She is at peace. She kneels down and touches the etched letters in the gravestone.

"Thank you, my dear friend, for everything you have given us. We touched worlds, found life, and brought a part of it back for you. Humanity's first starship bears your name, and it has seen wonders. I can only hope that we've lived up to your dreams."

Encased within the glass cube is a trumpet-like purple bell plant, taken from one of the samples Isaac and Ava collected on Astris, one of the truly native plants they found not far from the sea. A flower, for Bernard's grave, carried four light-years to this spot.

Ananke closes her eyes, smiles slightly, and then stands, approaching James.

"Bernard would be proud," James says.

Ananke sets her hand on his shoulder and smiles, the two standing side-by-side in the sunlit field with the spring breeze scattering the blossom petals like stars.

THE SCIENCE OF THE STORIES

Growing up, I watched shows like *Bill Nye Science Guy* and *MacGyver*. There always was a bit of magic in them, as if the secret rules of how and why things worked had been laid bare before me. Many years later I encountered Andy Weir's *The Martian*. Andy is a guy who asked "What if MacGyver were trapped on Mars?" *The Martian's* astronaut, Mark Watney, uses chemistry to make water, duct tapes his way through things, and generally gives you the sense that, like MacGyver with a potato battery, if you had these things, you too could survive.

Because of this, I always include a section babbling about the underlying science in my stories. It's a bit like pulling back the curtain and taking a peek behind-the-scenes. I hope you enjoy the Bill Nye-ing as much as I do.

Janus 2

In 1978, I huddled around the tv awaiting the opening credits of one of my favorite series. Ethereal music overlaid glowing nebula as a wise man's voice said, "There are those that believe, that life here, began out there." Moments later trumpets fanfared as Cylon raiders spun to attack, Imperial vipers responding.

Six years later, in 1984 a few geologists riding snowmobiles in the Alan Hills region of Antartica found a four-billion-year-old meteorite. The rock was duly titled "Alan Hills 84001," sounding a bit more like an 80s rock album than a meteorite. It's no surprise that it wasn't from Earth — it is a meteorite, after all — but what was interesting is that it was a little piece of Mars which made its way to our blue world. Far more intriguing was the presence of magnetite crystals. On Earth, such crystals are formed exclusively by microbes. This little rock from 1984 posed a huge question: did Mars once harbor life? It also rekindled our Mars fancy, resulting in a series of missions which included the now-famous Curiosity rover, and a series of Hollywood movies ranging from awful (Red Planet) to cheesy but watchable (Mission to Mars) to excellent (The Martian).

But I diverge.

In 2018, Curiosity Rover drilled into an ancient lakebed and found all the ingredients necessary to support life. If Mars were once warmer and had lakes and rivers, and pieces of Mars have landed on Earth, could Martian life have piggybacked here? The concept of life originating elsewhere - panspermia - has been around since at least the nineteenth century. More recently, in 2013 scientists proposed a concept that RNA (DNA's precursor) would have disintegrated on early Earth due to a lack of boron. Without RNA, we wouldn't have DNA. But Mars, with its evidence of ancient lakes and rivers, has plenty of boron. So, they asked, could RNA have developed on Mars, rode a meteor to Earth, and led to DNA-based life?

As we travel to other worlds, we face a type of reverse panspermia. NASA has strict sterilization protocols for the Mars rovers to prevent accidentally transplanting Earth life to Mars. Certainly, if a Mars rock can carry RNA to Earth, then an Earth rock could conceivable carry Earth microbes to other planets and moons. It is entirely possible that if we do find life in our solar system, it will be an offshoot of Earth's tree of life, because it is an immigrant from Earth.

In *Janus 2*, Ava tells the "throw a rock to the stars" story. The distance between stars is great, but so is the timescale of Earth's existence. If you calculate how far it is to Alpha Centauri, then divide that distance by the speed of an average baseball pitch, a baseball could get there in sixty million years. That seems like a long time, but keep in mind that tyrannosaurus rexs were running around sixty-five million years ago, right about the time when the giant asteroid that wiped out seventy-five percent of Earth's plant and animal life formed the Chicxulub Crater. Probably some bits of Earth got blown into space from that impact. Imagine for a moment a bit of tyrannosaur-DNA heading off to Alpha Centauri. By now, it would have arrived. This sounds like a great idea for my next story.

Switching gears, a key scene in *Janus 2* occurs in a complex crater ringed with towering ice spikes called penitente. This term recently got some attention due to the New Horizons Pluto mission, which found penitente on Pluto's Tarturus Dorsus region (which, as an aside, is an awesome name). Penitente are formed when ice erodes, usually through sublimation, creating dagger-like structures rising from the ground. If you'd like to see some first hand, you can find them on Earth in the Dry Andes. Jupiter's icy moon, Europa — another candidate for life itself — also is home to penitente. If you're an Arthur C. Clarke fan, you may recognize Europa from the ending of *2010: Odyssey Two*, where the monolith creators warn, "All these worlds are yours except Europa. Attempt no landings there." Perhaps the penitente will keep humans away, a spiked fortification warning off visitors.

Thanks again for reading *Janus 2*!

Bernard's Promise

Alpha Centauri is probably the most famous star which you've never seen. If you asked me to point it out, I couldn't. It resides in the aptly-named Centaurus constellation which is only visible from the southern hemisphere. Even if I lived in the southern hemisphere, I couldn't point to the star Alpha Centauri. It's a bit of a trick question because it isn't a star at all, but a star system consisting of two yellow stars and a distant red dwarf. Those two yellow stars, Alpha Centauri A and B, got renamed by the International Astronomical Union in 2016 to Rigil Kentaurus and Toliman. I admit Rigil is a bit confusing, and I spent half of my first draft spelling it Rigel, which is an entirely different star located 870 light-years away in the constellation Orion and known to Star Trek fans for things like Rigelian Fever. The much-closer Rigil Kentaurus comes from the Arabic *Rigil Qantūris*, meaning *the foot of the centaur*, and Toliman comes from *al-Zulmān*, meaning *the ostriches*. The third star, Proxima Centauri, kept its name and is often simply called Proxima, which is fitting for our closest stellar neighbor. In 2016, a planet was discovered in Proxima's habitable zone, dubbed Proxima B. In *Bernard's Promise*, that planet is named Aeolus and is where the crew finds the Silver Star wreck, although x-ray radiation from Proxima's flares has rendered the planet lifeless.

Imagine what it's like living in the Alpha Centauri system. You'd have the Sun, which your planet orbits, and then you'd have a second Sun, located where Saturn is for us. That second sun would have its own planets. What will really bake your noodle is that there will be other planets, even further out, which orbit in giant ellipses encompassing both suns. If you set two marbles on the floor, eight feet apart, to represent your two yellow suns, the marble you place for Proxima Centauri will be two-and-a-half miles away. In your sky, it would be no more than a red star.

On Alpha Centauri's Astris, one of the concerns the crew faces is infection. There's certainly a long history in science fiction of alien diseases having disastrous consequences. Yet, if you consider the eight million species of living creatures on good old planet Earth, the number that can make you sick is incredibly small. It is true that some diseases, called zoonoses, can be transmitted to humans from animals, but on the most part you cannot give your dog a cold even though you are both mammals (although, interestingly, you can give your cat a cold). However, it's really unlikely your potted petunia will catch anything from you. Now imagine life so far removed from the human evolutionary path that it's not even the same life chemistry. What will happen on an alien world? I'm not sure, although I'd probably still wash my hands before eating.

Speaking of eating, plants were thoughtful enough to evolve on Earth three billion years ago. A happy merger of cyanobacterium and a eukaryote paved the way for photosynthesizing algae. Originally Earth did not have an oxygen atmosphere, but you and I can literally breathe a sigh of relief due to photosynthesis. Also, you need oxygen for ozone, which, if the 80s taught us anything, is an important layer to have. Less than a half billion years ago, vascular plants like Cooksonia emerged. We had to wait until everyone's favorite period, the Jurassic, before finding the first flowers.

The plants and native life on Astris use peptide nucleic acid (PNA), an alternative to deoxyribonucleic acid (DNA). It's interesting that we've found other ways to store genetic information, and also that the familiar double helix isn't the only geometry. I don't think you could make an edible salad out of Astris plants, but with a bit of Mark Watney's terraforming expertise from *the Martian*, I'm sure you could grow some nice potatoes.

The catalyst for the story is the launch of the Proxima probe in 2054, which travels at 20% of light speed. In real life, project *Breakthrough Starshot* was announced in 2016. The goal is to design and send a fleet of 1,000 postage-stamp-sized light sails, called StarChips (mmm, StarChips...nom, nom, nom), to Proxima Centauri at 15% to 20% of light speed. Each StarChip will get accelerated by a laser from Earth orbit and achieve target speed in only ten minutes. Just imagine the type of acceleration required to take something to 20% c in ten minutes. This is like Riggs-drive type stuff. Who knows? Maybe we won't need to wait until 2080, after all, to see what's going on at Proxima.

In *Bernard's Promise*, James Hayden took humanity interstellar, exploring the strange life of the Centauri worlds and finding hints of where the Silver Stars have gone. After returning to an Earth that's advanced nine time-dilated years, he encounters an emerging technology that will force mankind to either fill the worlds of the solar system or search the stars for new Earths. One man can't do it alone, and he'll need a fleet spanning decades if they are to succeed. But the Silver Stars are still out there, and James's dreams of first contact may die light-years from home.

BEFORE YOU GO

Thanks for hopping in the pilot's seat and coming along on this voyage to faraway worlds. Hopefully you enjoyed the bit of nostalgia peppered with science. More Hayden's World shorts lie in the future. Check out www.sdfalchetti.com for the latest updates (and some random sci-fi musings).

Can I ask a favor before you leave? Would you leave a review of this book? You may have noticed I'm an indie author. I don't have a big ad agency to help others find my stories, but I do have awesome readers like you.

Thanks again, and keep dreaming big.

ABOUT THE AUTHOR

S.D. Falchetti is a mechanical engineer by day who dreams of fantastic voyages and far, far away places at night. He thinks that *The Empire Strikes Back* was the best of the Star Wars movies, and still has an original AT-AT from his childhood. He lives in the Northeastern United States.

www.sdfalchetti.com
sd@sdfalchetti.com

CPSIA information can be obtained
at www.ICGtesting.com
Printed in the USA
LVHW091701121021
700248LV00010B/209/J